Sanders & Bones
The African Adventures: 1

Sanders & Bones
The African Adventures: 1

Sanders of the River

The People of the River

Edgar Wallace

LEONAUR

Sanders & Bones
The African Adventures: 1
Sanders of the River
and
The People of the River
by Edgar Wallace

First published under the titles
Sanders of the River
and
The People of the River

Leonaur is an imprint of Oakpast Ltd

Copyright in this form © 2011 Oakpast Ltd

ISBN: 978-0-85706-457-8 (hardcover)
ISBN: 978-0-85706-458-5 (softcover)

http://www.leonaur.com

Publisher's Notes

Contents

Sanders of the River

Contents

CHAPTER 1

The Education of the King

Mr. Commissioner Sanders had graduated to West Central Africa by such easy stages that he did not realise when his acquaintance with the back lands began. Long before he was called upon by the British Government to keep a watchful eye upon some quarter of a million cannibal folk, who ten years before had regarded white men as we regard the unicorn; he had met the Basuto, the Zulu, the Fingo, the Pondo, Matabele, Mashona, Barotse, Hottentot, and Bechuana. Then curiosity and interest took him westward and northward, and he met the Angola folk, then northward to the Congo, westward to the Masai, and finally, by way of the Pigmy people, he came to his own land.

Now, there is a subtle difference between all these races, a difference that only such men as Sanders know.

It is not necessarily a variety of colour, though some are brown and some yellow, and some—a very few—jet black. The difference is in character. By Sanders' code you trusted all natives up to the same point, as you trust children, with a few notable exceptions. The Zulu were men, the Basuto were men, yet childlike in their grave faith. The black men who wore the *fez* were subtle, but trustworthy; but the browny men of the Gold Coast, who talked English, wore European clothing, and called one another "Mr.," were Sanders' pet abomination.

Living so long with children of a larger growth, it follows that he absorbed many of their childlike qualities. Once, on furlough in London, a confidence trick was played on him, and only his natural honesty pulled him out of a ridiculous scrape. For, when the gold-brick man produced his dull metal ingot, all Sanders' moral nerves stood endways, and he ran the confiding "*bunco steerer*" to the nearest station, charging him, to the astonishment of a sorely-puzzled police-

11

man, with "I.G.B.," which means illicit gold buying. Sanders did not doubt that the ingot was gold, but he was equally certain that the gold was not honestly come by. His surprise when he found that the "gold" was gold-leaf imposed upon the lead of commerce was pathetic.

You may say of Sanders that he was a statesman, which means that he had no exaggerated opinion of the value of individual human life. When he saw a dead leaf on the plant of civilisation, he plucked it off, or a weed growing with his "flowers" he pulled it up, not stopping to consider the weed's equal right to life. When a man, whether he was *capita* or slave, by his bad example endangered the peace of his country, Sanders fell upon him. In their unregenerate days, the Isisi called him "*Ogani Isisi*," which means "The Little Butcher Bird," and certainly in that time Sanders was prompt to hang. He governed a people three hundred miles beyond the fringe of civilisation. Hesitation to act, delay in awarding punishment, either of these two things would have been mistaken for weakness amongst a people who had neither power to reason, nor will to excuse, nor any large charity.

In the land which curves along the borders of Togo the people understand punishment to mean pain and death, and nothing else counts. There was a foolish Commissioner who was a great humanitarian, and he went up to Akasava—which is the name of this land—and tried moral suasion.

It was a raiding *palaver*. Some of the people of Akasava had crossed the river to Ochori and stolen women and goats, and I believe there was a man or two killed, but that is unimportant. The goats and the women were alive, and cried aloud for vengeance. They cried so loud that down at headquarters they were heard and Mr. Commissioner Niceman—that was not his name, but it will serve—went up to see what all the noise was about. He found the Ochori people very angry, but more frightened.

"If," said their spokesman, "they will return our goats, they may keep the women, because the goats are very valuable."

So Mr. Commissioner Niceman had a long, long *palaver* that lasted days and days, with the chief of the Akasava people and his councillors, and in the end moral suasion triumphed, and the people promised on a certain day, at a certain hour, when the moon was in such a quarter and the tide at such a height, the women should be returned and the goats also.

So Mr. Niceman returned to headquarters, swelling with admiration for himself and wrote a long report about his genius and his administrative abilities, and his knowledge of the native, which was afterwards published in *Blue Book* (*Africa*) 7943-96.

It so happened that Mr. Niceman immediately afterwards went home to England on furlough, so that he did not hear the laments and woeful wailings of the Ochori folk when they did not get their women or their goats.

Sanders, working round the Isisi River, with ten Houssas and an attack of malaria, got a helio message:

Go Akasava and settle that infernal woman *palaver*.—Administration.

So Sanders girded up his loins, took 25 grains of quinine, and leaving his good work—he was searching for M'Beli, the witchdoctor, who had poisoned a friend—trekked across country for the Akasava.

In the course of time he came to the city and was met by the chief.

"What about these women?" he asked.

"We will have a *palaver*," said the chief. "I will summon my headmen and my councillors."

"Summon nothing," said Sanders shortly. "Send back the women and the goats you stole from the Ochori."

"Master," said the chief, "at full moon, which is our custom, when the tide is so, and all signs of gods and devils are propitious, I will do as you bid."

"Chief, said Sanders, tapping the ebony chest of the other with the thin end of his walking-stick, "moon and river, gods or devils, those women and the goats go back to the Ochori folk by sunset, or I tie you to a tree and flog you till you bleed."

"Master," said the chief, "the women shall be returned."

"And the goats," said Sanders.

"As to the goats," said the chief airily, "they are dead, having been killed for a feast."

"You will bring them back to life," said Sanders.

"Master, do you think I am a magician?" asked the chief of the Akasava.

"I think you are a liar," said Sanders impartially, and there the *palaver* finished.

That night goats and women returned to the Ochori, and Sanders prepared to depart.

He took aside the chief, not desiring to put shame upon him or to weaken his authority.

"Chief," he said, "it is a long journey to Akasava, and I am a man fulfilling many tasks. I desire that you do not cause me any further journey to this territory."

"Master," said the chief truthfully, "I never wish to see you again."

Sanders smiled aside, collected his ten Houssas, and went back to the Isisi River to continue his search for M'Beli.

It was not a nice search for many causes, and there was every reason to believe, too, that the king of Isisi himself was the murderer's protector. Confirmation of this view came one morning when Sanders, encamped by the Big River, was taking a breakfast of tinned milk and toast. There arrived hurriedly Sato-Koto, the brother of the king, in great distress of mind, for he was a fugitive from the king's wrath. He babbled forth all manner of news, in much of which Sanders took no interest whatever. But what he said of the witchdoctor who lived in the king's shadow was very interesting indeed, and Sanders sent a messenger to headquarters, and, as it transpired, headquarters despatched in the course of time Mr. Niceman—who by this time had returned from furlough—to morally "suade" the king of the Isisi.

From such evidence as we have been able to collect it is evident that the king was not in a melting mood. It is an indisputable fact that poor Niceman's head, stuck on a pole before the king's hut, proclaimed the king's high spirits.

H.M.S. *St. George*, H.M.S. *Thrush*, H.M.S. *Philomel*, H.M.S. *Phoebe* sailed from Simonstown, and H.M.S. *Dwarf* came down from Sierra Leone *hec dum*, and in less than a month after the king killed his guest he wished he hadn't.

Headquarters sent Sanders to clear up the political side of the mess.

He was shown round what was left of the king's city by the flag-lieutenant of the *St. George*.

"I am afraid," said that gentleman, apologetically, "I am afraid that you will have to dig out a new king; we've rather killed the old one."

Sanders nodded.

"I shall not go into mourning," he said.

There was no difficulty in finding candidates for the vacant post. Sato-Koto, the dead king's brother, expressed his willingness to assume the cares of office with commendable promptitude.

"What do you say?" asked the admiral, commanding the expedition.

"I say no, sir," said Sanders, without hesitation. "The king has a son, a boy of nine; the kingship must be his. As for Sato-Koto, he shall be regent at pleasure."

And so it was arranged, Sato-Koto sulkily assenting.

They found the new king hidden in the woods with the women folk, and he tried to bolt, but Sanders caught him and led him back to the city by the ear.

"My boy," he said kindly, "how do people call you?"

"Peter, master," whimpered the wriggling lad; "in the fashion of the white people."

"Very well," said Sanders, "you shall be King Peter, and rule this country wisely and justly according to custom and the law. And you shall do hurt to none, and put shame on none nor shall you kill or raid or do any of the things that make life worth living, and if you break loose, may the Lord help you!"

Thus was King Peter appointed monarch of the Isisi people, and Sanders went back to headquarters with the little army of blue jackets and Houssas, for M'Beli, the witchdoctor, had been slain at the taking of the city, and Sanders' work was finished.

The story of the taking of Isisi village, and the crowning of the young king, was told in the London newspapers, and lost nothing in the telling. It was so described by the special correspondents, who accompanied the expedition, that many dear old ladies of Bayswater wept, and many dear young ladies of Mayfair said: "How sweet!" and the outcome of the many emotions which the description evoked was the sending out from England of Miss Clinton Calbraith, who was an M.A., and unaccountably pretty.

She came out to "mother" the orphan king, to be a mentor and a friend. She paid her own passage, but the books which she brought and the school paraphernalia that filled two large packing cases were subscribed for by the tender readers of *Tiny Toddlers*, a magazine for infants. Sanders met her on the landing-stage, being curious to see what a white woman looked like.

He put a hut at her disposal and sent the wife of his coast clerk to look after her.

"And now, Miss Calbraith," he said, at dinner that night, "what do you expect to do with Peter?"

She tilted her pretty chin in the air reflectively.

"We shall start with the most elementary of lessons—the merest kindergarten, and gradually work up. I shall teach him calisthenics, a little botany—Mr. Sanders, you're laughing."

"No, I wasn't," he hastened to assure her; "I always make a face like that—er—in the evening. But tell me this—do you speak the language—Swaheli, Bomongo, Fingi?"

"That will be a difficulty," she said thoughtfully.

"Will you take my advice?" he asked.

"Why, yes."

"Well, learn the language." She nodded. "Go home and learn it." She frowned. "It will take you about twenty-five years."

"Mr. Sanders," she said, not without dignity, "you are pulling—you are making fun of me."

"Heaven forbid!" said Sanders piously, "that I should do anything so wicked."

The end of the story, so far as Miss Clinton Calbraith was concerned, was that she went to Isisi, stayed three days, and came back incoherent.

"He is not a child!" she said wildly; "he is—a—a little devil!"

"So I should say," said Sanders philosophically.

"A king? It is disgraceful! He lives in a mud hut and wears no clothes. If I'd known!"

"A child of nature," said Sanders blandly. "You didn't expect a sort of Louis Quinze, did you?"

"I don't know what I expected," she said desperately; "but it was impossible to stay—quite impossible."

"Obviously," murmured Sanders.

"Of course, I knew he would be black," she went on; "and I knew that—oh, it was too horrid!"

"The fact of it is, my dear young lady," said Sanders, "Peter wasn't as picturesque as you imagined him; he wasn't the gentle child with pleading eyes; and he lives messy—is that it?"

This was not the only attempt ever made to educate Peter. Months afterwards, when Miss Cailbraith had gone home and was busily writing her famous book, *Alone in Africa: by an English Gentlewoman*, Sanders heard of another educative raid. Two members of an Ethiopian mission came into Isisi by the back way. The Ethiopian mission is made up of Christian black men, who, very properly, basing their creed upon Holy Writ, preach the gospel of Equality. A black man is as good as a white man any day of the week, and infinitely better on Sundays if he happens to be a member of the Reformed Ethiopian Church.

They came to Isisi and achieved instant popularity, for the kind of talk they provided was very much to the liking of Sato-Koto and the king's councillors.

Sanders sent for the missioners. The first summons they refused to obey, but they came on the second occasion, because the message Sanders sent was at once peremptory and ominous.

They came to headquarters, two cultured American negroes of good address and refined conversation. They spoke English faultlessly, and were in every sense perfect gentlemen.

"We cannot understand the character of your command," said one, "which savours somewhat of interference with the liberty of the subject."

"You'll understand me better," said Sanders, who knew his men, "when I tell you that I cannot allow you to preach sedition to my people."

"Sedition, Mr. Sanders!" said the negro in shocked tones. "That is a grave charge."

Sanders took a paper from a pigeon-hole in his desk; the interview took place in his office.

"On such a date," he said, "you said this, and this, and that."

In other words he accused them of overstepping the creed of Equality and encroaching upon the borderland of political agitation.

"Lies!" said the elder of the two, without hesitation.

"Truth or lies," he said, "you go no more to Isisi."

"Would you have the heathen remain in darkness?" asked the man, in reproach. "Is the light we kindle too bright, master?"

"No," said Sanders, "but a bit too warm."

So he committed the outrage of removing the Ethiopians from the scene of their earnest labours, in consequence of which questions were asked in Parliament.

Then the chief of the Akasava people—an old friend—took a hand in the education of King Peter. Akasava adjoins that king's territory, and the chief came to give hints in military affairs.

He came with drums a-beating, with presents of fish and bananas and salt.

"You are a great king!" he said to the sleepy-eyed boy who sat on a stool of state, regarding him with open-mouthed interest. "When you walk the world shakes at your tread; the mighty river that goes flowing down to the big water parts asunder at your word, the trees of the forest shiver, and the beasts go slinking to cover when your mightiness

17

goes abroad."

"*Oh, ko, ko!*" giggled the king, pleasantly tickled.

"The white men fear you," continued the chief of the Akasava; "they tremble and hide at your roar."

Sato-Koto, standing at the king's elbow, was a practical man.

"What seek ye, chief?" he asked, cutting short the compliments.

So the chief told him of a land peopled by cowards, rich with the treasures of the earth, goats, and women.

"Why do you not take them yourself?" demanded the regent.

"Because I am a slave," said the chief; "the slave of Sandi, who would beat me. But you, lord, are of the great; being king's headman, Sandi would not beat you because of your greatness."

There followed a *palaver*, which lasted two days.

"I shall have to do something with Peter," wrote Sanders despairingly to the Administrator; "the little beggar has gone on the war-path against those unfortunate Ochori. I should be glad if you would send me a hundred men, a Maxim, and a bundle of rattan canes; I'm afraid I must attend to Peter's education myself."

★★★★★★

"Lord, did I not speak the truth?" said the Akasava chief in triumph. "Sandi has done nothing! Behold, we have wasted the city of the Ochori, and taken their treasure, and the white man is dumb because of your greatness! Let us wait till the moon comes again, and I will show you another city."

"You are a great man," bleated the king, "and some day you shall build your hut in the shadow of my palace."

"On that day," said the chief, with splendid resignation, "I shall die of joy."

When the moon had waxed and waned and come again, a pencilled silver hoop of light in the eastern sky, the Isisi warriors gathered with spear and broad-bladed sword, with *ingola* on their bodies, and clay in their hair .

They danced a great dance by the light of a huge fire, and all the women stood round, clapping their hands rhythmically.

In the midst of this there arrived a messenger in a canoe, who prostrated himself before the king, saying:

"Master, one day's march from here is Sandi; he has with him five score of soldiers and the brass gun which says: '*Ha-ha-ha-ha-ha!*'"

A silence reigned in court circles, which was broken by the voice of the Akasava chief.

"I think I will go home," he said. "I have a feeling of sickness; also, it is the season when my goats have their young."

"Do not be afraid," said Sato-Koto brutally. "The king's shadow is over you, and he is so mighty that the earth shakes at his tread, and the waters of the big river part at his footfall; also, the white men fear him."

"Nevertheless," said the chief, with some agitation, "I must go, for my youngest son is sickening with fever, and calls all the time for me."

"Stay!" said the regent, and there was no mistaking his tone.

Sanders did not come the next day, nor the next. He was moving leisurely, traversing a country where many misunderstandings existed that wanted clearing up. When he arrived, having sent a messenger ahead to carry the news of his arrival, he found the city peaceably engaged.

The women were crushing corn, the men smoking, the little children playing and sprawling about the streets.

He halted at the outskirts of the city, on a hillock that commanded the main street, and sent for the regent.

"Why must I send for you?" he asked "Wiry does the king remain in his city when I come? This is shame."

"Master," said Sato-Koto, "it is not fitting that a great king should so humble himself."

Sanders was neither amused nor angry. He was dealing with a rebellious people, and his own fine feelings were as nothing to the peace of the land.

"It would seem that the king has had bad advisers," he reflected aloud, and Sato-Koto shuffled uneasily.

"Go, now, and tell the king to come—for I am his friend."

The regent departed, but returned again alone.

"Lord, he will not come," he said sullenly.

"Then I will go to him," said Sanders.

King Peter, sitting before his hut, greeted Mr. Commissioner with downcast eyes.

Sanders' soldiers, spread in a semi-circle before the hut, kept the rabble at bay.

"King," said Sanders—he carried in his hand a rattan cane of familiar shape, and as he spoke he whiffled it in the air, making a little humming noise—"stand up!"

19

"Wherefore?" said Sato-Koto.

"That you shall see," said Sanders.

The king rose reluctantly, and Sanders grabbed him by the scruff of his neck.

Swish!

The cane caught him most undesirably, and he sprang into the air with a yell.

Swish, swish, swish!

Yelling and dancing, throwing out wild hands to ward off the punishment, King Peter blubbered for mercy.

"Master!" Sato-Koto, his face distorted with rage, reached for his spear.

"Shoot that man if he interferes," said Sanders, without releasing the king.

The regent saw the levelled rifles and stepped back hastily.

"Now," said Sanders, throwing down the cane, "now we will play a little game."

"*Wow-wow—oh, ko!*" sobbed His Majesty.

"I go back to the forest," said Sanders. "By and by a messenger shall come to you, saying that the Commissioner is on his way. Do you understand?"

"*Yi-hi!*" sobbed the king.

"Then will you go out with your councillors and your old men and await my coming according to custom. Is that clear?"

"Ye-es, master," whimpered the boy.

"Very good," said Sanders, and withdrew his troops.

In half an hour came a grave messenger to the king, and the court went out to the little hill to welcome the white man.

This was the beginning of King Peter's education, for thus was he taught obedience.

Sanders went into residence in the town of Isisi, and held court.

"Sato-Koto," he said on the second day, "do you know the village of Ikan?"

"Yes, master; it is two days' journey into the bush."

Sanders nodded.

"You will take your wives, your children, your servants, and your possessions to the village of Ikan, there to stay until I give you leave to return. The *palaver* is finished."

Next came the chief of the Akasava, very ill at ease.

"Lord, if any man says I did you wrong, he lies," said the chief.

"Then I am a liar!" said Sanders. "For I say that you are an evil man, full of cunning."

"If it should be," said the chief, "that you order me to go to my village as you have ordered Sato-Koto, I will go, since he who is my father is not pleased with me."

"That I order," said Sanders; "also, twenty strokes with a stick, for the good of your soul. Furthermore, I would have you remember that down by Tembeli on the great river there is a village where men labour in chains because they have been unfaithful to the Government and have practised abominations."

So the chief of the Akasava people went out to punishment.

There were other matters requiring adjustment, but they were of a minor character, and when these were all settled to the satisfaction of Sanders, but by no means to the satisfaction of the subjects, the Commissioner turned his attention to the further education of the king.

"Peter," he said, "tomorrow when the sun comes up I go back to my own village, leaving you without councillors."

"Master, how may I do without councillors, since I am a young boy?" asked the king, crestfallen and chastened.

"By saying to yourself when a man calls for justice: 'If I were this man how should I desire the king's justice?'"

The boy looked unhappy.

"I am very young," he repeated; "and today there come many from outlying villages seeking redress against their enemies."

"Very good," said Sanders. "Today I will sit at the king's right hand and learn of his wisdom."

The boy stood on one leg in his embarrassment, and eyed Sanders askance.

There is a hillock behind the town. A worn path leads up to it, and a-top is a thatched hut without sides. From this hillock you see the broad river with its sandy shoals, where the crocodiles sleep with open mouth; you see the rising ground toward Akasava, hills that rise one on top of the other, covered with a tangle of vivid green. In this house sits the king in judgment, beckoning the litigants forward. Sato-Koto was wont to stand by the king, bartering justice.

Today Sato-Koto was preparing to depart and Sanders sat by the king's side.

There were indeed many litigants.

There was a man who had bought a wife, giving no less than a thousand rods and two bags of salt for her. He had lived for three months with her, when she departed from his house.

"Because," said the man philosophically, "she had a lover. Therefore, Mighty Sun of Wisdom, I desire the return of my rods and my salt."

"What say you?" said Sanders.

The king wriggled uncomfortably.

"What says the father?" he said hesitatingly, and Sanders nodded.

"That is a wise question," he approved, and called the father, a voluble and an eager old man.

"Now, king," he said hurriedly, "I sold this woman, my daughter; how might I know her mind? Surely I fulfil my contract when the woman goes to the man. How shall a father control when a husband fails?"

Sanders looked at the king again, and the boy drew a long breath.

"It would seem, M'bleni, that the woman, your daughter, lived many years in your hut, and if you do not know her mind you are either a great fool or she is a cunning one. Therefore, I judge that you sold this woman knowing her faults. Yet the husband might accept some risk also. You shall take back your daughter and return 500 rods and a bag of salt, and if it should be that your daughter marries again, you shall pay one-half of her dowry to this man."

Very, very slowly he gave judgment, hesitatingly, anxiously, glancing now and again to the white man for his approval.

"That was good," said Sanders, and called forward another pleader.

"Lord king," said the new plaintiff, "a man has put an evil curse on me and my family, so that they sicken."

Here was a little poser for the little judge, and he puzzled the matter out in silence, Sanders offering no help.

"How does he curse you?" at last asked the king.

"With the curse of death," said the complainant in a hushed voice.

"Then you shall curse him also," said the king, "and it shall be a question of whose curse is the stronger."

Sanders grinned behind his hand, and the king, seeing the smile, smiled also.

From here onward Peter's progress was a rapid one, and there came to headquarters from time to time stories of a young king who was a Solomon in judgment.

So wise he was (who knew of the formula he applied to each case?), so beneficent, so peaceable, that the chief of the Akasava, from whom was periodically due, took advantage of the gentle administration, and sent neither corn nor fish nor grain. He did this after a journey to faraway Ikan, where he met the king's uncle, Sato-Koto, and agreed upon common action. Since the crops were good, the king passed the first fault, but the second tribute became due, and neither Akasava nor Ikan sent, and the people of Isisi, angry at the insolence, murmured, and the king sat down in the loneliness of his hut to think upon a course which was just and effective.

******

"I really am sorry to bother you," wrote Sanders to the Administrator again, "but I shall have to borrow your Houssas for the Isisi country. There has been a tribute *palaver*, and Peter went down to Ikan and wiped up his uncle; he filled in his spare time by giving the Akasava the worst licking they have ever had. I thoroughly approve of all that Peter has done, because I feel that he is actuated only by the keenest sense of justice and a desire to do the right thing at the right time—and it was time Sato-Koto was killed—though I shall have to reprimand Peter for the sake of appearances. The Akasava chief is in the bush, hiding."

Peter came back to his capital after his brief but strenuous campaign, leaving behind him two territories that were all the better for his visit, though somewhat sore.

The young king brought together his old men, his witchdoctors, and other notabilities.

"By all the laws of white men," he said, "I have done wrong to Sandi, because he has told me I must not fight, and, behold, I have destroyed my uncle, who was a dog, and I have driven the chief of the Akasava into the forest. But Sandi told me also that I must do what was just, and that I have done according to my lights, for I have destroyed a man who put my people to shame. Now, it seems to me that there is only one thing to do, and that is to go to Sandi, telling the truth and asking him to judge."

"Lord king," said the oldest of his councillors, "what if Sandi puts you to the chain-gang?"

"That is with tomorrow," quoth the king, and gave orders for preparations to be made for departure.

Half-way to headquarters the two met; King Peter going down and Sanders coming up. And here befell the great incident.

No word was spoken of Peter's fault before sunset; but when blue

23

smoke arose from the fires of Houssa and warrior, and the little camp in the forest clearing was all a-chatter, Sanders took the king's arm and led him along the forest path.

Peter told his tale and Sanders listened.

"And what of the chief of the Akasava?" he asked.

"Master," said the king, "he fled to the forest cursing me, and with him went many bad men."

Sanders nodded again gravely.

They talked of many things till the sun threw long shadows, and then they turned to retrace their footsteps. They were within half a mile of the camp and the faint noise of men laughing, and the faint scent of fires burning came to them, when the chief of the Akasava stepped out from behind a tree and stood directly in their path. With him were some eight fighting men fully armed.

"Lord king," said the chief of the Akasava, "I have been waiting for you."

The king made neither movement nor reply, but Sanders reached for his revolver.

His hand closed on the butt, when something struck him and he went down like a log.

"Now we will kill the king of the Isisi, and the white man also." The voice was the chief's, but Sanders was not taking any particular interest in the conversation, because there was a hive of wild bees buzzing in his head, and a maze of pain; he felt sick.

"If you kill me it is little matter," said the king's voice, "because there are many men who can take my place; but if you slay Sandi, you slay the father of the people, and none can replace him."

"He whipped you, little king," said the chief of the Akasava mockingly.

"I would throw him into the river," said a strange voice after a long interval; "thus shall no trace be found of him, and no man will lay his death to our door."

"What of the king?" said another. Then came a crackling of twigs and the voices of men.

"They are searching," whispered a voice. "King, if you speak I will kill you now."

"Kill!" said the young king's even voice, and shouted, "Oh, M'sabo! Beteli! Sandi is here!"

That was all Sandi heard.

★★★★★★

Two days later he sat up in bed and demanded information. There was a young doctor with him when he woke, who had providentially arrived from headquarters.

"The king?" he hesitated. "Well, they finished the king, but he saved your life. I suppose you know that?"

Sanders said "Yes" without emotion.

"A plucky little beggar," suggested the doctor.

"Very," said Sanders. Then: "Did they catch the chief of the Akasava?"

"Yes; he was so keen on finishing you that he delayed his bolting. The king threw himself on you and covered your body."

"That will do."

Sanders' voice was harsh and his manner brusque at the best of times, but now his rudeness was brutal.

"Just go out of the hut, doctor—I want to sleep."

He heard the doctor move, heard the rattle of the "chick" at the hut door, then he turned his face to the wall and wept.

Chapter 2

Keepers of the Stone

There is a people who live at Ochori in the big African forest on the Ikeli River, who are called in the native tongue "The Keepers of the Stone."

There is a legend that years and years ago, *cala-cala*, there was a strange, flat stone, "inscribed with the marks of the devils" (so the grave native story-teller puts it), which was greatly worshipped and prized, partly for its magic powers, and partly because of the two ghosts who guarded it.

It was a fetish of peculiar value to the mild people who lived in the big forest, but the Akasava, who are neither mild nor reverential, and being, moreover, in need of gods, swooped down upon the Ochori one red morning and came away with this wonderful stone and other movables. Presumably, the "ghosts of brass" went also. It was a great business, securing the stone, for it was set in a grey slab in the solid rock, and many spear-heads were broken before it could be wrenched from its place. But in the end it was taken away, and for several years it was the boast of the Akasava that they derived much benefit from this sacred possession. Then of a sudden the stone disappeared, and with it all the good fortune of its owners. For the vanishing of the stone coincided with the arrival of British rule, and it was a bad thing for the Akasava.

There came in these far-off days ('95?) a ridiculous person in white with an escort of six soldiers. He brought a message of peace and good fellowship, and talked of a new king and a new law. The Akasava listened in dazed wonderment, but when they recovered they cut off his head, also the heads of the escort. It seemed to be the only thing to do under the circumstances.

Then one morning the Akasava people woke to find the city full of strange white folk, who had come swiftly up the river in steamboats. There were too many to quarrel with, so the people sat quiet, a little frightened and very curious, whilst two black soldiers strapped the hands and feet of the Akasava chief prior to hanging him by the neck till he was dead.

Nor did the bad luck of the people end here; there came a lean year, when the manioc, (there is a tremendous amount of free hydrocyanic acid [prussic acid] in manioc), root was bad and full of death-water, when goats died, and crops were spoilt by an unexpected hurricane. There was always a remedy at hand for a setback of this kind. If you have not the thing you require, go and take it. So, following precedents innumerable, the Akasava visited the Ochori, taking away much grain, and leaving behind dead men and men who prayed for death. In the course of time the white men came with their steamboats, their little brass guns, and the identical block and tackle, which they fastened to the identical tree and utilised in the inevitable manner.

"It appears," said the new chief—who was afterwards hanged for the killing of the king of the Isisi—"that the white man's law is made to allow weak men to triumph at the expense of the strong. This seems foolish, but it will be well to humour them."

His first act was to cut down the hanging-tree—it was too conspicuous and too significant. Then he set himself to discover the cause of all the trouble which had come upon the Akasava. The cause required little appreciation. The great stone had been stolen, as he well knew, and the remedy resolved itself into a question of discovering the thief. The wretched Ochori were suspect.

"If we go to them," said the chief of the Akasava thoughtfully, "killing them very little, but rather burning them, so that they told where this godstone was hidden, perhaps the Great Ones would forgive us."

"In my young days," said an aged councillor, "when evil men would not tell where stolen things were buried, we put hot embers in their hands and bound them tightly."

"That is a good way," approved another old man, wagging his head applaudingly; "also to the men in the path of the soldier-ants has been known to make them talkative."

"Yet we may not go up against the Ochori for many reasons," said the chief; "the principal of which is that if the stone be with them we shall not overcome them owing to the two ghosts—though I do not remember that the ghosts were very potent in the days when the stone was with us," he added, not without hope.

The little raid which followed and the search for the stone are told briefly in official records. The search was fruitless, and the Akasava folk must needs content themselves with such picking as came to hand.

Of how Mr. Niceman, the deputy commissioner, and then Sanders himself, came up, I have already told. That was long ago, as the natives say, *cala-cala*, and many things happened subsequently that put from the minds of the people all thought of the stone.

In course of time the chief of the Akasava died the death for various misdoings, and peace came to the land that fringes Togo.

★★★★★★

Sanders has been surprised twice in his life. Once was at Ikeli, which in the native tongue means "little river." It is not a little river at all, but, on the contrary, a broad, strong, sullen stream that swirls and eddies and foams as it swings the corner of its tortuous course seaward. Sanders sat on a deckchair placed under the awning of his tiny steamer, and watched the river go rushing past. He was a contented man, for the land was quiet and the crops were good. Nor was there any crime.

There was sleeping sickness at Bofabi, and *beriberi* at Akasava, and in the Isisi country somebody had discovered a new god, and, by all accounts that came down river, they worshipped him night and day.

He was not bothering about new gods, because gods of any kind were a beneficent asset. Milini, the new king of the Isisi, had sent him word:

"Master," said his mouthpiece, the messenger, "this new god lives in a box which is borne upon the shoulders of priests. It is so long and so wide, and there are four sockets in which the poles fit, and the god inside is a very strong one, and full of pride."

"*Ko, ko!*" said Sanders, with polite interest, "tell the lord king, your master, that so long as this god obeys the law, he may live in the Isisi country, paying no tax. But if he tells the young men to go fighting, I shall come with a much stronger god, who will eat your god up. The *palaver* is finished."

Sanders, with his feet stretched out on the rail of the boat, thought of the new god idly. When was it that the last had come? There was one in the N'Gombi country years ago, a sad god who lived in a hut which no man dare approach; there was another god who came with thunder demanding sacrifice—human sacrifice. This was an exceptionally bad god, and had cost the British Government six hundred thousand pounds, because there was fighting in the bush and a country unsettled. But, in the main, the gods were good, doing harm to none, for it is customary for new gods to make their appearance after the crops are gathered, and before the rainy season sets in.

So Sanders thought, sitting in the shade of a striped awning on the foredeck of the little *Zaire*.

The next day, before the sun came up, he turned the nose of the steamer upstream, being curious as to the welfare of the shy Ochori folk, who lived too near the Akasava for comfort, and, moreover, needed nursing. Very slow was the tiny steamer's progress, for the current was strong against her. After two days' travel Sanders got into Lukati, where young Carter had a station.

The deputy commissioner came down to the beach in his pyjamas, with a big pith helmet on the back of his head, and greeted his chief boisterously.

"Well?" said Sanders; and Carter told him all the news. There was a land *palaver* at Ebibi; Otabo, of Bofabi, had died of the sickness; there were two leopards worrying the outlying villages, and——

"Heard about the Isisi god?" he asked suddenly; and Sanders said that he had.

"It's an old friend of yours," said Carter. "My people tell me that this old god-box contains the stone of the Ochori."

"Oh!" said Sanders, with sudden interest.

He breakfasted with his subordinate, inspected his little garrison of thirty, visited his farm, admired his sweet potatoes, and patronised his tomatoes.

Then he went back to the boat and wrote a short dispatch in the tiniest of handwriting on the flimsiest of paper slips. "In case!" said Sanders.

"Bring me 14," he said to his servant, and Abiboo came back to him soon with a pigeon in his hand.

"Now, little bird," said Sanders, carefully rolling his letter round the red leg of the tiny courier and fastening it with a rubber band, "you've got two hundred miles to fly before sunrise tomorrow—and 'ware hawks!"

Then he gathered the pigeon in his hand, walked with it to the stern of the boat, and threw it into the air.

His crew of twelve men were sitting about their cooking-pot— that pot which everlastingly boils.

"Yoka!" he called, and his half-naked engineer came bounding down the slope.

"Steam," said Sanders; "get your wood aboard; I am for Isisi."

★★★★★★

There was no doubt at all that this new god was an extremely powerful one. Three hours from the city the *Zaire* came up to a long canoe with four men standing at their paddles singing dolefully. Sanders remembered that he had passed a village where women, their bodies decked with green leaves, wailed by the river's edge.

He slowed down till he came abreast of the canoe, and saw a dead man lying stark in the bottom.

"Where go you with this body?" he asked.

"To Isisi, lord," was the answer.

"The middle river and the little islands are places for the dead," said Sanders brusquely. "It is folly to take the dead to the living."

' Lord," said the man who spoke, "at Isisi lives a god who breathes life; this man"—he pointed downwards—"is my brother, and he died very suddenly because of a leopard. So quickly he died that he could not tell us where he had hidden his rods and his salt. Therefore we take him to Isisi, that the new god may give him just enough life to make his relations comfortable."

"The middle river," said Sanders quietly, and pointed to such a lone island, all green with tangled vegetation, as might make a burying ground. "What is your name?"

"Master, my name is N'Kema," said the man sullenly.

"Go, then, N'Kema," he said, and kept the steamer slow ahead whilst he watched the canoe turn its blunt nose to the island and disembark its cargo.

Then he rang the engines full ahead, steered clear of a sandbank, and regained the fairway.

He was genuinely concerned.

The stone was something exceptional in fetishes, needing delicate handling. That the stone existed, he knew. There were legends innumerable about it; and an explorer had, in the early days, seen it through his glasses. Also the "ghosts clad in brass" he had heard about—these fantastic and warlike shades who made peaceable men go out to battle—all except the Ochori, who were never warlike, and whom no number of ghosts could incite to deeds of violence.

You will have remarked that Sanders took native people seriously, and that, I remark in passing, is the secret of good government. To him,

30

ghosts were factors, and fetishes potent possibilities. A man who knew less would have been amused, but Sanders was not amused, because he had a great responsibility. He arrived at the city of Isisi in the afternoon, and observed, even at a distance, that something unusual was occurring. The crowd of women and children that the arrival of the Commissioner usually attracted did not gather as he swung in from midstream and followed the water-path that leads to shoal.

Only the king and a handful of old men awaited him, and the king was nervous and in trouble.

"Lord," he blurted, "I am no king in this city because of the new god; the people are assembled on the far side of the hill, and there they sit night and day watching the god in the box."

Sanders bit his lip thoughtfully, and said nothing.

"Last night," said the king, "'The Keepers of the Stone' appeared walking through the village."

He shivered, and the sweat stood in big beads on his forehead, for a ghost is a terrible thing.

"All this talk of keepers of stones is folly," said Sanders calmly; "they have been seen by your women and your unblooded boys."

"Lord, I saw them myself," said the king simply; and Sanders was staggered, for the king was a sane man.

"The devil you have!" said Sanders in English; then, "What manner of ghost were these?"

"Lord," said the king, "they were white of face, like your greatness. They wore brass upon their heads and brass upon their breasts. Their legs were bare, but upon the lower legs was brass again."

"Any kind of ghost is hard enough to believe," said Sanders irritably, "but a brass ghost I will not have at any price." He spoke English again, as was his practice when he talked to himself, and the king stood silent, not understanding him.

"What else?" said Sanders.

"They had swords," continued the chief, "such as the elephant-hunters of the N'Gombi people carry. Broad and short, and on their arms were shields."

Sanders was nonplussed.

"And they cry 'war,'" said the chief. "This is the greatest shame of all, for my young men dance the death dance and streak their bodies with paint and talk boastfully."

"Go to your hut," said Sanders; "presently I will come and join you."

He thought and thought, smoking one black cigar after another, then he sent for Abiboo, his servant.

"Abiboo," he said, "by my way of thinking, I have been a good master to you."

"That is so, lord," said Abiboo.

"Now I will trust you to go amongst my crew discovering their gods. If I ask them myself, they will lie to me out of politeness, inventing this god and that, thinking they please me.".

Abiboo chose the meal hour, when the sun had gone out and the world was grey and the trees motionless. He came back with the information as Sanders was drinking his second cup of coffee in the loneliness of the tiny deck-house.

"Master," he reported, "three men worship no god whatever, three more have especial family fetishes, and two are Christians more or less, and the four Houssas are with me in faith."

"And you?"

Abiboo, the Kano boy, smiled at Sanders' assumption of innocence.

"Lord," he said, "I follow the Prophet, believing only in the one God, beneficent and merciful."

"That is good," said Sanders. "Now let the men load wood, and Yoka shall have steam against moonrise, and all shall be ready for slipping."

At ten o'clock by his watch he fell-in his four Houssas, serving out to each a short carbine and a *bandoleer*. Then the party went ashore.

The king in his patience sat in his hut, and Sanders found him.

"You will stay here, Milini," he commanded, "and no blame shall come to you for anything that may happen this night."

"What will happen, master?"

"Who knows!" said Sanders, philosophically.

The streets were in pitch darkness, but Abiboo, carrying a lantern, led the way. Only occasionally did the party pass a tenanted hut. Generally they saw by the dull glow of the log that smouldered in every habitation that it was empty. Once a sick woman called to them in passing. It was near her time, she said, and there was none to help her in the supreme moment of her agony.

"God help you, sister!" said Sanders, ever in awe of the mysteries of birth. "I will send women to you. What is your name?"

"They will not come," said the plaintive voice. "Tonight the men go out to war, and the women wait for the great dance."

"Tonight?"

"Tonight, master—so the ghosts of brass decree."

Sanders made a clicking noise with his mouth.

"That we shall see," he said, and went on.

The party reached the outskirts of the city. Before them, outlined against a bronze sky, was the dark bulk of a little hill, and this they skirted.

The bronze became red, and rose, and dull bronze again, as the fires that gave it colour leapt or fell. Turning the shoulder of the hill, Sanders had a full view of the scene.

Between the edge of the forest and slope of the hill was a broad strip of level land. On the left was the river, on the right was swamp and forest again.

In the very centre of the plain a huge fire burnt. Before it, supported by its poles, on two high trestles, a square box.

But the people!

A huge circle, squatting on its haunches, motionless, silent; men, women, children, tiny babies, at their mothers' hips they stretched; a solid wheel of humanity, with the box and the fire as a hub.

There was a lane through which a man might reach the box—a lane along which passed a procession of naked men, going and returning. These were they who replenished the fire, and Sanders saw them dragging fuel for that purpose. Keeping to the edge of the crowd, he worked his way to the opening. Then he looked round at his men.

"It is written," he said, in the curious Arabic of the Kano people, "that we shall carry away this false god. As to which of us shall live or die through this adventure, that is with Allah, who knows all things."

Then he stepped boldly along the lane. He had changed his white ducks for a dark blue uniform suit, and he was not observed by the majority until he came with his Houssas to the box. The heat from the fire was terrific, overpowering. Close at hand he saw that the fierceness of the blaze had warped the rough-hewn boards of the box, and through the opening he saw in the light a slab of stone.

"Take up the box quickly," he commanded, and the Houssas lifted the poles to their shoulders. Until then the great assembly had sat in silent wonder, but as the soldiers lifted their burden, a yell of rage burst from five thousand throats, and men leapt to their feet.

Sanders stood before the fire, one hand raised, and silence fell, curiosity dominating resentment.

"People of the Isisi," said Sanders, "let no man move until the godstone has passed, for death comes quickly to those who cross the path of gods."

He had an automatic pistol in each hand, and the particular deity he was thinking of at the moment was not the one in the box.

The people hesitated, surging and swaying, as a mob will sway in its uncertainty. With quick steps the bearers carried their burden through the lane; they had almost passed unmolested when an old woman shuffled forward and clutched at Sanders' arm.

"Lord, lord!" she quavered, "what will you do with our god?"

"Take him to the proper place," said Sanders, "being by Government appointed his keeper."

"Give me a sign," she croaked, and the people in her vicinity repeated, "A sign, master!"

"This is a sign," said Sanders, remembering the woman in labour. "By the god's favour there shall be born to Ifabi, wife of Adako, a male child."

He heard the babble of talk; he heard his message repeated over the heads of the crowd; he saw a party of women go scurrying back to the village; then he gave the order to march. There were murmurings, and once he heard a deep-voiced man begin the war-chant, but nobody joined him. Somebody—probably the same man—clashed his spear against his wicker shield, but his warlike example was not followed. Sanders gained the village street. Around him was such a press of people that he followed the swaying box with difficulty. The river was in sight; the moon, rising a dull, golden ball over the trees, laced the water with silver, and then there came a scream of rage.

"He lies! He lies! Ifabi, the wife of Adako, has a female child."

Sanders turned swiftly like a dog at bay; his lips upcurled in a snarl, his white, regular teeth showing.

"Now," said Sanders, speaking very quickly, "let any man raise his spear, and he dies."

Again they stood irresolute, and Sanders, over his shoulder, gave an order.

For a moment only the people hesitated; then, as the soldiers gripped the poles of the god-box, with one fierce yell they sprang forward.

A voice screamed something; and, as if by magic, the tumult ceased, and the crowd darted backward and outward, falling over one another in their frantic desire to escape.

Sanders, his pistol still loaded, stood in open-mouthed astonishment at the stampede.

Save for his men he was alone; and then he saw.

Along the centre of the street two men were walking. They were clad alike in short crimson kilts that left their knees bare; great brass helmets topped their heads, and brass *cuirasses* covered their breasts.

Sanders watched them as they came nearer, then: "If this is not fever, it is madness," he muttered, for what he saw were two Roman centurions, their heavy swords girt about their waists.

He stood still, and they passed him, so close that he saw on the boss of one shield the rough-moulded letters:—

AUGUSTUS CAE.

"Fever" said Sanders emphatically, and followed the box to the ship.

******

When the steamer reached Lukati, Sanders was still in a condition of doubt, for his temperature was normal, and neither fever nor sun could be held accountable for the vision. Added to which, his men had seen the same thing.

He found the reinforcements his pigeon had brought, but they were unnecessary now.

"It beats me," he confessed to Carter, telling the story; "but we'll get out the stone; it might furnish an explanation. Centurions—bah!"

The stone, exposed in the light of day, was of greyish granite, such as Sanders did not remember having seen before.

"Here are the 'devil marks,'" he said, as he turned it over. "Possibly—whew!"

No wonder he whistled, for closely set were a number of printed characters; and Carter, blowing the dust, saw—

> *MARIUS ET AUGUSTUS*
> *CENT. . . . . . . NERO*
> *IMPERAT. . . . . . IN DEUS*
> *DULCE.*

That night, with great labour, Sanders, furbishing his rusty Latin, and filling in gaps, made a translation:

> *Marius and Augustus,*
> *Centurions of Nero, Caesar and*
> *Emperor,*

35

Sleep sweetly with the gods.

We are they who came beyond the wild lands which Hanno, the Carthaginian, found . . .

Marcus Septimus went up into Egypt, and with him Decimus Superbus, but by the will of Caesar, and the favour of the gods, we sailed to the black seas beyond. . . . Here we lived, our ships suffering wreck, being worshipped by the barbarians, teaching them warlike practices

. . . . You who come after . . . bear greetings to Rome to Cato Hippocritus, who dwells by the gate.

Sanders shook his head when he had finished reading, and said it was "rum."

CHAPTER 3

Bosambo of Monrovia

For many years have the Ochori people formed a sort of grim comic relief to the tragedy of African colonisation. Now it may well be that we shall laugh at the Ochori no more. Nor, in the small hours of the night, when conversation flags in the little circle about the fires in fishing camps, shall the sleepy-eyed be roused to merriment by stories of Ochori meekness. All this has come about by favour of the Liberian Government, though at present the Liberian Government is not aware of the fact.

With all due respect to the Republic of Liberia, I say that the Monrovians are naturally liars and thieves.

Once upon a time, that dignity might be added to the State, a warship was acquired—if I remember aright it was presented by a disinterested shipowner. The Government appointed three admirals, fourteen captains, and as many officers as the ship would hold, and they all wore gorgeous but ill-fitting uniforms. The Government would have appointed a crew also, but for the fact that the ship was not big enough to hold any larger number of people than its officers totalled.

This tiny man-of-war of the black republic went to sea once, the admirals and captains taking it in turn to stoke and steer—a very pleasing and novel sensation, this latter.

Coming back into the harbour, one of the admirals said—

"It is my turn to steer now," and took the wheel.

The ship struck a rock at the entrance of the harbour and went down. The officers escaped easily enough, for your Monrovian swims like a fish, but their uniforms were spoilt by the sea water. To the suggestion that salvage operations should be attempted to refloat the warship, the Government very wisely said no, they thought not.

"We know where she is," said the President—he was sitting on

37

the edge of his desk at Government House, eating sardines with his fingers—"and if we ever want her, it will be comforting to know she is so close to us."

Nothing more would have been done in the matter but for the fact that the British Admiralty decided that the wreck was a danger to shipping, and issued orders forthwith for the place where it lay to be buoyed.

The Liberian Government demurred on account of expense, but on pressure being applied (I suspect the captain of H.M.S. *Dwarf*, who was a man with a bitter tongue) they agreed, and the bell-buoy was anchored to the submerged steamer.

It made a nice rowdy, clanging noise, did that bell, and the people of Monrovia felt they were getting their money's worth.

But all Monrovia is not made up of the freed American slaves who were settled there in 1821. There are people who are described in a lordly fashion by the true Monrovians as "indigenous natives," and the chief of these are the Kroomen, who pay no taxes, defy the Government, and at intervals tweak the official nose of the Republic.

The second day after the bell was in place, Monrovia awoke to find a complete silence reigning in the bay, and that in spite of a heavy swell. The bell was still, and two ex-admirals, who were selling fish on the foreshore, borrowed a boat and rowed out to investigate. The explanation was simple—the bell had been stolen.

"Now!" said the President of the Liberian Republic in despair, "may Beelzebub, who is the father and author of all sin, descend upon these thieving Kroomen!"

Another bell was attached. The same night it was stolen. Yet another bell was put to the buoy, and a boat-load of admirals kept watch. Throughout the night they sat, rising and falling with the swell, and the monotonous "clang-jangle-clong" was music in their ears. All night it sounded, but in the early morning, at the dark hour before the sun comes up, it seemed that the bell, still tolling, grew fainter and fainter.

"Brothers," said an admiral, "we are drifting away from the bell."

But the explanation was that the bell had drifted away from them, for, tired of half measures, the Kroomen had come and taken the buoy, bell and all, and to this day there is no mark to show where a some-time man-of-war rots in the harbour of Monrovia.

The ingenious soul who planned and carried out this theft was one Bosambo, who had three wives, one of whom, being by birth

Congolaise, and untrustworthy, informed the police, and with some ceremony Bosambo was arrested and tried at the Supreme Court, where he was found guilty of "theft and high treason "and sentenced to ten years' penal servitude.

They took Bosambo back to prison, and Bosambo interviewed the black gaoler.

"My friend," he said, "I have a big *ju-ju* in the forest, and if you do not release me at once you and your wife shall die in great torment."

"Of your *ju-ju* I know nothing," said the gaoler philosophically, "but I receive two dollars a week for guarding prisoners, and if I let you escape I shall lose my job."

"I know a place where there is much silver hidden," said Bosambo with promptitude. "You and I will go to this place, and we shall be rich."

"If you knew where there was silver, why did you steal bells, which are of brass and of no particular value?" asked his unimaginative guard.

"I see that you have a heart of stone," said Bosambo, and went away to the forest settlement to chop down trees for the good of the State.

Four months after this, Sanders, Chief Commissioner for the Isisi, Ikeli, and Akasava countries, received, *inter alia*, a communication of a stereotyped description—

TO WHOM IT MAY CONCERN.
Wanted,—on a warrant issued by H.E. the President of Liberia, Bosambo Krooboy, who escaped from the penal settlement near Monrovia, after killing a guard. He is believed to be making for your country.

A description followed.

Sanders put the document away with other such notices—they were not infrequent in their occurrence—and gave his mind to the eternal problem of the Ochori.

Now, as ever, the Ochori people were in sad trouble. There is no other tribe in the whole of Africa that is as defenceless as the poor Ochori. The Fingoes, slaves as they are by name and tradition, were ferocious as the Masai, compared with the Ochori.

Sanders was a little impatient, and a deputation of three, who had journeyed down to headquarters to lay the grievances of the people before him, found him unsympathetic.

He interviewed them on his verandah.

"Master, no man leaves us in peace," said one. "Isisi folk, N'Gombi people from far-away countries, they come to us demanding this and that, and we give, being afraid."

"Afraid of what?" asked Sanders wearily.

"We fear death and pain, also burning and the taking of our women," said the other.

"Who is chief of you?" asked Sanders, wilfully ignorant.

"I am chief lord," said an elderly man, clad in a leopard skin.

"Go back to your people, chief, if indeed chief you are, and not some old woman without shame; go back and bear with you a fetish—a most powerful fetish—which shall be, as me, watching your interest and protecting you. This fetish you shall plant on the edge of your village that faces the sun at noon. You shall mark the place where it shall be planted, and at midnight, with proper ceremony, and the sacrifice of a young goat, you shall set my fetish in its place. And after that whosoever ill-treats you or robs you shall do so at some risk."

Sanders said this very solemnly, and the men of the deputation were duly impressed. More impressed were they when, before starting on their homeward journey, Sanders placed in their hands a stout pole, to the end of which was attached a flat board inscribed with certain marks.

They carried their trophy six days' journey through the forest, then four days' journey by canoe along the Little River, until they came to Ochori. There, by the light of the moon, with the sacrifice of two goats (to make sure), the pole was planted so that the board inscribed with mystic characters would face the sun at noon.

News travels fast in the back lands, and it came to the villages throughout the Isisi and the Akasava country that the Ochori were particularly protected by white magic. Protected they had always been, and many men had died at the white man's hand because the temptation to kill the Ochori folk had proved irresistible.

"I do not believe that Sandi has done this thing," said the chief of the Akasava. "Let us go across the river and see with our own eyes, and if they have lied we shall beat them with sticks, though let no man kill, because of Sandi and his cruelty."

So across the water they went, and marched until they came within sight of the Ochori city, and the Ochori people, hearing that the Akasava people were coming, ran away into the woods and hid, in accordance with their custom.

The Akasava advanced until they came to the pole stuck in the ground and the board with the devil marks.

Before this they stood in silence and in awe, and having made obeisance to it and sacrificed a chicken (which was the lawful property of the Ochori) they turned back.

After this came a party from Isisi, and they must needs come through the Akasava country.

They brought presents with them and lodged with the Akasava for one night.

"What story is this of the Ochori?" asked the Isisi chief in command; so the chief of the Akasava told him.

"You may save yourself the journey, for we have seen it."

"That," said the Isisi chief, "I will believe when I have seen."

"That is bad talk," said the Akasava people, who were gathered at the *palaver,* "these dogs of Isisi call us liars."

Nevertheless there was no bloodshed, and in the morning the Isisi went on their way.

The Ochori saw them coming, and hid in the woods, but the precaution was unnecessary, for the Isisi departed as they came.

Other folk made a pilgrimage to the Ochori, N'Gombi, Bokeli, and the Little People of the Forest, who were so shy that they came by night, and the Ochori people began to realise a sense of their importance.

Then Bosambo, a Krooman and an adventurer at large, appeared on the scene, having crossed eight hundred miles of wild land in the earnest hope that time would dull the memory of the Liberian Government and incidentally bring him to a land of milk and honey.

Now Bosambo had in his life been many things. He had been steward on an Elder Dempster boat, he had been scholar at a mission school—he was the proud possessor of a bound copy of *The Lives of the Saints,* a reward of industry—and among his accomplishments was a knowledge of English.

The hospitable Ochori received him kindly, fed him with sweet manioc and sugar-cane, and told him about Sandi's magic. After he had eaten, Bosambo walked down to the post and read the inscription—

TRESPASSERS BEWARE.

He was not impressed, and strolled back again thinking deeply.

"This magic," he said to the chief, "is good magic. I know, because I have white man's blood in my veins."

41

In support of this statement he proceeded to libel a perfectly innocent British official at Sierra Leone.

The Ochori were profoundly moved. They poured forth the story of their persecutions, a story which began in remote ages, when Tiganobeni, the great king, came down from the north and wasted the country as far south as the Isisi.

Bosambo listened—it took two nights and the greater part of a day to tell the story, because the official storyteller of the Ochori had only one method of telling—and when it was finished Bosambo said to himself—

"This is the people I have long sought. I will stay here."

Aloud he asked:

"How often does Sandi come to you?"

"Once every year, master," said the chief, "on the twelfth moon, and a little after."

"When came he last?"

"When this present moon is at full, three moons since; he comes after the big rains."

"Then," said Bosambo, again to himself, "for nine months I am safe."

They built him a hut and planted for him a banana grove and gave him seed. Then he demanded for wife the daughter of the chief, and although he offered nothing in payment the girl came to him. That a stranger lived in the chief village of the Ochori was remarked by the other tribes, for news of this kind spreads, but since he was married, and into the chief's family at that, it was accepted that the man must be of the Ochori folk, and such was the story that came to headquarters. Then the chief of the Ochori died. He died suddenly in some pain; but such deaths are common, and his son ruled in his place. Then the son died after the briefest reign, and Bosambo called the people together, the elders, the wise men, and the headmen of the country.

"It appears," he said, "that the many gods of the Ochori are displeased with you, and it has been revealed to me in a dream that I shall be chief of the Ochori. Therefore, O chiefs and wise men and headmen, bow before me, as is the custom, and I will make you a great people."

It is characteristic of the Ochori that no man said "nay" to him, even though in the assembly were three men who by custom might claim the chieftainship.

Sanders heard of the new chief and was puzzled.

"Etabo?" he repeated—this was how Bosambo called himself—"I do not remember the man—yet if he can put backbone into the people I do not care who he is."

Backbone or cunning, or both, Bosambo was certainly installed.

"He has many strange practices," reported a native agent to Sanders. "Every day he assembles the men of the village and causes them to walk past a *pelebi* (table) on which are many eggs. And it is his command that each man as he passes shall take an egg so swiftly that no eye may see him take it. And if the man bungle or break the egg, or be slow, this new chief puts shame upon him, whipping him."

"It is a game," said Sanders; but for the life of him he could not see what game it was. Report after report reached him of the new chief's madness. Sometimes he would take the unfortunate Ochori out by night, teaching them such things as they had never known before. Thus he instructed them in what manner they might seize upon a goat so that the goat could not cry. Also how to crawl on their bellies inch by inch so that they made no sound or sign. All these things the Ochori did, groaning aloud at the injustice and the labour of it.

"I'm dashed if I can understand it!" said Sanders, knitting his brows, when the last report came in. "With anybody but the Ochori this would mean war. But the Ochori!"

Notwithstanding his contempt for their fighting qualities, he kept his Police Houssas ready.

But there was no war. Instead, there came complaint from the Akasava that "many leopards were in the woods."

Leopards will keep, thought Sanders, and, anyway, the Akasava were good enough hunters to settle that *palaver* without outside help. The next report was alarming. In two weeks these leopards had carried off three score of goats, twenty bags of salt, and much ivory.

Leopards eat goats; there might conceivably be fastidious leopards that cannot eat goats without salt; but a leopard does not take ivory tusks even to pick his teeth with. So Sanders made haste to journey up the river, because little things were considerable in a country where people strain at gnats and swallow whole caravans.

"Lord, it is true," said the chief of the Akasava, with some emotion, "these goats disappear night by night, though we watch them; also the salt and ivory, because that we did not watch."

"But no leopard could take these things," said Sanders irritably. "These are thieves."

The chief's gesture was comprehensive.

"Who could thieve?" he said. "The N'Gombi people live very far away; also the Isisi. The Ochori are fools, and, moreover, afraid."

Then Sanders remembered the egg games, and the midnight manoeuvres of the Ochori.

"I will call on this new chief," he said; and crossed the river that day.

Sending a messenger to herald his coming, he waited two miles out of the city, and the councillors and wise men came out to him with offerings of fish and fruit.

"Where is your chief?" he asked.

"Lord, he is ill," they said gravely. "This day there came to him a feeling of sickness, and he fell down moaning. We have carried him to his hut."

Sanders nodded.

"I will see him," he said grimly.

They led him to the door of the chief's hut, and Sanders went in. It was very dark, and in the darkest corner lay a prostrate man. Sanders bent over him, touched his pulse lightly, felt gingerly for the swelling on the neck behind the ears for a sign of sleeping sickness. No symptom could he find; but on the bare shoulder, as his fingers passed over the man's flesh, he felt a scar of singular regularity; then he found another, and traced their direction. The convict brand of the Monrovian Government was familiar to him.

"I thought so," said Sanders, and gave the moaning man a vigorous kick.

"Come out into the light, Bosambo of Monrovia," he said; and Bosambo rose obediently and followed the Commissioner into the light.

They stood looking at one another for several minutes; then Sanders, speaking in the dialect of the Pepper Coast, said—

"I have a mind to hang you, Bosambo."

"That is as your Excellency wishes," said Bosambo.

Sanders said nothing, tapping his boot with his walking-stick and gazing thoughtfully downward.

"Having made thieves, could you make men of these people?" he said, after a while.

"I think they could fight now, for they are puffed with pride because they have robbed the Akasava," said Bosambo.

Sanders bit the end of his stick like a man in doubt.

"There shall be neither theft nor murder," he said. "No more chiefs

44

or chiefs' sons shall die suddenly," he added significantly.

"Master, it shall be as you desire."

"As for the goats you have stolen, them you may keep, and the teeth (ivory) and the salt also. For if you hand them back to Akasava you will fill their stomachs with rage, and that would mean war."

Bosambo nodded slowly.

"Then you shall remain, for I see you are a clever man, and the Ochori need such as you. But if—"

"Master, by the fat of my heart I will do as you wish," said Bosambo; "for I have always desired to be a chief under the British."

Sanders was half-way back to headquarters before he missed his field-glasses, and wondered where he could have dropped them. At that identical moment Bosambo was exhibiting the binoculars to his admiring people.

"From this day forth," said Bosambo, "there shall be no lifting of goats nor stealing of any kind. This much I told the great Sandi, and as a sign of his love, behold, he gave me these things of magic that eat up space."

"Lord," said a councillor in awe, "did you know the Great One?"

"I have cause to know him," said Bosambo modestly, "for I am his son."

Fortunately Sanders knew nothing of this interesting disclosure.

CHAPTER 4

The Drowsy One

There were occasions when Sanders came up against the outer world, when he learnt, with something like bewilderment, that beyond the farthermost forests, beyond the lazy, swelling, blue sea, there were men and women who lived in houses and carefully tabooed such subjects as violent death and such horrid happenings as were daily features of his life.

He had to treat with folk who, in the main, were illogical and who believed in spirits. When you deal in the abstract with government of races so influenced, a knowledge of constitutional law and economics is fairly valueless.

There is one type of man that can rule native provinces wisely, and that type is best represented by Sanders.

There are other types, as, for instance:

Once upon a time a young man came from England with a reputation. He was sent by the Colonial Office to hold a district under Sanders as Deputy Commissioner. He was a Bachelor of Law, had read Science, and had acquired in a methodical fashion a working acquaintance with Swaheli, bacteriology, and medicines. He was a very grave young man, and the first night of his arrival he kept Sanders (furtively yawning) out of his bed whilst he demonstrated a system whereby the aboriginal could be converted—not converted spiritually, but from unproductive vagrancy to a condition of good citizenship,

Sanders said nothing beyond using the conventional expressions of polite interest, and despatched the young man and his tremendous baggage to an up-country station, with his official blessing.

Torrington—this was the grave young man's name—established himself at Entoli, and started forth to instil into the heathen mind the elementary principles of applied mechanics. In other words he taught

46

them, through the medium of Swaheli—which they imperfectly understood—and a tin kettle, the lesson of steam. They understood the kettle part, but could not quite comprehend what meat he was cooking, and when he explained for the fortieth time that he was only cooking water, they glanced significantly one at the other and agreed that he was not quite right in his head.

They did not tell him this much to his face, for cannibals have very good manners—though their table code leaves much to be desired.

Mr. Torrington tried them with chemical experiments, showing them how sulphuric acid applied to sugar produced Su^3, Su^4, or words to that effect. He gained a reputation as a magician as a result, and in more huts than one he was regarded and worshipped as a Great and Clever Devil—which in a sense he was. But the first time he came up against the spirit of the people, his science, his law, and his cut-and-dried theories went *phutt!* And that is where Sanders came in— Sanders who had forgotten all the chemistry he ever knew, and who, as a student of Constitutional Law, was the rankest of failures.

It came about in this way.

There was a young man in Isisi who prophesied that on such a day, at such an hour, the river would rise and drown the people. When Mr. Torrington heard of this prophecy he was amused, and at first took no notice of it. But it occurred to him that here might be a splendid opportunity for revealing to the barbarian a little of that science with which he was so plentifully endowed.

So he drew a large sectional plan, showing—

(a) the bed of the river;

(b) the height of the banks;

(c) the maximum rise of the river;

(d) the height of the surrounding country; and demonstrated as plainly as possible the utter absurdity of the prophecy.

Yet the people were unconvinced, and were preparing to abandon the village when Sanders arrived on the scene. He sent for the prophet, who was a young man of neurotic tendencies, and had a wooden prison cage built on the bank of the river, into which the youth was introduced.

"You will stay here," said Sanders, "and when the river rises you must prophesy that it will fall again, else assuredly you will be drowned."

Whereupon the people settled down again in their homes and waited for the river to drown the prophet and prove his words. But the river at this season of the year was steadily falling, and the prophet, like many another, was without honour in his own country.

Sanders went away; and, although somewhat discouraged, Mr. Torrington resumed his experiments. First of all, he took up sleeping sickness, and put in three months' futile work, impressing nobody save a gentleman of whom more must be written in a further chapter. Then he dropped that study suddenly and went to another.

He had ideas concerning vaccination, but the first baby he vaccinated died of croup, and Torrington came flying down the river telling Sanders a rambling story of a populace infuriated and demanding his blood. Then Torrington went home.

"The country is now quiet," wrote Sanders to the Administrator, with sardonic humour. "There are numerous *palavers* pending, but none of any particular moment. The Isisi people are unusually quiet, and Bosambo, the Monrovian, of whom I have written your Excellency, makes a model chief for the Ochori. No thefts have been traced to him for three months. I should be grateful if full information could be supplied to me concerning an expedition which at the moment is traversing this country under the style of the Isisi Exploitation Syndicate."

Curiously enough, Torrington had forgotten the fact that a member of this expedition had been one of the most interested students of his sleeping sickness clinics.

The Isisi Exploitation Syndicate, Limited, was born between the entree and the sweet at the house of a gentleman whose Christian name was Isidore, and who lived in Maida Vale. At dinner one night with a dear friend—who called himself McPherson every day of the year except on Yum Kippur, when he frankly admitted that he had been born Isaacs—the question of good company titles came up, and Mr. McPherson said he had had the "Isisi Exploitation" in his mind for many years. With the aid of an atlas the Isisi country was discovered. It was one of those atlases on which are inscribed the staple products of the lands, and across the Isisi was writ fair "Rubber," "Kola-nut," "Mahogany," and "Tobacco."

I would ask the reader to particularly remember "Tobacco."

"There's a chief I've had some correspondence with," said Mr. McPherson, chewing his cigar meditatively; "we could get a sort of concession from him. It would have to be done on the quiet, because the country is a British Protectorate. Now, if we could get a man who'd put up the stuff, and send him out to fix the concession, we'd have a company floated before you could say knife."

Judicious inquiry discovered the man in Claude Hyall Cuthbert, a plutocratic young gentleman, who, on the strength of once having nearly shot a lion in Uganda, was accepted by a large circle of acquaintances as an authority on Africa.

Cuthbert, who dabbled in stocks and shares, was an acquisition to any syndicate, and on the understanding that part of his duty would be the obtaining of the concession, he gladly financed the syndicate to the extent of seven thousand pounds, four thousand of which Messrs. Isidore and McPherson very kindly returned to him to cover the cost of his expedition.

The other three thousand were earmarked for office expenses.

As Mr. McPherson truly said:

"Whatever happens, we're on velvet, my boy," which was perfectly true.

Before Cuthbert sailed, McPherson offered him a little advice.

"Whatever you do," he said, "steer clear of that dam' Commissioner Sanders. He's one of those pryin', interferin'———"

"I know the breed," said Cuthbert wisely. "This is not my first visit to Africa. Did I ever tell you about the lion I shot in Uganda?"

A week later he sailed.

★★★★★★

In course of time came a strange white man through Sanders' domain. This white man, who was Cuthbert, was following the green path to death—but this he did not know. He threw his face to the forest, as the natives say, and laughed, and the people of the village of O'Tembi, standing before their wattle huts, watched him in silent wonder.

It was a wide path between huge trees, and the green of the undergrowth was flecked with sunlight, and, indeed, the green path was beautiful to the eye, being not unlike a parkland avenue.

N'Beki, chief of this village of the O'Tembi, a very good old man, went out to the path when the white man began his journey.

"White man," he said solemnly, "this is the road to hell, where all manner of devils live. Night brings remorse, and dawn brings self-hatred, which is worse than death."

Cuthbert, whose Swaheli was faulty, and whose Bomongo talk was nil, grinned impatiently as his coastboy translated unpicturesquely.

"Dam nigger done say, this be bad place, no good; he say bimeby you libe for die."

"Tell him to go to blazes!" said Cuthbert noisily; "and, look here, Flagstaff, ask him where the rubber is, see? Tell him we know all about the forest, and ask him about the elephants, where their playground is?"

Cuthbert was broad-shouldered and heavily built, and under his broad sun-helmet his face was very hot and moist.

"Tell the white man," said the chief quietly, "there is no rubber within seven days' journey, and that we do not know ivory; elephants there were *cala cala*—but not now."

"He's a liar!" was Cuthbert's only comment. "Get these beggars moving, Flagstaff. Hi, *alapa', avanti, trek!*"

"These beggars," a straggling line of them, resumed their loads uncomplainingly. They were good carriers, as carriers go, and only two had died since the march began.

Cuthbert stood and watched them pass, using his stick dispassionately upon the laggards. Then he turned to go.

"Ask him," he said finally, "why he calls this the road to what-d'ye-call-it?"

The old man shook his head.

"Because of the devils," he said simply.

"Tell him he's a silly ass!" bellowed Cuthbert and followed his carriers.

This natural path the caravan took extended in almost a straight line through the forest. It was a strange path because of its very smoothness, and the only drawback lay in the fact that it seemed to be the breeding-place of flies—little black flies, as big as the house-fly of familiar shape, if anything a little bigger.

They terrified the natives for many reasons, but principally because they stung. They did not terrify Cuthbert, because he was dressed in *tapai* cloth; none the less, there were times when these black flies found joints in his armour and roused him to anger. This path extended ten miles and made pleasant travelling. Then the explorer struck off into the forest, following another path, well beaten, but more difficult.

By devious routes Mr. Cuthbert came into the heart of Sanders' territories, and he was successful in this, that he avoided Sanders. He had with him a caravan of sixty men and an interpreter, and in due course he reached his objective, which was the village of a great chief ruling a remarkable province—Bosambo, of the Ochori, no less; sometime Krooman, steward of the Elder Dempster line, chief on sufferance, but none the less an interesting person. Bosambo, you may be sure, came out to greet his visitor.

"Say to him," said Cuthbert to his interpreter, "that I am proud to meet the great chief."

"Lord chief," said the interpreter in the vernacular, "this white man is a fool, and has much money."

"So I see," said Bosambo.

"Tell him," said Cuthbert, with all the dignity of an ambassador, "that I have come to bring him wonderful presents."

"The white man says," said the interpreter, "that if he is sure you are a good man he will give you presents. Now," said the interpreter carefully, "as I am the only man who can speak for you, let us make arrangements. You shall give me one-third of all he offers. Then will I persuade him to continue giving, since he is the father of mad people."

"And you," said Bosambo briefly, "are the father of liars."

He made a sign to his guard, and they seized upon the unfortunate interpreter and led him forth. Cuthbert, in a sweat of fear, pulled a revolver.

"Master," said Bosambo loftily, "you no make urn fuss. Dis dam' nigger, he no good; he make you speak bad t'ings. I speak um English proper. You sit down, we talk um."

So Cuthbert sat down in the village of Ochori, and for three days there was a great giving of presents, and signing of concessions. Bosambo conceded the Ochori country—that was a small thing. He granted forest rights of the Isisi, he sold the Akasava, he bartered away the Lulungo territories and the "native products thereof"—I quote from the written document now preserved at the Colonial Office and bearing the scrawled signature of Bosambo—and he added, as a lordly afterthought, the Ikeli district.

"What about river rights?" asked the delighted Cuthbert.

"What will you give um?" demanded Bosambo cautiously.

"Forty English pounds?" suggested Cuthbert.

"I take um," said Bosambo.

It was a remarkably simple business; a more knowledgeable man than Cuthbert would have been scared by the easiness of his success, but Cuthbert was too satisfied with himself to be scared at anything.

It is said that his leave-taking with Bosambo was of an affecting character, that Bosambo wept and embraced his benefactor's feet.

Be that as it may, his "concessions" in his pocket, Cuthbert began his coast ward journey, still avoiding Sanders.

He came to Etebi and found a deputy-commissioner, who received him with open arms. Here Cuthbert stayed a week.

Mr. Torrington at the time was tremendously busy with a scheme for stamping out sleeping sickness. Until then, Cuthbert was under the impression that it was a pleasant disease, the principal symptom of which was a painless coma. Fascinated, he extended his stay to a fortnight, seeing many dreadful sights, for Torrington had established a sort of amateur clinic, and a hundred cases a day came to him for treatment.

"And it comes from the bite of a tsetse fly?" said Cuthbert. "Show me a tsetse."

Torrington obliged him, and when the other saw the little black insect he went white to the lips.

"My God!" he whispered, "I've been bitten by that!"

"It doesn't follow——" began Torrington;

but Cuthbert was blundering and stumbling in wild fear to his carriers' camp.

"Get your loads!" he yelled. "Out of this cursed country we get as quick as we can!"

Torrington, with philosophical calm, endeavoured to reassure him, but he was not to be appeased.

He left Etebi that night and camped in the forest. Three days later he reached a mission station, where he complained of headaches and pains in the neck (he had not attended Torrington's clinics in vain). The missionary, judging from the man's haggard appearance and general incoherence that he had an attack of malaria, advised him to rest for a few days; but Cuthbert was all a-fret to reach the coast. Twenty miles from the mission, Cuthbert sent his carriers back, and said he would cover the last hundred miles of the journey alone.

To this extraordinary proposition the natives agreed—from that day Cuthbert disappeared from the sight of man.

★★★★★★

Sanders was taking a short cut through the forest to avoid the interminable twists and bends of the river, when he came suddenly upon a village of death—four sad little huts, built hastily amidst a tangle of underwood. He called, but nobody answered him. He was too wary to enter any of the crazy habitations.

He knew these little villages in the forest. It was the native custom to take the aged and the dying—especially those who died sleepily—to far-away places, beyond the reach of man, and leave them there with a week's food and a fire, to die in decent solitude.

He called again, but only the forest answered him. The chattering, noisy forest, all a-crackle with the movements of hidden things. Yet there was a fire burning which told of life.

Sanders resumed his journey, first causing a quantity of food to be laid in a conspicuous place for the man who made the fire.

He was on his way to take evidence concerning the disappearance of Cuthbert. It was the fourth journey of its kind he had attempted. There had been *palavers* innumerable.

Bosambo, chief of the Ochori, had sorrowfully disgorged the presents he had received, and admitted his fault.

"Lord!" he confessed, "when I was with the white man on the coast I learnt the trick of writing—it is a cursed gift—else all this trouble would not have come about. For, desiring to show my people how great a man I was, I wrote a letter in the English fashion, and sent it by messenger to the coast and thence to friends in Sierra Leone, telling them of my fortune. Thus the people in London came to know of the treasure of this land."

Sanders, in a few illuminative sentences, conveyed his impression of Bosambo's genius.

"You slave and son of a slave," he said, "whom I took from a prison to rule the Ochori, why did you deceive this white man, selling him lands that were not yours?"

"Lord!" said Bosambo simply, "there was nothing else I could sell."

But there was no clue here as to Cuthbert's whereabouts, nor at the mission station, nor amongst the carriers detained on suspicion. One man might have thrown light upon the situation, but Torrington was at home fulfilling the post of assistant examiner in mechanics at South Kensington (more in his element there) and filling in his spare time with lecturing on *The Migration of the Bantu Races*.

So that the end of Sanders' fourth quest was no more successful than the third, or the second, or the first, and he retraced his steps to headquarters, feeling somewhat depressed.

He took the path he had previously traversed, and came upon the Death Camp late in the afternoon. The fire still burnt, but the food he had placed had disappeared. He hailed the hut in the native tongue, but no one answered him. He waited for a little while, and then gave orders for more food to be placed on the ground.

"Poor devil!" said Sanders, and gave the order to march. He himself had taken half a dozen steps, when he stopped. At his feet something glittered in the fading light. He stooped and picked it up. It was an exploded cartridge. He examined it carefully, smelt it—it had been recently fired. Then he found another. They were Lee-Metford, and bore the mark "'07," which meant that they were less than a year old.

He was still standing with the little brass cylinders in his hand, when Abiboo came to him.

"Master," said the Houssa, "who ties monkeys to trees with ropes?"

"Is that a riddle?" asked Sanders testily, for his mind was busy on this matter of cartridges.

Abiboo for answer beckoned him.

Fifty yards from the hut was a tree, at the foot of which, whimpering and chattering and in a condition of abject terror, were two small black monkeys tethered by ropes.

They spat and grinned ferociously as Sanders approached them. He looked from the cartridges to the monkeys and back to the cartridges again, then he began searching the grass. He found two more empty shells and a rusting lancet, such as may be found in the pocket-case of any explorer.

Then he walked back to the hut before which the fire burnt, and called softly—

"Mr. Cuthbert!"

There was no answer, and Sanders called again—

"Mr. Cuthbert!"

From the interior of the hut came a groan.

"Leave me alone. I have come here to die!" said a muffled voice.

"Come out and be civil," said Sanders coolly; "you can die afterwards."

After a few moments' delay there issued from the door of the hut the wreck of a man, with long hair and a month-old beard, who stood sulkily before the Commissioner.

"Might I ask," said Sanders, "what your little game is?"

The other shook his head wearily. He was a pitiable sight. His clothes were in tatters; he was unwashed and grimy.

"Sleeping sickness," he said wearily. "Felt it coming on—seen what

54

horrible thing it was—didn't want to be a burden. Oh, my God! What a fool I've been to come to this filthy country!"

"That's very likely," said Sanders. "But who told you that you had sleeping sickness?"

"Know it—know it," said the listless man.

"Sit down," said Sanders. The other obeyed, and Sanders applied the superficial tests.

"If you've got sleeping sickness," said Sanders, after the examination, "I'm suffering from religious mania—man, you're crazy!"

Yet there was something in Cuthbert's expression that was puzzling. He was dull, heavy, and stupid. His movements were slow and lethargic.

Sanders watched him as he pulled a black wooden pipe from his ragged pocket, and with painful slowness charged it from a skin pouch.

"It's got me, I tell you," muttered Cuthbert, and lit the pipe with a blazing twig from the fire. "I knew it (puff) as soon as that fellow Torrington (puff) described the symptoms (puff);—felt dull and sleepy—got a couple of monkeys and injected my blood (puff)—*they* went drowsy, too—sure sign——"

"Where did you get that tobacco from?" demanded Sanders quickly.

Cuthbert took time to consider his answer.

"Fellow gave it me—chief fellow, Bosambo. Native tobacco, but not bad—he gave me a devil of a lot."

"So I should say," said Sanders, and reaching over took the pouch and put it in his pocket.

★★★★★★

When Sanders had seen Mr. Cuthbert safe on board a homeward-bound steamer, he took his twenty Houssas to the Ochori country to arrest Bosambo, and expected Bosambo would fly; but the imperturbable chief awaited his coming, and offered him the customary honours.

"I admit I gave the white man the hemp," he said. "I myself smoke it, suffering no ill. How was I to know that it would make him sleep?"

"Why did you give it to him?" demanded Sanders.

Bosambo looked the Commissioner full in the face.

"Last moon you came, lord, asking why I gave him the Isisi country and the rights of the little river, because these were not mine to give.

Now you come to me saying why did I give the white man native tobacco—Lord, that was the only thing I gave him that was mine."

CHAPTER 5

The Special Commissioner

The Hon. George Tackle had the good fortune to be the son of his father; otherwise I am free to confess he had no claim to distinction. But his father, being the proprietor of the *Courier* and *Echo* (with which are incorporated I don't know how many dead and gone stars of the Fleet Street firmament), George had a "pull" which no amount of competitive merit could hope to contend with, and when the stories of atrocities in the district of Lukati began to leak out and questions were asked in Parliament, George opened his expensively-bound Gazetteer, discovered that the district of Lukati was in British territory, and instantly demanded that he should be sent out to investigate these crimes, which were a blot upon our boasted civilisation.

His father agreed, having altogether a false appreciation of his son's genius, and suggested that George should go to the office and "get all the facts" regarding the atrocities. George, with a good-natured smile of amusement at the bare thought of anybody instructing him in a subject on which he was so thoroughly conversant, promised; but the *Courier and Echo* office did not see him, and the librarian of the newspaper, who had prepared a really valuable dossier of newspaper cuttings, pamphlets, maps, and health hints for the young man's guidance, was dismayed to learn that the confident youth had sailed without any further instruction in the question than a man might secure from the hurried perusal of the scraps which from day to day appeared in the morning press.

As a special correspondent, I adduce, with ill-suppressed triumph, the case of the Hon. George Tackle as an awful warning to all newspaper proprietors who allow their parental affections to overcome their good judgment.

All that the Hon. George knew was that at Lukati there had been four well-authenticated cases of barbarous acts of cruelty against natives, and that the Commissioner of the district was responsible for the whippings and the torture.

He thought, did the Hon. George, that this was all that it was necessary to know. But this is where he made his big mistake.

Up at Lukati all sorts of things happened, as Commissioner Sanders knows, to his cost. Once he visited the district and left it tranquil, and for Carter, his deputy, whom he left behind, the natives built a most beautiful hut, planting gardens about, all off their own bat.

One day, when Carter had just finished writing an enthusiastic report on the industry of his people, and the whole-hearted way they were taking up and supporting the new regime, the chief of the village, whom Carter had facetiously named O'Leary (his born name was indeed Olari), came to him.

Carter at the moment was walking through the well-swept street of the village with his hands in his coat pockets and his big white helmet tipped on the back of his head because the sun was setting at his back.

"Father," said the Chief Olari, "I have brought these people to see you."

He indicated with a wave of his hand six strange warriors carrying their shields and spears, who looked at him dispassionately.

Carter nodded.

"They desire," said Olari, "to see the wonderful little black fetish that my father carries in his pocket that they may tell their people of its powers."

"Tell your people," said Carter good-humouredly, "that I have not got the fetish with me—if they will come to my hut I will show them its wonders."

Whereupon Olari lifted his spear and struck at Carter, and the six warriors sprang forward together. Carter fought gamely, but he was unarmed.

When Sanders heard the news of his subordinate's death he did not faint or fall into a fit of insane cursing. He was sitting on his broad verandah at headquarters when the dusty messenger came. He rose with pursed lips and frowning eyes, fingering the letter—this came from Tollemache, inspector of police at Bokari—and paced the verandah.

"Poor chap, poor chap!" was all that he said.

He sent no message to Olari; he made no preparations for a punitive raid; he went on signing documents, inspecting Houssas, attending dinner parties, as though Carter had never lived or died. All these things the spies of Olari reported, and the chief was thankful.

Lukati being two hundred miles from headquarters, through a savage and mountainous country, an expedition was no light undertaking, and the British Government, rich as it is, cannot afford to spend a hundred thousand pounds to avenge the death of a subordinate official. Of this fact Sanders was well aware, so he employed his time in collecting and authenticating the names of Carter's assassins. When he had completed them he went a journey seventy miles into the bush to the great witchdoctor Kelebi, whose name was known throughout the coast country from Dakka to the Eastern borders of Togoland.

"Here are the names of men who have put shame upon me," he said; "but principally Olari, chief of the Lukati people."

"I will put a spell upon Olari," said the witchdoctor; "a very bad spell, and upon these men. The charge will be six English pounds."

Sanders paid the money, and "dashed" two bottles of square-face and a piece of proper cloth. Then he went back to headquarters.

One night through the village of Lukati ran a whisper, and the men muttered the news with fearful shivers and backward glances.

"Olari, the chief, is cursed!"

Olari heard the tidings from his women, and came out of his hut into the moonlight, raving horribly.

The next day he sickened, and on the fifth day he was near to dead and suffering terrible pains, as also were six men who helped in the slaying of Carter. That they did not die was no fault of the witchdoctor, who excused his failure on account of the great distance between himself and his subjects.

As for Sanders, he was satisfied, saying that even the pains were cheap at the price, and that it would give him great satisfaction to write "*finis*" to Olari with his own hand.

A week after this, Abiboo, Sanders' favourite servant, was taken ill. There was no evidence of fever or disease, only the man began to fade as it were.

Making inquiries, Sanders discovered that Abiboo had offended the witchdoctor Kelebi, and that the doctor had sent him the death message.

Sanders took fifty Houssas into the bush and interviewed the witchdoctor.

"I have reason," he said, "for believing you to be a failure as a slayer of men."

"Master," said Kelebi in extenuation, "my magic cannot cross mountains, otherwise Olari and his friends would have died."

"That is as it may be," said Sanders. I lam now concerned with magic nearer at hand, and I must tell you that the day after Abiboo dies I will hang you."

"Father," said Kelebi emphatically, "under those circumstances Abiboo shall live."

Sanders gave him a sovereign, and rode back to headquarters, to find his servant on the high road to recovery.

I give you this fragment of Sanders' history, because it will enable you to grasp the peculiar environment in which Sanders spent the greater part of his life, and because you will appreciate all the better the irony of the situation created by the coming of the Hon. George Tackle.

Sanders was taking breakfast on the verandah of his house. From where he sat he commanded across the flaming beauties of his garden a view of a broad, rolling, oily sea, a golden blaze of light under the hot sun. There was a steamer lying three miles out (only in five fathoms of water at that), and Sanders, through his glasses, recognised her as the Elder Dempster boat that brought the monthly mail. Since there were no letters on his table, and the boat had been "in" for two hours, he gathered that there was no mail for him, and was thankful, for he had outlived the sentimental period of life when letters were pleasant possibilities.

Having no letters, he expected no callers, and the spectacle of the Hon. George being carried in a hammock into his garden was astonishing.

The Hon. George carefully alighted, adjusted his white pith helmet, smoothed the creases from his immaculate ducks, and mounted the steps that led to the *stoep*.

"How do?" said the visitor. "My name is Tackle—George Tackle." He smiled, as though to say more was an insult to his hearer's intelligence.

Sanders bowed, a little ceremoniously for him. He felt that his visitor expected this.

"I'm out on a commission," the Hon. George went on. "As you've doubtless heard, my governor is the proprietor of the *Courier and Echo*, and so he thought I'd better go out and see the thing for myself. I've no doubt the whole thing is exaggerated—"

"Hold hard," said Sanders, a light dawning on him. "I gather that you are a sort of correspondent of a newspaper?"

"Exactly."

"That you have come to inquire into—"

"Treatment of natives, and all that," said the Hon. George easily.

"And what is wrong with the treatment of the native?" asked Sanders sweetly.

The hon. gentleman made an indefinite gesture.

"You know—things in newspapers—missionaries," he said rapidly, being somewhat embarrassed by the realisation that the man, if any, responsible for the outrages was standing before him.

"I never read the newspapers," said Sanders, "and—"

"Of course," interrupted the Hon. George eagerly, "we can make it all right as far as you are concerned."

"Oh, thank you!" Sanders' gratitude was a little overdone, but he held out his hand. "Well, I wish you luck—let me know how you get on."

The Hon. George Tackle was frankly nonplussed.

"But excuse me," he said, "where—how Hang it all, where am I to put up?"

"Here?"

"Yes—dash it, my kit is on shore! I thought—"

"You thought I'd put you up?"

"Well, I did think——"

"That I'd fall on your neck and welcome you?"

"Not exactly, but——"

"Well," said Sanders, carefully folding his napkin, "I'm not so glad to see you as all that."

"I suppose not," said the Hon. George, bridling.

"Because you're a responsibility—I hate extra responsibility. You can pitch your tent just wherever you like—but I cannot offer you the hospitality you desire."

"I shall report this matter to the Administrator," said the Hon. George ominously.

"You may report it to my grandmother's maiden aunt," said Sanders politely.

Half an hour later he saw the Hon. George rejoin the ship that brought him to Isisi Bassam, and chuckled. George would go straight to the Administrator, and would receive a reception beside which a Sahara storm would be zephyrs of Araby.

At the same time Sanders was a little puzzled, and not a little hurt.

61

There never had been a question of atrocities in his district, and he was puzzled to account for the rumours that had brought the "commissioner" on his tour of investigation—could it be a distorted account of Olari's punishment?

"Go quickly to the ship, taking a book to the lord who has just gone from here," was his command to a servant, and proceeded to scribble a note:—

"I am afraid," he wrote, "I was rather rude to you—not understanding what the devil you were driving at. An overwhelming curiosity directs me to invite you to share my bungalow until such time as you are ready to conduct your investigation."

The Hon. George read this with a self-satisfied smirk.

"The way to treat these fellows," he said to the Elder Dempster captain, "is to show 'em you'll stand no nonsense. I thought he'd climb down."

The Elder Dempster captain, who knew Sanders by repute, smiled discreetly, but said nothing. Once more the special correspondent's mountain of baggage was embarked in the surf boat, and the Hon. George waved a farewell to his friends on the steamer.

The Elder Dempster skipper, leaning over the side of his bridge, watched the surf boat rising and falling in the swell.

"There goes a man who's looking for trouble," he said, "and I wouldn't take a half-share of the trouble he's going to find for five hundred of the best. Is that blessed anchor up yet, Mr. Simmons? Half ahead—set her due west, Mr. What's-your-name."

It was something of a triumph for the Hon. George. There were ten uniformed policemen awaiting him on the smooth beach to handle his baggage, and Sanders came down to his garden gate to meet him.

"The fact of it is—" began Sanders awkwardly; but the magnanimous George raised his hand.

"Let bygones," he said, "be bygones."

Sanders was unaccountably annoyed by this generous display. Still more so was he when the correspondent refused to reopen the question of atrocities.

"As your guest," said George solemnly, "I feel that it would be better for all concerned if I pursued an independent investigation. I shall endeavour as far as possible, to put myself in your place, to consider all extenuating circumstances—"

"Oh, have a gin-swizzle!" said Sanders rudely and impatiently;

"you make me tired."

"Look here," he said later, "I will only ask you two questions. Where are these atrocities supposed to have taken place?"

"In the district of Lukati," said the Hon. George.

"Olari," thought Sanders. "Who was the victim?" he asked.

"There were several," said the correspondent, and produced his notebook. "You understand that I'd really much rather not discuss the matter with you, but, since you insist," he read, "Efembi of Wastambo."

"Oh!" said Sanders, and his eyebrows rose.

"Kabindo of Machembi."

"Oh, lord!" said Sanders.

The Hon. George read six other cases, and with everyone a line was wiped from Sanders' forehead.

When the recital was finished the Commissioner said slowly—

"I can make a statement to you which will save you a great deal of unnecessary trouble."

"I would rather you didn't," said George, in his best judicial manner.

"Very good," said Sanders; and went away whistling to order dinner.

Over the meal he put it to the correspondent:

"There are a number of people on this station who are friends of mine. I won't disguise the fact from you—there is O'Neill, in charge of the Houssas; the doctor, Kennedy, the chap in charge of the survey party; and half a dozen more. Would you like to question them?"

"They are friends of yours?"

"Yes, personal friends."

"Then," said the Hon. George, gravely, "per haps it would be better if I did not see them."

"As you wish," said Sanders.

With an escort of four Houssas, and fifty carriers recruited from the neighbouring villages, the Hon. George departed into the interior, and Sanders saw him off.

"I cannot, of course, guarantee your life," he said, at parting, "and I must warn you that the Government will not be responsible for any injury that comes to you."

"I understand," said the Hon. George knowingly, "but I am not to be deterred. I come from a stock——"

"I dare say," Sanders cut his genealogical reminiscences short; "but the last traveller who was 'chopped' in the bush was a D'Arcy, and his people came over with the Conqueror."

The correspondent took the straight path to Lukati, and at the end of the third day's march came to the village of Mfabo, where lived the great witchdoctor, Kelebi.

George pitched his camp outside the village, and, accompanied by his four Houssas, paid a call upon the chief, which was one of the first mistakes he made, for he should have sent for the chief to call upon him; and if he called upon anybody, he should have made his visit to the witchdoctor, who was a greater man than forty chiefs.

In course of time, however, he found himself squatting on the ground outside the doctor's house, engaged, through the medium of the interpreter he had brought from Sierra Leone, in an animated conversation with the celebrated person.

"Tell him," said George to his interpreter, "that I am a great white chief whose heart bleeds for the native."

"Is he a good man?" asked George.

The witchdoctor, with the recollection of Sanders' threat, said "No!"

"Why?" asked the Hon. George eagerly. "Does he beat the people?"

Not only did he beat the people, explained the witchdoctor with relish, but there were times when he burnt them alive.

"This is a serious charge," said George, wagging his head warningly; nevertheless he wrote with rapidity in his diary:—

"Interviewed Kelebi, respected native doctor, who states:

"'I have lived all my life in this district, and have never known so cruel a man as Sandi (Sanders). I remember once he caused a man to be drowned, the man's name I forget; on another occasion he burned a worthy native alive for refusing to guide him and his Houssas through the forest. I also remember the time when he put a village to the fire, causing the people great suffering.

"'The people of the country groan under his oppressions, for from time to time he comes demanding money and crops, and if he does not receive all that he asks for he flogs the villagers until they cry aloud.'"

(I rather suspect that there is truth in the latter statement, for Sanders finds no little difficulty in collecting the hut-tax, which is the Government's due.)

George shook his head when he finished writing.

"This," he said, "looks very bad."

He shook hands with the witchdoctor, and that aged villain looked surprised, and asked a question in the native tongue.

"You no be fit to dash him somet'ing," said the interpreter.

"Dash him?"

"Give 'um present—bottle gin."

"Certainly not," said George. "He may be satisfied with the knowledge that he is rendering a service to humanity; that he is helping the cause of a downtrodden people."

The witchdoctor said something in reply, which the interpreter very wisely refrained from putting into English.

★★★★★★

"How go the investigations?" asked the captain of Houssas three weeks later.

"As far as I can gather," said Sanders, "our friend is collecting a death-roll by the side of which the records of the Great Plague will read like an advertisement of a health resort."

"Where is he now?"

"He has got to Lukati—and I am worried"; and Sanders looked it.

The Houssa captain nodded, for all manner of reports had come down from Lukati country. There had been good crops, and good crops mean idleness, and idleness means mischief. Also there had been devil dances, and the mild people of the Bokari district, which lies contiguous to Lukati, had lost women.

"I've got a free hand to nip rebellion in the bud," Sanders reflected moodily; "and the chances point to rebellion What do you say? Shall we make a report and wait for reinforcements, or shall we chance our luck?"

"It's your funeral," said the Houssa captain, "and I hate to advise you. If things go wrong you'll get the kicks; but if it were mine I'd go, like a shot—naturally."

"A hundred and forty men," mused Sanders.

"And two Maxims," suggested the other. . "We'll go," said Sanders; and half an hour later a bugle blared through the Houssas' lines, and Sanders was writing a report to his chief in far-away Lagos.

The Hon. George, it may be said, had no idea that he was anything but welcome in the village of Lukati.

Olari the chief had greeted him pleasantly, and told him stories of Sanders' brutality—stories which, as George wrote, "if true, must of necessity sound the death-knell of British integrity in our native possessions."

Exactly what that meant, I am not disposed to guess.

George stayed a month as the guest of Lukati. He had intended to stay at the most three days, but there was always a reason for postponing his departure.

Once the carriers deserted, once the roads were not safe, once Olari asked him to remain that he might see his young men dance. George did not know that his escort of four Houssas were feeling uneasy, because his interpreter—as big a fool as himself—could not interpret omens. George knew nothing of the significance of a dance in which no less than six witchdoctors took part, or the history of the tumble-down hut that stood in solitude at one end of the village. Had he taken the trouble to search that hut, he would have found a table, a chair, and a truckle bed, and on the table a report, soiled with dust and rain, which began:

> I have the honour to inform your Excellency that the natives maintain their industrious and peaceable attitude.

For in this hut in his lifetime lived Carter, Deputy Commissioner; and the natives, with their superstitious regard for the dead, had moved nothing.

It was approaching the end of the month, when the Hon. George thought he detected in his host a certain scarcely-veiled insolence of tone, and in the behaviour of the villagers something more threatening.

The dances were a nightly occurrence now, and the measured stamping of feet, the clash of spear against cane shield, and the never-ending growl of the song the dancers sang, kept him awake at nights. Messengers came to Olari daily from long distances, and once he was awakened in the middle of the night by screams. He jumped out of bed and pushed aside the fly of his tent to see half a dozen naked women dragged through the streets—the result of a raid upon the unoffending Bokari. He dressed, in a sweat of indignation and fear, and went to the chief's hut, fortunately without his interpreter, for what Olari said would have paralysed him.

In the morning (after this entirely unsatisfactory interview) he paraded his four Houssas and such of his carriers as he could find, and prepared to depart.

"Master," said Olari, when the request was interpreted, "I would rather you stayed. The land is full of bad people, and I have still much to tell you of the devilishness of Sandi. Moreover," said the chief, "to-night there is to be a great dance in your honour," and he pointed to where three slaves were engaged in erecting a big post in the centre of the village street.

"After this I will let you go," said Olari, "for you are my father and my mother."

The Hon. George was hesitating, when, of a sudden, at each end of the street there appeared, as if by magic, twenty travel-stained Houssas. They stood at attention for a moment, then opened outwards, and in the centre of each party gleamed the fat water-jacket of a Maxim gun.

The chief said nothing, only he looked first one way and then the other, and his brown face went a dirty grey. Sanders strolled leisurely along toward the group. He was unshaven, his clothes were torn with bush-thorn, in his hand was a long-barrelled revolver.

"Olari," he said gently; and the chief stepped forward.

"I think, Olari," said Sanders, "you have been chief too long."

"Master, my father was chief before me, and his father," said Olari, his face twitching.

"What of Tagondo, my friend?" asked Sanders, speaking of Carter by his native name.

"Master, he died," said Olari; "he died of the sickness *mongo*—the sickness itself."

"Surely," said Sanders, nodding his head, "surely you also shall die of the same sickness."

Olari looked round for a way of escape.

He saw the Hon. George looking from one to the other in perplexity, and he flung himself at the correspondent's feet.

"Master!" he cried, "save me from this man who hates me!"

George understood the gesture; his interpreter told him the rest; and, as a Houssa servant reached out his hand to the chief, the son of the house of Widnes, strong in the sense of his righteousness, struck it back.

"Look here, Sanders," forgetting all his previous misgivings and fears concerning the chief, "I should say that you have punished this poor devil enough!"

"Take that man, sergeant," said Sanders sharply; and the Houssa gripped Olari by the shoulder and flung him backward.

"You shall answer for this!" roared the Hon. George Tackle, in impotent wrath. "What are you going to do with him? My God! No, no!—not without a trial!"

He sprang forward, but the Houssas caught him and restrained him.

★★★★★★

"For what you have done," said the correspondent—this was a month after, and he was going aboard the homeward steamer—"you shall suffer!"

"I only wish to point out to you," said Sanders, "that if I had not arrived in the nick of time, you would have done all the suffering— they were going to sacrifice you on the night I arrived. Didn't you see the post?"

"That is a lie!" said the other. "I will make England ring with your infamy. The condition of your district is a blot on civilisation!"

★★★★★★

"There is no doubt," said Mr. Justice Keneally, summing up in the libel action, Sanders *v. The Courier and Echo* and another, "that the defendant Tackle did write a number of very libellous and damaging statements, and, to my mind, the most appalling aspect of the case is that, commissioned as he was to investigate the condition of affairs in the district of Lukati, he did not even trouble to find out where Lukati was. As you have been told, gentlemen of the jury, there are no less than four Lukatis in West Africa, the one in Togoland being the district in which it was intended the defendant should go. How he came to mistake Lukati of British West Africa for the Lukati of German Togoland, I do not know, but in order to bolster up his charges against a perfectly-innocent British official he brought forward a number of unsupported statements, each of which must be regarded as damaging to the plaintiff, but more damaging still to the newspaper that in its colossal ignorance published them."

The jury awarded Sanders nine thousand seven hundred and fifty pounds.

Chapter 6

The Dancing Stones

Heroes should be tall and handsome, with flashing eyes; Sanders was not so tall, was yellow of face, moreover had grey hair. Heroes should also be of gentle address, full of soft phrases, for such tender women who come over their horizon; Sanders was a dispassionate man who swore on the slightest provocation, and had no use for women any way.

When you place a man upon a throne, even though that throne be a wooden stool worth in the mart fourpence more or less, you assume a responsibility which greatly outweighs all the satisfaction or personal gratification you may derive from your achievement. There is a grave in Toledo, a slab of brass, over a great king-maker who lived long enough to realise his insignificance. The epitaph upon that brass tomb of his is eloquent of his sum knowledge of life and human effort.

PULVIS
ET
NIHIL

. . .says the inscription, and Powder and Nothing is the ultimate destiny of all king-makers.

Sanders was a maker of kings in the early days. He helped break a few, so it was in obedience to the laws of compensation that he took his part in reconstructive work.

He broke Esindini, Matabini, T'saki—to name three—and helped, in the very old days, and in another country, to break Lobengula, the Great Bull.

King-maker he was beyond question—you could see Republicanism written legibly in the amused grin with which he made them—but the kings he made were little ones—that is the custom of the

British- African rule, they break a big king and put many little kings in his place, because it is much safer.

Somewhere about 12 north, and in longitude 0°, is a land which is peculiar for the fact that it is British, French, German, and Italian—according to which map of Africa you judge it by.

At the time of which I write it was neither, but it was ruled by Mensikilimbili for the Great King. He was the most powerful of monarchs, and, for the matter of that, the most cruel. His dominion stretched "from moonrise to sunset," said the natives, and he held undisputed sway.

He had a court, and sat upon an ivory throne, and wore over the leopard skins of his rank a mantle woven of gold thread and scarlet thread, and he administered justice. He had three hundred wives and forty thousand fighting men, and his acquaintance with white men began and ended with the coming of a French Mission, who presented him with a tall hat, a barrel organ, and one hundred thousand *francs* in gold.

This was Limbili, the great King of Yitingi.

The little kings of the Southern lands spoke of him with bated breath; his name was uttered in a low voice, as of a god; he was the symbol of majesty and of might—the Isisi people, themselves a nation of some importance, and boastful likewise, referred to themselves disparagingly when the kingdom of Yitingi was mentioned.

Following the French Mission, Sanders went up as envoy to the Limbilu, carrying presents of a kind and messages of goodwill.

He was escorted into the territory by a great army and was lodged in the city of the king.

After two days' waiting he was informed that his Majesty would see him, and was led to the Presence.

The Presence was an old man, a vicious old man, if Sanders was any judge of character, who showed unmistakable signs of anger and contempt when the Commissioner displayed his presents.

"And what are these, white man?" said the king. "Toys for my women, or presents for my little chiefs?"

"These are for your Greatness," said Sanders quietly, "from a people who do not gauge friendship by the costliness of presents."

The king gave a little sniff.

"Tell me, white man," he said; "in your travels have you ever seen so great a king as I?"

"Lord king," said Sanders, frank to a fault. "I have seen greater."

The king frowned, and the crowd about his sacred person muttered menacingly.

"There you lie," said the king calmly; "for there never was a greater king than I."

"Let the white man say who is greater," croaked an aged councillor, and a murmur of approval arose.

"Lord," said Sanders, looking into the eyes of the old man who sat on the throne, "I have seen Lo Ben." (Lo Bengola, the King of the Matabele).

The king frowned again, and nodded.

"Of him I have heard," he said; "he was a great king and an eater-up of nations—who else?"

"King," lied Sanders, "also Ketcewayo"; and something like a hush fell upon the court, for the name of Ketcewayo was one that travelled north.

"But of white kings," persisted the chief; "is there a white king in the world whose word when it goes forth causes men to tremble?"

Sanders grinned internally, knowing such a king, but answered that in all his life he had never met such a king.

"And of armies," said the king, "have you ever seen an army such as mine?"

And so through the category of his possessions he ran; and Sanders, finding that the lie was to save himself a great deal of trouble, lied and acclaimed King Limbili as the greatest king in all the world, commander of the most perfect army, ruler of a sublime kingdom.

It may be said that the kingdom of Yitingi owed its integrity to its faults, for, satisfied with the perfection of all his possessions, the great king confined his injustices, his cruelties, and his little wars within the boundaries of his state. Also he sought relaxation therein.

One day, just after the rains, when the world was cool and the air filled with the faint scent of African spring, Sanders made a tour through the little provinces. These are those lands which lie away from the big rivers. Countries curled up in odd corners, bisected sharply on the map by this or that international boundary line, or scattered on the fringe of the wild country vaguely inscribed by the chartographer as "Under British Influence."

It was always an interesting journey—Sanders made it once a year—for the way led up strange rivers and through unfamiliar scenes, past villages where other white men than Sanders were never seen. After a month's travel the Commissioner came to Icheli, which lies on the border of the great king's domain, and with immense civility he was received by the elders and the chiefs.

"Lord, you have come at a good moment," said the chief solemnly, "tonight Daihili dances."

"And who is Daihili?" asked Sanders.

They told him; later they brought for his inspection a self-conscious girl, a trifle pert, he thought, for a native.

A slim girl, taller than the average woman, with a figure perfectly modelled, a face not unpleasant even from the European standpoint, graceful in carriage, her every movement harmonious. Sanders, chewing the end of his cigar, took her in at one glance.

"My girl, they tell me that you dance," he said.

"That is so, master," she said; "I am the greatest dancer in all the world."

"So far I cannot go," said the cautious Commissioner; "but I do not doubt that your dancing is very wonderful."

"Lord," she said, with a gesture, "when I dance men go mad, losing their senses. Tonight when the moon is high I will show you the dance of the Three Lovers."

"Tonight," said Sanders briefly, "I shall be in bed—and, I trust, asleep."

The girl frowned a little, was possibly piqued, being a woman of fifteen, and in no wise different to women elsewhere in the world. This Sanders did not know, and I doubt whether the knowledge would have helped him much if he did.

He heard the *tom-tom* beating, that night as he lay in bed, and the rhythmical clapping of hands, and fell asleep wondering what would be the end of a girl who danced so that men went mad.

The child was the chief's daughter, and at parting Sanders had a few words to say concerning her.

"This daughter of yours is fifteen, and it would be better if she were married," he said.

"Lord, she has many lovers, but none rich enough to buy her," said the proud father, "because she is so great a dancer. Chiefs and headmen from villages far distant come to see her." He looked round and lowered his voice. "It is said," he whispered, "that the Great One himself has spoken her. Perhaps he will send for her, offering this and that. In such a case," said the chief hopefully, "I will barter and bargain, keeping him in suspense, and every day the price will rise "

"If the Great One need her, let her go," said Sanders, "lest instead of money presents he sends an army. I will have no war, or women *palaver*, which is worse than war, in my country—mark that, chief."

"Lord, your word is my desire," said the chief conventionally.

Sanders went back to his own people by easy stages. At Isisi he was detained for over a week over a question of witchcraft; at Belembi (in the Isisi country) he stopped three days to settle a case of murder by fetish. He was delivering judgment, and Abiboo, the Sergeant of Police, was selecting and testing his stoutest cane for the whipping which was to follow, when the chief of the Icheli came flying down the river with three canoes, and Sanders, who, from where he sat, commanded an uninterrupted view of the river, knew there was trouble—and guessed what that trouble was.

"Justice!" demanded the chief, his voice trembling with the rage and fear he had nursed, "justice against the Old One, the stealer of girls, the destroyer of cities—may death go to him. *Iwa!*—"

The very day Sanders had left, the messenger of the great king had come, and with him a hundred warriors, demanding the dancing girl. True to his pre-arranged scheme, the chief began the inevitable bargaining over terms. The presents offered were too small. The girl was worth a hundred thousand rods—nay, a thousand bags of salt.

"You were mad," said Sanders calmly; "no woman is worth a thousand bags of salt."

"Well, that might be," admitted the outraged father; "yet it would be folly to begin by naming a price too low. The bargaining went on through the night and all the next day, and in the end the envoy of the great king grew impatient.

"Let the woman be sent for," he said, and obedient to the summons came Daihili, demure enough, yet with covert glances of encouragement to the unemotional ambassador, and with subtle exhibitions of her charms.

"Woman," said the messenger, "the greatest of kings desires you, will you come?"

"Lord," said the girl, "I wish for nothing better."

With that, the hundred armed warriors in attendance at the *palaver* closed round the girl.

"And so," said Sanders, "you got nothing?"

"Lord, it is as you say," moaned the old chief.

"It is evident," said Sanders, "that an injustice has been done; for no man may take a woman unless he pay. I think," he added, with a flash of that mordant humour which occasionally illuminated his judgments, "that the man pays twice, once to the father, and all his life to his wife—but that is as may be."

Six weeks later, after consultation, Sanders sent a messenger to the great king, demanding the price of the woman.

What happened to the messenger I would rather not describe. That he was killed, is saying the least. Just before he died, when the glaze of death must have been on his eyes, and his poor wrecked body settling to the rest of oblivion, he was carried to a place before the king's hut, and Daihili danced the Dance of the Spirits. This much is now known.

Sanders did nothing; nor did the British Government, but hurried notes were exchanged between ambassadors and ministers in Paris, and that was the end of the incident.

Two Icheli spies went up into the great king's country. One came back saying that the dancing girl was the favourite wife of the old king, and that her whims swayed the destinies of the nation. Also he reported that because of this slim girl who danced, many men, councillors, and captains of war had died the death.

The other spy did not come back.

It may have been his discovery that induced the girl to send an army against the Icheli, thinking perchance that her people were spying upon her.

One day the city of Icheli was surrounded by the soldiers of the great king, and neither man, woman nor child escaped.

The news of the massacre did not come to Sanders for a long time. The reason was simple: there was none to carry the message, for the Icheli are isolated folk. One day, however, an Isisi hunting party, searching for elephants, came upon a place where there was a smell of burning and many skeletons—and thus Sanders knew——

"We cannot," wrote Monsieur Leon Marchassa, Minister for Colonial Affairs, "accept responsibility for the misdoings of the king of the Yitingi, and my Government would regard with sympathetic interest any attempt that was made by His Majesty's Government to pacify this country."

But the British Government did nothing, because war is an expensive matter, and Sanders grinned and cursed his employers genially.

Taking his life in his hands, he went up to the border of Yitingi, with twenty policemen, and sent a messenger;—a Yitingi messenger—to the king. With the audacity which was not the least of his assets, he demanded that the king should come to him for a *palaver*.

This adventure nearly proved abortive at the beginning, for just as the *Zaire* was steaming to the borders Sanders unexpectedly came upon traces of a raiding expedition. There were unmistakable signs as to the author.

"I have a mind to turn back and punish that cursed Bosambo, Chief of the Ochori," he said to Sergeant Abiboo, "for having sworn by a variety of gods and devils that he would keep the peace; behold he has been raiding in foreign territory."

"He will keep, master," said Abiboo, "besides which, he is in the neighbourhood, for his fires are still warm."

So Sanders went on, and sent his message to the king.

He kept steam in his little boat—he had chosen the only place where the river touches the Yitingi border—and waited, quite prepared to make an ignominious, if judicious, bolt.

To his astonishment, his spies brought word that the king was coming. He owed this condescension to the influence of the little dancing girl, for she, woman-like, had a memory for rebuffs, and had a score to settle with Mr. Commissioner Sanders.

The great king arrived, and across the meadow-like lands that fringe the river on both sides Sanders watched the winding procession with mingled feelings. The king halted a hundred yards from the river, and his big scarlet umbrella was the centre of a black line of soldiers spreading out on either hand for three hundred yards.

Then a party detached itself and came towards the dead tree by the water side, whereon hung limply in the still air the ensign of England.

"This," said Sanders to himself, "is where I go dead one time."

It is evidence of the seriousness of the situation, as it appealed to him, that he permitted himself to descend to Coast English.

"The king, the Great One, awaits you, white man, offering you safety in his shadow," said the king's messenger; and Sanders nodded. He walked leisurely toward the massed troops, and presently appeared before the old man squatting on a heap of skins and blinking like an ape in the sunlight.

"Lord king, live forever," said Sanders glibly, and as he raised his hand in salute he saw the girl regarding him from under knit brows.

"What is your wish, white man?" said the old king; "what rich presents do you bring, that you call me many days' journey?"

"Lord, I bring no presents," said Sanders boldly; "but a message from a king who is greater than you, whose soldiers outnumber the sands of the river, and whose lands extend from the east to the west, from the north to the south."

"There is no such king," snarled the old man. "You lie, white man, and I will cut your tongue into little strips."

"Let him give his message, master," said the girl.

"This is the message," said Sanders. He stood easily, with his hands in the pockets of his white uniform jacket, and the king was nearer death than he knew. "My master says: 'Because the Great King of Yitingi has eaten up the Icheli folk: because he has crossed the borderland and brought suffering to my people, my heart is sore. Yet, if the Great King will pay a fine of one thousand head of cattle and will allow free access to his country for my soldiers and my commissioners, I will live in peace with him.'"

The old man laughed, a wicked, cackling laugh.

"*Oh, ko!*" he chuckled; "a great king!"

Then the girl stepped forward.

"Sandi," she said, "once you put me to shame, for when I would have danced for you, you slept."

"To you, Daihili," said Sanders steadily, "I say nothing; I make no *palaver* with women, for that is not the custom or the law. Still less do I talk with dancing girls. My business is with Limbili the king."

The king was talking rapidly behind his hand to a man who bent over him, and Sanders, his hands still in his jacket pockets, snapped down the safety catches of his automatic Colts.

All the time the girl spoke he was watching from the corners of his eyes the man who talked with the king. He saw him disappear in the crowd of soldiers who stood behind the squatting figures, and prepared for the worst.

"Since I may not dance for you," the girl was saying, "my lord the king would have you dance for me."

"That is folly," said Sanders: then he saw the line on either side wheel forward, and out came his pistols.

"*Crack! Crack!*"

The shot intended for the king missed him, and broke the leg of a soldier behind.

It had been hopeless from the first; this Sanders realised with some philosophy, as he lay stretched on the baked earth, trussed like a fowl, and exceedingly uncomfortable. At the first shot Abiboo, obeying his instructions, would turn the bows of the steamer downstream; this was the only poor satisfaction he could derive from the situation.

Throughout that long day, with a pitiless sun beating down upon him, he lay in the midst of an armed guard, waiting for the death which must come in some dreadful form or other.

He was undismayed, for this was the logical end of the business. Toward the evening they gave him water, which was most acceptable. From the gossip of his guards he gathered that the evening had been chosen for his exit, but the manner of it he must guess.

From where he lay he could see, by turning his head a little, the king's tent, and all the afternoon men were busily engaged in heaping flat stones upon the earth before the pavilion. They were of singular uniformity, and would appear to be specially hewn and dressed for some purpose. He asked his guard a question.

"They are the dancing stones, white man," said the soldier, "they come from the mountain near the city."

When darkness fell a huge fire was lit; it was whilst he was watching this that he heard of the *Zaire's* escape, and was thankful.

He must have been dozing, exhausted in body and mind, when he was dragged to his feet, his bonds were slipped, and he was led before the king. Then he saw what form his torture was to take.

The flat stones were being taken from the fire with wooden pincers and laid to form a rough pavement before the tent.

"White man," said the king, as rude hands pulled off the Commissioner's boots, "the woman Daihili would see you dance."

"Be assured, king," said Sanders, between his teeth, "that some ay you shall dance in hell in more pleasant company, having first danced at the end of a rope."

"If you live through the dancing," said the king, "you will be sorry."

A ring of soldiers with their spears pointing inward surrounded the pavement, those on the side of the tent crouching so that their bodies might not interrupt the Great One's view.

"Dance," said the king; and Sanders was thrown forward. The first stone he touched was only just warm, and on this he stood still till a spear-thrust sent him to the next . It was smoking hot, and he leapt up with a stifled cry. Down he came to another, hotter still, and leapt again—

"Throw water over him," said the amused king, when they dragged the fainting man off the stones, his clothes smouldering where he lay in an inert heap.

"Now dance," said the king again—when out of the darkness

about the group leapt a quivering pencil of yellow light.

Ha-ha-ha-ha-a-a-a!

Abiboo's Maxim-gun was in action at a range of fifty yards, and with him five hundred Ochori men under that chief of chiefs, Bosambo.

For a moment the Yitingi stood, and then, as with a wild yell which was three-parts fear, the Ochori charged, the king's soldiers broke and fled.

They carried Sanders to the steamer quickly, for the Yitingi would re-form, being famous night fighters. Sanders, sitting on the deck of the steamer nursing his burnt feet and swearing gently, heard the scramble of the Ochori as they got into their canoes, heard the grunting of his Houssas hoisting the Maxim on board, and fainted again.

"Master," said Bosambo in the morning, "many moons ago you made charge against the Ochori, saying they would not fight. That was true, but in those far-off days there was no chief Bosambo. Now, because of my teaching, and because I have put fire into their stomachs, they have defeated the soldiers of the Great King."

He posed magnificently, for on his shoulders was a mantle of gold thread woven with blue, which was not his the night before.

"Bosambo," said Sanders, "though I have a score to settle with you for breaking the law by raiding, I am grateful that the desire for the properties of others brought you to this neighbourhood. Where did you get that cloak?" he demanded.

"I stole it," said Bosambo frankly, "from the tent of the Great King; also I brought with me one of the stones upon which my lord would not stand. I brought this, thinking that it would be evidence."

Sanders nodded, and bit his cigar with a little grimace. "On which my lord would not stand," was very prettily put.

"Let me see it," he said; and Bosambo himself carried it to him.

It had borne the heat well enough, but rough handling had chipped a corner; and Sanders looked at this cracked corner long and earnestly.

"Here," he said, "is an argument that no properly constituted British Government can overlook—I see Limbili's finish."

★★★★★★

The rainy season came round and the springtime, before Sanders again stood in the presence of the Great King. All around him was desolation and death. The plain was strewn with the bodies of men, and the big city was a smoking ruin. To the left, three regiments of Houssas were encamped; to the right, two battalions of African Rifles sat at "chop," and the snappy notes of their bugles came sharply through the still air.

"I am an old man," mumbled the king; but the girl who crouched at his side said nothing. Only her eyes never left the brick-red face of Sanders.

"Old you are," he said, "yet not too old to die."

"I am a great king," whined the other, "and it is not proper that a great king should hang."

"Yet if you live," said Sanders, "many other great kings will say, 'We may commit these abominations, and because of our greatness we shall live.'"

"And what of me, lord?" said the girl in a low voice.

"You!" Sanders looked at her. "*Ho, hi,*" he said, as though he had just remembered her. "You are the dancing girl? Now we shall do nothing with you, Daihili—because you are nothing."

He saw her shrink as one under a lash.

After the execution, the Colonel of the Houssas and Sanders were talking together.

"What I can't understand," said the Colonel, "is why we suddenly decided upon this expedition. It has been necessary for years—but why this sudden activity?"

Sanders grinned mysteriously.

"A wonderful people, the English," he said airily. "Old Man Limbili steals British subjects, and I report it. 'Very sad,' says England. He wipes out a nation. 'Deplorable!' says England. He makes me dance on the original good-intention stones of Hades. 'Treat it as a joke,' says England; but when I point out that these stones assay one ounce ten penny-weights of refined gold, and that we've happed upon the richest reef in Central Africa, there's an army here in six months!"

I personally think that Sanders may have been a little unjust in his point of view. After all, wars cost money, and wars of vengeance are notoriously unprofitable.

CHAPTER 7

The Forest of Happy Dreams

Sanders was tied up at a "wooding," being on his way to collect taxes and administer justice to the folk who dwell on the lower Isisi River.

By the river-side the little steamer was moored. There was a tiny bay here, and the swift currents of the river were broken to a gentle flow; none the less, he inspected the shore-ends of the wire hawsers before he crossed the narrow plank that led to the deck of the *Zaire*. The wood was stacked on the deck, ready for to-morrow's run. The new water-gauge had been put in by Yoka, the engineer, as he had ordered; the engines had been cleaned; and Sanders nodded approvingly. He stepped lightly over two or three sleeping forms curled up on the deck, and gained the shore. "Now I think I'll turn in," he muttered, and looked at his watch. It was nine o'clock. He stood for a moment on the crest of the steep bank, and stared back across the river. The night was black, but he saw the outlines of the forest on the other side. He saw the jewelled sky, and the pale reflection of stars in the water. Then he went to his tent, and leisurely got into his pyjamas. He jerked two tabloids from a tiny bottle, swallowed them, drank a glass of water, and thrust his head through the tent opening. "*Ho*, Sokani!" he called, speaking in the vernacular, "let the *lo-koli* sound!"

He went to bed.

He heard the rustle of men moving, the gurgles of laughter as his subtle joke was repeated, for the Cambul people have a keen sense of humour, and then the penetrating rattle of sticks on the native drum—a hollow tree-trunk. Fiercely it beat—furiously, breathlessly, with now and then a deeper note as the drummer, using all his art, sent the message of sleep to the camp.

In one wild *crescendo*, the *lo-koli* ceased, and Sanders turned with a sigh of content and closed his eyes—he sat up suddenly. He must have dozed; but he was wide awake now.

He listened, then slipped out of bed, pulling on his mosquito boots. Into the darkness of the night he stepped, and found N'Kema, the engineer, waiting.

"You heard, master?" said the native.

"I heard," said Sanders, with a puzzled face, "yet we are nowhere near a village."

He listened.

From the night came a hundred whispering noises, but above all these, unmistakable, the faint clatter of an answering drum. The white man frowned in his perplexity. "No village is nearer than the Bongindanga," he muttered, "not even a fishing village; the woods are deserted—"

The native held up a warning finger, and bent his head, listening. He was reading the message that the drum sent. Sanders waited; he knew the wonderful fact of this native telegraph, how it sent news through the trackless wilds. He could not understand it, no European could; but he had respect for its mystery.

"A white man is here," read the native; "he has the sickness."

"A white man!"

In the darkness Sanders' eyebrows rose incredulously.

"He is a foolish one," N'Kema read; "he sits in the Forest of Happy Thoughts, and will not move."

Sanders clicked his lips impatiently. "No white man would sit in the Forest of Happy Thoughts," he said, half to himself, "unless he were mad."

But the distant drum monotonously repeated the outrageous news. Here, indeed, in the heart of the loveliest glade in all Africa, encamped in the very centre of the Green Path of Death, was a white man, a sick white man—in the Forest of Happy Thoughts—a sick white man.

So the drum went on and on, till Sanders, rousing his own *lo-koli* man, sent an answer crashing along the river, and began to dress hurriedly.

In the forest lay a very sick man. He had chosen the site for the camp himself. It was in a clearing, near a little creek that wound between high elephant-grass to the river. Mainward chose it, just before the sickness came, because it was pretty. This was altogether an inadequate reason; but Mainward was a sentimentalist, and his life was a long record of choosing pretty camping places, irrespective of danger.

"He was," said a newspaper, commenting on the crowning disaster which sent him a fugitive from justice to the wild lands of Africa, "over-burdened with imagination." Mainward was cursed with ill-timed confidence; this was one of the reasons he chose to linger in that deadly strip of land of the Ituri, which is clumsily named by the natives "The Lands-where-all-bad-thoughts-become-good-thoughts" and poetically adapted by explorers and daring traders as "The Forest of Happy Dreams." Over-confidence had generally been Mainward's undoing—over-confidence in the ability of his horses to win races; over-confidence in his own ability to secure money to hide his defalcations—he was a director in the Welshire County Bank once—over-confidence in securing the love of a woman, who, when the crash came, looked at him blankly and said she was sorry, but she had no idea he felt towards her like that——

Now Mainward lifted his aching head from the pillow and cursed aloud at the din. He was endowed with the smattering of pigeon-English which a man may acquire from a three months' sojourn divided between Sierra Leone and Grand Bassam.

"Why for they make 'em cursed noise, eh?" he fretted. "You plenty fool-man, Abiboo."

"*Si, senor*," agreed the Kano boy, calmly.

"Stop it, d'ye hear? stop it!" raved the man on the tumbled bed; "this noise is driving me mad—tell them to stop the drum."

The *lo-koli* stopped of its own accord, for the listeners in the sick man's camp had heard the faint answer from Sanders.

"Come here, Abiboo—I want some milk; open a fresh tin; and tell the cook I want some soup, too."

The servant left him muttering and tossing from side to side on the creaking camp bedstead. Mainward had many strange things to think about. It was strange how they all clamoured for immediate attention; strange how they elbowed and fought one another in their noisy claims to his notice. Of course, there was the bankruptcy and the discovery at the bank—it was very decent of that inspector fellow to clear out—and Ethel, and the horses, and—and——

The Valley of Happy Dreams! That would make a good story if Mainward could write; only, unfortunately, he could not write. He could sign things, sign his name "three months after date pay to the order of——" He could sign other people's names; he groaned, and winced at the thought.

But here was a forest where bad thoughts became good, and, God knows, his mind was ill-furnished. He wanted peace and sleep and happiness—he greatly desired happiness. Now suppose "Fairy Lane" had won the Wokingham Stakes? It had not, of course (he winced again at the bad memory), but suppose it had? Suppose he could have found a friend who would have lent him £16,000, or even if Ethel——

"Master," said Abiboo's voice, "dem puck-a-puck, him lib for come."

"Eh, what's that?"

Mainward turned almost savagely on the man.

"*Puck-a-puck*—you hear 'um?"

But the sick man could not hear the smack of the *Zaire's* stern wheel, as the little boat breasted the downward rush of the river—he was surprised to see that it was dawn, and grudgingly admitted to himself that he had slept. He closed his eyes again and had a strange dream. The principal figure was a small, tanned, clean-shaven man in a white helmet, who wore a dingy yellow overcoat over his pyjamas.

"How are you feeling?" said the stranger.

"Rotten bad," growled Mainward, "especially about Ethel; don't you think it was pretty low down of her to lead me on to believe she was awfully fond of me, and then at the last minute to chuck me?"

"Shocking," said the strange, white man gravely, "but put her out of your mind just now; she isn't worth troubling about. What do you say to this?"

He held up a small, greenish pellet between his forefinger and thumb, and Mainward laughed weakly.

"Oh, rot!" he chuckled faintly. "You're one of those Forest of Happy Dreams Johnnies; what's that? A love philtre?" He was hysterically amused at the witticism.

Sanders nodded.

"Love or life, it's all one," he said, but apparently unamused. "Swallow it!"

Mainward giggled and obeyed.

"And now," said the stranger—this was six hours later—"the best thing you can do is to let my boys put you on my steamer and take you down river."

Mainward shook his head. He had awakened irritable and lamentably weak.

"My dear chap, it's awfully kind of you to have come—by the way, I suppose you are a doctor?"

Sanders shook his head.

"On the contrary, I am the Commissioner of this district," he said flippantly—"but you were saying——"

"I want to stay here—it's devilish pretty."

"Devilish is the very adjective I should have used—my dear man, this is the plague spot of the Congo; it's the home of every death-dealing fly and bug in Africa."

He waved his hand to the hidden *vistas* of fresh green glades, of gorgeous creepers shown in the light of the camp fires.

"Look at the grass," he said; "it's homeland grass—that's the seductive part of it; I nearly camped here myself. Come, my friend, let me take you to my camp."

Mainward shook his head obstinately.

"I'm obliged, but I'll stay here for a day or so. I want to try the supernatural effects of this pleasant place," he said with a weary smile. "I've got so many thoughts that need treatment."

"Look here," said Sanders roughly, "you know jolly well how this forest got its name; it is called Happy Dreams because it's impregnated with fever, and with every disease from *beriberi* to sleeping sickness. You don't wake from the dreams you dream here. Man, I know this country, and you're a newcomer; you've trekked here because you wanted to get away from life and start all over again."

"I beg your pardon." Mainward's face flushed; and he spoke a little stiffly.

"Oh, I know all about you—didn't I tell you I was the Commissioner? I was in England when things were going rocky with you, and I've read the rest in the papers I get from time to time. But all that is nothing to me. I'm here to help you start fair. If you had wanted to commit suicide, why come to Africa to do it? Be sensible and shift your camp; I'll send my steamer back for your men. Will you come?"

"No," said Mainward sulkily. "I don't want to, I'm not keen; besides, I'm not fit to travel."

Here was an argument which Sanders could not answer. He was none too sure upon that point himself, and he hesitated before he spoke again.

"Very well," he said at length, "suppose you stay another day to give you a chance to pull yourself together. I'll come along tomorrow with a tip-top invalid chair for you—is it a bet?"

Mainward held out his shaking hand, and the ghost of a smile puckered the corners of his eyes. "It's a bet," he said.

He watched the Commissioner walk through the camp, speaking to one man after another in a strange tongue. A singular, masterful man this, thought Mainward. Would he have mastered Ethel? He watched the stranger with curious eyes, and noted how his own lazy devils of carriers jumped at his word.

"Goodnight," said Sanders' voice; and Mainward looked up. "You must take another of these pellets, and tomorrow you'll be as fit as a donkey-engine. I've got to get back to my camp tonight, or I shall find half my stores stolen in the morning; but if you'd rather I stopped—"

"No, no," replied the other hastily. He wanted to be alone. He had lots of matters to settle with himself. There was the question of Ethel, for instance.

"You won't forget to take the tabloid?"

"No. I say, I'm awfully obliged to you for coming. You've been a good white citizen."

Sanders smiled. "Don't talk nonsense!" he said good-humouredly. "This is all brotherly love. White to white, and kin to kin, don't you know? We're all alone here, and there isn't a man of our colour within five hundred miles. Goodnight, and please take the tabloid "

Mainward lay listening to the noise of departure. He thought he heard a little bell tingle. That must be for the engines. Then he heard the puck-a-puck of the wheel—so that was how the steamer got its name.

Abiboo came with some milk. "You take um medicine, master?" he inquired.

"I take um," murmured Mainward; but the green tabloid was underneath his pillow.

Then there began to steal over him a curious sensation of content. He did not analyse it down to its first cause. He had had sufficient introspective exercise for one day. It came to him as a pleasant shock to realise that he was happy.

He opened his eyes and looked round.

His bed was laid in the open, and he drew aside the curtains of his net to get a better view.

A little man was walking briskly toward him along the velvet stretch of grass that sloped down from the glade, and Mainward whistled.

"Atty," he gasped. "By all that's wonderful."

Atty, indeed, it was: the same wizened Atty as of yore; but no longer pulling the long face to which Mainward had been accustomed. The little man was in his white riding-breeches, his diminutive top-boots were splashed with mud, and on the crimson of his silk jacket there was evidence of a hard race. He touched his cap jerkily with his whip, and shifted the burden of the racing saddle he carried to the other arm.

"Why, Atty," said Mainward, with a smile, "what on earth are you doing here?"

"It's a short way to the jockey's room, sir," said the little man. "I've just weighed in. I thought the Fairy would do it, sir, and she did."

Mainward nodded wisely. "I knew she would, too," he said.

"Did she give you a smooth ride?"

The jockey grinned again. "She never does that," he said. "But she ran gamely enough. Coming up out of the Dip, she hung a little, but I showed her the whip, and she came on as straight as a die. I thought once the Stalk would beat us—I got shut in, but I pulled her round, and we were never in difficulties. I could have won by ten lengths," said Atty.

"You could have won by ten lengths," repeated Mainward in wonder. "Well, you've done me a good turn, Atty. This win will get me out of one of the biggest holes that ever a reckless man tumbled into—I shall not forget you, Atty."

"I'm sure you won't, sir," said the little jockey gratefully; "if you'll excuse me now, sir——"

Mainward nodded and watched him, as he moved quickly through the trees.

There were several people in the glade now, and Mainward looked down ruefully at his soiled duck suit. "What an ass I was to come like this," he muttered in his annoyance. "I might have known that I should have met all these people."

There was one he did not wish to see; and as soon as he sighted Venn, with his shy eyes and his big nose, Mainward endeavoured to slip back out of observation. But Venn saw him, and came tumbling through the trees, with his big, flabby hand extended and his dull eyes aglow.

"Hullo, hullo!" he grinned, "been looking for you."

Mainward muttered some inconsequent reply. "Rum place to find you, eh?" Venn removed his shining silk hat and mopped his brow with an awesome silk handkerchief.

"But look here, old feller—about that money?"

"Don't worry, my dear man," Mainward interposed easily. "I shall pay you now."

"That ain't what I mean," said the other impetuously; "a few hundred more or less does not count. But you wanted a big sum—"

"And you told me you'd see me—"

"I know, I know," Venn put in hastily; "but that was before *Kaffirs* started jumpin'. Old feller, you can have it!"

He said this with grotesque emphasis, standing with his legs wide apart, his hat perched on the back of his head, his plump hands dramatically outstretched: and Mainward laughed outright.

"Sixteen thousand?" he asked.

"Or twenty," said the other impressively.

"I want to show you—" Somebody called him, and with a hurried apology he went blundering up the green slope, stopping and turning back to indulge in a little dumb show illustrative of his confidence in Mainward and his willingness to oblige.

Mainward was laughing, a low, gurgling laugh of pure enjoyment. Venn, of all people! Venn, with his accursed questions and talk of securities. Well! Well!

Then his merriment ceases, and he winced again, and his heart beat faster and faster, and a curious weakness came over him——

How splendidly cool she looked.

She walked in the clearing, a white, slim figure; he heard the swish of her skirt as she came through the long grass—white, with a green belt all encrusted with gold embroidery. He took in every detail hungrily—the dangling gold ornaments that hung from her belt, the lace collar at her throat, the——

She did not hurry to him, that was not her way.

But in her eyes dawned a gradual tenderness—those dear eyes that dropped before his shyly.

"Ethel!" he whispered, and dared to take her hand.

"Aren't you wonderfully surprised?" she said.

"Ethel! Here!"

"I—I had to come."

She would not look at him, but he saw the pink in her cheek and heard the faltering voice with a wild hope. "I behaved so badly, dear—so very badly."

She hung her head.

"Dear! dear!" he muttered, and groped toward her like a blind man.

She was in his arms, crushed against his breast, the perfume of her presence in his brain.

"I had to come to you." Her hot cheek was against his. "I love you so."

"Me—love me? Do you mean it?" He was tremulous with happiness, and his voice broke—"Dearest."

Her face was upturned to his, her lips so near; he felt her heart beating as furiously as his own. He kissed her—her lips, her eyes, her dear hair

"O, God, I'm happy!" she sobbed, "so—so happy—"

★★★★★★

Sanders sprang ashore just as the sun was rising, and came thoughtfully through the undergrowth to the camp. Abiboo, squatting by the curtained bed, did not rise. Sanders walked to the bed, pulled aside the mosquito netting, and bent over the man who lay there.

Then he drew the curtains again, lit his pipe slowly, and looked down at Abiboo.

"When did he die?" he asked.

"In the dark of the morning, master," said the man.

Sanders nodded slowly. "Why did you not send for me?"

For a moment the squatting figure made no reply, then he rose and stretched himself.

"Master," he said, speaking in Arabic—which is a language which allows of nice distinctions—"this man was happy; he walked in the Forest of Happy Thoughts; why should I call him back to a land where there was neither sunshine nor happiness, but only night and pain and sickness?"

"You're a philosopher," said Sanders irritably.

"I am a follower of the Prophet," said Abiboo, the Kano boy; "and all things are according to God's wisdom."

Chapter 8

The Akasavas

You who do not understand how out of good evil may arise must take your spade to some virgin grassland, untouched by the hand of man from the beginning of time. Here is soft, sweet grass, and never a sign of nettle, or rank, evil weed. It is as God made it. Turn the soil with your spade, intent on improving His handiwork, and next season—weeds, nettles, lank creeping things, and coarse-leafed vegetation cover the ground.

Your spade has aroused to life the dormant seeds of evil, germinated the ugly waste life that all these long years has been sleeping out of sight—in twenty years, with careful cultivation, you may fight down the weeds and restore the grassland, but it takes a lot of doing.

Your intentions may have been the best in disturbing the primal sod; you may have had views of roses flourishing where grass was; the result is very much the same.

I apply this parable to the story of a missionary and his work. The missionary was a good man, though of the wrong colour. He had large ideas on his duty to his fellows; he was inspired by the work of his cloth in another country; but, as Sanders properly said, India is not Africa.

Kenneth McDolan came to Mr. Commissioner Sanders with a letter of introduction from the new Administration.

Sanders was at "chop" one blazing morning when his servant, who was also his sergeant, Abiboo, brought a card to him. It was a nice card, rounded at the corners, and gilt-edged, and in the centre, in old English type, was the inscription—

Rev. KENNETH McDOLAN.

Underneath was scribbled in pencil: "*On a brief visit.*" Sanders sniffed impatiently, for "reverend" meant "missionary," and "missionary" might mean anything. He looked at the card again and frowned in his perplexity. Somehow the old English and the reverendness of the visiting card did not go well with the rounded corners and the gilt edge.

"Where is he?" he demanded.

"Master," said Abiboo, "he is on the verandah. Shall I kick him off?" Abiboo said this very naturally and with simple directness, and Sanders stared at him.

"Son of sin!" he said sternly, "is it thus you speak of God-men, and of white men at that?"

"This man wears the clothes of a God-man," said Abiboo serenely; "but he is a black man, therefore of no consequence."

Sanders pulled a pair of mosquito boots over his pyjamas and swore to himself.

"White missionaries, yes," he said wrathfully, "but black missionaries I will not endure."

The Reverend Kenneth was sitting in Sanders' basket-chair, one leg flung negligently over one side of the chair to display a silk sock. His finger-tips were touching, and he was gazing with good-natured tolerance at the little green garden which was the Commissioner's special delight.

He was black, very black; but his manners were easy, and his bearing self-possessed.

He nodded smilingly to Sanders and extended a lazy hand.

"Ah, Mr. Commissioner," he said in faultless English, "I have heard a great deal about you."

"Get out of that chair," said Sanders, who had no small talk worth mentioning, "and stand up when I come out to you! What do you want?"

The Reverend Kenneth rose quickly, and accepted the situation with a rapidity which will be incomprehensible to any who do not know how thumbnail deep is the cultivation of the cultured savage.

"I am on a brief visit," he said, a note of deference in his tone. "I am taking the small towns and villages along the coast, holding services, and I desire permission to speak to your people."

This was not the speech he had prepared. He had come straight from England, where he had been something of a lion in Bayswater society, and where, too, his theological attainments had won him regard and no small amount of fame in even a wider circle.

"You may speak to my people," said Sanders; "but you may not address the Kano folk nor the Houssas, because they are petrified in the faith of the Prophet."

Regaining his self-possession, the missionary smiled.

"To bring light into dark places "he began.

"Cut it out," said Sanders briefly; "the *palaver* is finished." He turned on his heel and re-entered the bungalow.

Then a thought struck him.

"Hi!" he shouted, and the retiring missionary turned back.

"Where did you pick up the 'Kenneth McDolan'?" he asked.

The negro smiled again.

"It is the patronymic bestowed upon me at Sierra Leone by a good Christian white man, who brought me up and educated me as though I were his own son," he recited.

Sanders showed his teeth.

"I have heard of such cases," he said unpleasantly.

The next day the missionary announced his intention of proceeding up country. He came in to see Sanders as though nothing had happened. Perhaps he expected to find the Commissioner a little ashamed of himself; but if this was so he was disappointed, for Sanders was blatantly unrepentant.

"You've got a letter from the Administration," he said, "so I can't stop you."

"There is work for me," said the missionary, "work of succour and relief. In India some four hundred thousand—"

"This is not India," said Sanders shortly; and with no other word the native preacher went his way.

Those who know the Akasava people best know them for their laziness—save in matter of vendetta, or in the settlement of such blood feuds as come their way, or in the lifting of each other's goats, in all which matters they display an energy and an agility truly inexplicable. 'He is an Akasava man—he points with his foot,' is a proverb of the Upper River, and the origin of the saying goes back to a misty time when (as the legend goes) a stranger happened upon a man of the tribe lying in the forest.

"Friend," said the stranger, "I am lost. Show me the way to the river"; and the Akasava warrior, raising a leg from the ground, pointed with his toe to the path.

Though this legend lacks something in point of humour, it is regarded as the acme of mirth-provoking stories from Bama to the Lado country.

It was six months after the Reverend Kenneth McDolan had left for his station that there came to Sanders at his headquarters a woeful deputation, arriving in two canoes in the middle of the night, and awaiting him when he came from his bath to the broad *stoep* of his house in the morning—a semi-circle of chastened and gloomy men, who squatted on the wooden *stoep*, regarding him with the utmost misery.

"Lord, we are of the Akasava people," said the spokesman, "and we have come a long journey."

"So I am aware," said Sanders, with acrid dryness, "unless the Akasava country has shifted its position in the night. What do you seek?"

"Master, we are starving," said the speaker, "for our crops have failed, and there is no fish in the river; therefore we have come to you, who are our father."

Now this was a most unusual request; for the Central African native does not easily starve, and, moreover, there had come no news of crop failure from the Upper River.

"All this sounds like a lie," said Sanders thoughtfully, "for how may a crop fail in the Akasava country, yet be more than sufficient in Isisi? Moreover, fish do not leave their playground without cause, and if they do they may be followed."

The spokesman shifted uneasily.

"Master, we have had much sickness," he said, "and whilst we cared for one another the planting season had passed; and, as for the fish, our young men were too full of sorrow for their dead to go long journeys." Sanders stared.

"Therefore we have come from our chief asking you to save us, for we are starving."

The man spoke with some confidence, and this was the most surprising thing of all. Sanders was nonplussed, frankly confounded. For all the eccentric course his daily life took, there was a certain regularity even in its irregularity. But here was a new and unfamiliar situation. Such things mean trouble, and he was about to probe this matter to its depth.

"I have nothing to give you," he said, "save this advice—that you return swiftly to where you came from and carry my word to your chief. Later I will come and make inquiries."

The men were not satisfied, and an elder, wrinkled with age, and sooty-grey of head spoke up.

"It is said, master," he mumbled, through his toothless jaws, "that in other lands when men starve there come many white men bringing grain and comfort."

"Eh?"

Sanders' eyes narrowed.

"Wait," he said, and walked quickly through the open door of his bungalow.

When he came out he carried a pliant whip of rhinoceros-hide, and the deputation, losing its serenity, fled precipitately.

Sanders watched the two canoes paddling frantically up stream, and the smile was without any considerable sign of amusement. That same night the *Zaire* left for the Akasava country, carrying a letter to the Reverend Kenneth McDolan, which was brief, but unmistakable in its tenor.

> Dear Sir,(—it ran—)You will accompany the bearer to head-quarters, together with your belongings. In the event of your refusing to comply with this request, I have instructed my sergeant to arrest you.
>
> Yours faithfully,
>
> H. Sanders, Commissioner.

"And the reason I am sending you out of this country," said Sanders, "is because you have put funny ideas into the heads of my people."

"I assure you" began the negro.

"I don't want your assurance," said Sanders, "you are not going to work an Indian Famine Fund in Central Africa."

"The people were starving—"

Sanders smiled.

"I have sent word to them that I am coming to Akasava," he said grimly, "and that I will take the first starved-looking man I see and beat him till he is sore."

The next day the missionary went, to the intense relief, be it said, of the many white missionaries scattered up and down the river; for, strange as it may appear, a negro preacher who wears a black coat and silk socks is regarded with a certain amount of suspicion.

True to his promise, Sanders made his visit, but found none to thrash, for he came to a singularly well-fed community that had spent a whole week in digging out of the secret hiding-places the foodstuffs which, at the suggestion of a too zealous seeker after fame, it had concealed.

"Here," said Sanders, wickedly, "endeth the first lesson."

But he was far from happy. It is a remarkable fact that once you interfere with the smooth current of native life all manner of things happen. It cannot be truthfully said that the events that followed on the retirement from active life of the Reverend Kenneth McDolan were immediately traceable to his ingenious attempt to engineer a famine in Akasava. But he had sown a seed, the seed of an idea that somebody was responsible for their well-being—he had set up a beautiful idol of Pauperism, a new and wonderful fetish. In the short time of his stay he had instilled into the heathen mind the dim, vague, and elusive idea of the Brotherhood of Man.

This Sanders discovered, when, returning from his visit of inspection, he met, drifting with the stream, a canoe in which lay a prone man, lazily setting his course with half-hearted paddle strokes.

Sanders, on the bridge of his tiny steamer, pulled the little string that controlled the steam whistle, for the canoe lay in his track. Despite the warning, the man in the canoe made no effort to get out of his way, and since both were going with the current, it was only by putting the wheel over and scraping a sandbank that the steamer missed sinking the smaller craft.

"Bring that man on board!" fumed Sanders, and when the canoe had been unceremoniously hauled to the *Zaire*'s side by a boat-hook, and the occupant rudely pulled on board, Sanders let himself go.

"By your infernal laziness," he said, "I see that you are of the Akasava people; yet that is no reason why you should take the middle of the channel to yourself."

"Lord, it is written in the books of your gods," said the man, "that the river is for us all, black and white, each being equal in the eyes of the white gods."

Sanders checked his lips impatiently.

"When you and I are dead," he said, "we shall be equal, but since I am quick and you are quick, I shall give you ten strokes with a whip to correct the evil teaching that is within you."

He made a convert.

But the mischief was done.

Sanders knew the native mind much better than any man living, and he spent a certain period every day for the next month cursing the Reverend Kenneth McDolan. So far, however, no irreparable mischief had been done, but Sanders was not the kind of man to be caught napping. Into the farthermost corners of his little kingdom his secret-service men were dispatched, and Sanders sat down to await developments.

At first the news was good; the spies sent back stories of peace, of normal happiness; then the reports became less satisfactory. The Akasava country is unfortunately placed, for it is the very centre territory, the ideal position for the dissemination of foolish propaganda, as Sanders had discovered before.

The stories the spies sent or brought were of secret meetings, of envoys from tribe to tribe, envoys that stole out from villages by dead of night, of curious rites performed in the depth of the forest and other disturbing matters.

Then came a climax.

Tigili, the king of the N'Gombi folk, made preparations for a secret journey. He sacrificed a goat and secured good omens; likewise three witchdoctors in solemn conclave gave a favourable prophecy.

The chief slipped down the river one night with fourteen paddlers, a drummer, his chief headsman, and two of his wives, and reached the Akasava city at sunset the next evening. Here the chief of the Akasava met him, and led him to his hut.

"Brother," said the Akasava chief, not without a touch of pompousness, "I have covered my bow with the skin of a monkey."

Tigili nodded gravely.

"My arrows are winged with the little clouds," he said in reply.

In this cryptic fashion they spoke for the greater part of an hour, and derived much profit therefrom.

In the shadow of the hut without lay a half-naked man, who seemed to sleep, his head upon his arm, his legs doubled up comfortably.

One of the Akasava guard saw him, and sought to arouse him with the butt of his spear, but he only stirred sleepily, and, thinking that he must be a man of Tigili's retinue, they left him.

When the king and the chief had finished their *palaver*, Tigili rose from the floor of the hut and went back to his canoe, and the chief of the Akasava stood on the bank of the river watching the craft as it went back the way it had come.

The sleeper rose noiselessly and took another path to the river. Just outside the town he had to cross a path of moonlit clearing, and a man challenged him.

This man was an Akasava warrior, and was armed, and the sleeper stood obedient to the summons.

"Who are you?"

"I am a stranger," said the man.

The warrior came nearer and looked in his face.

"You are a spy of Sandi," he said, and then the other closed with him.

The warrior would have shouted, but a hand like steel was on his throat. The sentinel made a little sound like the noise a small river makes when it crosses a shallow bed of shingle, then his legs bent limply, and he went down.

The sleeper bent down over him, wiped his knife on the bare shoulder of the dead man, and went on his way to the river. Under the bush he found a canoe, untied the native rope that fastened it, and stepping in, he sent the tiny dug-out down the stream.

★★★★★★

"And what do you make of all this?" asked Sanders. He was standing on his broad *stoep*, and before him was the spy, a lithe young man, in the uniform of a sergeant of Houssa Police.

"Master, it is the secret society, and they go to make a great killing," said the sergeant.

The Commissioner paced the verandah with his head upon his breast, his hands clasped behind his back.

These secret societies he knew well enough, though his territories had been free of them. He knew their mushroom growth; how they rose from nothingness with rituals and practices ready-made. He knew their influence up and down the Liberian coast; he had some knowledge of the "silent ones" of Nigeria, and had met the "white faces" in the Kassai. And now the curse had come to his territory. It meant war, the upsetting of twenty years' work—the work of men who died and died joyfully, in the faith that they had brought peace to the land—it meant the undermining of all his authority.

He turned to Abiboo.

"Take the steamer," he said, "and go quickly to the Ochori country, telling Bosambo, the chief, that I will come to him—the *palaver* is finished." He knew he could depend upon Bosambo if the worst came.

In the days of waiting he sent a long message to the Administration, which lived in ease a hundred miles down the coast. He had a land wire running along the seashore, and when it worked it was a great blessing. Fortunately it was in good order now, but there had been times when wandering droves of elephants had pulled up the poles and twisted a mile or so of wire into a hopeless tangle.

The reply to his message came quickly.

Take extreme steps to wipe out society. If necessary arrest Tigili. I will support you with four hundred men and a gunboat; prefer you should arrange the matter without fuss.
                    Administration.

Sanders took a long walk by the sea to think out the situation and the solution. If the people were preparing for war, there would be simultaneous action, a general rising. He shook his head. Four hundred men and a gunboat more or less would make no difference. There was a hope that one tribe would rise before the other? he could deal with the Akasava; he could deal with the Isisi plus the Akasava; he was sure of the Ochori—that was a comfort—but the others? He shook his head again. Perhaps the inherent idleness of the Akasava would keep them back. Such a possibility was against their traditions.

He must have come upon a solution suddenly, for he stopped dead in his walk, and stood still, thinking profoundly, with his head upon his breast. Then he turned and walked quickly back to his bungalow.

What date had been chosen for the rising we may never know for certain. What is known is that the Akasava, the N'Gombi, the Isisi, and the Boleki folk were preparing in secret for a time of killing, when there came the great news.

Sandi was dead.

A canoe had overturned on the Isisi River, and the swift current had swept the Commissioner away, and though men ran up and down the bank no other sign of him was visible but a great white helmet that floated, turning slowly, out of sight.

So a man of the Akasava reported, having learnt it from a sergeant of Houssas, and instantly the *lo-koli* beat sharply, and the headmen of the villages came panting to the *palaver* house to meet the paramount chief of the Akasava.

"Sandi is dead," said the chief solemnly. "He was our father and our mother and carried us in his arms; we loved him and did many disagreeable things for him because of our love. But now that he is dead, and there is none to say 'Yea' or 'Nay' to us, the time of which I have spoken to you secretly has come; therefore let us take up our arms and go out, first against the God-men who pray and bewitch us with the sprinkling of water, then against the chief of the Ochori, who for many years have put shame upon us."

"Master," said a little chief from the fishing village which is near to the Ochori border, "is it wise—our Lord Sandi having said there shall be no war?"

"Our Lord Sandi is dead," said the paramount chief wisely; "and being dead, it does not greatly concern us what he said; besides which," he said, as a thought struck him, "last night I had a dream and saw Sandi; he was standing amidst great fires, and he said, 'Go forth and bring me the head of the chief of the Ochori.'"

No further time was wasted.

That night the men of twenty villages danced the dance of killing, and the great fire of the Akasava burnt redly on the sandy beach to the embarrassment of a hippo family that lived in the high grasses nearby.

In the grey of the morning the Akasava chief mustered six hundred spears and three score of canoes, and he delivered his oration:

> First, we will destroy the mission men, for they are white, and it is not right that they should live and Sandi be dead; then we will go against Bosambo, the chief of the Ochori. When rains came in the time of kidding, he who is a foreigner and of no human origin brought many evil persons with him and destroyed our fishing villages, and Sandi said there should be no killing. Now Sandi is dead, and, I do not doubt, in hell, and there is none to hold our pride.

Round the bend of the river, ever so slowly, for she was breasting a strong and treacherous current, came the nose of the *Zaire*. It is worthy of note that the little blue flag at her stern was not at half-mast. The exact significance of this was lost on the Akasava. Gingerly the little craft felt its way to the sandy strip of beach, a plank was thrust forth, and along it came, very dapper and white, his little ebony stick with the silver knob swinging between his fingers, Mr. Commissioner Sanders, very much alive, and there were two bright Maxim-guns on either side of the gangway that covered the beach.

A nation, paralysed by fear and apprehension, watched the *debarquement*, the chief of the Akasava being a little in advance of his painted warriors.

On Sanders' face was a look of innocent surprise. "Chief," said he, "you do me great honour that you gather your young men to welcome me; nevertheless, I would rather see them working in their gardens."

He walked along one row of fighting men, plentifully besmeared with camwood, and his was the leisurely step of some great personage inspecting a guard of honour.

"I perceive," he went on, talking over his shoulder to the chief who, fascinated by the unexpected vision, followed him, "I perceive that each man has a killing spear, also a fighting shield of wicker work, and many have N'Gombi swords."

"Lord, it is true," said the chief, recovering his wits, "for we go hunting elephant in the Great Forest."

"Also that some have the little bones of men fastened about their necks—that is not for the elephant."

He said this meditatively, musingly, as he continued his inspection, and the chief was frankly embarrassed.

"There is a rumour," he stammered, "it is said—there came a spy who told us—that the Ochori were gathering for war, and we were afraid—"

"Strange," said Sanders, half to himself, but speaking in the vernacular, "strange indeed is this story, for I have come straight from the Ochori city, and there I saw nothing but men who ground corn and hunted peacefully; also their chief is ill, suffering from a fever."

He shook his head in well-simulated bewilderment.

"Lord," said the poor chief of the Akasava, "perhaps men have told us lies—such things have happened—"

"That is true," said Sanders gravely. "This is a country of lies; some say that I am dead; and, lo! the news has gone around that there is no law in the land, and men may kill and war at their good pleasure."

"Though I die at this minute," said the chief virtuously, "though the river turn to fire and consume my inmost stomach, though every tree become a tiger to devour me, I have not dreamt of war."

Sanders grinned internally.

"Spare your breath," he said gently. "You who go hunting elephants, for it is a long journey to the Great Forest, and there are many swamps to be crossed, many rivers to be swum. My heart is glad that I have come in time to bid you farewell."

There was a most impressive silence, for this killing of elephants was a stray excuse of the chief's. The Great Forest is a journey of two months, one to get there and one to return, and is moreover through the most cursed country, and the Akasava are not a people that love long journeys save with the current of the river.

The silence was broken by the chief.

"Lord, we desire to put off our journey in your honour, for if we go, how shall we gather in *palaver*?"

Sanders shook his head.

"Let no man stop the hunter," quoth he. "Go in peace, chief, and you shall secure many teeth, (tusks)." He saw a sudden light come to the chief's eyes, but continued, "I will send with you a sergeant of Houssas, that he may carry back to me the story of your prowess"—the light died away again—"for there will be many liars who will say that you never reached the Great Forest, and I shall have evidence to confound them."

Still the chief hesitated, and the waiting ranks listened, eagerly shuffling forward, till they ceased to bear any semblance to an ordered army, and were as a mob.

"Lord," said the chief, "we will go to morrow—"

"The smile was still on Sanders' lips, but his face was set, and his eyes held a steely glitter that the chief of the Akasava knew.

"You go today, my man," said Sanders, lowering his voice till he spoke in little more than a whisper, "else your warriors march under a new chief, and you swing on a tree."

"Lord, we go," said the man huskily," though we are bad marchers and our feet are very tender."

Sanders, remembering the weariness of the Akasava, found his face twitching.

"With sore feet you may rest," he said significantly; "with sore backs you can neither march nor rest—go!"

At dawn the next morning the N'Gombi people came in twenty-five war canoes to join their Akasava friends, and found the village tenanted by women and old men, and Tigili, the king, in the shock of the discovery, surrendered quietly to the little party of Houssas on the beach.

"What comes to me, lord?" asked Tigili, the king.

Sanders whistled thoughtfully.

"I have some instructions about you somewhere," he said.

CHAPTER 9

The Wood of Devils

Four days out of M'Sakidanga, if native report be true, there is a
trickling stream that meanders down from N'Gombi country. Native
report says that this is navigable even in the dry season. The missionaries at Bonginda ridicule this report; and Arburt, the young chief of
the station, with a gentle laugh in his blue eyes, listened one day to the
report of Elebi about a fabulous land at the end of this river, and was
kindly incredulous.

"If it be that ivory is stored in this place," he said in the vernacular,
"or great wealth lies for the lifting, go to Sandi, for this ivory belongs
to the Government. But do you, Elebi, fix your heart more upon
God's treasures in heaven, and your thoughts upon your unworthiness
to merit a place in His kingdom, and let the ivory go."

Elebi was known to Sanders as a native evangelist of the tornado
type, a thunderous, voluble sub-minister of the service; he had, in his
ecstatic moments, made many converts. But there were days of reac-
tion, when Elebi sulked in his mud hut, and reviewed Christianity
calmly.

It was a service, this new religion. You could not work yourself
to a frenzy in it, and then have done with the thing for a week. You
must needs go on, on, never tiring, never departing from the straight
path, exercising irksome self-restraint, leaving undone that which you
would rather do.

"Religion is prison," grumbled Elebi, after his interview, and
shrugged his broad, black shoulders.

In his hut he was in the habit of discarding his European coat for
the loin cloth and the blanket, for Elebi was a savage—an imitative
savage—but still barbarian. Once, preaching on the River of Devils, he
had worked himself up to such a pitch of enthusiastic fervour that he

had smitten a scoffer, breaking his arm, and an outraged Sanders had him arrested, whipped, and fined a thousand rods. Hereafter Elebi had figured in certain English missionary circles as a Christian martyr, for he had lied magnificently, and his punishment had been represented as a form of savage persecution.

But the ivory lay buried three days' march beyond the Secret River; thus Elebi brooded over the log that smouldered in his hut day and night. Three days beyond the river, branching off at a place where there were two graves, the country was reputably full of devils, and Elebi shuddered at the thought; but, being a missionary and a lay evangelist, and, moreover, the proud possessor of a copy of the Epistle to the Romans (laboriously rendered into the native tongue), he had little to fear. He had more to fear from a certain White Devil at a faraway headquarters, who might be expected to range the lands of the Secret River, when the rains had come and gone.

It was supposed that Elebi had one wife, conforming to the custom of the white man, but the girl who came into the hut with a steaming bowl of fish in her hands was not the wife that the missionaries recognised as such.

"Sikini," he said, "I am going a journey by canoe."

"In the blessed service?" asked Sikini, who had come under the influence of the man in his more elated periods.

"The crackling of a fire is like a woman's tongue," quoted Elebi; "and it is easier to keep the lid on a boiling pot than a secret in a woman's heart."

Elebi had the river proverbs at his finger-tips, and the girl laughed, for she was his favourite wife, and knew that in course of time the information would come to her.

"Sikini," said the man suddenly, "you know that I have kept you when the Blood Taker would have me put you away."

(Arburt had a microscope and spent his evenings searching the blood of his flock for signs of trynosomiasis.)

"You know that for your sake I lied to him who is my father and my protector, saying: 'There shall be but one wife in my house, and that Tombolo, the coast woman.'"

The girl nodded, eyeing him stolidly.

"Therefore I tell you that I am going beyond the Secret River, three days' march, leaving the canoe at a place where there are two graves."

"What do you seek?" she asked.

"There are many teeth in that country," he said; "dead ivory that the people brought with them from a distant country, and have hidden, fearing one who is a Breaker of Stones, (*Bula Matidi, i.e.,* "Stone Breaker," is the native name for the Congo Government). I shall come back rich, and buy many wives who shall wait upon you and serve you, and then I will no longer be Christian, but will worship the red fetish as my father did, and his father."

"Go," she said, nodding thoughtfully.

He told her many things that he had not revealed to Arburt—of how the ivory came, of the people who guarded it, of the means by which he intended to secure it.

Next morning before the mission *lo-koli* sounded, he had slipped away in his canoe; and Arburt, when the news came to him, sighed and called him a disappointing beggar—for Arburt was human, Sanders, who was also human, sent swift messengers to arrest Elebi, for it is not a good thing that treasure-hunting natives should go wandering through a strange country, such excursions meaning war, and war meaning, to Sanders at any rate, solemn official correspondence, which his soul loathed.

Who would follow the fortunes of Elebi must paddle in his wake as far as Okau, where the Barina meets the Lapoi, must take the left river path, past the silent pool of the White Devil, must follow the winding stream till the elephants' playing ground be reached. Here the forest has been destroyed for the sport of the Great Ones; the shore is strewn with tree trunks, carelessly uprooted and as carelessly tossed aside by the gambolling mammoth. The ground is innocent of herbage or bush; it is a flat wallow of mud, with the marks of pads where the elephant has passed.

Elebi drew his canoe up the bank, carefully lifted his cooking-pot, full of living fire, and emptied its contents, heaping thereon fresh twigs and scraps of dead wood. Then he made himself a feast, and went to sleep.

A wandering panther came snuffling and howling in the night, and Elebi rose and replenished the fire. In the morning he sought for the creek that led to the Secret River, and found it hidden by the hippo grass.

Elebi had many friends in the N'Gombi country. They were gathered in the village of Tambango—to the infinite embarrassment of the chief of that village—for Elebi's friends laid hands upon whatsoever they desired, being strangers and well armed, and, moreover, outnumbering the men of the village three to one. One, O'Sako, did the chief hold in greatest dread, for he said little, but stalked tragically through the untidy street of Tambango, a bright, curved execution knife in the crook of his left arm. O'Sako was tall and handsome. One broad shoulder gleamed in its nakedness, and his muscular arms were devoid of ornamentation. His thick hair was plastered with clay till it was like a European woman's, and his body was smeared with *ingola* dust.

Once only he condescended to address his host.

"You shall find me three young men against the Lord Elebi's arrival, and they shall lead us to the land of the Secret River."

"But, master," pleaded the chief, "no man may go to the Secret River, because of the devils."

"Three men," said O'Sako softly; "three young men swift of foot, with eyes like the N'Gombi, and mouths silent as the dead."

"——the devils," repeated the chief weakly, but O'Sako stared straight ahead and strode on.

When the sun blazed furiously on the rim of the world in a last expiring effort, and the broad river was a flood of fire, and long shadows ran through the clearings, Elebi came to the village. He came unattended from the south, and he brought with him no evidence of his temporary sojourn in the camps of civilisation. Save for his loin cloth, and his robe of panther skin thrown about his shoulders, he was naked.

There was a *palaver* house at the end of the village, a thatched little wattle hut perched on a tiny hill, and the Lord Elebi gathered there his captains and the chief of the village. He made a speech.

"*Cala, cala*" he began—and it means "long ago," and is a famous opening to speeches—"before the white man came, and when the Arabi came down from the northern countries to steal women and ivory, the people of the Secret River buried their 'points' in a Place of Devils. Their women they could not bury, so they lost them. Now all the people of the Secret River are dead. The Arabi killed some, Bula Matadi killed others, but the sickness killed most of all. Where their villages were the high grass has grown, and in their gardens only the weaver bird speaks. Yet I know of this place, for there came to me a vision and a voice that said—"

The rest of the speech from the European standpoint was pure blasphemy, because Elebi had had the training of a lay preacher, and had an easy delivery.

When he had finished, the chief of the village of Tambangu spoke.

It was a serious discourse on devils. There was no doubt at all that in the forest where the *caché* was there was a veritable stronghold of devildom. Some had bad faces and were as tall as the gum-trees—taller, for they used whole trees for clubs; some were small, so small that they travelled on the wings of bees, but all were very potent, very terrible, and most effective guardians of buried treasure. Their greatest accomplishment lay in leading astray the traveller: men went into the forest in search of game or copal or rubber, and never came back, because there were a thousand ways in and no way out.

Elebi listened gravely.

"Devils of course there are," he said, "including the Devil, the Old One, who is the enemy of God. I have had much to do with the casting out of devils—in my holy capacity as a servant of the Word. Of the lesser devils I know nothing, though I do not doubt they live. Therefore I think it would be better for all if we offered prayer."

On his instruction the party knelt in full view of the village, and Elebi prayed conventionally but with great earnestness that the Powers of Darkness should not prevail, but that the Great Work should go on triumphantly.

After which, to make doubly sure, the party sacrificed two fowls before a squat *bete* that stood before the chief's door, and a crazy witchdoctor anointed Elebi with human fat.

"We will go by way of Ochori," said Elebi, who was something of a strategist. "These Ochori folk will give us food and guides, being a cowardly folk and very fearful."

He took farewell of the old chief and continued his journey, with O'Sako and his warriors behind him. So two days passed. An hour's distance from the city of the Ochori he called a conference.

"Knowing the world," he said, "I am acquainted with the Ochori, who are slaves: you shall behold their chief embrace my feet. Since it is fitting that one, such as I, who know the ways of white men and their magic, should be received with honour; let us send forward a messenger to say that the Lord Elebi comes, and bid them kill so many goats against our coming."

"That is good talk," said O'Sako, his lieutenant, and a messenger was despatched.

Elebi with his caravan followed slowly.

It is said that Elebi's message came to Bosambo of Monrovia, chief of the Ochori, when he was in the despondent mood peculiar to men of action who find life running too smoothly.

It was Bosambo's practice—and one of which his people stood in some awe—to reflect aloud in English in all moments of crisis, or on any occasion when it was undesirable that his thoughts should be conveyed abroad.

He listened in silence, sitting before the door of his hut and smoking a short wooden pipe, whilst the messenger described the quality of the coming visitor, and the unparalleled honour which was to fall upon the Ochori.

Said Bosambo at the conclusion of the recital, "Damn nigger."

The messenger was puzzled by the strange tongue.

"Lord Chief," he said, "my master is a great one, knowing the ways of white men."

"I also know something of white men," said Bosambo calmly, in the River dialect, "having many friends, including Sandi, who married my brother's wife's sister, and is related to me. Also," said Bosambo daringly, "I have shaken hands with the Great White King who dwells beyond the big water, and he has given me many presents."

With this story the messenger went back to the slowly advancing caravan, and Elebi was impressed and a little bewildered.

"It is strange," he said, "no man has ever known an Ochori chief who was aught but a dog and the son of a dog—let us see this Bosambo. Did you tell him to come out and meet me?"

"No," replied the messenger frankly, "he was such a great one, and was so haughty because of Sandi, who married his brother's wife's sister; and so proud that I did not dare tell him."

There is a spot on the edge of the Ochori city where at one time Sanders had caused to be erected a warning sign, and here Elebi found the chief waiting and was flattered. There was a long and earnest conference in the little *palaver* house of the city, and here Elebi told as much of his story as was necessary, and Bosambo believed as much as he could.

"And what do you need of me and my people?" asked Bosambo at length.

"Lord chief," said Elebi, "I go a long journey, being fortified with the blessed spirit of which you know nothing, that being an especial mystery of the white men."

"There is no mystery which I did not know," said Bosambo loftily, "and if you speak of spirits, I will speak of certain saints, also of a Virgin who is held in high respect by white men."

"If you speak of the blessed Paul—" began Elebi, a little at sea.

"Not only of Paul but Peter, John, Luke, Matthew, Antonio, and Thomas," recited Bosambo rapidly. He had not been a scholar at the Catholic mission for nothing. Elebi was nonplussed.

"We will let these magic matters rest," said Elebi wisely; "it is evident to me that you are a learned man. Now I go to seek some wonderful treasures. All that I told you before was a lie. Let us speak as brothers. I go to the wood of devils, where no man has been for many years. I beg you, therefore, to give me food and ten men for carriers."

"Food you can have but no men," said Bosambo, "for I have pledged my word to Sandi, who is, as you know, the husband of my brother's wife's sister, that no man of mine should leave this country."

With this Elebi had to be content, for a new spirit had come to the Ochori since he had seen them last, and there was a defiance in the timid eyes of these slaves of other days, which was disturbing. Besides they seemed well armed.

Every few hundred yards the party stopped, and Elebi tied one of the strips to a branch of a tree.

"In this way," he communicated to his lieutenant, "we may be independent of gods, and fearless of devils, for if we cannot find the ivory we can at least find our way back again."

(There had been such an experiment made by the missionaries in traversing the country between Bonguidga and the Big River, but there were no devils in that country.)

In two days' marches they came upon a place of graves. There had been a village there, for Isisi palms grew luxuriously, and pushing aside the grass they came upon a rotting roof. Also there were millions of weaver birds in the nut-palms, and a choked banana grove.

The graves, covered with broken cooking pots, Elebi found, and was satisfied.

In the forest, a league beyond the dead village, they came upon an old man, so old that you might have lifted him with a finger and thumb.

"Where do the young men go in their strength?" he mumbled childishly; "into the land of small devils? Who shall guide them back to their women? None, for the devils will confuse them, opening new roads and closing the old. *Oh, Ko Ko!*"

He snivelled miserably.

"Father," said Elebi, dangling strips of red flannel from his hand, "this is white man's magic, we come back by the way we go."

Then the old man fell into an insane fit of cursing, and threw at them a thousand deaths, and Elebi's followers huddled back in frowning fear.

"You have lived too long," said Elebi gently, and passed his spear through the old man's neck.

★★★★★★

They found the ivory two days' journey beyond the place of killing. It was buried under a mound, which was overgrown with rank vegetation, and there was by European calculation some £50,000 worth.

In the morning the party set forth and Bosambo, who took no risks, saw them started on their journey. He observed that part of the equipment of the little caravan were two big baskets filled to the brim with narrow strips of red cloth.

"This is my magic," said Elebi mysteriously, when he was questioned, "it is fitting that you should know its power."

Bosambo yawned in his face with great insolence.

Clear of Ochori by one day's march, the party reached the first straggling advance guard of the Big Forest. A cloud of gum-trees formed the approach to the wood, and here the magic of Elebi's basket of cloth strips became revealed.

"We will go back and find carriers," said Elebi, "taking with us as many of the teeth as we can carry."

Two hours later the party began its return journey, following the path where at intervals of every half-mile a strip of scarlet flannelette hung from a twig.

There were many paths they might have taken, paths that looked as though they had been made by the hand of man, and Elebi was glad that he had blazed the way to safety.

For eight hours the caravan moved swiftly, finding its direction with no difficulty; then the party halted for the night.

Elebi was awakened in the night by a man who was screaming, and he leapt up, stirring the fire to a blaze.

"It is the brother of Olambo of Kinshassa, he has the sickness *mongo*" said an awe-stricken voice, and Elebi called a council.

"There are many ways by which white men deal with this sickness," he said wisely, "by giving certain powders and by sticking needles into arms, but to give medicine for the sickness when madness comes is useless—so I have heard the fathers at the station say, because madness only comes when the man is near death."

"He was well last night," said a hushed voice. "There are many devils in the forest, let us ask him what he has seen."

So a deputation went to the screaming, writhing figure that lay trussed and tied on the ground, and spoke with him. They found some difficulty in gaining an opening, for he jabbered and mouthed and laughed and yelled incessantly.

"On the question of devils," at last Elebi said.

"Devils," screeched the madman. "*Yi!* I saw six devils with fire in their mouths—death to you, Elebi! Dog—"

He said other things which were not clean.

"If there were water here," mused Elebi, "we might drown him; since there is only the forest and the earth, carry him away from the camp, and I will make him silent."

So they carried the lunatic away, eight strong men swaying through the forest, and they came back, leaving Elebi alone with his patient. The cries ceased suddenly and Elebi returned, wiping his hands on his leopard skin.

"Let us sleep," said Elebi, and lay down.

Before the dawn came up the party were on the move.

They marched less than a mile from their camping ground and then faltered and stopped.

"There is no sign, lord," the leader reported, and Elebi called him a fool and went to investigate.

But there was no red flannel, not a sign of it. They went on another mile without success.

"We have taken the wrong path, let us return," said Elebi, and the party retraced its steps to the camp they had abandoned. That day was spent in exploring the country for three miles on either side, but there was no welcome blaze to show the trail.

"We are all N'Gombi men," said Elebi, "let us tomorrow go forward, keeping the sun at our back; the forest has no terrors for the N'Gombi folk—yet I cannot understand why the white man's magic failed."

"Devils!" muttered his lieutenant sullenly.

Elebi eyed him thoughtfully.

"Devils sometimes desire sacrifices," he said with significance, "the wise goat does not bleat when the priest approaches the herd."

In the morning a great discovery was made. A crumpled piece of flannel was found on the outskirts of the camp. It lay in the very centre of a path, and Elebi shouted in his joy.

Again the caravan started on the path. A mile farther along another little red patch caught his eye, half a mile beyond, another.

Yet none of these were where he had placed them, and they all bore evidence of rude handling, which puzzled the lay brother sorely. Sometimes the little rags would be missing altogether, but a search party would come upon one some distance off the track, and the march would go on.

Near sunset Elebi halted suddenly and pondered. Before him ran his long shadow; the sun was behind him when it ought to have been in front.

"We are going in the wrong direction," he said, and the men dropped their loads and stared at him.

"Beyond any doubt," said Elebi after a pause, "this is the work of devils—let us pray."

He prayed aloud earnestly for twenty minutes, and darkness had fallen before he had finished.

They camped that night on the spot where the last red guide was, and in the morning they returned the way they had come. There was plenty of provision, but water was hard to come by, and therein lay the danger. Less than a mile they had gone before the red rags had vanished completely, and they wandered helplessly in a circle.

"This is evidently a matter not for prayer, but for sacrifice," concluded Elebi, so they slew one of the guides.

Three nights later, O'Sako, the friend of Elebi, crawled stealthily to the place where Elebi was sleeping, and settled the dispute which had arisen during the day as to who was in command of the expedition.

★★★★★★

"Master," said Bosambo of Monrovia, "all that you ordered me to do, that I did."

Sanders sat before the chief's hut in his camp chair and nodded.

"When your word came that I should find Elebi—he being an enemy of the Government and disobeying your word—I took fifty of my young men and followed on his tracks. At first the way was easy, because he had tied strips of cloth to the trees to guide him on the backward journey, but afterwards it was hard, for the N'Kema that live in the wood "

"Monkeys?" Sanders raised his eyebrows.

"Monkeys, master," Bosambo nodded his head, ' the little black monkeys of the forest who love bright colours—they had come down from their trees and torn away the cloths and taken them to their houses after the fashion of the monkey people. Thus Elebi lost himself and with him his men, for I found their bones, knowing the way of the forest."

"What else did you find?" asked Sanders.

"Nothing, master," said Bosambo, looking him straight in the eye.

"That is probably a lie!" said Sanders.

Bosambo thought of the ivory buried beneath the floor of his hut and did not contradict him.

CHAPTER 10

The Loves of M'lino

When a man loves one woman, whether she be alive or dead, a deep and fragrant memory or a very pleasant reality, he is apt to earn the appellation of "woman-hater," a hasty judgment which the loose-minded pass upon any man whose loves lack promiscuity, and who does not diffuse his passions. Sanders was described as a woman-hater by such men who knew him sufficiently little to analyse his character, but Sanders was not a woman-hater in any sense of the word, for he bore no ill-will toward woman kind, and certainly was innocent of any secret love.

There was a young man named Ludley who had been assistant to Sanders for three months, at the end of which time Sanders sent for him—he was stationed at Isisi City.

"I think you can go home," said Sanders.

The young man opened his eyes in astonishment.

"Why?" he said.

Sanders made no reply, but stared through the open doorway at the distant village.

"Why?" demanded the young man again.

"I've heard things," said Sanders shortly—he was rather uncomfortable, but did not show it.

"Things—like what?"

Sanders shifted uneasily in his chair.

"Oh—things," he said vaguely, and added:

"You go home and marry that nice girl you used to rave about when you first came out."

Young Ludley went red under his tan.

"Look here, chief!" he said, half angrily, half apologetically, "you're surely not going to take any notice—you know it's the sort of thing that's done in black countries—oh, damn it all, you're not going to act as censor over my morals, are you?"

Sanders looked at the youth coldly.

"Your morals aren't worth worrying about," he said truthfully. "You could be the most depraved devil in the world—which I'll admit you aren't—and I should not trouble to reform you. No. It's the morals of my cannibals that worry me. Home you go, my son; get married, crescit *sub pondere virtus*—you'll find the translation in the foreign phrase department of any respectable dictionary. As to the sort of things that are done in black countries, they don't do them in our black countries—monkey tricks of that sort are good enough for the Belgian Congo, or for Togoland, but they aren't good enough for this little strip of wilderness."

Ludley went home.

He did not tell anybody the real reason why he had come home, because it would not have sounded nice. He was a fairly decent boy, as boys of his type go, and he said nothing worse about Sanders than that he was a woman-hater.

The scene that followed his departure shows how little the white mind differs from the black in its process of working. For, after seeing his assistant safely embarked on a homeward-bound boat, Sanders went up the river to Isisi, and there saw a woman who was called M'Lino.

The average black woman is ugly of face, but beautiful of figure, but M'Lino was no ordinary woman, as you shall learn. The Isisi people, who keep extraordinary records in their heads, the information being handed from father to son, say that M'Lino came from an Arabi family, and certainly if a delicately-chiselled nose, a refinement of lip, prove anything, they prove M'Lino came from no pure Bantu stock.

She came to Sanders when he sent for her, alert, suspicious, very much on her guard.

Before he could speak, she asked him a question.

"Lord, where is Lijingii?" This was the nearest the native ever got to the pronunciation of Ludley's name.

"Lijingii has gone across the black water," said Sanders gently, "to his own people."

"You sent him, lord," she said quickly, and Sanders made no reply.

"Lord," she went on, and Sanders wondered at the bitterness in her tone, "it is said that you hate women."

"Then a lie is told," said Sanders. "I do not hate women; rather I greatly honour them, for they go down to the caves of hell when they bear children; also I regard them highly because they are otherwise brave and very loyal."

She said nothing. Her head was sunk till her chin rested on her bare, brown breast, but she looked at him from under her brows, and her eyes were filled with a strange luminosity. Something like a panic awoke in Sanders' heart—had the mischief been done? He cursed Ludley, and breathed a fervent, if malevolent, prayer that his ship would go down with him. But her words reassured him.

"I made Lijingii love me," she said, "though he was a great lord, and I was a slave; I also would have gone down to hell, for some day I hoped I should bear him children, but now that can never be."

"And thank the Lord for it!" said Sanders, under his breath.

He would have given her some words of cheer, but she turned abruptly from him and walked away. Sanders watched the graceful figure as it receded down the straggling street, and went back to his steamer.

He was ten miles down the river before he remembered that the reproof he had framed for the girl had been undelivered.

"That is very extraordinary," said Sanders, with some annoyance, "I must be losing my memory."

Three months later young Penson came out from England to take the place of the returned Ludley. He was a fresh-faced youth, bubbling over with enthusiasm, and, what is more important, he had served a two-years' apprenticeship at Sierra Leone.

"You are to go up to Isisi," said Sanders, "and I want to tell you that you've got to be jolly careful."

"What's the racket?" demanded the youth eagerly. "Are the beggars rising?"

"So far as I know," said Sanders, putting his feet up on the rail of the verandah, "they are not—it is not bloodshed, but love that you've got to guard against."

And he told the story of M'Lino, even though it was no creditable story to British administration.

"You can trust me," said young Penson, when he had finished.

"I trust you all right," said Sanders, "but I don't trust the woman—let me hear from you from time to time; if you don't write about her I shall get suspicious, and I'll come along in a very unpleasant mood."

"You can trust me," said young Penson again; for he was at the age when a man is very sure of himself.

Remarkable as it may read, from the moment he left to take up his new post until he returned to headquarters, in disgrace, a few months later, he wrote no word of the straight, slim girl, with her wonderful eyes. Other communications came to hand, official reports, terse and to the point, but no mention of M'Lino, and Sanders began to worry.

The stories came filtering through, extraordinary stories of people who had been punished unjustly, of savage floggings administered by order of the sub-commissioner, and Sanders took boat and travelled up the river *hec dum*.

He landed short of the town, and walked along the river bank. It was not an easy walk, because the country hereabouts is a riot of vegetation. Then he came upon an African idyll—a young man, who sat playing on a squeaky violin, for the pleasure of M'Lino, lying face downwards on the grass, her chin in her hands.

"In the name of a thousand devils!" said Sanders wrathfully; and the boy got up from the fallen tree on which he sat, and looked at him calmly, and with no apparent embarrassment. Sanders looked down at the girl and pointed.

"Go back to the village, my woman," he said softly, for he was in a rage.

"Now, you magnificent specimen of a white man," he said, when the girl had gone—slowly and reluctantly—"what is this story I hear about your flogging O'Sako?"

The youth took his pipe from his pocket and lit it coolly.

"He beat M'Lino," he said, in the tone of one who offered full justification.

"From which fact I gather that he is the unfortunate husband of that attractive nigger lady you were charming just now when I arrived?"

"Don't be beastly," said the other, scowling. "I know she's a native and all that sort of thing, but my people at home will get used to her colour—"

"Go on board my boat," said Sanders quietly. "Regard yourself as my prisoner."

Sanders brought him down to headquarters without troubling to investigate the flogging of O'Sako, and no word passed concerning M'Lino till they were back again at headquarters.

"Of course I shall send you home," said Sanders.

"I supposed you would," said the other listlessly. He had lost all his self-assurance on the journey down river, and was a very depressed young man indeed.

"I must have been mad," he admitted, the day before the mail boat called *en route* for England; "from the very first I loved her—good heavens, what an ass I am!"

"You are," agreed Sanders, and saw him off to the ship with a cheerful heart.

"I will have no more sub-commissioners at Isisi," he wrote acidly to the Administration. "I find my work sufficiently entertaining without the additional amusement of having to act as chaperon to British officials."

He made a special journey to Isisi to straighten matters out, and M'Lino came unbidden to see him.

"Lord, is he gone, too?" she asked.

"When I want you, M'Lino," said Sanders, "I will send for you."

"I loved him," she said, with more feeling than Sanders thought was possible for a native to show.

"You are an easy lover," said Sanders.

She nodded.

"That is the way with some women," she said. "When I love, I love with terrible strength; when I hate, I hate forever and ever—I hate you, master!"

She said it very simply.

"If you were a man," said the exasperated Commissioner, "I would tie you up and whip you."

"F—f—b!" said the girl contemptuously, and left him staring.

To appreciate the position, you have to realise that Sanders was lord of all this district; that he had the power of life and death, and no man dared question or disobey his word. Had M'Lino been a man, as he said, she would have suffered for her treason—there is no better word for her offence—but she was a woman, and a seriously gifted woman, and, moreover, sure of whatever powers she had.

He did not see her again during the three days he was in the city, nor (this is the extraordinary circumstance) did he discuss her with the chief. He learned that she had become the favourite wife of O'Sako; that she had many lovers and scorned her husband, but he sought no news of her. Once he saw her walking towards him, and went out of his way to avoid her. It was horribly weak and he knew it, but he had no power to resist the impulse that came over him to give her a wide berth.

116

Following this visit, Sanders was coming down stream at a leisurely pace, he himself at the steering wheel, and his eyes searching the treacherous river for sand banks. His mind was filled with the problem of M'Lino, when suddenly in the bush that fringes the Isisi River, something went "*woof*," and the air was filled with flying potlegs. One struck his cabin, and splintered a panel to shreds, many fell upon the water, one missed Sergeant Abiboo's head and sent his *tarbosh* flying.

Sanders rang his engines astern, being curious to discover what induced the would-be assassin to fire a blunderbuss in his direction, and Abiboo, bare-headed, went pattering forward and slipped the canvas cover from the gleaming little Maxim.

Then four Houssa soldiers jumped into the water and waded ashore, holding their rifles above their heads with the one hand and their ammunition in the other, and Sanders stood by the rail of the boat, balancing a sporting Lee-Enfield in the crook of his arm.

Whoever fired the shot had chosen the place of killing very well. The bush was very thick, the approach to land lay through coarse grass that sprang from the swamp, vegetation ran rank, and a tangle of creeper formed a screen that would have been impenetrable to a white man.

But the Houssas had a way—they found the man with his smoking gun, waiting calmly.

He was of the Isisi people—a nation of philosophers—and he surrendered his weapon without embarrassment.

"I think," he said to Sergeant Abiboo, as they hurried down the bank to the river-side, "this means death."

"Death and the torments of hell to follow," said Abiboo, who was embittered by the loss of his *tarbosh*, which had cost him five *francs* in the French territory.

Sanders put up his rifle when he saw the prisoner. He held an informal court in the shattered deck cabin.

"Did you shoot at me?" he asked.

"I did, master," said the man.

"Why?"

"Because," the prisoner replied, "you are a devil and exercise witchcraft."

Sanders was puzzled a little.

"In what particular section of the devil department have I been busy?" he asked in the vernacular.

The prisoner was gazing at him steadily.

117

"Master," he replied, "it is not my business to understand these things. It is said to me, 'kill'—and I kill."

Sanders wasted no more time in vain questions. The man was put in irons, the nose of the steamer turned again downstream, and the Commissioner resumed his vigil.

Midway between B'Fani and Lakaloli he came to a tying-up place. Here there were dead trees for the chopping, and he put his men to replenish his stock of fuel.

He was annoyed, not because a man had attempted to take his life, nor even because his neat little cabin forward was a litter of splinters and broken glass where the potleg had struck, but because he nosed trouble where he thought all was peace and harmony.

He had control of some sixteen distinct and separate nations, each isolated and separated from the other by custom and language. They were distinct, not as the French are from the Italian, but as the Slav is from the Turk.

In the good old times before the English came there were many wars, tribe against tribe, people against people. There were battles, murders, raidings, and wholesale crucifixions, but the British changed all that. There was peace in the land.

Sanders selected with care a long, thin cigar from his case, nibbled at the end and lit it.

The prisoner sat on the steel deck of the *Zaire* near the men's quarters. He was chained by the leg-iron to a staple, and did not seem depressed to any extent. When Sanders made his appearance, a camp-stool in his hand, the Commissioner seated himself, and began his inquisition.

"How do they call you, my man?"

"Bofabi of Isisi."

"Who told you to kill me?"

"Lord, I forget."

"A man or a woman?"

"Lord, it may have been either."

More than that Sanders could not learn, and the subsequent examination at Isisi taught Sanders nothing, for, when confronted with M'Lino, the man said that he did not know her.

Sanders went back to his base in a puzzled frame of mind, and Bofabi of Isisi was sent to the convict establishment at the river's mouth. There matters stood for three months, and all that Sanders learnt of the girl was that she had a new lover whose name was Tebeki, and

118

who was chief of the Akasava.

There were three months of peace and calm, and then Tebeki, coveting his neighbour's wife, took three hundred spears down into the Isisi country, burnt the village that sheltered her, crucified her husband, and carried her back with him.

In honour of this achievement Tebeki gave a feast and a beer dance. There were great and shameless orgies that lasted five days, and the strip of forest that fringes the river between the Isisi and the lower river became a little inferno.

At the end of the five days Tebeki sat down to consider his position. He was in the act of inventing justification for his crime, when Sanders came on the scene. More ominous were the ten Houssas and the Maxim which accompanied the brown-faced little man.

Sanders walked to Tebeki's hut and called him out, and Tebeki, blear-eyed and shaky, stepped forth into the hot sunshine, blinking.

"Tebeki," said Sanders, "what of O'Sako and his village?"

"Master," said Tebeki, slowly, "he put shame upon me—"

"Spare me your lies," said Sanders coldly, and signed to the Houssas.

Then he looked round for a suitable tree. There was one behind the hut—a great copal-gum.

"In half an hour I shall hang you," said Sanders, looking at his watch.

Tebeki said nothing; only his bare feet fidgeted in the dust.

There came out of the hut a tall girl, who stood eyeing the group with curiosity; then she came forward, and laid her hand on Tebeki's bare shoulder.

"What will you do with my man?" she asked. "I am M'Lino, the wife of O'Sako."

Sanders was not horrified, he showed his teeth in a mirthless grin and looked at her.

"You will find another man, M'Lino," he said, "as readily as you found this one." Then he turned away to give directions for the hanging. But the woman followed him, and boldly laid her hand on his arm.

"Master," she said, "if any was wronged by O'Sako's death, was it not I, his wife? Yet I say let Tebeki go free, for I love him."

"You may go to the devil," said Sanders politely; "I am getting tired of you and your lovers."

He hanged Tebeki, expeditiously and with science, and the man died immediately, because Sanders was very thorough in this sort of business.

Then he and the Houssa corps marched away, and the death song of the woman sounded fainter and fainter as the forest enveloped him. He camped that night on the Hill of Trees, overlooking the sweeping bend of the river, and in the morning his orderly came to tell him that the wife of O'Sako desired to see him.

Sanders cursed the wife of O'Sako, but saw her.

She opened her mission without preliminary.

"Because of the death I brought to O'Sako, my husband, and Tebeki, my lover, the people have cast me forth," she said. "Every hand is against me, and if I stay in this country I shall die."

"Well?" said Sanders.

"So I will go with you, until you reach the Sangar River, which leads to the Congo. I have brothers there."

"All this may be true," said Sanders dispassionately; "on the other hand, I know that your heart is filled with hate because I have taken two men from you, and hanged a third. Nevertheless, you shall come with us as far as the Sangar River, but you shall not touch the 'chop' of my men, nor shall you speak with them."

She nodded and left him, and Sanders issued orders for her treatment.

In the middle of the night Abiboo, who, in addition to being Sanders' servant, was a sergeant of the Houssas, came to Sanders' tent, and the Commissioner jumped out of bed and mechanically reached for his Express.

"Leopards?" he asked briefly.

"Master," said Sergeant Abiboo, "it is the woman M'Lino—she is a witch."

"Sergeant," said the exasperated Sanders, "if you wake me up in the middle of the night with that sort of talk, I will break your infernal head."

"Be that as it may, master," said the sergeant stolidly, "she is a witch, for she has talked with my men and done many wonderful things— such as causing them to behold their children and far-away scenes."

"Have I an escort of babies?" asked Sanders despairingly. "I wish," he went on, with quiet savageness, "I had chosen Kroomen or Bushmen"—the sergeant winced—"or the mad people of the Isisi River, before I took a half-company of the King's Houssas."

The sergeant gulped down the insult, saying nothing.

"Bring the woman to me," said Sanders. He scrambled into his clothing, and lit his tent lantern.

After a while he heard the pattering of bare feet, and the girl came into his tent, and regarded him quietly.

"M'Lino," said Sanders, "I told you that you were not to speak with my men."

"Lord," she said, "they spoke with me first."

"Is this true?"

The sergeant at the tent door nodded. "Tembeli, the son of Sekambano, spoke with her, thus disobeying orders, and the other men followed," he said.

"Bushmen by gad!" fumed Sanders. "You will take Tembeli, the son of Sekambano, tie him to a tree, and give him twenty lashes."

The sergeant saluted, produced a tawdry little notebook, all brass binding and gold edges, and made a laborious note.

"As for you," said Sanders to the woman, "you drop your damned bush-mesmerism, or I'll treat you in the same way—*alaki?*"

"Yes, lord," she said meekly, and departed.

Two Houssas tied Tembeli to a tree, and the sergeant gave him twenty-one with a pliable hippo-hide—the extra one being the sergeant's perquisite.

In the morning the sergeant reported that Tembeli had died in the night, and Sanders worried horribly.

"It isn't the flogging," he said; "he has had the *chicotte* before."

"It is the woman," said the sergeant wisely. "She is a witch; I foresaw this when she joined the column."

They buried Tembeli, the son of Sekambano, and Sanders wrote three reports of the circumstances of the death, each of which he tore up.

Then he marched on.

That night the column halted near a village, and Sanders sent the woman, under escort, to the chief, with orders to see her safely to the Sangar River. In half an hour she returned, with the escort, and Sergeant Abiboo explained the circumstances.

"The chief will not take her in, being afraid."

"Afraid?" Sanders spluttered in his wrath; "Afraid? What is he afraid of?"

"Her devilry," said the sergeant; "the *lo-koli* has told him the story of Tebeki, and he will not have her."

Sanders swore volubly for five minutes; then he went off to interview the chief of the village.

The interview was short and to the point. Sanders knew this native very well, and made no mistakes.

"Chief," he said at the end of the *palaver*, "two things I may do; one is to punish you for your disobedience, and the other is to go on my way."

"Master," said the other earnestly, "if you give my village to the fire, yet I would not take the woman M'Lino."

"So much I realise," said Sanders; "therefore I will go on my way."

He marched at dawn on the following day, the woman a little ahead of the column, and under his eye. Halting for a "chop "and rest at midday, a man of the Houssas came to him and said there was a dead man hanging from a tree in the wood. Sanders went immediately with the man to the place of the hanging, for he was responsible for the peace of the district.

"Where?" he asked, and the man pointed to a straight gum-tree that stood by itself in a clearing.

"Where?" asked Sanders again, for there was no evidence of tragedy. The man still pointed at the tree, and Sanders frowned.

"Go forward and touch his foot," said the Commissioner, and, after a little hesitation, the soldier walked slowly to the tree and put out his hand. But he touched nothing but air, as far as Sanders could see.

"You are mad," he said, and whistled for the sergeant.

"What do you see there?" asked Sanders, and the sergeant replied instantly:

"Beyond the hanging man—"

"There is no hanging man," said Sanders coolly—for he began to appreciate the need for calm reasoning—"nothing but a tree and some shadows."

The Houssa looked puzzled, and turned a grave face to his.

"Master, there is a man hanging," he said.

"That is so," said Sanders quietly; ' we must investigate this matter." And he signed for the party to return to the camp.

On the way he asked carelessly if the sergeant had spoken with the woman M'Lino.

"I saw her, but she did not speak, except with her eyes."

Sanders nodded. "Tell me," he said, "where did you bury Tembeli, the son of Sekambano?"

"Master, we left him, in accordance with our custom, on the ground at the foot of a tree."

Sanders nodded again, for this is not the custom of the Houssas.

"We will go back on our tracks to the camping place where the woman came to us," he said.

They marched until sundown, and whilst two men pitched his tent Sanders strolled round the little camp. The men were sitting about their cooking-pots, but the woman M'Lino sat apart, her elbows on her knees, her face between her hands.

"M'Lino," he said to her, halting suddenly before her, "how many men have you killed in your life?"

She looked at him long and fixedly, and he returned the stare; then she dropped her eyes. "Many men," she said.

"So I think," said Sanders.

He was eating his dinner when Abiboo came slowly toward him.

"Master, the man has died," he said.

Sanders looked at him narrowly.

"Which man?"

"The man you *chicotted* with your own hand," said Abiboo.

Now, the Commissioner had neither *chicotted* a man, nor had he ordered punishment, but he replied in a matter-of-fact tone, "I will see him."

On the edge of the camp there was a little group about a prostrate figure. The Houssas fell apart with black looks as Sanders came near, and there was some muttering. Though Sanders did not see it, M'Lino looked strangely at Ahmid, a Houssa, who took up his rifle and went stealthily into the bush.

The Commissioner bent over the man who lay there, felt his breast, and detected no beat of heart.

"Get me my medicine chest," he said, but none obeyed him.

"Sergeant," he repeated, "bring my medicine chest!"

Abiboo saluted slowly, and, with every appearance of reluctance, went.

He came back with the case of undressed skin, and Sanders opened it, took out the ammonia bottle, and applied it to the man's nose. He made no sign.

"We shall see," was all that Sanders said when the experiment failed. He took a hypodermic syringe and filled the little tube with a solution of strychnine. This he jabbed unceremoniously into the patient's back. In a minute the corpse sat up, jerkily.

"Ha!" said Sanders, cheerfully; "I am evidently a great magician!"

He rose to his feet, dusted his knees, and beckoned the sergeant.

"Take four men and return to the place where you left Tembeli. If the leopards have not taken him, you will meet him on the road, because by this time he will have waked up."

He saw the party march off, then turned his attention to M'Lino.

"My woman," he said, "it is evident to me that you are a witch, although I have met your like before"—it was observed that the face of Sanders was very white. "I cannot flog you, because you are a woman, but I can kill you."

She laughed.

Their eyes met in a struggle for mastery, and so they stared at one another for a space of time which seemed to Sanders a thousand years, but which was in all probability less than a minute.

"It would be better if you killed yourself," she said.

"I think so," said Sanders dully, and fumbled for his revolver.

It was half drawn, his thumb on the hammer, when a rifle banged in the bushes and the woman fell forward without a word.

Ahmid, the Houssa, was ever a bad shot.

******

"I believe," said Sanders, later, "that you took your rifle to kill me, being under the influence of M'Lino, so I will make no bad report against you."

"Master," said the Houssa simply, "I know nothing of the matter."

"That I can well believe," said Sanders, and gave the order to march.

CHAPTER 11

The Witchdoctor

Nothing surprised Sanders except the ignorance of the average stay-at-home Briton on all matters pertaining to the savage peoples of Africa. Queer things happened in the "black patch"—so the coast officials called Sanders' territory—miraculous, mysterious things, but Sanders was never surprised. He had dealings with folks who believed in ghosts and personal devils, and he sympathised with them, realising that it is very difficult to ascribe all the evils of life to human agencies.

Sanders was an unquiet man, or so his constituents thought him, and a little mad; this also was the native view. Worst of all, there was no method in his madness.

Other commissioners might be depended upon to arrive after the rains, sending word ahead of their coming. This was a good way—the Isisi, the Ochori, and the N'Gombi people, everlastingly at issue, were agreed upon this—because, with timely warning of the Commissioner's approach, it was possible to thrust out of sight the ugly evidence of fault, to clean up and make tidy the muddle of folly.

It was bad to step sheepishly forth from your hut into the clear light of the rising sun, with all the debris of an overnight feast mutely testifying to your discredit, and face the cold, unwavering eyes of a little brown-faced man in immaculate white. The switch he carried in his hand would be smacking his leg suggestively, and there were always four Houssa soldiers in blue and scarlet in the background, immobile, but alert, quick to obey.

Once Sanders came to a N'Gombi village at dawn, when by every known convention he should have been resting in his comfortable bungalow some three hundred miles downriver.

Sanders came strolling through the village street just as the sun topped the trees and long shadows ran along the ground before the flood of lemon-coloured light.

The village was silent and deserted, which was a bad sign, and spoke of overnight orgies. Sanders walked on until he came to the big square near the *palaver* house, and there the black ruin of a dead fire smoked sullenly.

Sanders saw something that made him go raking amongst the embers.

"Pah!" said Sanders, with a wry face.

He sent back to the steamer for the full force of his Houssa guard, then he walked into the chief's hut and kicked him till he woke.

He came out blinking and shivering, though the morning was warm.

"Telemi, son of O'ari," said Sanders, "tell me why I should not hang you—man-eater and beast."

"Lord," said the chief, "we chopped this man because he was an enemy, stealing into the village at night, and carrying away our goats and our dogs. Besides which, we did not know that you were nearby."

"I can believe that," said Sanders.

A *lo-koli* beat the villages to wakefulness, and before a silent assembly the headman of the N'Gombi village was scientifically flogged.

Then Sanders called the elders together and said a few words of cheer and comfort.

"Only hyenas and crocodiles eat their kind," he said, "also certain fishes." (There was a general shudder, for amongst the N'Gombi to be likened to a fish is a deadly insult.) "Cannibals I do not like, and they are hated by the King's Government. Therefore when it comes to my ears—and I have many spies—that you chop man, whether he be enemy or friend, I will come quickly and I will flog sorely; and if it should again happen I will bring with me a rope, and I will find me a tree, and there will be broken huts in this land."

Again they shuddered at the threat of the broken hut, for it is the custom of the N'Gombi to break down the walls of a dead man's house to give his spirit free egress.

Sanders carried away with him the chief of the village, with leg-irons at his ankles, and in course of time the prisoner arrived at a little labour colony on the coast, where, he worked for five years in company with other indiscreet headmen who were suffering servitude for divers offences.

They called Sanders in the Upper River districts by a long and sonorous name, which may be euphemistically translated as "The man who has a faithless wife," the little joke of Bosambo, chief of the Ochori, and mightily subtle because Sanders was wedded to his people.

North and south, east and west, he prowled. He travelled by night and by day. Sometimes his steamer would go threshing away up river, and be watched out of sight by the evil-doing little fishing-villages.

"Go you," said Sarala, who was a little headman of the Akasava, "go you three hours' journey in your canoe and watch the river for Sandi's return. And at first sign of his steamer—which you may see if you climb the hill at the river's bend—come back and warn me, for I desire to follow certain customs of my father in which Sandi has no pleasure."

He spoke to two of his young men and they departed. That night by the light of a fire, to the accompaniment of dancing and drum-beating, the son of the headman brought his firstborn, ten hours old, squealing noisily, as if with knowledge of the doom ahead, and laid it at his father's feet.

"People," said the little chief, "it is a wise saying of all, and has been a wise saying since time began, that the firstborn has a special virtue; so that if we sacrifice him to sundry gods and devils, good luck will follow us in all our doings."

He said a word to the son, who took a broad-bladed spear and began turning the earth until he had dug a little grave. Into this, alive, the child was laid, his little feet kicking feebly against the loose mould.

"Oh, gods and devils," invoked the old man, "we shed no blood, that this child may come to you unblemished."

The son stirred a heap of loose earth with his foot, so that it fell over the baby's legs; then into the light of the fire stepped Sanders, and the chief's son fell back.

Sanders was smoking a thin cigar, and he smoked for fully a minute without saying a word, and a minute was a very long time. Then he stepped to the grave, stooped, and lifted the baby up awkwardly, for he was more used to handling men than babes, gave it a little shake to clear it of earth, and handed it to a woman.

"Take the child to its mother," he said, "and tell her to send it to me alive in the morning, otherwise she had best find a new husband."

Then he turned to the old chief and his son.

"Old man," he said, "how many years have you to live?"

"Master," said the old man, "that is for you to say."

Sanders scratched his chin reflectively, and the old man watched him with fear in his eyes.

"You will go to Bosambo, chief of the Ochori, telling him I have sent you, and you shall till his garden, and carry his water until you die," said Sanders.

"I am so old that that will be soon," said the old man.

"If you were younger it would be sooner," said Sanders. "As for your son, we will wait until the morning."

The Houssas in the background marched the younger man to the camp Sanders had formed down river—the boat that had passed had been intended to deceive a chief under suspicion—and in the morning, when the news came that the child was dead—whether from shock, or injury, or exposure, Sanders did not trouble to inquire—the son of the chief was hanged.

I tell these stories of Sanders of the River, that you may grasp the type of man he was and learn something of the work he had to do. If he was quick to punish, he acted in accordance with the spirit of the people he governed, for they had no memory; and yesterday, with its faults, its errors and its teachings, was a very long time ago, and a man resents an unjust punishment for a crime he has forgotten.

It is possible to make a bad mistake, but Sanders never made one, though he was near to doing so once.

Sanders was explaining his point of view in regard to natives to Professor Sir George Carsley, when that eminent scientist arrived unexpectedly at headquarters, having been sent out by the British Government to study tropical disease at first hand.

Sir George was a man of some age, with a face of exceptional pallor and a beard that was snowy white.

"There was a newspaper man who said I treated my people like dogs," said Sanders slowly, for he was speaking in English, a language that was seldom called for. "I believe I do. That is to say, I treat them as if they were real good dogs, not to be petted one minute and kicked the next; not to be encouraged to lie on the drawing-room mat one day, and the next cuffed away from the dining-room hearthrug."

Sir George made no answer. He was a silent man, who had had some experience on the coast, and had lived for years in the solitude of a Central African province, studying the habits of the malarial mosquito.

Sanders was never a great conversationalist, and the three days the professor spent at headquarters were deadly dull ones for the Commissioner.

On one subject alone did the professor grow talkative.

"I want to study the witchdoctor," he said. "I think there is no appointment in the world that would give me a greater sense of power than my appointment by a native people to that post."

Sanders thought the scientist was joking, but the other returned to the subject again and again, gravely, earnestly, and persistently, and for his entertainment Sanders recited all the stories he had ever heard of witchdoctors and their tribe.

"But you don't expect to learn anything from these people?" said Sanders, half in joke.

"On the contrary," said the professor, seriously; "I anticipate making valuable scientific discoveries through my intercourse with them."

"Then you're a silly old ass," said Sanders; but he said it to himself.

The pale professor left him at the end of the fourth day, and beyond an official notification that he had established himself on the border, no further news came of the scientist for six months, until one evening came the news that the pale-faced old man had been drowned by the upsetting of a canoe. He had gone out on a solitary excursion, taking with him some scientific apparatus, and nothing more was heard of him until his birch-bark canoe was discovered, bottom up, floating on the river.

No trace of Sir George was found, and in the course of time Sanders collected the dead man's belongings and forwarded them to England.

There were two remarkable facts about this tragedy, the first being that Sanders found no evidence either in papers or diaries, of the results of any scientific research work performed by the professor other than a small note-book. The second was, that in his little book the scientist had carefully recorded the stories Sanders had told him of witch doctors.

(Sanders recognised at least one story which he had himself invented on the spur of the moment for the professor's entertainment.)

Six more or less peaceful months passed, and then began the series of events which make up the story of the Devil Man.

It began on the Little River.

There was a woman of the Isisi people who hated her husband, though he was very good to her, building her a hut and placing an older wife to wait upon her. He gave her many presents, including a great neck-ring of brass, weighing pounds, that made her the most envied woman on the Isisi River. But her hatred for her husband was unquenched; and one morning she came out from her hut, looking dazed and frightened, and began in a quavering voice to sing the Song of the Dead, mechanically pouring little handfuls of dust on her head, and the villagers went in, to find the man stark and staring, with a twisted grin on his dead face and the pains of hell in his eyes.

In the course of two days they burned the husband in the Middle River; and as the canoe bearing the body swept out of sight round a bend of the river, the woman stepped into the water and laved the dust from her grimy body and stripped the green leaves of mourning from her waist.

Then she walked back to the village with a light step, for the man she hated best was dead and there was an end to it.

Four days later came Sanders, a grim little man, with a thin, brown face and hair inclined to redness.

"M'Fasa," he said, standing at the door of her hut and looking down at her, as with a dogged simulation of indifference she pounded her grain, "they tell me your man has died."

"Lord, that is true," she said. "He died of a sudden sickness."

"Too sudden for my liking," said Sanders, and disappeared into the dark interior of the hut. By and by Sanders came back into the light and looked down on her. In his hand was a tiny glass phial, such as Europeans know very well, but which was a remarkable find in a heathen village.

"I have a fetish," he said, "and my fetish has told me that you poisoned your husband, M'Fasa."

"Your fetish lies," she said, not looking up.

"I will not argue that matter," said Sanders wisely, for he had no proofs beyond his suspicions; and straightway he summoned to him the chief man of the village.

There was a little wait, the woman pounding her corn slowly, with downcast eyes, pausing now and then to wipe the sweat from her forehead with the back of her hand, and Sanders, his helmet on the back of his head, a half-smoked cheroot in his mouth, hands thrust deep into his duck-pockets and an annoyed frown on his face, looking at her.

By and by came the chief tardily, having been delayed by the search for a soldier's scarlet coat, such as he wore on great occasions.

"Master, you sent for me," he said.

Sanders shifted his gaze.

"On second thoughts," he said, "I do not need you."

The chief went away with a whole thanksgiving service in his heart, for there had been certain secret doings on the river for which he expected reprimand.

"M'Fasa, you will go to my boat," said Sanders, and the woman, putting down her mortar, rose and went obediently to the steamer. Sanders followed slowly, having a great many matters to consider. If he denounced this woman to the elders of the village, she would be stoned to death; if he carried her to headquarters and tried her, there was no evidence on which a conviction might be secured. There was no place to which he could deport her, yet to leave her would be to open the way for further mischief.

She awaited him on the deck of the *Zaire*, a straight, shapely girl of eighteen, fearless, defiant.

"M'Fasa," said Sanders, "why did you kill your husband?"

"Lord, I did not kill him; he died of the sickness," she said, as doggedly as before.

Sanders paced the narrow deck, his head on his breast, for this was a profound problem Then he looked up.

"You may go," he said; and the woman, a little puzzled, walked along the plank that connected the boat with the shore, and disappeared into the bush.

Three weeks later his spies brought word that men were dying unaccountably on the Upper River. None knew why they died, for a man would sit down strong and full of cheer to his evening meal, and lo! in the morning, when his people went to wake him, he would be beyond waking, being most unpleasantly dead.

This happened in many villages on the Little River.

"It's getting monotonous," said Sanders to the captain of the Houssas. "There is some wholesale poisoning going on, and I am going up to find the gentleman who dispenses the dope."

It so happened that the first case claiming investigation was at Isisi City. It was a woman who had died, and this time Sanders suspected the husband, a notorious evil-doer.

"Okali," he said, coming to the point, "why did you poison your wife?"

"Lord," said the man, "she died of the sickness. In the evening she was well, but at the dark hour before sun came she turned in her sleep saying '*Ah! oh!*' and straightway she died."

Sanders drew a long breath.

"Get a rope," he said to one of his men, and when the rope arrived Abiboo scrambled up to the lower branch of a copal-gum and scientifically lashed a block and tackle.

"Okali," said Sanders, "I am going to hang you for the murder of your wife, for I am a busy man and have no time to make inquiries; and if you are not guilty of her murder, yet there are many other abominable deeds you have been guilty of, therefore I am justified in hanging you."

The man was grey with terror when they slipped the noose over his neck and strapped his hands behind him.

"Lord, she was a bad wife to me and had many lovers," he stammered. "I did not mean to kill her, but the Devil Man said that such medicine would make her forget her lovers—"

"Devil Man! What Devil Man?" asked Sanders quickly.

"Lord, there is a devil greatly respected in these parts, who wanders in the forest all the time and gives many curious medicines."

"Where is he to be found?"

"Lord, none know. He comes and goes, like a grey ghost, and he has a fetish more powerful than a thousand ordinary devils. Master, I gave the woman, my wife, that which he gave to me, and she died. How might I know that she would die?"

"*Cheg'li,*" said Sanders shortly to the men at the rope-end, and *cheg'li* in the dialect of the River means "pull."

★★★★★★

"Stop!"

Sanders was in a changeable mood, and a little irritable by reason of the fact that he knew himself to be fickle.

"How came this drug to you? In powder, in liquid, or—"

The man's lips were dry. He could do no more than shake his head helplessly.

"Release him," said Sanders; and Abiboo loosened the noose and unstrapped the man's hands.

"If you have lied to me," said Sanders, "you die at sunset. First let me hear more of this Devil Man, for I am anxious to make his acquaintance."

He gave the man ten minutes to recover from the effects of his fear, then sent for him.

"Lord," said he, "I know nothing of the Devil Man save that he is

132

the greatest witchdoctor in the world, and on nights when the moon is up and certain stars are in their places he comes like a ghost, and we are all afraid. Then those of us who need him go forth into the forest, and he gives to us according to our desires."

"How carried he the drug?

"Lord, it was in a crystal rod, such as white men carry their medicines in. I will bring it to you."

He went back to his hut and returned a few minutes later with a phial, the fellow to that which was already in Sanders' possession. The Commissioner took it and smelt at the opening. There was the faintest odour of almonds, and Sanders whistled, for he recognised the after-scent of cyanide of potassium, which is not such a drug as untutored witchdoctors know, much less employ.

★★★★★★

"I can only suggest," wrote Sanders to headquarters, "that by some mischance the medicine chest of the late Sir George Carsley has come into the possession of a native 'doctor.' You will remember that the chest was with the professor when he was drowned. It has possibly been washed up and discovered. . . . In the meantime, I am making diligent inquiries as to the identity of the Devil Man, who seems to have leapt into fame so suddenly."

There were sleepless nights ahead for Sanders, nights of swift marchings and doublings, of quick runs up the river, of unexpected arrivals in villages, of lonely vigils in the forest and by strange pools. But he had no word of the Devil Man, though he learnt many things of interest. Most potent of his magical possessions was a box, "so small," said one who had seen it, and indicated a six-inch square. In this box dwelt a small and malicious god who pinched and scratched (yet without leaving a mark), who could stick needles into the human body and never draw blood.

"I give it up," said Sanders in despair, and went back to his base to think matters out.

He was sitting at dinner one night, when far away on the river the drum be it. It was not the regular *lo-koli* roll, but a seres of staccato tappings, and, stepping softly to the door, the Commissioner listened.

He had borrowed the Houssa signalling staff from headquarters, and stationed them at intervals along the river. On a still night the tapping of a drum carries far, but the rattle of iron-wood sticks on a hollowed tree-trunk carries farthest of all.

"*Clok-clok, clockitty-clock.*"

It sounded like the far-away croaking of a bull-frog; but Sanders picked out the letters:

"Devil Man sacrifices tomorrow night in the Forest of Dreams."

As he jotted down the message on the white sleeve of his jacket, Abiboo came running up the path.

"I have heard," said Sanders briefly. "There is steam in the *puc̄apuc̄*?"

"We are ready, master," said the man.

Sanders waited only to take a hanging revolver from the wall and throw his overcoat over his arm, for his travelling kit was already deposited on the *Zaire*, and had been for three days.

In the darkness the sharp nose of his little boat swung out to the stream, and ten minutes after the message came the boat was threshing a way against the swift river.

All night long the steamer went on, tacking from bank to bank to avoid the shoals.

Dawn found her at a wooding, where her men, working at fever speed, piled logs on her deck until she had the appearance of a timber-boat.

Then off again, stopping only to secure news of the coming sacrifice from the spies who were scattered up and down the river.

Sanders reached the edge of the Dream Forest at midnight and tied up. He had ten Houssa policemen with him, and at the head of these he stepped ashore into the blackness of the forest. One of the soldiers went ahead to find the path and keep it, and in single file the little force began its two-hour march. Once they came upon two leopards fighting; once they stumbled over a buffalo sleeping in their path. Twice they disturbed strange beasts that slunk into the shadows as they passed, and came snuffling after them, till Sanders flashed a white beam from his electric lamp in their direction. Eventually they came stealthily to the place of sacrifice.

There were at least six hundred people squatting in a semi-circle before a rough altar built of logs. Two huge fires blazed and crackled on either side of the altar; but Sanders' eyes were for the Devil Man, who leant over the body of a young girl, apparently asleep, stretched upon the logs.

Once the Devil Man had worn the garb of civilisation; now he was clothed in rags. He stood in his grimy shirt-sleeves, his white beard wild and uncombed, his pale face tense, and a curious light in his eyes.

In his hand was a bright scalpel, and he was speaking—and, curiously enough, in English.

"This, gentlemen," said he, leaning easily against the rude altar, and speaking with the assurance of one who had delivered many such lectures, "is a bad case of trynosomiasis. You will observe the discoloration of skin, the opalescent pupils, and now that I have placed the patient under anaesthetics you will remark the misplacement of the cervical glands, which is an invariable symptom."

He paused and looked benignly around.

"I may say that I have lived for a great time amongst native people. I occupied the honourable position of witchdoctor in Central Africa—"

He stopped and passed his hand across his brow, striving to recall something; then he picked up the thread of his discourse.

All the time he spoke the half-naked assembly sat silent and awe-stricken, comprehending nothing save that the witchdoctor with the white face, who had come from nowhere and had done many wonderful things—his magic box proved to be a galvanic battery—was about to perform strange rites.

"Gentlemen," the old man went on, tapping the breast of his victim with the handle of his scalpel, "I shall make an incision—"

Sanders came from his place of concealment, and walked steadily towards the extemporised operating-table.

"Professor," he said gently, and the madman looked at him with a puzzled frown.

"You are interrupting the clinic," he said testily; "I am demonstrating—"

"I know, sir."

Sanders took his arm, and Sir George Carsley, a great scientist, consulting surgeon to St. Mark's Hospital, London, and the author of many books on tropical diseases, went with him like a child.

CHAPTER 12

The Lonely One

Mr. Commissioner Sanders had lived so long with native people that he had absorbed not a little of their simplicity. More than this, he had acquired the uncanny power of knowing things which he would not and could not have known unless he were gifted with the prescience which is every aboriginal's birthright.

He had sent three spies into the Isisi country—which lies a long way from headquarters and is difficult of access—and after two months of waiting they came to him in a body, bearing good news.

This irritated Sanders to an unjustifiable degree.

"Master, I say to you that the Isisi are quiet," protested one of the spies; "and there is no talk of war."

"H'm!" said Sanders, ungraciously. "And you?"

He addressed the second spy.

"Lord," said the man, "I went into the forest, to the border of the land, and there is no talk of war. Chiefs and headmen told me this."

"Truly you are a great spy," scoffed Sanders; "and how came you to the chiefs and headmen? And how did they greet you? 'Hail! secret spy of Sandi'? Huh!"

He dismissed the men with a wave of his hand, and putting on his helmet went down to the Houssa lines, where the blue-coated soldiers gambled in the shade of their neat white barracks.

The Houssa captain was making palatable medicine with the aid of a book of cigarette papers and a six-ounce bottle of quinine sulphide.

Sanders observed his shaking hand, and talked irritably.

"There's trouble in the Isisi," he said, "I can smell it. I don't know what it is—but there's devilry of sorts."

"Secret societies?" suggested the Houssa.

"Secret grandmothers," snarled Sanders. "How many men have you got?"

"Sixty, including the lame 'uns," said the Houssa officer, and swallowed a paperful of quinine with a grimace.

Sanders tapped the toe of his boot with his thin ebony stick, and was thoughtful.

"I may want 'em," he said. "I'm going to find out what's wrong with these Isisi people."

★★★★★★

By the little river that turns abruptly from the River of Spirits, Imgani, the Lonely One, built a house. He built it in proper fashion, stealing the wood from a village five miles away. In this village there had been many deaths, owing to The Sickness; and it is the custom on the Upper River that whenever a person dies, the house wherein he died shall die also.

No man takes shelter under the accursed roof where under the Spirit sits brooding; the arms of the dead man are broken and scattered on his shallow grave, and the cooking-pots of his wives are there likewise.

By and by, under the combined influences of wind and rain, the reed roof sags and sinks, the doorposts rot; elephant-grass, coarse and strong, shoots up between crevices in wall and roof; then come a heavier rain and a heavier wind, and the forest has wiped the foul spot clean.

Imgani, who said he was of the N'Gombi people, and was afraid of no devils—at any rate, no Isisi devil—stole doorposts and native rope fearlessly. He stole them by night, when the moon was behind the trees, and mocked the dead spirits, calling them by evil and tantalising names.

Yet he went cautiously to work; for whilst he did not hold spirits in account, he was wholesomely respectful of the live Isisi, who would have put him to death had his sacrilege been detected, though, strangely enough, death was the thing he feared least.

So he stole the accursed supports and accursed roof-props, and would have stolen the roofs as well, but for the fact that they were very old and full of spiders.

All these things he came and took, carrying them five miles to the turn of the river, and there, at his leisure, he built a little house. In the daytime he slept, in the night he trapped beasts and caught fish, but he made no attempt to catch the big bats that come over from the middle island of the river, though these are very edible, and regarded as a delicacy.

One day, just before the sun went down, he went into the forest on the track of zebra. He carried two big hunting-spears, such as the N'Gombi make best; a wickerwork shield, and on his back, slung by a strip of hide, a bunch of dried fish he had caught in the river.

A man of middle height was Imgani, spare of build, but broad of shoulder. His skin shone healthily, and his step was light. As he walked, you saw the muscles of his back ripple and weave like the muscles of a well-trained thoroughbred.

He was half an hour's journey within the forest f when he came upon a girl. She was carrying a bundle of *manioc* root on her head, and walked gracefully.

When she saw Imgani she stopped dead, and the fear of death and worse came in her eyes, for she knew him to be an outcast man, with no tribe and no people. Such men are more dreadful than the *ingali*, who rears up from the grass and plunges his poison-fangs in your leg.

They stood watching one another, the man leaning with both hands on the spears, his cheek against them; the girl trembled.

"Woman, where do you go?" said Imgani.

"Master, I go to the village which is by the river, this being the path," she flurried.

"What have you there?"

"*Manioc*, for bread," she whispered thickly.

"You are a root-eater," said Imgani, nodding his head.

"Master, let me go," she said, staring at him.

Imgani jerked his head.

"I see you are afraid of me—yet I want nothing from you," he said. "I am Imgani, which means the Lonely One; and I have no desire for wives or women, being too high a man for such folly. You are safe, root-eater, for if I wished I would fill this forest with the daughters of chiefs, all very beautiful, all moaning for me."

The girl's fear had disappeared, and she looked at him curiously. Moreover, she recognised that there was truth in his claim of austerity. Possibly she was a little piqued, for she said tartly enough, employing an Isisi proverb:

"*Only the goat bleats at the mouth of the leopard's cave—the Isisi grow fat on strangers.*"

He looked at her, his head cocked on one side.

"They say in the lower country that the Isisi sell men to the Arabi," he said musingly. "That is bad talk; you may go."

With another jerk of his head he dismissed her.

She had gone some little distance when he called her back.

"Root-eater," he said, "if men ask you who I be, you shall say that I am Imgani the Lonely One, who is a prince amongst the princes; also that I have killed many men in my day—so many that I cannot count them. Also say that from my house, which I have built by the river, to as far as a man can see in every way, is my kingdom, and let none stray therein, except to bring gifts in their hands, for I am very terrible and very jealous."

"Lord," said the girl, "I will say all this."

And she went, half running, in the direction of the village, leaving Imgani to continue on his way.

Now this village had many young men eager to please the girl, who carried *manioc*, for she was a chief's daughter, and she was, moreover, fourteen, a marriageable age. So when she came flying along the village street, half hysterical in her fear, crying, babbling, incoherent, there was not wanting sympathy nor knight valiant to wipe out the insult.

Six young men, with spears and short swords, danced before the chief and the chief's daughter (how important she felt, any woman of any race will tell you), and one of them, E'kebi, a man gifted with language, described from sunset to moonrise, which is roughly four hours, exactly what would happen to Imgani when the men of the Isisi fell upon him; how his eyes would shrivel as before a great and terrible fire, and his limbs wither up, and divers other physiological changes which need not be particularised.

"That is good talk," said the chief; "yet, since Sandi is our master and has spies everywhere, do not shed blood, for the smell of blood is carried farther than a man can see. And Sandi is very devilish on this question of killing. Moreover, this Lonely One is a stranger, and if we catch him we may sell him to the Arabi, who will give us cloth and gin for him."

Having heard all this, they sacrificed a young goat and marched. They came upon the house of Imgani, but the Lonely One was not there, for he was trapping beasts in the forest; so they burnt his house, uprooted his poor garden, and, being joined by many other Isisi people, who had followed at a respectful distance, lest Imgani's estimate of his own prowess were justified by results, they held high revel, until of a sudden the sun came up over the middle island, and all the little stars in the sky went out.

Imgani saw all this, leaning on his spears in the shadow of the forest, but was content to be a spectator.

For, he reasoned, if he went out against them they would attempt to kill him or beat him with rods, and that his high spirit could not endure.

He saw the flames lick away the house he had built with such labour.

"They are foolish people," he mused, "for they burn their own, and perhaps the spirits of the dead will be displeased and give them boils."

When all that was left of his habitation was a white heap of ash, a dark-red glow, and a hazy wisp of smoke, Imgani turned his face to the forest.

All day long he walked, halting only to eat the fish he carried, and at night time he came upon another Isisi village, which was called O'Fasi.

He came through the village street with his shoulders squared, his head erect, swinging his spears famously. He looked neither to the left nor to the right; and the villagers, crowding to the doors of their huts, put their clenched knuckles to their mouths, and said: "*O ho!*" which means that they were impressed.

So he stalked through the entire length of the village, and was making for the forest-path beyond, when a messenger came pattering after him.

"Lord," said the messenger, "the *capita* of this village, who is responsible to the Government for all people who pass, and especially for thieves who may have escaped from the Village of Irons, desires your presence, being sure that you are no thief, but a great one, and wishing to do honour to you."

Thus he recited, and being a peaceable man, who had been chosen for the part because he was related by marriage to the principal wife of the chief, he kept a cautious eye on the broad-headed spear, and determined the line of his flight.

"Go back to your master, slave," said Imgani, "and say to him that I go to find a spot of sufficient loneliness, where I may sleep this night and occupy myself with high thoughts. When I have found such a place I will return. Say, also, that I am a prince of my own people, and that my father has legions of such quantity that, if every righting man of the legions were to take a handful of sand from the bottom of the river, the river would be bottomless; also say that I am named Imgani, and that I love myself better than any man has loved himself since the moon went white that it might not look like the sun."

He went on, leaving the messenger filled with thought.

True to his promise, Imgani returned.

He came back to find that there was a *palaver* in progress, the subject of the *palaver* being the unfortunate relative by marriage to the chief's principal wife.

"Who," the chief was saying, "has put shame upon me, being as great a fool as his cousin, my wife."

"Master," said the poor relation humbly, "I entreated him to return; but he was a man of great pride, and, moreover, impatient to go."

"Your mother was a fool," said the chief; "her mother also was a fool, and your father, whoever he was, and no man knows, was a great fool."

This interesting beginning to a crude address on hereditary folly was interrupted by the return of Imgani, and as he came slowly up the little hillock the assembly took stock of him, from the square, steel razor stuck in the tight-fitting leopard-skin cap to the thin bangles of brass about his ankles.

The chief, a portly man of no great courage, observed the spears, noting that the hafts were polished smooth by much handling.

"Lord," said he mildly, "I am chief of this village, appointed by the Government, who gave me a medal to wear about my neck, bearing on one side the picture of a great man with a beard, and on the other side certain devil marks and writings of vast power. This was given to me that all people might know I was chief, but I have lost the medal. None the less, I am chief of this village, as this will show."

He fumbled in the bosom of his cloth and brought out a bag of snake skin, and from this he extracted a very soiled paper.

With tender care he unfolded it, and disclosed a sheet of official notepaper with a few scrawled words in the handwriting of Mr. Commissioner Sanders. They ran:

To all Sub-Commissioners, Police Officers, and Commanders of Houssa Ports:
Arrest and detain the bearer if found in any other territory than the Isisi.

There was a history attached to this singular document. It had to do with an unauthorised raid upon certain Ochori villages and a subsequent trial at headquarters, where a chief, all aquiver with apprehension, listened to a terse but knowledgeable prophecy as to what fate awaited him if he put foot out of his restricted dominion.

Imgani took the paper in his hand and was interested. He turned it about, rubbed the writing lightly with his fingers to see whether it was permanent, and returned it to the chief.

"That is very wonderful, though I do not fear magic, except an especial kind such as is practised by a certain witchdoctor of my father's," he said; "nor do I know any government which can govern me."

After which he proceeded to tell them of his father, and of his legions and wives, and various other matters of equal interest.

"I do not doubt that you will understand me," he said. "I am a Lonely One, hating the company of men, who are as changeable as the snow upon the mountains. Therefore, I have left my house with my wives, who were faithful as women go, and I have taken with me no legion, since they are my father's."

The chief was puzzled.

"Why you are lonely, I cannot tell," he said; "but certainly you did right to leave your father's legions. This is a great matter, which needs a *palaver* of older men."

And he ordered the *lo-koli* to be sounded and the elders of the village to be assembled.

They came, bringing their own carved stools, and sat about the thatched shelter, where the chief sat in his presidency.

Again Imgani told his story; it was about fifty wives, and legions of warriors as countless as the sand of the river's beach; and the trustful Isisi listened and believed.

"And I need this," said Imgani, in his peroration; "a little house built on the edge of the river, in such a place that no path passes me and no human being comes within sight of me, for I am very lonely by nature—and a great hater of men."

Imgani went to live in the clearing Nature had made for him, and in a hut erected by his new-found friends. Other hospitalities he refused.

"I have no wish for wives," he stated, "being full of mighty plans to recover my kingdom from evil men who are my father's councillors." Lonely he was in very truth, for none saw him except on very special occasions. It was his practice to go hunting by night and to sleep away the hot days. Sometimes, when the red ball of the sun dropped down behind the trees on the western bank of the river, the villagers saw the straight, blue film of his smoke as he cooked his evening meal; sometimes a homeward-bound boatman saw him slipping silently through the thin edge of the forest on his way to a kill.

They called him the Silent One, and he enjoyed a little fame.

More than this, he enjoyed the confidence of his hosts. The Isisi country is within reach of the Foreign River, down which strangely-shaped boats come by night empty, and return by night full of people who are chained neck to neck, and the officials of French West Africa—which adjoins the Isisi country—receive stories of raids and of burnings which they have not the facilities for investigating, for the Isisi border is nearly six hundred miles from the French headquarters, and lies through a wilderness.

Imgani, in his hunting trips, saw things which might have filled him with amazement, but for the fact that he was a man who was not given to emotion.

He saw little caravans that came stealing from the direction of the territory of France, with whimpering women and groaning men in bondage.

He saw curious midnight shippings of human souls, and grew to know the white-robed Arabs who handled the whip so deftly.

One night as he stood watching all these things, El Mahmud, that famous trader, espied him in the moonlight and saw that he was of a strange people.

"What man are you?" he asked.

"Lord," said Imgani, "I am of a strange people—the N'Gombi."

"That is a lie," said the slaver, "for you have not the face marks of the N'Gombi; you are a half-bred Arab," and he addressed him in Arabic.

Imgani shook his head.

"He does not understand," said the slaver to his lieutenant; "find out where this man's hut is; one night we will take him, for he is worth money."

He spoke in Arabic, and his subordinate nodded.

When the slaver came again three men visited Imgani's house, but he was hunting, and he was hunting every time the long boats came by night to O'Fasi.

143

★★★★★★

Sanders did not go to O'Fasi for six months, during which time, it should be emphasised, nothing happened which by any stretch of imagination could be held to justify any loss of prestige.

He was due to make his half-yearly visit to the Isisi. The crops had been good, the fish plentiful, the rains gentle, and there had been no sickness. All these facts you may bear in mind.

One morning, when swirls of grey mist looped from tree to tree and the east was growing grey, Imgani came back from the forest bearing on his shoulders all that was material of a small buck which he had snared in the night.

When he saw a little fire before his hut and a man squatting chin on knee, he twirled those spears of his cheerfully and went on, for he was afraid of no man.

"Is the world so full of people that you come to disturb my loneliness?" he asked. "I have a thought that I shall kill you and fry your heart, for I do not like to see you sitting by a fire before my hut."

He said all this with a ferocious mien, and the man before the fire shifted uneasily.

"Master, I expected this," he said, "for I see you are a proud man; but I come because of your pride, knowing your wisdom."

Imgani tossed the buck to one side and sat down, staring threateningly and laying the haft of his spears across his bare knee.

Then the other man craned his neck forward and spoke eagerly.

The sun came up and flushed the world rosy; but still he sat talking with great force, Imgani listening.

"So, master," he concluded, "we will kill Sandi when he comes to *palaver*. Ifiba, M'bwka, and a cousin of my mother's, will put spears into him very quickly, and we shall be a great people."

Imgani nodded his head wisely.

"That is true," he said, "people who kill white men must be greatly honoured, because all the other nations will say: 'Behold, these are the people who kill white men!'"

"And when he is dead," the messenger went on, "many young men will go to the boat that smokes and slay all who are with him."

"That is wise also," said Imgani; "when I kill white men I also kill their friends."

He discussed his deeds to some length and with great detail. After the man had gone, Imgani made a meal of fish and manioc, polished the steel blades of his spears with wet sand, dried them carefully with grass, and laid himself down in the shade of the hut to sleep.

He was awake in the early part of the afternoon, and went plunging into the river, swimming far towards the middle stream with great, strong strokes.

Then he swam back to shore, let the sun dry him, and dressed himself in his leopard skin.

He came to the village slowly, and found it agitated. More especially so was the chief, that wise *capita*, for news had arrived that Sandi was coming in the night, and that even now his steamer was rounding the bend of the river.

A plan had miscarried; Sanders was two days ahead of time, and Ifiba and M'bwka, his trusty men, were away on an expedition, and there was no time to substitute unseasoned assassins.

The steamer drifted broadside to the shore, one stern wheel revolving lazily, and then they saw, Imgani amongst the rest, that the decks were crowded with soldiers, impassive brown men in blue uniforms and *fezes*.

A plank bumped down, and holding their rifles high the soldiers came pattering to the shore, and with them a white officer—but not Sandi.

It was a brusque, white man.

"Who is the chief here?" he said crossly.

"Lord, I am that man," said the stout chief, all a-flutter.

"Take that man."

A sergeant of Houssas grasped the chief and deftly swung him round; a corporal of Houssas snapped a pair of handcuffs on his wrists.

"Lord," he whined, "why this shame?"

"Because you are a great thief," said the Houssa ofhcer, "a provoker of war and a dealer in slaves."

"If any man says that, it is a lie," said the chief, "for no Government man has witnessed such abominations."

Imgani stepped forward.

"Chief," he said, "I have seen it."

"You are a great liar," fumed the portly *capita*, trembling with rage, "and Sandi, who is my friend, will not believe you."

"I am Sandi," said Imgani, and smiled crookedly.

CHAPTER 13

The Seer

There are many things that happen in the very heart of Africa that no man can explain; that is why those who know Africa best hesitate to write stories about it.

Because a story about Africa must be a mystery story, and your reader of fiction requires that his mystery shall be, in the end, X-rayed so that the bones of it are visible.

You can no more explain many happenings which are the merest commonplaces in latitude 2° N., longitude (say) 46 W., than you can explain the miracle of faith, or the wonder of telepathy, as this story goes to show.

In the dead of a night Mr. Commissioner Sanders woke.

His little steamer was tied up by a wooding—a wooding he had prepared for himself years before by lopping down trees and leaving them to rot.

He was one day's steam either up or down the river from the nearest village, but he was only six hours' march from the Amatombo folk, who live in the very heart of the forest, and employ arrows poisoned by tetanus.

Sanders sat up in bed and listened.

A night bird chirped monotonously; he heard the "*clug-clug*" of water under the steamer's bows and the soft rustling of leaves as a gentle breeze swayed the young boughs of the trees that overhung the boat. Very intently he listened, then reached down for his mosquito boots and his socks.

He drew them on, found his flannel coat hanging behind the door of his tiny cabin, and opened the door softly. Then he waited, standing, his head bent.

In the darkness he grinned unpleasantly, and, thumbing back the leather strap that secured the flap of the holster which hung by his bunk he slipped out the Colt-automatic, and noiselessly pulled back the steel envelope.

He was a careful man, not easily flurried, and his every movement was methodical. He was cautious enough to push up the little safety-catch which prevents premature explosion, tidy enough to polish the black barrel on the soft sleeve of his coat, and he waited a long time before he stepped out into the hot darkness of the night.

By and by he heard again the sound which had aroused him. It was the faint twitter of a weaver bird.

Now weaver birds go to sleep at nights like sensible people, and they live near villages, liking the society of human beings. Certainly they do not advertise their presence so brazenly as did this bird, who twittered and twittered at intervals.

Sanders watched patiently.

Then suddenly, from close at hand, from the very deck on which he stood, came an answering call.

Sanders had his little cabin on the bridge of the steamer; he walked farther away from it. In the corner of the bridge he crouched down, his thumb on the safety-catch.

He felt, rather than saw, a man come from the forest; he knew that there was one on board the steamer who met him.

Then creeping round the deck-house came two men. He could just discern the bulk of them as they moved forward till they found the door of the cabin and crept in. He heard a little noise, and grinned again, though he knew that their spear-heads were making sad havoc of his bedclothes.

Then there was a little pause, and he saw one come out by himself and look around.

He turned to speak softly to the man inside.

Sanders rose noiselessly.

The man in the doorway said "*Kah!*" in a gurgling voice and went down limply, because Sanders had kicked him scientifically in the stomach, which is a native's weak spot. The second man ran out, but fell with a crash over the Commissioner's extended leg, and, falling, received the full weight of a heavy pistol barrel in the neighbourhood of his right ear.

"Yoka!" called Sanders sharply, and there was a patter of feet aft, for your native is a light sleeper, "tie these men up. Get steam, for we will go away from here; it is not a nice place."

Sanders, as I have tried to explain, was a man who knew the native; he thought like a native, and there were moments when he acted not unlike a barbarian.

Clear of the danger, he tied up to a little island in mid-stream just as the dawn spread greyly, and hustled his two prisoners ashore.

"My men," said he, "you came to kill me in the dark hours."

"Lord, that is true," said one, "I came to kill, and this other man, who is my brother, told me when to come—yet it might have been another whom he called, for I am but one of many."

Sanders accepted the fact that a chain of cheerful assassins awaited his advent without any visible demonstration of annoyance.

"Now you will tell me," he said, "who gave the word for the killing, and why I must die."

The man he addressed, a tall, straight youth of the Amatombo people, wiped the sweat from his forehead with his manacled hands.

"Lord, though you chop me," he said, "I will not tell you, for I have a great *ju-ju*, and there are certain fetishes which would be displeased."

Sanders tried the other man with no greater success. This other was a labourer he had taken on at a village four days' journey down stream.

"Lord, if I die for my silence I will say nothing," he said.

"Very good," said Sanders, and nodded his head to Abiboo. "I shall stake you out," he added, "flat on the ground, your legs and arms outstretched, and I will light a little fire on your chests, and by and by you will tell me all I want to know."

Staked out they were, with fluffy little balls of dried creeper on each breast, and Sanders took a lighted stick from the fire his servants had built.

The men on the ground watched his every movement. They saw him blow the red stick to a flame and advance toward them, then one said—

"Lord, I will speak."

"So I thought," said Sanders; "and speak truth, or I will make you uncomfortable."

If you ask me whether Sanders would have employed his lighted stick, I answer truthfully that I think it possible; perhaps Sanders knew his men better than I know Sanders.

The two men, released from their unhappy position, talked frankly, and Sanders was a busy man taking notes in English of the conversation which was mainly in Bomongo.

When his interrogation was completed, Sanders gathered up his notes and had the men taken on board the steamer. Two hours later the *Zaire* was moving at its fullest speed in the direction of a village of the Akasava, which is called in the native tongue Tukalala.

There was a missionary to Tukalala, a devoted young American Methodist, who had elected to live in the fever belt amongst heathen men that he might bring their hearts to the knowledge of God.

Sanders had no special regard for missionaries; indeed, he had views on the brotherhood which did him no particular credit, but he had an affection for the young man who laboured so cheerfully with such unpromising material, and now he paced the little bridge of his steamer impatiently, for it was very necessary that he should reach Tukalala before certain things happened.

He came round a bend of the little river just as the sun was going down behind the trees on the western bank, and the white beach before the mission station showed clearly.

He motioned with two fingers to the man at the wheel, and the little steamer swung almost broadside to the swift stream and headed for the bank, and the black water of the river humped up against his port bow as though it were a sluice gate.

Into the beach he steamed; *"pucka-pucka- pucka-puck,"* sang the stern wheel noisily.

Where the missionary's house had stood was a chaos of blackened debris, and out of it rose lazy little wisps of smoke.

He found the missionary dressed in white duck, greatly soiled, lying face downwards, and he found some difficulty in raising him, because he was pinned to the ground with a broad-bladed elephant spear which had been broken off flush with his shoulders.

Sanders turned him on his back, closed the patient's eyes, staring, it seemed, hungrily at. the darkening sky as though at the last questioning God's wisdom.

The Commissioner took a gaudy bandana handkerchief from his pocket, and laid it on the dead man's face.

"Abiboo," he said softly to his sergeant, "dig me a great hole by that copal gum, for this man was a great chief amongst his people, and had communion with gods."

"He was a Christ man," said Abiboo sagely, who was a devout follower of the Prophet, "and in the *Sura of Mary* it is written:

The sects have fallen to variance about Jesus, but woe, because of the assembly of a great day to those who believe not!

Abiboo bore the title of *Haj* because he had been to Mecca and knew the *Koran* better than most Christians know the *Bible*.

Sanders said nothing. He took a cigar from his pocket and lit it, casting his eyes around.

No building stood. Where the mission station with its trim garden had been, was desolation. He saw scraps of cloth in the fading light. These were other victims, he knew.

In the mellow light of the moon he buried the missionary, saying the *Lord's Prayer* over him, and reciting as much of the Burial Service as he could remember.

Then he went back to the *Zaire* and set a guard. In the morning Sanders turned the nose of the *Zaire* downstream, and at sunset came to the big river—he had been sailing a tributary—and where the two rivers meet is the city of the Akasava.

They brought the paramount chief of all the people to him, and there was a *palaver* on the little bridge with a lantern placed on the deck and one limp candle therein to give light to the assembly.

"Chief," said Sanders, "there is a dead white man in your territory, and I will have the hearts of the men who killed him, or by The Death I will have your head."

He said this evenly, without passion, yet he swore by *Ewa*, which means death and is a most tremendous oath. The chief, squatting on the deck, fidgeting with his hands, shivered.

"Lord," he said, in a cracked voice, "this is a business of which I know nothing; this thing has happened in my territory, but so far from my hand that I can neither punish nor reward."

Sanders was silent save for an unsympathetic sniff.

"Also, master," said the chief, "if the truth be told, this *palaver* is not of the Akasava alone, for all along the big river men are rebellious, obeying a new *ju-ju* more mighty than any other."

"I know little of *ju-jus*," said Sanders shortly, "only I know that a white man has died and his spirit walks abroad and will not rest until I have slain men. Whether it be you or another I do not care—the *palaver* is finished."

The chief rose awkwardly, brought up his hand in salute, and went shuffling down the sloping plank to land.

As for Sanders, he sat thinking, smoking one cigar after another.

He sat long into the night. Once he called his servant to replace the candle in the lantern and bring him a cushion for his head. He sat there until the buzzing little village hushed to sleep, until there was no sound but the whispering of bat wings as they came and went from the middle island—for bats love islands, especially the big vampire bats.

At two o'clock in the morning he looked at his watch, picked up the lantern, and walked aft.

He picked a way over sleeping men until he came to that part of the deck where a Houssa squatted with loaded carbine watching the two prisoners.

He stirred them gently with his foot, and they sat up blinking at his light.

"You must tell me some more," he said. "How came this bad *ju-ju* to your land?"

The man he addressed looked up at him.

"Lord, how comes rain or wind?" he said. "It was a sudden thought amongst the people. There were certain rites and certain dances, and we chopped a man; then we all painted our faces with camwood, and the maidens said 'Kill!'"

Sanders could be very patient.

"I am as your father and your mother," he said. "I carry you in my arms; when the waters came up and destroyed your gardens I came with *manioc* and salt and saved you; when the sickness came I brought white men who scraped your arms and put magic in your blood; I have made peace, and your wives are safe from M'Gombi and Isisi folk, yet you are for killing me."

The other nodded.

"That is true talk, master—but such is the way of *ju-jus*. They are very High Things, and do not remember."

Sanders was worried; this matter was out of his reach. "What said the *ju-ju*?"

"Lord, it said very clearly, speaking through the mouth of an old man, M'fabaka of Begeli—"

"M'fabaka of Begeli?" repeated Sanders softly, and noted the name for a speedy hanging. "This old man saw a vision, and in this vision, which he saw with great pain and foaming at the mouth and hot eyeballs, he saw white men slain by black men and their houses burnt."

"When was this?"

"When the moon was full"—six days ago, thought Sanders—"and

151

he saw a great king with many legions marching through the land making all white men fear him."

He went on to give, as only a native memory can recall, the minutest detail of the king's march; how he slew white men and women and put their house to flames; how his legions went dancing before him.

"And all this happened at the full of the moon," he finished; "therefore we, too, went out to slay, and, knowing that your Highness would be coming as is your custom to give judgment at this season of the year, it was thought wise to kill you, also the Christ-man."

He told all this in a matter-of-fact tone, and Sanders knew that he spoke the truth.

Another man would have been more affected by that portion of the narrative which touched him most nearly, but it was the king ("a great man, very large about the middle"), and his devastating legions who occupied the Commissioner's thoughts.

There was truth behind this, he did not doubt that. There was a rising somewhere that he had not heard of; very quickly he passed in mental review the kings of the adjoining territories and of his own lands.

Bosambo of Monrovia, that usurper of the Ochori chieftainship, sent him from time to time news of the outlying peoples. There was no war, north or south or east.

"I will see this old man M'fabaka of Begeli," he said.

Begeli is a village that lies on an in-running arm of the river, so narrow that it seems like a little river, so still that it is apparently a lake. Forests of huge trees slope down on either bank, and the trees are laced one to the other with great snake-like tendrils, and skirted at foot with rank undergrowth. The *Zaire* came cautiously down this stretch of calm water, two Maxim guns significantly displayed at the bridge.

A tiny little steamer this *Zaire*. She had the big blue of England drooping from the flagstaff high above the stern wheel—an ominous sign, for when Sanders flew the Commissioner's flag it meant trouble for somebody.

He stood on the deck coatless, signalling with his raised fingers to the man at the wheel.

"*Phew!*" An arrow was shivering in the wooden deck-house. He pulled it out and examined its hammered steel point carefully, then he threw it overboard.

"*Bang!*"

A puff of smoke from the veiling foliage—a bullet splintered the back of his deck-chair.

He reached down and took up a rifle, noticed the drift of the smoke and took careful aim.

"*Bang!*"

There was no sign to show where the bullet struck, and the only sound that came back was the echo and the shrill swish of it as it lashed its way through the green bushes.

There was no more shooting.

"*Puck-apuck-puck-apuck-puck*," went the stern wheel slowly, and the bows of the *Zaire* clove the calm waters and left a fan of foam behind. Before the village was in view six war canoes, paddling abreast, came out to meet the Commissioner. He rang the engines to "Stop," and as the noise of them died away he could hear in the still air the beating of drums; through his glasses he saw fantastically-painted bodies, also a head stuck upon a spear.

There had been a trader named Ogilvie in this part of the world, a mild, uncleanly man who sold cloth and bought wild rubber.

"Five hundred yards," said Sanders, and Sergeant Abiboo, fiddling with the grip of the port Maxim, gave the cartridge belt a little pull, swung the muzzle forward, and looked earnestly along the sights. At the same time the Houssa corporal, who stood by the tripod of the starboard gun, sat down on the little saddle seat of it with his thumb on the control.

There came a spurt of smoke from the middle canoe; the bullet fell short.

"Ogilvie, my man," soliloquised Sanders, "if you are alive—which I am sure you are not—you will explain to me the presence of these Schneiders."

Nearer came the canoes, the paddle plunging rhythmically, a low, fierce drone of song accompanying the movement.

"Four hundred yards," said Sanders, and the men at the Maxims readjusted the sights.

"The two middle canoes," said Sanders. "Fire!"

A second pause.

"*Ha, ha, ha, ha, ha, ha, ha, ha!*" laughed the guns sardonically.

Sanders watched the havoc through his glasses.

"The other canoes," he said briefly.

"*Ha, ha, ha, ha, ha, ha, ha, ha!*"

This gunner was a careful man, and fired spasmodically, desiring to see the effects of his shots.

Sanders saw men fall, saw one canoe sway and overturn, and the black heads of men in the water; he rang the steamer ahead full speed.

Somebody fired a shot from one of the uninjured canoes. The wind of the bullet fanned his face, he heard the smack of it as it struck the woodwork behind.

There came another shot, and the boy at the wheel turned his head with a little grin to Sanders.

"Lord," he mumbled in Arabic, "this was ordained from the beginning."

Sanders slipped his arm about his shoulder and lowered him gently to the deck.

"All things are with God," he said softly.

"*Blessed be His name,*" whispered the dying boy.

Sanders caught the wheel as it spun and beckoned another steersman forward.

The nose of the steamer had turned to the offending canoe. This was an unhappy circumstance for the men therein, for both guns now covered it, and they rattled together, and through the blue haze you saw the canoe emptied.

That was the end of the fight. A warrior in the fifth boat held his spear horizontally above his head in token of surrender, and ten minutes later the chief of the rebels was on board.

"Master," he said calmly, as they led him to Sanders' presence, "this is a bad *palaver*. How will you deal with me?"

Sanders looked at him steadily.

"I will be merciful with you," he said, "for as soon as we come to the village I shall hang you."

"So I thought," said the chief without moving a muscle; "and I have heard it said that you hang men very quickly so that they feel little pain."

"That is my practice," said Sanders of the River, and the chief nodded his head approvingly.

"I would rather it were so," he said.

It was to a sorrowful village that he came, for there were many women to wail their dead.

Sanders landed with his Houssas and held a high *palaver* under the trees.

"Bring me the old man M'fabaka who sees visions," he said, and they brought him a man so old that he had nothing but bones to shape him.

They carried him to the place of justice and set him down before the Commissioner.

"You are an evil man," said Sanders, "and because your tongue has lied many men have died; today I hang your chief upon a tree, and with him certain others. If you stand before your people and say, 'Such a story, and such a story was a lie and no other thing,' you may live your days; but, if you persist in your lying, by my God, and your god, you shall die!"

It was a long time before the old man spoke, for he was very old and very frightened, and the fear of death, which is the ghost of some old men, was on him.

"I spoke the truth," he quavered at last. "I spoke of what I saw and of what I knew—only that." Sanders waited.

"I saw the great king slay and burn; yesterday I saw him march his regiments to war, and there was a great shouting, and I saw smoke."

He shook his head helplessly.

"I saw these things. How can I say I saw nothing?"

"What manner of king?" asked Sanders.

Again there was a long interval of silence whilst the old man collected himself.

"A great king," he said shakily, "as big as a bull about the middle, and he wore great, white feathers and the skin of a leopard."

"You are mad," said Sanders, and ended the *palaver*.

★★★★★★

Six days later Sanders went back to headquarters, leaving behind him a chastened people.

Ill-news travels faster than steam can push a boat, and the little *Zaire*, keeping to midstream with the blue flag flying, was an object of interest to many small villages, the people of which crowded down to their beaches and stood with folded arms, or with clenched knuckles at their lips to signify their perturbation, and shouted in monotonous chorus after the boat.

"Oh, Sandi—father! How many evil ones have you slain today? Oh, killer of devils—oh, hanger of trees!—we are full of virtues and do not fear."

"*Ei-fo, Kalaba? Ei ko Sandi! Eiva fo elegi,*" etc.

Sanders went with the stream swiftly, for he wished to establish communication with his chief. Somewhere in the country there was a revolt—that he knew.

There was truth in all the old man had said before he died—for die he did of sheer panic and age.

Who was this king in revolt? Not the king of the Isisi, or of the M'Gombi, nor of the people in the forelands beyond the Ochori.

The *Zaire* went swinging in to the Government beach, and there was a captain of Houssas to meet him.

"Land wire working?" said Sanders as he stepped ashore.

The Houssa captain nodded.

"What's the *palaver?*" he asked.

"War of a kind," said Sanders; "some king or other is on the rampage."

And he told the story briefly.

The Houssa officer whistled.

"By Lord High Keeper of the Privy Purse!" he swore mildly, "that's funny!"

"You've a poisonous sense of humour!" Sanders snapped.

"Hold hard," said the Houssa, and caught his arm. "Don't you know that Lo Benguela is in rebellion? The description fits him."

Sanders stopped.

"Of course," he said, and breathed a sigh of relief.

"But," said the perplexed Houssa officer, "Matabeleland is three thousand miles away. Rebellion started a week ago. How did these beggars know?"

For answer Sanders beckoned a naked man of the Akasava people who was of his boat's crew, being a good chopper of wood.

"I'fasi," he said, "tell me, what do they do in your country today?" The man grinned sheepishly, and stood on one leg in his embarrassment, for it was an honour to common men that Sanders should address them by name.

"Lord, they go to hunt elephant," he said.

"How many?" said Sanders.

"Two villages," said the man, "for one village has sickness and cannot go."

"How do you know this?" said Sanders. "Is not your country four days by river and three days by land?"

The man looked uncomfortable.

"It is as you say, master—yet I know," he said.

Sanders turned to the Houssa with a smile.

"There is quite a lot to be learnt in this country," he said.

★★★★★★

A month later Sanders received a cutting from the *Cape Times*. The part which interested him ran:

> . . . the rumour generally credited by the Matebele rebels that their adherents in the north had suffered a repulse lacks confirmation. The Commissioner of Barotseland denies the native story of a rebellious tribe, and states that as far as he knows the whole of his people have remained quiet. Other northern Commissioners state the same. There has been no sympathetic rising, though the natives are emphatic that in a 'far-away land,' which they cannot define, such a rebellion has occurred. The idea is, of course, absurd.

Sanders smiled again.

Dogs of War

Chiefest of the restrictions placed upon the black man by his white protector is that which prevents him, when his angry passions rise, from taking his enemy by the throat and carving him with a broad, curved blade of native make. Naturally, even the best behaved of the tribes chafe under this prohibition the British have made.

You may be sure that the Akasava memory is very short, and the punishment which attended their last misdoing is speedily forgotten in the opportunity and the temptation which must inevitably come as the years progress. Thus, the Akasava, learning of certain misdoings on the part of the Ochori, found themselves in the novel possession of a genuine grievance, and prepared for war, first sending a message to "Sandi," setting forth at some length the nature of the insult the Ochori had offered them. Fortunately, Sanders was in the district, and came on the spot very quickly, holding *palaver*, and soothing an outraged nation as best he could. Sanders was a tactful man, and tact does not necessarily imply soft-handedness. For there was a truculent soul who sat in the council and interpolated brusque questions.

Growing bolder as the Commissioner answered suavely, he went, as a child or native will, across the border line which divides a good manner from a bad. Sanders turned on him.

"What base-born slave dog are you?" he asked; and whilst the man was carefully considering his answer, Sanders kicked him down the slope of the hill on which the *palaver* house stood, and harmony was once more restored.

Very soon on the heels of this *palaver* came a bitter complaint from the Isisi. It concerned fishing nets that had been ruthlessly destroyed by the Lulungo folk, and this was a more difficult matter for Sanders to settle. For one thing, all self-respecting people hate the Lulungo, a dour, wicked, mischievous people, without shame or salt. But the Isisi were pacified, and a messy war was averted. There were other and minor alarums—all these were in the days' work—but Sanders worried about the Lulungo, because of their general badness, and because of all his people, Isisi, Ikeli, Akasava, and Ochori, who hated the Lulungo folk with a deep-rooted hatred. In his own heart, Sanders knew that war could only be postponed, and so advised London, receiving in reply, from an agitated Under-Secretary in Whitehall, the urgent request that the postponement should cover and extend beyond the conclusion of "the present financial year—for heaven's sake!"

They had a proverb up in the Lulungo district—three days' march beyond the Akasava—and it is to this effect: "*When a man hath a secret enemy and cannot find him, pull down his own hut and search among the debris.*" This is a cumbersome translation. There is another proverb which says, "*Because of the enemy who lives in the shadow of your hut*"; also another which says, "*If you cannot find your enemy, kill your dearest friend.*" The tendency of all these proverbs is to show that the Lulungo people took a gloomy view of life, and were naturally suspicious.

Sanders had a cook of the Lulungo tribe, down at M'piti—which model city served as Mr. Commissioner's headquarters. He was a wanderer, and by way of being a cosmopolitan, having travelled as far north as Dacca, and as far south as Banana—and presumably up the Congo to Matadi. When he came to M'piti, applying for work, he was asked his name and replied in the "English" of the Coast

"Master, dey one call me Sixpence all'time. I make 'um cook fine; you look 'um for better cook, you no find 'um—savvy."

"And what," said Sanders, in the Lulungo dialect, "what mongrel talk do you call this?"

"Master, it is English," said the abashed native.

"It is monkey talk," said Sanders, cruelly; "the talk of krooboys and half-bred sailors who have no language. What are you called by your people?"

"Lataki, master," said the cook.

"So shall you be called," said Sanders. "Further, you shall speak no language but your own, and your pay will be ten shillings a month."

Lataki made a good cook, and was a model citizen for exactly three months, at the end of which time Sanders, returning unexpectedly from a hunting trip, found Lataki asleep in his master's bed—Lataki being very drunk, and two empty gin bottles by the bedside testifying mutely to his discredit. Sanders called his police, and Lataki was thrown into the lock-up to sober down, which he did in twenty-four hours.

"I would have you understand," said Sanders to the culprit the next day, "that I cannot allow my servants to get drunk; more especially I cannot allow my drunken servants to sleep off their potations on my bed."

"Lord, I am ashamed," said Lataki cheerfully; "such things happen to a man who has seen much of the world."

"You may say the same about the whipping you are about to receive," said Sanders, and gave an order to the sergeant of police.

Lataki was no stoic and when, tied to a tree, ten strokes were laid upon his stout back by a bored Houssa, he cried out very loudly against Sanders, and against that civilisation of which Sanders was the chosen instrument. After it was all over, and he had discovered that he was still alive, albeit sore, he confessed he had received little more than he deserved, and promised tearfully that the lesson should not be without result. Sanders, who had nothing more to say in the matter, dismissed him to his duties.

It was a week after this that the Commissioner was dining in solitude on palm-oil chop—which is a delicious kind of coast curry—and chicken. He had begun his meal when he stopped suddenly, went to his office, and brought in a microscope. Then he took a little of the "chop"—just as much as might go on the end of a pin—smeared it on a specimen glass, and focussed the instrument. What he saw interested him. He put away the microscope and sent for Lataki; and Lataki, in spotless white, came.

"Lataki," said Sanders carelessly, "knowing the ways of white men, tell me how a master might do his servant honour?"

The cook in the doorway hesitated.

"There are many ways," he said, after a pause. "He might—"

He stopped, not quite sure of his ground.

"Because you are a good servant, though possessed of faults," said Sanders, "I wish to honour you; therefore I have chosen this way; you, who have slept in my bed unbidden, shall sit at my table with me at my command."

The man hesitated, a little bewildered, then he shuffled forward and sat clumsily in the chair opposite his master.

"I will wait upon you," said Sanders, "according to the custom of your own people."

He heaped two large spoonfuls of palm-oil chop upon the plate before the man.

"Eat," he said.

But the man made no movement, sitting with his eyes upon the tablecloth.

"Eat," said Sanders again, but still Lataki sat motionless.

Then Sanders rose, and went to the open doorway of his bungalow and blew a whistle.

There was a patter of feet, and Sergeant Abiboo came with four Houssas.

"Take this man," said Sanders, "and put him in irons. Tomorrow I will send him down country for judgment."

He walked back to the table, when the men had gone with their prisoner, carefully removed the poisoned dish, and made a meal of eggs and bananas, into neither of which is it possible to introduce ground glass without running the risk of instant detection.

Ground glass—glass powdered so fine that it is like precipitated chalk to the touch—is a bad poison, because when it comes in contact with delicate membranes right down inside a man, it lacerates them and he dies, as the bad men of the coast know, and have known for hundreds of years. In the course of time Lataki came before a judge who sat in a big thatched barn of a courthouse, and Lataki brought three cousins, a brother, and a disinterested friend, to swear that Sanders had put the glass in his own "chop" with malice aforethought. In spite of the unanimity of the evidence—the witnesses had no less than four rehearsals in a little hut the night before the trial—the prisoner was sentenced to fifteen years' penal servitude.

Here the matter would have ended, but for the Lulungo people, who live far away in the north, and who chose to regard the imprisonment of their man as a *casus belli*.

They were a suspicious people, a sullen, loveless, cruel people, and they were geographically favoured, for they lived on the edge of a territory which is indisputably French, and, moreover, unreachable.

Sanders sent flying messages to all the white people who lived within striking distance of the Lulungo. There were six in all, made up of two missions, Jesuit and Baptist. They were most unsatisfactory people, as the following letters show:

The first from the Protestant:

Losebi Mission.

Dear Mr. Commissioner,—My wife and I are very grateful to

161

you for your warning, but God has called us to this place, and here we must stay, going about our Master's business, until He, in His wisdom, ordains that we shall leave the scene of our labours.

Father Holling wrote:

Ebendo River.

Dear Sanders,—I think you are wrong about the Lulungo people, several of whom I have seen recently. They are mighty civil, which is the only bad sign I have detected. I shall stay because I think I can fight off any attack they make. I have four Martini-Metford rifles, and three thousand rounds of ammunition, and this house, as you know, is built of stone. I hope you are wrong, but—

Sanders took his steamboat, his Maxim gun, and his Houssa police, and went up the river, as far as the little stern-wheeler would carry him. At the end of every day's journey he would come to a place where the forest had been cleared, and where, stacked on the beach, was an orderly pile of wood. Somewhere in the forest was a village whose contribution to the State this ever-replenished wood-pile was. Night and day two sounding men with long rods, sitting at the steamer's bow, "stubbed" the water monotonously. Shoal, sandbank, channel, shoal. Sometimes, with a shuddering jar, the boat would slide along the flat surface of a hidden bank, and go flop into the deep water on the other side; sometimes, in the night, the boat would jump a bank to find itself in a little "lake" from which impassable ridges of hidden sand barred all egress. Then the men would slip over the sides of the vessel and walk the sandy floor of the river, pushing the steamer into deep water. When sixty miles from the Baptist Mission, Sanders got news from a friendly native:

"Lord, the Lulungo came at early morning, taking away the missionary, his wife, and his daughter, to their city."

Sanders, yellow with fever, heavy-eyed from want of sleep, unshaven and grimy, wiped the perspiration from his head with the back of his hand.

"Take the steamer up the river," he said to Abiboo. "I must sleep."

He was awakened at four o'clock in the afternoon by the smashing of a water-bottle, which stood on a shelf by his bunk. It smashed for no apparent reason, and he was sprinkled with bits of glass and gouts of water.

Then he heard a rifle go "*pang!*" close at hand, and as he sprang up and opened the wire-woven door of his cabin, Abiboo came to report.

"There were two men firing from the bank," he said. "One I have shot."

They were nearing the village now, and turning a sharp bend of the river they came in sight of it, and the little *Zaire's* siren yelled and squealed defiantly.

Sanders saw a crowd of men come down to the beach, saw the glitter of spears, and through his glasses the paint on the bodies of the men. Then six canoes came racing out to meet the steamer.

A corporal of Houssas sat down nonchalantly on a little saddle-seat behind the brass Maxim, and gripped its handles.

"Five hundred yards," said Sanders, and the corporal adjusted the sight without perceptible hurry.

The canoes came on at a hurricane speed, for the current was with them. The man behind the gun polished a dull place on the brass water-jacket with the blue sleeves of his coat, and looked up.

Sanders nodded.

The canoes came nearer, one leading the rest in that race where hate nerved effort, and death was the prize.

Suddenly—

"*Ha-ha-ha-ha-ha-ha!*" laughed the little gun sardonically, and the leading canoe swung round broadside to the stream, because the men who steered it were dead, and half of the oarsmen also.

"*Ha-ha-ha-h-a-a!*"

There was a wild scramble on the second canoe; it swayed, capsized, and the river was full of black heads, and the air resounded with shrill cries.

As for the remainder of the flotilla it swung round and made for safety; the machine-gun corporal slipped in another belt of cartridges, and made good practice up to nine hundred yards, from which two canoes, frantically paddled, were comparatively safe.

Sanders put his tiny telegraph over to full speed ahead and followed.

On the shore the Lulungo made a stand, and missiles of many kinds struck the little steamer. But the Maxim sprayed the village noisily, and soon there came a nervous man waving a palm leaf, and Sanders ceased firing, and shouted through his megaphone that the messenger must swim aboard.

"Lord, we feel great shame," said the man. He stood in a wet place on the deck, and little rills of water dripped from him. "We did not know we fought Sandi the lion, Sandi the buffalo, before the stamp of whose mighty feet—"

Sanders cut him short.

"There is a white man, a white woman, and a young girl in your city," he said. "Bring them to the ship, and then I will sit in the *palaver*-house, and talk this matter over."

The man shuffled uneasily.

"Master," he said, "the white man died of the sickness; the woman is ill also; as for the girl, I know nothing."

Sanders looked at him, his head on one side like an inquisitive bird.

"Bring me the white man, alive or dead," he said softly; "also the white woman, well or ill, and the girl."

In an hour they brought the unfortunate missionary, having taken some time to make him look presentable. The wife of the missionary came in another canoe, four women holding her, because she was mad.

"Where is the girl?" asked Sanders, He spoke very little above a whisper.

The messenger made no answer.

"The girl?" said Sanders, and lashed him across the face with his thin stick.

"Master," muttered the man, with his head on his chest, "the chief has her."

Sanders took a turn up and down the deck, then he went to his cabin and came out with two revolvers belted to his hips.

"I will go and see this chief," he said. "Abiboo, do you run the boat's nose into the soft sand of the bank, covering the street with the Maxim whilst I go ashore."

He landed without opposition; neither gun banged nor spear flew as he walked swiftly up the broad street. The girl lay before the chief's hut quite dead, very calm, very still. The hand to cut short her young life had been more merciful than Sanders dared hope. He lifted the child in his arms, and carried her back to the ship. Once he heard a slight noise behind him, but three rifles crashed from the ship, and he heard a thud and a whimper of pain.

He brought the body on board, and laid it reverently on the little after-deck. Then they told him that the woman had died, and he nodded his head slowly, saying it was better so.

The *Zaire* backed out into midstream, and Sanders stood watching the city wistfully. He wanted the chief of the Lulungo badly; he wanted, in his cold rage, to stake him out in spread-eagle fashion, and kill him with slow fires. But the chief and his people were in the woods, and there were the French territories to fly to.

In the evening he buried the missionary and his family on a little island, then drove downstream, black rage in his soul, and a sense of his impotence, for you cannot fight a nation with twenty Houssa policemen.

He came to a little "wooding" at dusk, and tied up for the night. In the morning he resumed his journey, and at noon he came, without a moment's warning, into the thick of a war fleet.

There was no mistaking the character of the hundred canoes that came slowly upstream four abreast, paddling with machine-like regularity. That line on the right were Akasava men; you could tell that by the blunt noses of the dugouts. On the left were the Ochori; their canoes were streaked with red cornwood. In the centre, in lighter canoes of better make, he saw the white-barred faces of the Isisi people.

"In the name of heaven!" said Sanders, with raised eyebrows.

There was consternation enough in the fleet, and its irregular lines wavered and broke, but the *Zaire* went steaming into the midst of them. Then Sanders stopped his engines, and summoned the chiefs on board.

"What shame is this?" said Sanders.

Otako, of the Isisi, king and elder chief, looked uncomfortably to Ebeni of Akasava, but it was Bosambo, self-appointed ruler of the Ochori, who spoke.

"Lord," he said, "who shall escape the never-sleeping eye of Sandi? Lo! we thought you many miles away, but like the owl—"

"Where do you go?" asked Sanders.

"Lord, we will not deceive you," said Bosambo. "These great chiefs are my brothers, because certain Lulungo have come down upon our villages and done much harm, stealing and killing. Therefore, because we have suffered equally, and are one in misfortune, we go up against the Lulungo people, for we are human, and our hearts are sore."

A grin, a wicked, mirthless grin, parted Sanders' lips.

"And you would burn and slay?" he asked.

"Master, such was the pleasure we had before us."

"Burning the city and slaying the chief, and scattering the people

165

who hide in the forest?"

"Lord, though they hide in hell we will find them," said Bosambo; "yet, if you, who are as a father to us all, say 'nay,' we will assemble our warriors and tell them it is forbidden."

Sanders thought of the three new graves on a little island.

"Go!" he said, pointing up the river.

He stood on the deck of the *Zaire* and watched the last canoe as it rounded the bend, and listened to the drone of many voices, growing fainter and fainter, singing the Song of the Slayer, such as the Isisi sing before action.

The People of the River

Contents

To
SIR SAMUEL SCOTT,
BART, M.P.

CHAPTER 1

A Certain Game

Sanders had been away on a holiday.

The Commissioner, whose work lay for the main part in wandering through a malarial country in some discomfort and danger, spent his holiday in travelling through another malarial country in as great discomfort and at no less risk. The only perceptible difference, so far as could be seen, between his work and his holiday was that instead of considering his own worries he had to listen to the troubles of somebody else.

Mr. Commissioner Sanders derived no small amount of satisfaction from such a vacation, which is a sure sign that he was most human.

His holiday was a long one, for he went by way of St. Paul de Loanda overland to the Congo, shot an elephant or two in the French Congo, went by mission steamer to the Sangar River and made his way back to Stanley Pool.

At Matadi he found letters from his relief, a mild youth who had come from headquarters to take his place as a temporary measure, and was quite satisfied in his inside mind that he was eminently qualified to occupy the seat of the Commissioner.

The letter was a little discursive, but Sanders read it as eagerly as a girl reads her first love letter. For he was reading about a land which was very dear to him.

Umfebi, the headman of Kulanga, has given me a little trouble.
He wants sitting on badly, and if I had control . . .

Sanders grinned unpleasantly and said something about "impertinent swine," but did he not refer to the erring Umfeb?

I find M'laka, the chief of the Little River, a very pleasant man to deal with: he was most attentive to me when I visited his village and trotted out all his dancing girls for my amusement.

Sanders made a little grimace. He knew M'laka for a rascal and wondered. "A chief who has been most civil and courteous is Bosambo of the Ochori. I know this will interest you because Bosambo tells me that he is a special *protégé* of yours. He tells me how you had paid for his education as a child and had gone to a lot of trouble to teach him the English language. I did not know of this."

Sanders did not know of it either, and swore an oath to the brazen sky to take this same Bosambo, thief by nature, convict by the wise provision of the Liberian Government, and chief of the Ochori by sheer effrontery, and kick him from one end of the city to the other.

He is certainly the most civilised of your men,(the letter went on.) He has been most attentive to the astronomical mission which came out in your absence to observe the eclipse of the moon. They speak very highly of his attention and he has been most active in his attempt to recover some of their property which was either lost or stolen on their way down the river.

Sanders smiled, for he himself had lost property in Bosambo's territory.

"I think I will go home," said Sanders.

Home he went by the nearest and the quickest way and came to headquarters early one morning, to the annoyance of his relief, who had planned a great and fairly useless *palaver* to which all the chiefs of all the land had been invited.

"For," he explained to Sanders in a grieved tone, "it seems to me that the only way to ensure peace is to get at the minds of these people, and the only method by which one can get at their minds is to bring them all together."

Sanders stretched his legs contemptuously and sniffed. They sat at chop on the broad *stoep* before the Commissioner's house, and Mr. Franks—so the deputy Commissioner was named—was in every sense a guest. Sanders checked the vitriolic appreciation of the native mind which came readily to his lips, and inquired:

"When is this prec—when is this *palaver?*"

"This evening," said Franks.

Sanders shrugged his shoulders.

"Since you have gathered all these chiefs together," he said, "and they are present in my Houssa lines, with their wives and servants, eating my 'special expense' vote out of existence, you had better go through with it."

That evening the chiefs assembled before the residency, squatting in a semi-circle about the chair on which sat Mr. Franks—an enthusiastic young man with a very pink face and gold-mounted spectacles.

Sanders sat a little behind and said nothing, scrutinising the assembly with an unfriendly eye. He observed without emotion that Bosambo of the Ochori occupied the place of honour in the centre, wearing a leopard skin and loop after loop of glittering glass beads. He had ostrich feathers in his hair and bangles of polished brass about his arms and ankles and, chiefest abomination, suspended by a scarlet ribbon from that portion of the skin which covered his left shoulder, hung a large and elaborate decoration.

Beside him the kings and chiefs of other lands were mean, commonplace men. B'fari of the Larger Isisi, Kulala of the N'Gombi, Kandara of the Akasava, Etobi of the River-beyond-the-River, and a score of little kings and overlords might have been so many carriers.

It was M'laka of the Lesser Isisi who opened the *palaver*.

"Lord Franki," he began, "we are great chiefs who are as dogs before the brightness of your face, which is like the sun that sets through a cloud."

Mr. Franks, to whom this was interpreted, coughed and went pinker than ever.

"Now that you are our father," continued M'laka, "and that Sandi has gone from us, though you have summoned him to this *palaver* to testify to your greatness, the land has grown fruitful, sickness has departed, and there is peace amongst us."

He avoided Sanders' cold eye whilst the speech was being translated.

"Now that Sandi has gone," M'laka went on with relish, "we are sorry, for he was a good man according to some, though he had not the great heart and the gentle spirit of our lord Franki."

This he said, and much more, especially with regard to the advisability of calling together the chiefs and headmen that they might know of the injustice of taxation, the hardship of life under certain heartless lords—here he looked at Sanders—and need for restoring the old powers of chiefs.

Other orations followed. It gave them great sorrow, they said, because Sandi, their lord, was going to leave them. Sandi observed that the blushing Mr. Franks was puzzled, and acquitted him of spreading the report of his retirement.

Then Bosambo, sometime of Monrovia, and now chief of the Ochori, from-the-border-of-the-river-to-the mountains-by-the-forest.

"Lord Franki," he said, "I feel shame that I must say what I have to say, for you have been to me as a brother."

He said this much, and paused as one overcome by his feelings. Franks was doubly affected, but Sanders watched the man suspiciously.

"But Sandi was our father and our mother," said Bosambo; "in his arms he carried us across swift rivers, and with his beautiful body he shielded us from our enemies; his eyes were bright for our goodness and dim to our faults, and now that we must lose him my stomach is full of misery, and I wish I were dead."

He hung his head, shaking it slowly from side to side, and there were tears in his eyes when he lifted them. David lamenting Jonathan was no more woeful than Bosambo of Monrovia taking a mistaken farewell of his master.

"Franki is good," he went on, mastering himself with visible effort; "his face is very bright and pretty, and he is as innocent as a child; his heart is pure, and he has no cunning."

Franks shifted uneasily in his seat as the compliment was translated.

"And when M'laka speaks to him with a tongue of oil," said Bosambo, "lo! Franki believes him, though Sandi knows that M'laka is a liar and a breaker of laws, who poisoned his brother in Sandi's absence and is unpunished."

M'laka half rose from his seat and reached for his elephant sword.

"Down!" snarled Sanders; his hand went swiftly to his jacket pocket, and M'laka cowered.

"And when Kulala of the N'Gombi raids into Ala-mandy territory stealing girls, our lord is so gentle of spirit—"

"Liar and dog and eater of fish!"

The outraged Kulala was on his feet, his fat figure shaking with wrath.

But Sanders was up now, stiffly standing by his relief, and a gesture sent insulter and insulted squatting to earth.

All that followed was Greek to Mr. Franks, because nobody troubled to translate what was said.

"It seems to me," said Sanders, "that I may divide my chiefs into three parts, saying this part is made of rogues, this part of fools, and this, and the greater part, of people who are rogues in a foolish way. Now I know only one of you who is a pure rogue, and that is Bosambo of the Ochori, and for the rest you are like children.

"For when Bosambo spread the lie that I was leaving you, and when the master Franki called you together, you, being simpletons, who throw your faces to the shadows, thought, 'Now this is the time to speak evilly of Sandi and well of the new master.' But Bosambo, who is a rogue and a liar, has more wisdom than all of you, for the cunning one has said, 'I will speak well of Sandi, knowing that he will stay with us; and Sandi, hearing me, will love me for my kindness.'"

For one of the few times of his life Bosambo was embarrassed, and looked it.

"Tomorrow," said Sanders, "when I come from my house, I wish to see no chief or headman, for the sight of you already makes me violently ill. Rather I would prefer to hear from my men that you are hurrying back with all speed to your various homes. Later, I will come and there will be *palavers*—especially in the matter of poisoning. The *palaver* is finished."

He walked into the house with Franks, who was not quite sure whether to be annoyed or apologetic.

"I am afraid my ideas do not exactly tally with yours," he said, a little ruefully.

Sanders smiled kindly.

"My dear chap," he said, "nobody's ideas really tally with anybody's! Native folk are weird folk—that is why I know them. I am a bit of a weird bird myself."

When he had settled his belongings in their various places the Commissioner sent for Bosambo, and that worthy came, stripped of his gaudy furnishings, and sat humbly on the *stoep* before Sanders.

"Bosambo," he said briefly, "you have the tongue of a monkey that chatters all the time."

"Master, it is good that monkeys chatter," said the crestfallen chief, "otherwise the hunter would never catch them."

"That may be," said Sanders; "but it their chattering attracts bigger game to stalk the hunter, then they are dangerous beasts. You shall tell me later about the poisoning of M'laka's brother; but first you shall say why you desire to stand well with me. You need not lie, for we are men talking together."

Bosambo met his master's eye fearlessly.

"Lord," he said, "I am a little chief of a little people. They are not of my race, yet I govern them wisely. I have made them a nation of fighters where they were a nation of women."

Sanders nodded. "All this is true; if it were not so, I should have removed you long since. This you know. Also that I have reason to be grateful to you for certain happenings."

"Lord," said Bosambo, earnestly, "I am no beggar for favours, for I am, as you know, a Christian, being acquainted with the blessed Peter and the blessed Paul and other holy saints which I have forgotten. But I am a better man than all these chiefs and I desire to be a king."

"How much?" asked the astonished Sanders.

"A king, lord," said Bosambo, unashamed; "for I am fitted for kingship, and a witch doctor in the Kroo country, to whom I dashed a bottle of gin, predicted I should rule vast lands."

"Not this side of heaven," said Sanders decisively. He did not say "heaven," but let that pass.

Bosambo hesitated.

"Ochori is a little place and a little people," he said, half to himself; "and by my borders sits M'laka, who rules a large country three times as large and very rich——"

Sanders clicked his lips impatiently, then the humour of the thing took possession of him.

"Go you to M'laka," he said, with a little inward grin, "say to him all that you have said to me. If M'laka will deliver his kingdom into your hands I shall be content."

"Lord," said Bosambo, "this I will do, for I am a man of great attainments and have a winning way."

With the dignity of an emperor's son he stalked through the garden and disappeared.

The next morning Sanders said goodbye to Mr. Franks—a coasting steamer gave the Commissioner an excuse for hurrying him off. The chiefs had departed at sunrise, and by the evening life had resumed its normal course for Sanders.

It ran smoothly for two months, at the end of which time M'laka paid a visit to his brother-in-law, Kulala, a chief of N'Gombi, and a man of some importance, since he was lord of five hundred spears, and famous hunters.

They held a *palaver* which lasted the greater part of a week, and at the end there was a big dance.

It was more than a coincidence that on the last day of the *palaver* two shivering men of the Ochori were led into the village by their captors and promptly sacrificed.

The dance followed.

The next morning M'laka and his relative went out against the Ochori, capturing on their way a man whom M'laka denounced as a spy of Sandi's. Him they did to death in a conventional fashion, and he died uncomplainingly. Then they rested three days.

M'laka and his men came to the Ochori city at daybreak, and held a brief *palaver* in the forest.

"Now news of this will come to Sandi," he said; "and Sandi, who is a white devil, will come with his soldiers, and we will say that we were driven to do this because Bosambo invited us to a dance, and then endeavoured to destroy us."

"Bosambo would have destroyed us," chanted the assembly faithfully.

"Further, if we kill all the Ochori, we will say that it was not our people who did the killing, but the Akasava."

"Lord, the killing was done by the Akasava," they chanted again.

Having thus arranged both an excuse and an alibi, M'laka led his men to their quarry.

In the grey light of dawn the Ochori village lay defenceless. No fires spluttered in the long village street, no curl of smoke uprose to indicate activity.

M'laka's army in one long, irregular line went swiftly across the clearing which separated the city from the forest.

"Kill!" breathed M'laka; and along the ranks the order was taken up and repeated.

Nearer and nearer crept the attackers; then from a hut on the outskirts of the town stepped Bosambo, alone.

He walked slowly to the centre of the street, and M'laka saw, in a thin-legged tripod, something straight and shining and ominous.

Something that caught the first rays of the sun as they topped the trees of the forest, and sent them flashing and gleaming back again.

Six hundred fighting men of the N'Gombi checked and halted dead at the sight of it. Bosambo touched the big brass cylinder with his hand and turned it carelessly on its swivel until it pointed in the direction of M'laka, who was ahead of the others, and no more than thirty paces distant.

As if to make assurance doubly sure, he stooped and glanced along the polished surface, and M'laka dropped his short spear at his feet and raised his hands.

"Lord Bosambo," he said mildly, "we come in peace."

"In peace you shall go," said Bosambo, and whistled.

The city was suddenly alive with armed men. From every hut they came into the open.

"I love you as a man loves his goats," said M'laka fervently; "I saw you in a dream, and my heart led me to you."

"I, too, saw you in a dream," said Bosambo; "therefore I arose to meet you, for M'laka, the king of the Lesser Isisi, is like a brother to me."

M'laka, who never took his eyes from the brass-coated cylinder, had an inspiration.

"This much I beg of you, master and lord," he said; "this I ask, my brother, that my men may be allowed to come into your city and make joyful sacrifices, for that is the custom."

Bosambo scratched his chin reflectively.

"This I grant," he said; "yet every man shall leave his spear, stuck head downwards into earth—which is our custom before sacrifice."

M'laka shifted his feet awkwardly. He made the two little double-shuffle steps which native men make when they are embarrassed.

Bosambo's hand went slowly to the tripod.

"It shall be as you command," said M'laka hastily; and gave the order.

Six hundred dejected men, unarmed, filed through the village street, and on either side of them marched a line of Ochori warriors—who were not without weapons. Before Bosambo's hut M'laka, his brother-in-law, Kulala, his headmen, and the headmen of the Ochori, sat to conference which was half meal and half *palaver*.

"Tell me. Lord Bosambo," asked M'laka, "how does it come about that Sandi gives you the gun that says *'Ha-ha-ha'*? For it is forbidden that the chiefs and people of this land should be armed with guns."

Bosambo nodded.

"Sandi loves me," he said simply, "for reasons which I should be a dog to speak of, for does not the same blood run in his veins that runs in mine?"

"That is foolish talk," said Kulala, the brother-in-law; "for he is white and you are black."

"None the less it is true," said the calm Bosambo; "for he is my cousin, his brother having married my mother, who was a chief's daughter. Sandi wished to marry her," he went on reminiscently; "but there are matters which it is shame to talk about. Also he gave me these."

From beneath the blanket which enveloped his shoulders he produced a leather wallet. From this he took a little package. It looked like a short, stumpy *bato*. Slowly he removed its wrapping of fine native cloth, till there were revealed three small cups of wood. In shape they favoured the tumbler of commerce, in size they were like very large thimbles.

Each had been cut from a solid piece of wood, and was of extreme thinness. They were fitted one inside the other when he removed them from the cloth, and now he separated them slowly and impressively.

At a word, a man brought a stool from the tent and placed it before him.

Over this he spread the wisp of cloth and placed the cups thereon upside down.

From the interior of one he took a small red ball of *copal* and camwood kneaded together.

Fascinated, the marauding chiefs watched him.

"These Sandi gave me," said Bosambo, "that I might pass the days of the rains pleasantly; with these I play with my headman."

"Lord Bosambo," said M'laka, "how do you play?"

Bosambo looked up to the warm sky and shook his head sadly.

"This is no game for you, M'laka," he said, addressing the heavens; "but for one whose eyes are very quick to see; moreover, it is a game played by Christians."

Now the Isisi folk pride themselves on their keenness of vision. Is it not a proverb of the River, "The N'Gombi to hear, the Bushman to smell, the Isisi to see, and the Ochori to run"?

"Let me see what I cannot see," said M'laka; and, with a reluctant air, Bosambo put the little red ball on the improvised table behind the cup.

"Watch then, M'laka! I put this ball under this cup: I move the cup——"

Very leisurely he shifted the cups.

"I have seen no game like this," said M'laka; and contempt was in his voice.

"Yet it is a game which pleased me and my men of bright eyes," said Bosambo; "for we wager so much rods against so much salt that no man can follow the red ball."

The chief of the Lesser Isisi knew where the red ball was, because there was a slight scratch on the cup which covered it.

"Lord Bosambo," he said, quoting a saying, "only the rat comes to dinner and stays to ravage—yet if I did not sit in the shadow of your hut, I would take every rod from you."

"The *nukusa* is a Small animal, but he has a big voice," said Bosambo, giving saying for saying; "and I would wager you could not uncover the red ball."

M'laka leant forward.

"I will stake the spears of my warriors against the spears of the Ochori," he said.

Bosambo nodded.

"By my head," he said.

M'laka stretched forward his hand and lifted the cup, but the red ball was not there. Rather it was under the next cup, as Bosambo demonstrated.

M'laka stared.

"I am no blind man," he said roughly; "and your tongue is like the burning of dry sticks—*clack, clack, clack!*"

Bosambo accepted the insult without resentment.

"It is the eye," he said meditatively; "we Ochori folk see quickly."

M'laka swallowed an offensive saying.

"I have ten bags of salt in my house," he said shortly, "and it shall be my salt against the spears you have won."

"By my heart and life," said Bosambo, and put the ball under the cup.

Very lazily he moved the cup to and fro, changing their positions.

"My salt against your spears," said M'laka exultantly, for he saw now which was the cup. It had a little stain near the rim.

Bosambo nodded, and M'laka leant forward and lifted the cup. But the ball was not there.

M'laka drew a deep breath, and swore by Iwa—which is death—and by devils of kinds unknown; by sickness and by his father—who had been hanged, and was in consequence canonised. .

"It is the eye," said Bosambo sadly; "as they say by the River, 'The Ochori to see——"

"That is a lie!" hissed M'laka; "the Ochori see nothing but the way they run. Make this game again——"

And again Bosambo covered the red ball; but this time he bungled, for he placed the cup which covered the ball on an uneven place on the stool. And between the rim of the cup and the cloth there was a little space where a small ball showed redly—and M'laka was not blind.

"Bosambo," he said, holding himself, "I wager big things, for I am a chief of great possessions, and you are a little chief, yet this time I will wager my all."

"M'laka of the Isisi," responded Bosambo slowly, "I also am a great chief and a relative by marriage to Sandi. Also I am a God-man speaking white men's talk and knowing of Santa Antonio, Marki, Luki, the blessed Timothi, and similar magics. Now this shall be the wager; if you find a red ball you shall find a slave whose name is Bosambo of the Ochori, but if you lose the red one you shall lose your country."

"May the sickness mango come to me if I do not speak the truth," swore M'laka, "but to all this I agree."

He stretched out his hand and touched the cup.

"It is here!" he shouted and lifted the cover.

There was no red ball.

M'laka was on his feet breathing quickly through his nose.

He opened his mouth to speak, but there was no need, for an Ochori runner came panting through the street with news; before he could reach the hut where his overlord sat and tell it, the head of Sanders' column emerged from the forest path.

It is said that "the smell of blood carries farther than a man can see." It had been a tactical error to kill one of Sanders' spies.

The Commissioner was stained and soiled and he was unshaven, for the call of war had brought him by forced marches through the worst forest path in the world.

Into the open strode the column, line after line of blue-coated Houssas, bare-legged, sandal-footed, scarlet-headed, spreading out as smoke spreads when it comes from a narrow barrel. Forming in two straggling lines, it felt its way cautiously forward, for the Ochori city might hold an enemy.

Bosambo guessed the meaning of the demonstration and hurried forward to meet the Commissioner. At a word from Sanders the lines halted, and midway between the city and the wood they met—Bosambo and his master.

"Lord," said Bosambo conventionally, "all that I have is yours."

"It seems that you have your life, which is more than I expected," said Sanders. "I know that M'laka, chief of the Lesser Isisi, is sheltering in your village. You shall deliver this man to me for judgment."

"M'laka, I know," said Bosambo, carefully, "and he shall be delivered; but when you speak of the chief of the Lesser Isisi you speak of

183

me, for I won all his lands by a certain game."

"We will talk of that later," said Sanders.

He led his men to the city, posting them on its four sides, then he followed Bosambo to where M'laka and his headman awaited his coming—for the guest of a chief does not come out to welcome other guests.

"M'laka," said Sanders, "there are two ways with chiefs who kill the servants of Government. One is a high and short way, as you know."

M'laka's eyes sought a possible tree, and he shivered.

"The other way," said Sanders, "is long and tiresome, and that is the way for you. You shall sit down in the Village of Irons for my King's pleasure."

"Master, how long?" asked M'laka in a shaky voice.

"Whilst you live," said Sanders.

M'laka accepted what was tantamount to penal servitude for life philosophically—for there are worse things.

"Lord," he said, "you have always hated me. Also you have favoured other chiefs and oppressed me. Me, you deny all privilege; yet to Bosambo, your uncle——"

Sanders drew a long breath.

"——you give many favours, such as guns."

"If my word had not been given," said Sanders coldly, "I should hang you, M'laka, for you are the father of liars and the son of liars. What guns have I given Bosambo?"

"Lord, that is for you to see," said M'laka and jerked his head to the terrifying tripod.

Sanders walked towards the instrument.

"Bosambo," he said, with a catch in his voice, "I have in mind three white men who came to see the moon."

"Lord, that is so," said Bosambo cheerfully; "they were mad, and they looked at the moon through this thing; also at stars."

He pointed to the innocent telescope. "And this they lost?" said Sanders.

Bosambo nodded.

"It was lost by them and found by an Ochori man who brought it to me," said Bosambo. "Lord, I have not hidden it, but placed it here where all men can see it."

Sanders scanned the horizon. To the right of the forest was a broad strip of marshland, beyond, blurred blue in the morning sunlight rose the little hill that marks the city of the Lesser Isisi.

He stooped down to the telescope and focused it upon the hill. At its foot was a cluster of dark huts.

"Look," he said, and Bosambo took his place. "What do you see?" asked Sanders.

"The city of the Lesser Isisi," said Bosambo.

"Look well," said Sanders, "but that is the city you have won by a certain game."

Bosambo shifted uncomfortably.

"When I come to my new city——" he began.

"I also will come," said Sanders significantly. On the stool before the huts the three little wooden cups still stood, and Sanders had seen them, also the red ball. "Tomorrow I shall appoint a new chief to the Lesser Isisi. When the moon is at full I shall come to see the new chief," he said, "and if he has lost his land by 'a certain game' I shall appoint two more chiefs, one for the Isisi and one for the Ochori, and there will be sorrow amongst the Ochori, for Bosambo of Monrovia will be gone from them."

"Lord," said Bosambo, making one final effort for Empire, "you said that if M'laka gave, Bosambo should keep."

Sanders picked up the red ball and slipped it under one cup. He changed their positions slightly.

"If your game is a fair game," he said, "show me the cup with the ball."

"Lord, it is the centre one," said Bosambo without hesitation.

Sanders raised the cup.

There was no ball.

"I see," said Bosambo slowly, "I see that my lord Sandi is also a Christian."

"It was a jest," explained Bosambo to his headmen when Sanders had departed; "thus my lord Sandi always jested even when I nursed him as a child. Menchimis, let the *lokali* sound and the people be brought together for a greater *palaver* and I will tell them the story of Sandi, who is my half-brother by another mother."

CHAPTER 2

The Eloquent Woman

There was a woman of the N'Gombi people who had a suave tongue. When she spoke men listened eagerly, for she was of the kind peculiar to no race, being born with stirring words.

She stirred the people of her own village to such effect that they went one night and raided French territory, bringing great shame to her father; for Sanders came hurriedly north, and there were some summary whippings, and nearly a burying. Thereupon her father thought it wise to marry this woman to a man who could check her tongue.

So he married her to a chief, who was of the N'Gombi folk, and this chief liked her so much that he made her his principal wife, building a hut for her next to his. About her neck he had fixed a ring of brass, weighing some twenty-four pounds—a great distinction which his other wives envied.

This principal wife was nearly fifteen years old—which is approaching middle age on the River—and was, in consequence, very wise in the ways of men. Too wise, some thought, and certainly her lord had cause for complaint when, returning from a hunting expedition a day or two before he could possibly return, he found his wife more happy than was to his liking and none too lonely.

"M'fashimbi," he said, as she knelt before him with her arms folded meekly on her bare, brown bosom, "in the days of my father I should bend down a stripling tree and rope your neck to it, and when your head was struck from your body I should burn you and he that made me ashamed. But that is not the law of the white man, and I think you are too worthless a woman for me to risk my neck upon."

"Lord, I am of little good," she said.

For a whole day she lay on the ground surrounded by the whole of the village, to whom she talked whilst the workmen sawed away at the brass collar. At the end of that time the collar was removed from her neck, and the chief sent her back to the parent from whom he had most expensively bought her. He sent her back in the face of great opposition, for she had utilised her time profitably and the village was so moved by her eloquence that it was ripe for rebellion.

For no woman is put away from her man, whether she wears the feathers and silks of Paris or the camwood and oil of the N'Gombi, without harbouring for that man a most vengeful and hateful feeling, and no sooner had M'fashimbi paddled clear of her husband's village than she set herself the task of avenging herself upon him.

There accompanied her into exile the man with whom, and for whom, she had risked and lost so much. He was named Otapo, and he was a dull one.

As they paddled, she, kneeling in the canoe behind him, said: "Otapo, my husband has done me a great wrong and put dust on my head, yet you say nothing."

"Why should I speak when you have spoken so much?" asked Otapo calmly. "I curse the day I ever saw you, M'fashimbi, for my error has cost me a fishing-net, which was the best in the village, also a new piece of cloth I bought from a trader; these our lord chief has taken."

"If you had the heart of a man you would have killed Namani, my husband," she said.

"I have killed myself and lost my net," said Otapo; "also my piece of cloth."

"You are like a woman," she jeered.

"I could wish that my mother had borne a girl when she bore me," said Otapo, "then I should not have been disgraced."

She paddled in silence for a while, and then she said of a sudden:

"Let us go to the bank, for I have hidden some treasures of my husband near this spot."

Otapo turned the head of the canoe to the shore with one long stroke.

As they neared the bank she reached behind her and found a short spear, such as you use for hunting animals where the grass is thick.

She held it in both hands, laying the point on a level with the second rib beneath his shoulder blade.

As the prow of the canoe grounded gently on the sandy shore she drove her spear forward, with all her might. Otapo half rose like a man who was in doubt whether he would rise or not, then he tumbled languidly into the shallow water.

M'fashimbi waded to the shore, first securing the canoe, then she guided the body to land, and exerting all her strength, drew it to a place beneath some trees.

"Otapo, you are dead," she said to the figure, "and you are better dead than living, for by your death you shall revenge me, as living you feared to do."

She took the spear and flung it a few yards farther off from where the body lay. Then she got into the canoe, washed away such bloodstains as appeared on its side, and paddled downstream.

In a day's time she came to her father's village, wailing.

She wailed so loud and so long that the village heard her before she reached the shore and came out to meet her. Her comely body she had smeared with ashes, about her waist hung long green leaves, which is a sign of sorrow; but her grief she proclaimed long and loud, and her father, who was the chief of the village, said to his elders, as with languid strokes—themselves eloquent of her sorrow—she brought her canoe to land:

"This woman is either mad or she has suffered some great wrong."

He was soon to learn, for she came running up to the bank towards him and fell before him, clasping his feet.

"*Ewa!* Death to my husband, Namani, who has lied about me and beaten me, O father of fathers!" she cried.

"Woman," said the father, "what is this?"

She told him a story—an outrageous story. Also, which was more serious, she told a story of the killing of Otapo.

"This man, protecting me, brought me away from my husband, who beat me," she sobbed, "and my husband followed, and as we sat at a meal by the bank of the river, behold my husband stabbed him from behind. *Oe ai!*"

And she rolled in the dust at her father's feet.

The chief was affected, for he was of superior rank to Namani and, moreover, held the peace of that district for my lord the Commissioner.

"This is blood and too great a *palaver* for me," he said, "and, moreover, you being my daughter, it may be thought that I do not deal justice fairly as between man and man."

So he embarked on his canoe and made for Isau, where Sanders was.

The Commissioner was recovering from an attack of malarial fever, and was not pleased to see the chief. Less pleased was he when he heard the story the "Eloquent Woman" had to tell.

"I will go to the place of killing and see what is to be seen." He went on board the *Zaire*, and with steam up the little stern-wheeler made post-haste for the spot indicated by the woman. He landed where the marks of the canoe's prow still showed on the soft sand, for hereabouts the river neither rises nor falls perceptibly in the course of a month.

He followed the woman into the wood, and here he saw all that was mortal of Otapo; and he saw the spear.

M'fashimbi watched him closely.

"Lord," she said with a whimper, "here it was that Namani slew the young man Otapo as we sat at food."

Sanders' keen eyes surveyed the spot.

"I see no sign of a fire," said Sanders suddenly.

"A fire, lord?" she faltered.

"Where people sit at food they build a fire," said Sanders shortly, "and here no fire has been since the beginning of the world."

He took her on board again and went steaming upstream to the village of Namani.

"Go you," he said to the Houssa sergeant privately, "and if the chief does not come to meet me, arrest him, and if he does come you shall take charge of his huts and his women."

Namani was waiting to greet him and Sanders ordered him on board.

"Namani," said Sanders, "I know you as an honest man, and no word has been spoken against you. Now this woman, your wife, sayest you are a murderer, having killed Otapo."

"She is a liar!" said Namani calmly. "I know nothing of Otapo."

A diligent inquiry which lasted two days failed to incriminate the chief. It served rather to inflict some damage upon the character of M'fashimbi; but in a land where women have lovers in great numbers she suffered little.

At the end of the two days Sanders delivered judgment.

"I am satisfied Otapo is dead," he said; "for many reasons I am not satisfied that Namani killed him. I am in no doubt that M'fashimbi is a woman of evil acts and a great talker, so I shall banish her to a far country amongst strangers."

He took her on board his steamer, and the *Zaire* cast off.

In twenty-four hours he came to the "city of the forest," which is the Ochori city, and at the blast of his steamer's siren the population came running to the beach.

Bosambo, chief of the Ochori, was the last to arrive, for he came in procession under a scarlet umbrella, wearing a robe of tinselled cloth and having before him ten elder men bearing tinselled sticks.

Sanders watched the coming of the chief from the bridge of the steamer and his face betrayed no emotion. When Bosambo was come on board the Commissioner asked him:

"What childish folly is this, Bosambo?"

"Lord," said Bosambo, "thus do great kings come to greater kings, for I have seen certain pictures in a book which the god-woman gave me and by these I know the practice."

"Thus also do people dress themselves when they go out to make the foolish laugh," said Sanders unpleasantly. "Now I have brought you a woman who talks too much, and who has been put away by one man and has murdered another by my reckoning, and I desire that she shall live in your village."

"Lord, as you say," said the obedient Bosambo, and regarded the girl critically.

"Let her marry as she wishes," said Sanders; "but she shall be of your house, and you shall be responsible for her safe keeping until then."

"Lord, she shall be married this night," said Bosambo earnestly.

When Sanders had left and the smoke of the departing steamer had disappeared behind the trees, Bosambo summoned his headman and his captains to *palaver*.

"People," he said, "the Lord Sandi, who loves me dearly, has come bringing presents—behold this woman." He waved his hand to the sulky girl who stood by his side on the little knoll where the *palaver* house stood.

"She is the most beautiful of all the women of the N'Gombi," said Bosambo, "and her name is N'lami-n'safo, which means the Pearl, and Sandi paid a great price for her, for she dances like a leopard at play, and has many loving qualities."

The girl knew enough of the unfamiliar Ochori dialect to realise that her merits were being extolled, and she shifted her feet awkwardly.

"She is a wife of wives," said Bosambo impressively, "gentle and kind and tender, a great cooker of *manioc*, and a teller of stories—yet I may not marry her, for I have many wives and I am wax in their hands. So you shall take her, you who pay readily and fearlessly, for you buy that which is more precious than goats or salt."

For ten goats and a thousand rods this "gift" of Sandi's passed into the possession of his headman.

Talking to his chief wife of these matters, Bosambo said: "Thus is Sandi obeyed; thus also am I satisfied; all things are according to God's will."

"If you had taken her Mahomet," said the wife, who was a Kano woman and a true believer, "you would have been sorry."

"Pearl of bright light," said Bosambo humbly, "you are the first in my life, as God knows; for you I have deserted all other gods, believing in the one beneficent and merciful; for you also I have taken an umbrella of state after the manner of the Kano kings."

The next day Bosambo went hunting in the forest and did not return till a week was past.

It is the practice of the Ochori people, as it is of other tribes, to go forth to meet their chief on his return from hunting, and it was strange that none came to greet him with the Song of the Elephant.

With his twenty men he came almost unnoticed to his own hut.

Half-way along the village street he came upon an elder man, who ran to him.

"Lord," he said, "go not near the hut of Fabadimo, your chief headman."

"Has he sickness?" asked Bosambo.

"Worse, lord," said the old cynic. "He has a wife, and for six days and the greater part of six nights all the city has sat at her feet listening."

"What talk does she make?" asked Bosambo.

"Lord, she talks so that all things are clear," said the old man; "and all her words have meanings; and she throws a light like the very sun upon dark brains, and they see with her."

Bosambo had twenty men with him, men he could trust. The darkness was coming on, and at the far end of the city he could see the big fire where the "Eloquent Woman" talked and talked and talked.

He went first to his hut. He found his Kano wife alone, for the other women of his house had fled.

"Lord, I did not expect to see you alive," she said, "so I waited for death when the time came."

"That shall be many years away," said Bosambo.

He sent her with two of his men to the woods to wait his coming, then the rest of the party, in twos and threes, made their way to the outskirt of the throng before his headman's hut.

It was admirably placed for a forum. It stood on the crest of a sharp rise, flanked on either side by other huts.

Half-way down the slope a big fire blazed, and the leaping flames lit the slim figure that stood with arms outstretched before the hut.

". . . Who made you the slaves of a slave—the slave of Bosambo? Who gave him power to say 'Go forth' or 'Remain'? None. For he is a man like you, no different in make, no keener of eye, and if you stab him with a spear, will he not die just as you will die?

"And Sandi, is he not a man, though white? Is he stronger than Efambi or Elaki or Yako? Now I say to you that you will not be a free people whilst Bosambo lives or Sandi lives."

Bosambo was a man with keen animal instincts. He felt the insurrection in the air; he received through every tingling nerve the knowledge that his people were out of hand. He did not hesitate.

A solid mass of people stood between him and the woman. He could not reach her.

Never taking his eyes from her, he put his hand beneath his shield and drew his throwing spear. He had space for the swing; balanced and quivering, it lay on his open palm, his arm extended to the fullest.

"*Whew-w!*"

The light lance flickered through the air quicker than eye could follow.

But she had seen the outstretched arm and recognised the thrower, and leapt on one side.

The spear struck the man who stood behind her—and Fabadimo, the chief headman, died without speaking.

"Bosambo!" screamed the girl, and pointed. "Bosambo, kill—kill!"

He heard the rustle of disengaging spears, and fled into the darkness.

Sanders, at headquarters, was lying in a hammock swung between a pole of his verandah and a hook-fastened to the wall of his bungalow. He was reading, or trying to read, a long and offensive document from headquarters. It had to do with a census return made by Sanders, and apparently this return had fallen short in some respects.

Exactly how, Sanders never discovered, for he fell asleep three times in his attempt and the third time he was awakened by his orderly, who carried a tired pigeon in his hand.

"Master, here is a book," (any written thing—a letter, a note), said the man.

Sanders was awake instantly and out of his hammock in a second. Fastened about one red leg of the bird by a long india-rubber band was a paper twice the size of a cigarette paper and of the same texture. He smoothed it out.

Written in copying pencil were a few words in Arabic:

"From Abiboo, the servant of God, to Sandi, the ever-wakeful father of his people.

"Peace be to you and on your house. Declaring that there is but one God, the true and indivisible, I send you news that the woman you gave to Bosambo is causing great trouble. This has come to me by messengers, Bosambo having fled with twenty men to the edge of the Isisi country.

"Written at a place on the Isisi River, where there are three crocodile creeks meeting in the form of an arrow."

Now Abiboo had been left in the village from which M'fashimbi had been ejected. He had been left to clear up the mystery of Otapo's death and he was not a man easily alarmed.

Pulling on his mosquito boots, Sanders walked over to the house occupied by the officer of Houssa.

He found that gentleman sipping tea in solitary state.

"I shall want you," said Sanders; "there's a dust-up in the Ochori country."

The officer raised his eyebrows. He was a young man on the cynical side of twenty-five.

"Not the gentle Bosambo," he protested ironically; "not that mirror of chivalry?"

"Don't be comic, my man," snarled Sanders. "The Ochori are up, and there is a lady missionary somewhere on the border."

The Houssa captain sprang to his feet.

"Bless the woman, I forgot her!" he said in a worried tone. He took a whistle from his breast pocket and blew it, and a bare-legged bugler raced across the little parade ground from the guard hut.

"*Ta-ta-ta!*" said the Houssa captain, and the quavering note of the assembly sounded.

"What is the *palaver*?" demanded the officer, and briefly Sanders related the circumstances.

With a full head of steam the little *Zaire* pushed her way up-stream. Day and night she steamed till she came to the place "where three

193

crocodile creeks meet in the form of an arrow," and here Sanders stopped to relieve Abiboo and his handful of Houssas.

Sanders learnt with relief that the fighting had not threatened the mission stations.

"What of Bosambo?" he asked.

"Living or dead, I do not know," said Abiboo philosophically; "and if he is dead he died a believer, for the Kano woman he took to wife is a believer in the one Allah and of Mahmut, his prophet."

"All this may be true," said Sanders patiently, "yet I am less concerned by his prospects of immortality than the present disposition of his body."

About this Abiboo could tell him nothing, save that ten miles farther on Bosambo had held an island in the middle of the river, and that up to two days before he was still holding it.

Hereabouts the river twists and turns, and there was no sight of the middle island till the *Zaire* came curving round a sharp bend. "Stand by those maxims!" said Sanders sharply.

The Houssa captain sank on the saddle seat of one little brass-coated gun, and Abiboo took the other.

The water was alive with canoes.

The Ochori were attacking the island; the thunder of the *Zaire's* wheel drowned all sound.

"They're fighting all right," said the captain. "What do you say, Sanders?"

Sanders, with his hands on the wheel, waited, his eyes fixed ahead. Now he saw clearly. A party had landed, and there was fierce hand-to-hand fighting.

"Let 'em go," he said, and two trembling pencils of flame leapt from the guns.

For answer the canoes formed like magic into first two, then three, then four lines, and downstream they came at a furious rate.

Then one of the maxims jammed and as it did there came a shower of spears, one of which just missed Sanders.

In an instant the little boat was surrounded—the magic of the maxim had failed for the first time on the big river. It was so unexpected, so inexplicable, that a man might be excused if he lost his head; but Sanders' hand did not tremble as he swung the wheel over, and the steamer turned in a full circle.

The Houssas were shooting point-blank with their carbines; the Houssa captain, bleeding from the head, was re-adjusting the breech-

194

lock of the maxim without concern.

Downstream at full speed went the *Zaire*. The canoes could not keep up with it save one that had fastened itself to the side; the Houssas bayoneted the occupants without asking or accepting explanation.

"I've got the gun fixed," said the Houssa officer as he slipped in a fresh belt of cartridges.

Sanders nodded. A word to the steersman and the *Zaire* turned. She came back towards the lines of canoes, her maxim firing steadily.

The second line wavered and broke; the third never formed. In the centre of the fleeing canoes was one larger than another. At the stern stood a woman, waving her arms and talking.

"Abiboo," said Sanders, and the Houssa turned his gun over to a comrade and came to his master. "Do you see that woman in the canoe?"

"Lord, I see her," said Abiboo.

"It seems to me," said Sanders gravely, "that this woman would be better dead."

He rang the telegraph to stop, and the grind of the engines ceased. The *Zaire* moved slowly forward without a tremble, and Abiboo, lying on the deck with the butt of his rifle pressed to his cheek, took careful aim.

They found Bosambo conscious beneath a heap of dead. He lay across the Kano woman, who was also alive, for Bosambo had taken the spear-thrusts meant for her.

He had, as Sanders counted, twenty-five wounds.

"Lord," he whispered as Sanders stood by his side, "did I not tell you the Ochoris could fight?"

"They have fought to some purpose, my child," said Sanders grimly.

Bosambo grinned faintly.

"Lord," he said softly, "when I go back to them they will be sorry."

And sorry indeed they were, as I will tell you.

CHAPTER 3

The Affair of the Lady Missionary

The house of De Silva, Mackiney and Company is not so well known as, say, the Rockefeller or the house of Marshall Field; nor does it inspire the same confidence in circles of world-finance as, say, the house of Rothschild or Pierpoint Morgan. Yet on the coast De Silva and Mackiney (where they dug up the last ethnological abomination, I know not) held a position analogous to all the houses I have named in combination. They were the Rothschilds, the Marshall Fields, the Pierpoint Morgans, of that particular coast. It is said that they put up a proposition that they should coin their own money, but a conservative government—with a small "c"—politely declined to sanction the suggestion.

They had a finger in all the pies that were baked in that part of the world. They had interests in steamship companies, controlled banks, financed exploration and exploitation companies, helped in the creation of railways, floated gold mines, but before and above all, they sold things to the natives and received in exchange other things of infinitely greater value than they gave. The trading store and the trading caravan were the foundation of the house of De Silva and Mackiney—De Silva had long since retired from the business, and was the Marquis de Something-or-other of the Kingdom of Portugal—and even in the days of its greater prosperity native truck was its long suit.

A little steamer would come slowly to a sandy beach, where the only sign of civilisation was a tin-roofed shanty and a flagstaff. Great hogsheads bound together by rope would be cast overboard, and a steam *pinnace* would haul the consignment to land.

Then would follow lighter after lighter loaded with straw-packed cases, and these a solitary white man, sweating under a huge sun-helmet, would receive on behalf of Messrs. De Silva and Mackiney and carefully remove to the store of De Silva and Mackiney till the caravans which had been despatched by the same reputable firm had returned from the dark interior. Then would the carriers be paid their wages—in gin. Some there were who preferred rum, and for these the big hogsheads would be tapped; but in the main the favourite form of recompense was to be found in the lightly packed cases, where between straw lay the square-faced bottles of German spirit.

Emanuel Mackiney was worth, if rumour be true, something over a million and, like John Bright's visitor, that was all he was worth. He was immensely wealthy and immensely unscrupulous, so that while his cheques were honoured from French Dacca to Portuguese Benguela, he himself was not honoured anywhere.

Though his English was not perfect, though his origin was obvious, he invariably spoke of England as "home."

That is all it is necessary to tell about Emanuel Mackiney. His son is entitled to a distinct description.

Burney Mackiney had completed his education in England, having exploited it with less profit than his father had exploited the coast.

He was big and coarse and strong. He had lived long enough in England to elaborate the vices he had acquired on the coast—for he had grown up in the business, knew the language of a dozen peoples, and the habits of every nation from the borders of Dahomey to Angola. A tall man, with plump cheeks of bronze rosiness, full of lip and plump of chin, he had all the confidence in himself which unlimited possessions beget.

And Burney was in love.

He made the girl's acquaintance before the ship which was carrying him back to the handsome *stucco* mansion at Sierra Leone had reached Teneriffe.

A slim girl, with a wise, sad face, delicately moulded. This was Ruth Glandynne.

"Missionary, eh?" Burney's good-natured contempt, like Burney's wealth, was obvious. "Africa isn't the sort of place for a girl."

"I know worse," she said with a smile.

"And what part of the coast are you going to?" he asked.

"I am going to open a mission on the Isisi River."

"Alone?"

"It isn't very unusual, you know," she said. "There were two missionaries coming, but my companion fell sick—she will come out later."

"H'm!" said Burney. "Isisi River, eh?"

"Do you know it?"

She was interested. The grey eyes which had regarded him with suspicion and hostility were now alight with interest.

"Not exactly; we've never got in there, ye know. My governor does all the trade of the coast, but they've kept us out of the Isisi. There was a commissioner man there, perfect dog of a man, named Sanders. You'll hate him. He loathes missionaries and traders and all that."

This was the beginning of an acquaintance which led within two days to a proposal.

To Burney's intense amazement he was unhesitatingly rejected.

"It is most flattering that you should think that way," she said, meeting his eye without embarrassment; "but I have no wish to marry—anybody."

"One minute, Miss Glandynne," he said roughly; "don't make any mistake. You think my being rich and your being poor makes a difference. My father wouldn't mind——"

"I never gave your financial position a moment's thought," she said, rising; "and you really cannot be any judge of mine."

"I love you," he muttered. "I've never met a girl as stunning as you. Look here," he laid his hand on her arm, "I could have had the pick of women at home, on my word I could. Titled ladies, some of them; but there's something about you——"

They were alone on the promenade deck and it was dark and he had dined and was full of confidence.

"There's something about you"—he tightened his hold on her arm—"that gets into my blood—Ruth!"

In a second she was clasped in his strong arms, struggling.

"Let me go!" she cried.

For answer he bent and kissed her fiercely.

With a superhuman effort she freed herself and staggered back against the rail, pale and trembling.

"You blackguard!" she breathed.

The scorn in her steady grey eyes cowed him.

"I'm sorry," he muttered. "I'm a fool—I've had a little to drink——"

She walked swiftly along the deck and disappeared down the companion, and for three days he did not see her.

Another man would have been ashamed to meet her again, but Burney Mackiney was not of this kind. He had views on women, and had no other regret than that he had apologised. That was weak, he felt. The stronger, the more masterful you are with women, the better they like it. He waited his opportunity.

The night before the ship reached Sierra Leone he found her sitting on the forepart of the promenade deck, alone.

"Miss Glandynne!" he greeted; and she looked up with a cold stare. "Look here, what's the good of being bad friends. I've made up my mind to marry you."

She would have risen, but she feared a repetition of the scene in which she had been an unwilling actress. So she sat in silence and he misinterpreted her attitude.

"I can't get you out of my mind," he went on. "It's damnable to think of you on the Isisi River with nothing but cannibals and native brutes about you."

"Any variety of brute is preferable to you," she said; and the insult went home.

For a moment he stood incoherent with rage, then he loosed upon her a flood of invective.

She took advantage of his humiliation to make her escape. He did not see her again, though she saw him, for she watched the boat that carried him to land at Sierra Leone with heartfelt gratitude.

★★★★★★

Mr. Commissioner Sanders came down to the beach to meet her and he was in no amiable frame of mind.

She saw a man of medium height, dressed in spotless white, a big white helmet shading a face tanned to the colour of teak. His face was thin and clean-shaven, his eyes unwavering and questioning, his every movement conveying the impression of alert vitality.

"I suppose I ought to be glad to see you," he said, shaking his head reprovingly. "You're the first white woman I've seen for many rains— but you're a responsibility."

She laughed, and gave him a cool, soft hand to shake. "You don't like missionaries, do you?" she smiled.

"I don't," said Sanders; "but I've had all sorts of orders to see that you're made comfortable; and really there is a lot of work on the river—medical work amongst the women. You're the doctor, I suppose?"

She shook her head.

"I'm the nurse," she said; "the doctor was taken ill before I sailed."

"Humph!" said Sanders.

He had had a hut prepared for her, and two native women trained to the ways of white folk to wait upon her. He gave her dinner that night at his bungalow, and invited the Houssa captain to share the meal. It was the nearest approach to a chaperon he could find.

"I've had a hut built for you," he said; "and the stores and furniture which came for you have been sent up. There are three or four missionaries in the country. You will find Father O'Leary at Cosinkusu—that's about a hundred miles from you. He's a decent sort of chap. There's a man named Boyton—he's a Baptist, or something, and is always on the rampage against the father for proselytising his flock. Boyton lives about one hundred and fifty miles from you. They're the principal missionaries."

He gave her a brief history of the district in which she was to live; indeed, he told her much more than he ever intended telling, but those grey eyes were very compelling and those lips were so ready to smile.

She stayed two days at headquarters and on the third morning her belongings were packed on the *Zaire*.

Before this she met Bosambo of Monrovia, specially summoned.

"This man is chief of the tribe which lies nearest to your station," said Sanders; "though you are practically in the Isisi country. I have sent for him to—to——"

"Tell him to look after me," she smiled, and Sanders smiled responsively.

"Something like that. As a matter of fact, I wanted you to see him here so that he might know that you go as my guest and my friend."

He stammered a little, for Sanders was not used to saying pretty things.

When he had seen her on board he sent for Bosambo.

"Bosambo," he said, in the vernacular, "this lady is of my race, and she will be alone amongst my people, who are wicked and cunning, seeking to deceive her, for she is a God-woman, though she is also a doctor. Now to you I say guard her till your last breath of life, and be in my place, as me, in all matters that touch her."

Bosambo stretched out his hands, palm upwards.

"Master," he said earnestly, "if I swore by the Blessed Virgin whom I worshipped in Liberia, behold I do not know who I swear by, for I have forgotten the holy things that the fathers taught me. But by my head and spirit, and by my life-ghost, I will do as you say."

He turned and walked majestically to the boat. Half-way down the beach he turned about and came back to Sanders.

"Lord, when I have been faithful to your honour's satisfaction, will you buy for me at Sierra Leone a piece of gold cloth, such as a chief might wear?"

"Go, you bargaining child!" said Sanders, without irritation.

He watched the little steamer until it swept round a bend of the river out of sight, and then walked slowly to the bungalow, with—it must be confessed—a sigh.

In Sierra Leone, about this time, Burney Mackiney was engaged with his father.

The elder Mackiney was not pleasant to look upon, being grossly stout, puckered and yellow of face, and affected with stertorous breathing.

"It's worth trying," he said, after there had been long silence; "the country's full of rubber, and there's no law preventing the importation of liquor—except the law which gives the commissioner the right to make his own laws. How would you get in?"

"Through the French territory," said his son; "it's dead easy."

There was another long pause.

"But why do you want to go?" asked the elder. "It's not like you to go to a lot of trouble."

"I want to see the country," said the other carelessly. He wanted something more than that. For days he had been hatching his black plot—the Arabs had done such things, and it would not be difficult. Clear of civilisation, he would become an Arab—he spoke coast Arabic perfectly.

He could buy his way through the tribes; a swift dash across the French frontier, he could reach the Isisi River—stay long enough to establish the fact that it was an Arab trader who was the guilty man. She would have to marry him then.

This, in brief, was his plan.

He chose his caravan carefully, and a month later left Sierra Leone in an "S. and M." steamer for an unknown destination.

Exactly three months after he had said good-bye to the missionary, Mr. Commissioner Sanders was serenely and leisurely making his way along a small river, which leads to a distant section of the Lesser Isisi, when he met a common man, named I'fambi M'Waka—or M'Wafamba as he was called.

Sanders, at the time, was using a little launch, for the *Zaire* was in "dock"—in other words, she was beached.

The Commissioner was proceeding up stream, M'Wafamba was floating down in his battered iron-wood canoe and looking over the side, Sanders regarded the man with idle curiosity.

As they came abreast, M'Wafamba sat upright and turned his face.

"Ho, Sandi!" he called boisterously.

"Ho, man!" called Sanders. "Take your canoe nearer the shore, for my swift boat will make the waters dance and you may suffer."

For answer came a peal of hoarse laughter.

"Ho, Sandi!" bawled M'Wafamba; "white man, pig eater, white monkey!"

Sanders' hand tightened on the steering wheel, and he sent the launch round in a circle until he came up with the canoe.

One Houssa caught the canoe with a boat hook, another reached over and gripped the insolent M'Wafamba by the arm.

A little dazed, and resisting awkwardly, he was pulled into the launch.

"Either one of two things you are," said Sanders; "mad with sickness mango or a great rascal."

"You are a liar, and an eater of liars," said the reckless M'Wafamba; and when Sanders put out his hand to feel the neck of the man for tell-tale swellings, M'Wafamba tried to bite it.

Sanders drew back sharply, not from fear of the bite, but for another reason.

Whilst two of his men sat on the struggling prisoner's chest, he steered the boat for the bank.

"Get him ashore," said the commissioner; and the luckless captive was dragged to land without ceremony.

"Tie him to a tree and make ready for a flogging," said Sanders.

They strapped his hands above the trunk of a young gum tree and stripped his cloth from his shoulders, whilst Sanders walked up and down, his hands in his pockets, his head sunk on his breast, for of a sudden on that sunlit day there had risen a cloud which blotted out all brightness from his official life.

When his men had finished their work Sanders approached the prisoner, a little frightened now, though somewhat rambling of speech.

"How do they call you, my man?" asked the commissioner.

"I'fambi M'Waka," whimpered the man by the tree, "commonly M'Wafamba—of the village of the Pool of Devils."

"M'Wafamba," said Sanders, "being of the Isisi people, you know something of me and my way."

"Lord, I have seen you, and also your way," said the man.

"And if I say 'death' what do I mean?"

"Lord, you mean death, as all men on the river know," said M'Wafamba.

Sanders nodded.

"Now, I am going to flog you till you die," he Said grimly, "if you do not tell me where you found drink in my land—for you are drunk with a certain evil poison, which is called *ginni*, and it is forbidden by law that *ginni* shall be bought or sold in this territory."

Then the man rolled his head drunkenly.

"Strike, pig eater," he said heroically, "for I have sworn an oath that I will tell no man."

"So be it," said Sanders; "it is your oath against my whipping."

Abiboo, the sergeant of the Houssa, tall and strong of arm, took a firm grip of his hide-whip, stepped a little to one side and sent it whistling round his head, then—

"*Flack!*"

M'Wafamba woke the forest with a yell.

"Enough!" he screamed. "I speak!"

They loosed him.

"Lord," he wept, "it was an Arabi man, who came across the French border; this he gave me for certain rubber I collected, saying it would put the spirit of white men into my heart and make me equal in courage to the bravest. And so it did, lord; but now it has gone out of me, and my heart is like water."

"What manner of Arabi was this?" asked Sanders.

"Lord, he was big and strong, and had a fat face like a pig and he wore a ring."

"When did you see him?"

"Two days' journey from here, lord; but he has gone, for he has great matters on hand—so a man, who is my cousin, told me—for he goes to the Ochori country to lift the white woman, who gives us certain beastly waters to drink when we are sick."

The trees seemed of a sudden to spin and the ground to heave up under the Commissioner's feet. He staggered a little, and Abiboo, suspecting fever, leapt to his side and put his strong arm on his shoulders. Only for a second he stood thus, white as death; then—

"Into the boat!" he said.

There was wood enough on board for six hours' steaming—the mission station was twelve hours at the least.

He swept down the little river swiftly and turned to breast the strong currents of the Isisi. Six hours, almost to the minute, the wood lasted. It brought him to a fishing village, where a store of government wood awaited him.

But the "Arabi" had two days' start.

Mackiney had bribed and fought his way through the Mishadombi tribe (those "people-who-are-not-all-alike," about which I must tell you), which serve as a buffer State between French and British territory; he had corrupted the Isisi, and now, with a guide—the cousin of that same M'Wafamba—was moving rapidly on the mission station.

It had been built at the junction of two rivers, in the very spot where, a year before, Sanders had established himself as "the Silent One."

Mackiney had with him fifty men, mainly of the Kroo coast.

His plan was to take to one of the smaller streams that feed the Isisi. It was navigable for eighty miles and would bring him to within a month's march of the regular caravan route to Lago—by then he hoped the girl would be compliant.

His party reached within striking distance of his objective late in the afternoon.

The mission house was half a mile from the village, and he sent out spies who brought him word that beyond two native women and a couple of men there was no opposition to be feared.

He sat apart from his men as they cooked their evening meal.

In his long white *burnous*, his head enveloped in a filleted hood, he was an Arab to the life.

When night came his headman approached him. "Master," he asked, "what of this Kaffir?"

He spoke of the guide.

"Him you will kill," said Mackiney in Arabic; "for I do not know how much he guesses."

"He guesses too much," said the headman; "for he says that you are no Arab, but a white man."

"You must lose no time," said Mackiney shortly.

He sat waiting by the fire they had kindled for him. Soon he heard a little scuffle and turning his head saw a knot of swaying men and a muffled bellowing like that of a man with a cloth upon his face.

The group went staggering into the forest, disappearing in the darkness of the night.

By and by they came back laughing amongst themselves. The cousin of M'Wafamba, who went with them, did not come back.

"It is time," said his headman. "In two hours the moon will be here."

Very quickly the fires were extinguished and the cooking-pots stacked in the forepart of the big canoe, and in silence, with paddles striking evenly, they crossed the river.

The canoe was beached two hundred yards from the mission house, near a clump of bush. From here to the path was a few steps.

In single file, headed by the white-robed Arab, the party made its stealthy way along the twisting path. On either side the trees rose steeply, and save for the call of night birds there was no sound.

The forest ended abruptly. Ahead of them was a little clearing and in the centre the dark bulk of the mission hut.

"Now may Allah further our enterprise," breathed Mackiney, and took a step forward.

Out of the ground, almost at his feet, rose a dark figure.

"Who walks in the night?" asked a voice.

"Damn you!" grunted Mackiney in English.

The figure moved ever so slightly.

"Master," he said, "that is a white man's word, yet you have the dress of an Arabi."

Mackiney recovered himself.

"Man, whoever you are, stand on one side, for I have business with the God-woman."

"I also," was the calm reply, "for our Lord Sandi put me here; and I am as he; here have I stood every night save one."

Mackiney had a revolver in his hand, but he dare not fire for fear of alarming the occupants of the hut.

"Let me go on," he said. He knew, rather than saw, the long spear that was levelled at his breast in the darkness. "Let me be, and I will give you many bags of salt and rods more numerous than the trees of the forest."

He heard a little chuckle in the darkness.

"You give too much for too little," said the voice. "Oh, M'laka!"

Mackiney heard the pattering of feet; he was trapped, for somewhere ahead of him armed men were holding the path.

He raised his revolver and fired twice at the figure.

A spear whizzed past him, and he leapt forward and grappled with the man in his path.

He was strong as a young lion, but the man whose hand caught his throat was no weakling. For an instant they swayed, then fell, rolling over and over in the path.

Mackiney reached his hand for another revolver. It closed round the butt, when he felt a shock—something hit him smoothly in the left side—something that sent a thrill of pain through every nerve in his body.

"Oh, dear!" said Mackiney in English.

He never spoke again.

"Arabi, or white man, I do not know," said Bosambo of Monrovia; "and there is none to tell us, because my people were quick to kill, and only one of his followers is left alive and he knows nothing."

"What have you done with this Arabi?" asked Sanders.

They held their *palaver* in the mission house in the first hours of the dawn and the girl, pale and troubled, sat at the table looking from one man to the other, for she knew little of the language.

"Lord," said Bosambo, "him I buried according to my desire that no man should know of this raid, lest it put evil thoughts in their heads."

"You did wisely," said Sanders.

He went back to headquarters a little puzzled, for he knew none of the facts of the case.

And when, months after, urgent inquiries came to him respecting the whereabouts of one Burney Mackiney, he replied in all truth that he could give no information.

CHAPTER 4

The Swift Walker

They have a legend in the Akasava country of a green devil. He is taller than the trees, swifter than the leopard, more terrible than all other ghosts, for he is green—the fresh, young green of the trees in spring—and has a voice that is a strangled bark, like the hateful, rasping *gr-r-r* of a wounded crocodile.

This is *M'shimba-m'shamba*, the Swift Walker.

You sometimes find his erratic track showing clearly through the forest. For the space of twelve yards' width the trees are twisted, broken and uprooted, the thick undergrowth swept together in tangled heaps, as though by two huge clumsy hands.

This way and that goes the path of *M'shimba-m'shamba*, zigzag through the forest—and woe to the hut or the village that stands in his way!

For he will leave this hut intact, from this hut he will cut the propped verandah of leaves; this he will catch up in his ruthless fingers and tear it away swiftly from piece to piece, strewing the wreckage along the village street.

He has lifted whole families and flung them broken and dying into the forest; he has wiped whole communities from the face of the earth.

Once, by the Big River, was a village called N'kema-n-'kema, and means literally, "monkey-monkey." It was a poor village, and the people lived by catching fish and smoking the same. This they sold to inland villages, profiting on occasions to the equivalent of twelve shillings a week. Generally it was less; but, more or less, some fifty souls lived in comfort on the proceeds.

Some there were in that village that believed in *M'shimba-m'shamba,* and some who scoffed at him.

And when the votaries of the green devil went out to make sacrifices to him the others laughed. So acute did the division between the worshippers and the non-worshippers become, that the village divided itself into two, some building their dwellings on the farther side of the creek which ran near by, and the disbelievers remaining on the other bank.

For many months the sceptics gathered to revile the famous devil. Then one night *M'shimba-m'shamba* came. He came furiously, walking along the water of the creek—for he could do such miraculous things—stretching out his hairy arms to grab tree and bush and hut.

In the morning the worshippers were alone alive, and of the village of the faithless there was no sign save one tumbled roof, which heaved now and then very slightly, for under it was the chief of the village, who was still alive.

The worshippers held a *palaver*, and decided that it would be a sin to rescue him since their lord, *M'shimba-m'shamba,* had so evidently decreed his death. More than this, they decided that it would be a very holy thing and intensely gratifying to their green devil, if they put fire to the hut—the fallen roof of wood and plaited grass heaved pathetically at the suggestion—and completed the destruction.

At this moment there arrived a great chief of an alien tribe, Bosambo of the Ochori, who came up against the tide in his State canoe, with its fifty paddlers and his State drummer.

He was returning from a visit of ceremony and had been travelling before daylight, when he came upon the village and stopped to rest his paddlers and eat.

"Most wonderful chief," said the leader of the believers, "you have come at a moment of great holiness." And he explained the passing of *M'shimba-m'shamba*, and pointed to the fallen roof, which showed at long intervals a slight movement. "Him we will burn," said the headman simply; "for he has been a sinful reviler of our lord the devil, calling him by horrible names, such as 'snake eater' and 'sand drinker.'"

"Little man," said Bosambo magnificently, "I will sit down with my men and watch you lift that roof and bring the chief before me; and if he dies, then, by Damnyou—which is our Lord Sandi's own fetish—I will hang you up by your legs over a fire."

Bosambo did not sit down, but superintended the rescue of the unfortunate chief, accelerating the work—for the people of the village had no heart in it—by timely blows with the butt of his spear.

They lifted the roof and brought an old man to safety. There had been three others in the hut, but they were beyond help.

The old chief was uninjured, and had he been younger he would have required no assistance to free himself. They gave him water and a little corn to eat and he recovered sufficiently to express his contrition. For he had seen *M'shimba-m'shamba*, the green one.

"Higher than trees, he stood, lord," he said to the interested Bosambo; "and round about his head were little tearing clouds, that flew backwards and forwards to him and from him like birds."

He gave further anatomical particulars. He thought that one leg of the devil was longer than the other, and that he had five arms, one of which proceeded from his chest.

Bosambo left the village, having established the chief in his chieftainship and admonished his would-be murderers.

Now it need not be explained that Bosambo had no more right to establish chiefs or to admonish people of the Akasava than you and I have to vote in the Paris municipal elections. For Bosambo was a chief of the Ochori, which is a small, unimportant tribe, and himself was of no great consequence.

It was not to offer an apology that he directed his paddlers to make for the Akasava city. It lay nearly ten miles out of his way, and Bosambo would not carry politeness to such lengths.

When he beached his canoe before the wondering people of the city and marched his fifty paddlers (who became fifty spearmen by the simple expedient of leaving their paddles behind and taking their spears with them) through the main streets of the city, he walked importantly.

"Chief," he said to that worthy, hastily coming forth to meet him, "I come in peace, desiring a *palaver* on the high matter of *M'shimba-m'shamba*."

When the chief, whose name was Sekedimi, recognised him he was sorry that he had troubled to go out to greet him, for the Ochori were by all native reckoning very small fish indeed.

"I will summon the children," said Sekedimi sourly; "for they know best of ghosts and such stories."

"This is a *palaver* for men," said Bosambo, his wrath rising; "and though the Akasava, by my way of thinking, are no men, yet I am willing to descend from my highness, where Sandi's favour has put me, to talk with your people."

"Go to your canoe, little chief," snarled Sekedimi, "before I beat you with rods. For we Akasava folk are very jealous, and three chiefs of this city have been hanged for their pride. And if you meet *M'shimba-m'shamba*, behold you may take him with you."

Thus it came about that Bosambo, paramount chief of the Ochori, went stalking back to his canoe with as much dignity as he could summon, followed by the evil jests of the Akasava and the rude words of little boys.

Exactly what capital Bosambo could have made from his chance acquaintance with *M'shimba-m'shamba* need not be considered.

It is sufficient for the moment, at any rate, to record the fact that he returned to his capital, having lost something of prestige, for his paddlers, who took a most solemn oath not to tell one word of what had happened in the Akasava village, told none—save their several wives.

Bosambo was in many ways a model chief.

He dispensed a justice which was, on the whole, founded on the purest principles of equity. Somewhere, hundreds of miles away, sat Sanders of the River, and upon his method Bosambo, imitative as only a coast man can be, based his own. He punished quickly and obeyed the law himself as far as it lay within him to obey anything.

There was no chief as well disciplined as he, else it would have been a bad day's work for Sekedimi of the Akasava, for Bosambo was a man of high spirit and quick to resent affront to his dignity. And Sekedimi had wounded him deeply.

But Bosambo was a patient man; he had the gift which every native possesses of pigeon-holing his grievances. Therefore he waited, putting aside the matter and living down his people's disapproval.

He carried a pliant stick of hippo hide that helped him considerably in preserving their respect.

All things moved orderly till the rains had come and gone.

Then one day at sunset he came again to the Akasava City, this time with only ten paddlers. He walked through the street unattended, carrying only three light spears in his left hand and a wicker shield on the same arm. In his right hand he had nothing but his thin, pliant stick of hippo skin, curiously carved.

The chief of the Akasava had word of his coming and was puzzled, for Bosambo had arrived in an unaccustomed way—without ostentation.

"The dawn has come early," he said politely.

"I am the water that reflects the light of your face," replied Bosambo with conventional courtesy.

"You will find me in a kind mood," said Sekedimi; "and ready to listen to you."

He was fencing cautiously; for who knew what devilish lies Bosambo had told Sandi?

Bosambo seated himself before the chief.

"Sekedimi," said he, "though my skin is black, I am of white and paramount people, having been instructed in their magic, and knowing their gods intimately."

"So I have heard; though, for my part, I take no account of their gods, being, as they tell me, for women and gentle things."

"That is true," said Bosambo, "save one god, whose name was Petero, who was a great cutter off of ears."

Sekedimi was impressed.

"Him I have not heard about," he admitted.

"Knowing these," Bosambo went on, "I came before the rains to speak of *M'shimba-m'shamba,* the green one, who walks crookedly."

"This is the talk of children," said Sekedimi; "for *M'shimba-m'shamba* is the name our fathers gave to the whirlwind that comes through the forest—and it is no devil."

Sekedimi was the most enlightened chief that ever ruled the Akasava and his explanation of *M'shimba-m'shamba* was a perfectly true one.

"Lord chief," said Bosambo earnestly, "no man may speak with better authority on such high and holy matters as devils as I, Bosambo, for I have seen wonderful sights and know the world from one side to the other. For I have wandered far, even to the edge of the world which looks down into hell; and I have seen wild leopards so great that they have drunk up whole rivers and eaten trees of surprising height and thickness."

"*Ko, ko,*" said the awe-stricken counsellors of the chief who stood about his person; and even Sekedimi was impressed.

"Now I come to you," said Bosambo, "with joyful news, for my young men have captured *M'shimba-m'shamba,* the green one, and have carried him to the land of the Ochori."

This he said with fine dramatic effect, and was pleased to observe the impression he had created.

"We bound the green one," he went on, "with N'Gombi chains, and laid the trunk of a tree in his mouth to silence his fearful roaring. We captured him, digging an elephant pit so deep that only men of strongest eyesight could see the bottom, so wide that no man could shout across it and be heard. And we took him to the land of the Ochori on a hundred canoes."

Sekedimi sat with open mouth.

"The green one?" he asked incredulously.

"The green one," said Bosambo, nodding his head; "and we fastened together four shields, like that which I carry, and these we put over each of his eyes, that he might not see the way we took him or find his way back to the Akasava."

There was a long silence.

"It seems," said Sekedimi, after a while, "that you have done a wonderful thing; for you have removed a devil from our midst. Yet the Ochori people will be sorry, for the curse which you have taken from us you have given to your people, and surely they will rise against you."

"*E-wa!*" murmured his counsellors, nodding their heads wisely. "The Ochori will rise against their chief, for he has loosened an evil one in their midst."

Bosambo rose, for night was falling and he desired to begin the return stage of his journey.

"The Ochori are a very proud people," he said. "Never have they had a great devil before; the Isisi, the Akasava, the N'Gombi, the Bush folk, and the Lesser Isisi, the Bomongo, the Boungendi—all these tribes have devils in many variety, but the Ochori have had none and they were very sad. Now their stomachs are full of pride for *M'shimba-m'shamba,* the green one, is with them, roving the forest in which we have loosed him, in a most terrifying way."

He left the Akasava in a thoughtful mood, and set his State canoe for the juncture of the river.

That night the Akasava chief called together all his headmen, his elders, his chief fighting men and all men of consequence.

The *staccato* notes of the *lokali* called the little chiefs of outlying villages, and with them their elder men. From the fourth hour of night till the hour before dawn the *palaver* lasted.

"O chiefs and people," said Sekedimi, "I have called you together to tell you of a great happening. For *M'shimba-m'shamba,* who since the beginning of the world has been the own devil of the Akasava people, is now no longer ours. Bosambo, of the Ochori, has bound him and carried him away."

"This is certainly a shame," said one old man; "for *M'shimba-m'shamba* is our very own devil, and Bosambo is an evil man to steal that which is not his."

"That is as I think," said Sekedimi. "Let us go to Sandi, who holds

212

court by the border of the N'Gombi country, and he shall give us a book."

Sanders was at that time settling a marriage dispute, the principal article of contention being: if a man pays six thousand *matakos* (brass rods) for a wife, and in the first twelve months of her married life she develop sleeping-sickness, was her husband entitled to recover his purchase price from her father? It was a long, long *palaver*, requiring the attendance of many witnesses; and Sanders was deciding it on the very common-sense line that any person selling a damaged article, well knowing the same to be damaged, was guilty of fraud. The evidence, however, exonerated the father from blame, and there only remained a question of equity. He was in the midst of the second half of the trial when the chief of the Akasava, with his headman, his chief slave, and a deputation of the little chiefs waited upon him.

"Lord," said Sekedimi, without preliminary, "we have covered many miles of country and traversed rivers of surprising swiftness; also we encountered terrible perils by the way."

"I will excuse you an account of your adventures," said the Commissioner, "for I am in no mood for long *palavers*. Say what is to be said and have done."

Thereupon Sekedimi told the story of the filched devil from the beginning, when he had, with a fine sarcasm, presented the Swift Walker to the Ochori.

Now Sanders knew all about *M'shimba-m'shamba*. Moreover, he knew that until very recently the chief himself was in no doubt as to what the "green one" really was.

It was characteristic of him that he made no attempt to turn the chief to a sense of his folly.

"If Bosambo has taken *M'shimba-m'shamba*," he said gravely, "then he has done no more than you told him to do."

"Now I spoke in jest," said Sekedimi, "for this devil is very dear to us, and since we can no more hear his loud voice in our forests we are sad for one who is gone."

"Wait!" said Sanders, "for is this the season when *M'shimba-m'shamba* walks? Is it not rather midway between the rains that he comes so swiftly? Wait and he will return to you."

But Sekedimi was in no mood for waiting.

"Master, if I go to Bosambo," he said, "and speak kindly to him, will he not return the green one?"

"Who knows?" said Sanders wearily. "I am no prophet."

"If my lord gave me a book——" suggested Sekedimi.

"This is no book *palaver*," said Sanders briefly; "but justice between man and man. For if I give you a book to Bosambo, what shall I say when Bosambo asks me also for a book to you?"

"Lord, that is just," said Sekedimi, and he went his way. With twelve of his principal chiefs he made the journey to the Ochori City, carrying with him gifts of goats and fat dogs, salt and heavy rings of brass.

Bosambo received him ceremoniously, accepted his gifts but declined to favour him.

"Sekedimi," he said, "I am wax in the hands of my people. I fear to anger them; for they love *M'shimba-m'shamba* better than they love their goats or their salt or their wives."

"But no one sees him till the middle time between the rains," said Sekedimi.

"Last night we heard him," persisted Bosambo steadily; "very terrible he was, and my people trembled and were proud."

For many hours the chief of the Akasava pleaded and argued, but without avail.

"I see that you have a heart of brass," said Sekedimi at length; "therefore, Bosambo, return me the presents I brought, and I will depart."

"As to the presents," said Bosambo, "they are dispersed, for swift messengers have carried them to the place where *M'shimba-m'shamba* sits and have put them where he may find them, that he may know the Akasava remember him with kindness."

Empty-handed the chief returned.

He sent courier after courier in the course of the next month, without effect. And as time wore on his people began to speak against him. The crops of two villages failed, and the people cursed him, saying that he had sold the ghost and the spirit of fortune.

At last, in desperation, he paid another visit to Bosambo.

"Chief," he said, when all ceremonies had been observed, "I tell you this: I will give you fifty bags of salt and as much corn as ten canoes can hold if you will return to me our green one. And if your pride resists me, then I will call my spears, though Sandi hang me for it."

Bosambo was a wise man. He knew the limit of human endurance. Also he knew who would suffer if war came, for Sanders had given him private warning.

"My heart is heavy," he said. "Yet since you are set upon this matter I will return you *M'shimba-m'shamba*, though I shall be shamed before my people. Send me the salt and the corn, and when the tide of the river is so high and the moon is nearly full I will find the green one and bring him back to your land."

Sekedimi went back to his city a happy man. In a week the salt and the corn were delivered and the canoes that brought them carried a message back. On such a day, at such an hour, the green one would be cut loose in the forest of the Akasava. Afterwards, Bosambo would come in state to announce the transfer.

At the appointed time the chief of the Akasava waited by the river beach, two great fires burning behind him to guide Bosambo's canoe through the night. And behind the fires the population of the city and the villages about stood awed and expectant, biting its knuckles.

'*Tom-tom! Tom-tom! Tom-tom!* Over the water came the faint sound of Bosambo's drum and the deep-chested chant of his paddlers. In half an hour his canoe grounded and he waded ashore.

"Lord Sekedimi," he greeted the chief, "this night I have loosened *M'shimba-m'shamba,* the green one, the monster. And he howled fearfully because I left him. My heart is sore, and there is nothing in my poor land which gives me pleasure."

"Fifty sacks of my salt I sent you," said Sekedimi unpleasantly; "also corn."

"None the less, I am as an orphan who has lost his father and his mother," moaned Bosambo.

"Let the *palaver* finish, chief," said Sekedimi, "for my heart is also sore, having lost salt and corn."

"I see that you have no stomach for pity," Said Bosambo, and re-embarked.

Clear of the Akasava city, Bosambo regained his spirits, though the night was stormy and great spots of rain fell at intervals.

The further he drew from the Akasava chief the more jovial he became, and he sang a song.

"There are fools in the forest," he bawled musically; "such as the *ingonona* who walks with his eyes shut; but he is not so great a fool as Sekedimi.

"He is like a white man who is newly come to this land.

"He is like a child that burns his fingers.

"He is simple and like a great worm."

He sang all this, and added libellous and picturesque particulars.

"Lord chief," said the headman suddenly, arresting his song, "I think we will make for the shore."

Over the trees on the right bank of the river lightning flickered with increasing brightness, and there was a long continuous rumble of thunder in the air.

"To the middle island," ordered Bosambo.

The headman shivered.

"Lord, the middle island is filled with spirits," he said.

"You are a fool," said Bosambo; but he ordered the canoe to the left bank.

Brighter and more vivid grew the lightning, louder and louder the crackle and crash of thunder. The big raindrops fell fitfully.

Then above the noise of thunder came a new sound—a weird howling that set the paddlers working with quicker strokes.

"*Whow-w-w!*"

A terrifying shriek deafened them.

The man nearest him dropped his paddle with a frightened whimper, and Bosambo caught it.

"Paddle, dogs!" he thundered.

They were within a dozen yards of the shore when, by the quick flashing lightning he saw a jagged path suddenly appear in the forest on the bank before him.

It was as though giant hands were plucking at trees. They twisted and reeled like drunken men—cracked, and fell over.

"Paddle!"

Then something caught Bosambo and lifted him from the canoe. Up, up he went; then as swiftly down to the water; up again, and down. He struck out for the shore, choked and half-conscious.

His fingers caught the branches of a stricken tree, and he drew himself to land. He stumbled forward on his hands and knees, panting heavily.

Overhead the storm raged, but Bosambo did not heed it. His forty paddlers, miraculously cast ashore by the whirlwind, lay around him laughing and moaning, according to their temperaments.

But these he forgot.

For he was engaged in the composition of a hurried and apologetic prayer to *M'shimba-m'shamba*, the green one, the Swift Walker.

CHAPTER 5

Brethren of the Order

Native men loved Sanders of the River well enough to die for him. Some hated him well enough to kill him. These things have a trick of balancing themselves, and the story of Tambeli the Strong, and a member of that sinister organisation, the Silent Ones of Nigeria, offers an object lesson on this point.

From the Big River which empties itself into the Atlantic Ocean somewhere between Dacca and Banana Point—this is a fairly vague location—run a number of smaller rivers, east, west, and northerly, more or less.

The Isisi, or "Little River," is one of these. It runs to the conjunction of the Baranga River, and it is a moot point among geographers whether the right confluence is the true Isisi and the left confluence the Baranga, or vice versa.

Commissioner Sanders, in defiance of all cartographers, traces the Isisi to the right, because the left river runs through the land of lawless tribes, which are called in the native tongue Nushadombi, or literally, "the-Men-Who-Are-Not-All-Alike."

Beyond the deep forest through which for twenty miles the Baranga runs, beyond and northward of the swampland where the crocodiles breed, lies a lake with a score of outlets, none of which are navigable. Here, at one time, was a village, and to this village had drifted the outcast men of a hundred tribes. Men bloodguilty, survivors of unlawful feuds, evaders of taxes, the sinful and the persecuted of every tribe and people within a hundred miles came drifting into Nushadombi.

So that in course of time what had once been a village grew to a city, and that city the hub of a nation.

They dwelt apart, a sullen, hateful people, defiant of all laws save the laws of self-preservation. Successive expeditions were sent against them. They were near the border of the German territory, and took that which pleased them, contemptuous of border line or defined sphere.

Germany sent a native army through a swamp to destroy them—that army drifted back in twos and threes, bringing stories of defeat and the unpleasant consequences thereof.

France, from the south-east dispatched an expedition with no better success.

Sanders neither sent armed forces nor peace mission.

He knew a great deal more about this strange nation than he ever put into the dispatches, the production of which, for the benefit of an Under-Secretary of Colonial Affairs, was a monthly nightmare.

The commissioner ignored the existence of the People-Who-Were-Not-All-Alike. He might have continued in this attitude of wilful ignorance but for the advent into his official orbit of one Tambeli.

Tambeli had three gods. One was a fierce god, who came into his life when the rains came and the great winds howled through the forest, lifting up and casting down trees; when vivid flashes of lightning lit the forest with incessant stabbings of white flame, and the heavens crashed and crackled. He had another god, burnt and carved from a certain hard wood which is found in the N'Gombi country, and he had yet another god, which was himself.

Tambeli was the handsomest man of all the Isisi.

He was very tall, his shoulders were broad, his arms were perfectly moulded, the muscles being gathered in cordlike pads, properly. His hair he loved to dress with clay so that it billowed on either side of his head.

Wearing the skin of a leopard, and leaning on the long elephant spear, he would stand for hours by the edge of the river, the admiration of women who came to the shallow places to fill their cooking-pots. This was as Tambeli desired, for he was a man of gallantry. More so than was to the liking of certain husbands, so it is said; and there was an evening when, as Tambeli went stalking through the village, one M'fabo, an outraged man, sprang upon him from a hiding-place, roaring hoarsely in his mad anger. But Tambeli was as lithe as a cat and as strong as the leopard whose skin he wore. He grasped M'fabo by the throat, lifted him clear of the ground, and, swinging him round and round, as a mischievous boy might swing a rat by the tail, flung him into the hut he had quitted.

Thereafter no man raised his hand openly against Tambeli, though there were some who sought to injure him by stealth. A foreigner—a Congolaise man—slipped into his hut one night with a sharpened razor.

It was the little square razor that the Congo folk wear tucked away in their hair, and his pleasure was to cut Tambeli's throat. This Congo-man was never seen again—the river was very handy, and Tambeli was very strong—but his razor was found by the river's edge and it was stained with blood.

Tambeli was a rich man, having goats and brass rods and salt in sacks. He had six wives, who tended his gardens and cooked for him, and they were proud of their lord, and gloried in his discreditable exploits. For Tambeli was a trader, though few knew it, and it was his practice to absent himself three months in the year on business of his own.

One day the chief of the village died, and the women having decked their bodies with green leaves, danced the death dance locked arm in arm.

Tambeli, watching the reeling line making its slow progress through the village street, had a thought, and when they laid the body on the bottom of a canoe and paddled it upriver to the middle island, where the dead were buried, Tambeli was swept downstream, four of his wives paddling till, after a long day and a night, he came to the Isisi city where the king lived. To that great man he went. And the king, who was drunk, was neither sorry nor glad to see him.

"Lord King," said he, "I am Tambeli of Isaukasu by the little river, and I have served you many times, as you well know."

The king blinked at him with dull eyes, and said nothing.

"We are a people without a chief," said Tambeli; "and the men of my village desire that I shall rule them in place of C'fari, who is dead."

The king scratched his neck thoughtfully, but said nothing for a while; then he asked: "What do you bring?"

Tambeli detailed a magnificent list, which comprehended goats, salt, and rods to a fabulous amount. He added a gift which was beyond price.

"Go back to your people—chief," said the king, and Tambeli embraced the knees of his master, and called him his father and his mother.

That is how Tambeli came to be sitting on the stool of chieftainship when Mr. Commissioner Sanders arrived unexpectedly from the south in his tiny steamboat.

★★★★★★

Now, Isaukasu lay on the very border line of the Ochori country, and was a village of some importance since the back country produced rubber and gum. It was the kind of village which became a city in the twinkling of an eye.

The steamer was tied up to the bank, a gangway was thrown ashore and Sanders, in shining white, came briskly to the beach.

Tambeli, a picturesque figure, awaited him.

"Lord Master," he said, "C'fari has died, and I am chief of this town by order of my father the king."

Sanders perked his head on one side, like a curious bird, and eyed the man with interest.

"Your father the king is king no more," he said softly, "being at this moment on my ship, very sick; and though he were well and on his throne, no man says who may be chief of town or village save I. And truly, Tambeli, you are no chief for me."

Tambeli stuck out his jaw a little, for he was a very determined man.

"I have paid for my honour with salt and rods," he said.

"And gin," said Sanders gently. "Now you shall tell me how gin comes into my country when I forbid it."

Tambeli faced the white man squarely. "Master," said he, twiddling the brass-bound haft of his spear, "I have been in many countries, and know many customs; also, they tell me, the black people of the coast, that there is no law, white or black, which prevents a man from buying or selling square-faces if he so wishes."

"I am the law," said Sanders, and his voice was softer than ever. "If I say thus, it is thus. And gin you shall neither buy nor sell nor barter, though the black lawgivers of the coast be as wise as gods."

"In this matter of chiefship——" said Tambeli.

"You are no chief for me," said Sanders, "neither now nor at any time, for you are an evil man and a robber of that which men prize dearly. I have spoken; the *palaver's* finished."

Tambeli hesitated. Behind Sanders stood a sergeant and two men of the Houssas, and as Tambeli stood irresolutely, the sergeant stepped forward and grasped him by the shoulder.

"*Aleki!*" he said, which is an invitation to hurried movement.

As the sergeant's grip tightened, Tambeli, the strong one, caught him by the slack of his uniform jacket and sent him spinning—then he stood stiffly, for the warm muzzle of Sanders' revolver was pressing against his stomach, and Tambeli, who had, as he claimed, a knowledge of countries and customs, knew Sanders for a man with little or no regard for human life.

They handcuffed Tambeli and ironed his leg to a staple in the deck of the *Zaire*, for he had shamed the authority of the Crown, had unceremoniously flung a full sergeant of Houssas down the bank that leads to the river, and such things are not good for people to see.

The steamer went thrashing down the river towards headquarters and Sanders gave himself over to the question of Tambeli.

There was, as he had boldly said, no law prohibiting the sale of strong drink in the territory under his care; but Sanders never consulted constitutions. He had kept his lands free of the gin curse, and he had no intention of adding to the list of his responsibilities, which was already too long.

There was drink in the country; this he had reason to know. Polambi of Isisi, Sakalana of the Akasava, Nindino of the N'Gombi, all chiefs of parts, had gone from the straight path. There had been certain indiscretions which had sent Sanders hurrying "all ways at once." There had been, too, some drastic readjustment of authority.

The gin problem was half solved by the arrest of Tambeli; there remained the problem of the man. This he settled for himself.

The *Zaire* was tied to a wooding, and Sanders had retired to his cabin and was sleeping when a noise on deck aroused him and he came out in a hurry to find Tambeli, the strong man, gone, and with him the chain that fastened him to the staple and the staple that fastened him to the deck. He left behind him a private of Houssas with a cracked head.

Sanders whistled a little tune to himself all the way to headquarters. He sat in a deck-chair under the striped awning, whistling tunefully and very softly for the greater part of two days and his men, who knew him well and understood his mood, were careful to keep out of his way.

He arrived at headquarters still whistling. He was the only white man on the station and was thankful. He had put one of his guests, a somewhat frightened king of the Isisi, under escort, but that was no satisfaction to him, for Tambeli had set the law at defiance and had broken for the bush.

News came down from Nushadombi at fitful intervals, because there was good reason why no courier should come from that country; better reason why its inhabitants should be bad travellers. Sanders hated Nushadombi with all the fierce hatred which a lawgiver extends to a lawless community. He hated it worse because there was always at the back of his mind the uneasy conviction that he was rightly responsible for its government.

This responsibility he had triumphantly repudiated on more occasions than one; but, none the less, there was a voice which spoke very softly to Sanders in his silent moments, and that voice said: "Nushadombi is British, if you've the courage."

It was as a sop to conscience that he spied upon the People-Who-Were-Not-All-Alike. His spies came and went. He lost a few men in the process, but that was the luck of the game. He learnt of little murders, of family feuds, and the like, but nothing of moment.

On a sultry afternoon in March Sanders was sitting on a rock overlooking the mouth of the big river, fishing for Cape salmon, and thinking, curiously enough, of the Nushadombi folk. Whilst so engaged Sergeant Abiboo, his Houssa orderly, ran towards him, picking a dainty way over the sharp stones, his long bayonet flapping his thigh with every wild leap he made.

Sanders looked up inquiringly.

"Lord," explained Abiboo, his hand steadfast at the salute, "there has come a listener from Nushadombi, having much to tell your honour."

"Let him come here," said Sanders.

"Lord, he cannot walk," said Abiboo simply; "for the Men-Who-Are-All-Not-Alike caught him, and he dies tonight by my way of thinking."

Sanders threw down his line and followed the Houssa back to the residency.

He found the spy lying on a rough, stretcher in the shade of the *stoep*.

The man looked round with a twisted grin as Sanders came up the steps that led to the verandah.

"*Ho*, Bogora!" said Sanders quietly, "what bad talk they make of you?"

"There is no talk worth the talking after tonight," said the man painfully. "As for me, I will make my report and sleep; and, lord, if I did not love you I would have died three nights ago."

Sanders made a brief examination of the man's injuries. He did not turn sick, for that was not his way—he covered the tortured limbs

222

with the blanket again.

"One Tambeli, a man of Isisi, now sits down with the people of Nushadombi!" gasped the spy, "and is regarded fearfully, being a chief; also it is said that he is a member of a great *ju-ju*, and has powerful friends among the chiefs. He knew me when other men would have passed me by, and by his orders they did what they did. Also, lord, they are for attacking different nations, such as the Isisi, the Ochori, and the N'Gombi."

"How soon?" asked Sanders.

"When the second moon comes after the rains."

"That we shall see," said Sanders. "As for Tambeli, I will settle with him, Bogoro, my brother, for I will carry your blood upon my hands and at my hands he shall die; all gods witness my words."

The wreck on the stretcher smiled.

"Sandi," he said slowly, "it is worth all to hear you call me brother."

And he closed his eyes as if to sleep, and died as Sanders watched him.

Bosambo came from his hut one morning just before the dawn. The city of the Ochori was very silent. There had been a dance the night before and in the very centre of the city a dull glow showed where the great fire had been.

Bosambo drew on his cloak of monkey skins, for the morning air was chill, and walked to the end of the village street, past the gardens and through the little jungle path that led to his own plantation. Here he paused, listening.

There was no sound save the distant "*hush, hush,*" of the small river as it swept over the rocks on its way to the River Beyond.

He squatted down in the shadow of a gum-tree and waited patiently. In an hour the sun would be up; before then he expected things to happen.

He had not been sitting longer than five minutes when he saw a figure moving towards him, coming from an opposite direction. It moved cautiously, halting now and then as though not certain of its ground. Bosambo rose without sound. "Friend," he said, "you move in silence."

"That is the royal way," said the figure.

"Life is full of silences," said Bosambo.

"None are so silent as the dead," was the response. They said these things glibly, as men repeating a ritual, as, indeed, they were.

"Sit with me, my brother," said Bosambo, and the other came to his side and sank down on his haunches.

"This I say to you, Bosambo," said the stranger, "that oaths are oaths, and men who swear to blood brotherhood do live and die one for the other."

"That is true," said Bosambo; "hence I have come; for when yesterday a strange forest man brought me a little water in a shell, and in that water a berry, I knew that the Silent Ones had need of me." The stranger nodded his head.

"Yes, it is many years since I swore the oath," mused Bosambo; "and I was very young, and the Silent Ones do not walk in the Ochori country, but in Nigeria, which is a month of marches away."

The man by his side made a little clicking noise with his mouth.

"I am here," he said importantly. "I, Tambeli, a traveller, also, by some accounted king of the People-Who-Are-Not All-Alike. Also a high man in the Order of the Silent Ones, ruthless avengers of slights and controllers of *ju-jus*."

"Lord, I gathered so much," said the humble Bosambo, "by your honour's summons. Now tell me how I may serve my brother, who is alone in this country?"

There was a note of careless interrogation in his voice, and the hand farthest from his visitor fingered the thin, long blade of a knife.

"Not alone, brother," said Tambeli, with decision, "for there are many brethren of our society who watch my coming and going."

"That is as well," said Bosambo truthfully, and quietly slipped the knife back into its wooden sheath.

"Now you can serve me thus," said Tambeli. "I am the king of a vengeful people who hate Sandi, and, behold, he is coming with soldiers to punish them. And in his coming he must pass through the Ochori country, sitting down with you for a day."

"All this is true," said Bosambo conventionally, and waited.

Tambeli put his hand beneath his robe and brought forth a short stick of bamboo.

"Bosambo," he said, "there is a spirit in this which will do little good to Sandi. For if you cut away the gum which seals one end you will find a powder such as the witchdoctors of my people make, and this can be emptied on the 'chop' of Sandi, and he will know nothing, yet he will die."

Bosambo took the stick without a word, and placed it in a little bag which hung at his waist.

"This you will do in fear of the Silent Ones, who are merciless."

"This I will do," said Bosambo gravely.

No more was said, the two men parting without further speech.

Bosambo returned to his hut as the eastern sky went pearl-grey, as though a shutter of heaven had been suddenly opened. He was a silent man that morning, and not even Fatima, his wife, evoked the response of speech.

In the afternoon he caught a dog straying in the forest, and, dragging it to a place where none could see, he gave it meat. It died very quickly, because Bosambo had sprinkled the food with the powder which Tambeli had brought.

Bosambo watched the unpleasant experiment without emotion. When he had hidden all evidence of his crime he returned to the village.

At night-time came Sanders, and Bosambo, warned of the urgency of his visit, alike by *lokali* message, and the evident fact that Sanders was travelling by night, had a great fire kindled on the beach to guide the *Zaire* to land.

The little stern wheeler came slowly into the light; naked men splashed overboard and waded ashore with hawsers at their shoulders, and the boat was safely moored.

Then Sanders came. "I sit with you for one day," he said, "being on my way to do justice."

"Lord, my house is in the hollow of your hands, and my life also," replied Bosambo magnificently. "There is the new hut which I built for you in the shadow of my house."

"I sleep on board," said Sanders shortly. "Tomorrow at dawn I am for the People-Who-Are-Not-All-Alike."

They walked together through the village, Sanders to stretch his legs; Bosambo, as his host, from courtesy. The chief knew that eyes were watching him, because he had received an intimation that the Silent Ones awaited his report at no great distance in the forest.

They reached the end of the village and turned to stroll back.

"Lord," said Bosambo, speaking earnestly, "if I say a thing to you which is of great moment, I beg your honour not to stand still in this place showing your anger."

"Speak on," said Sanders.

"If," continued Bosambo, "there came from your ship when you sleep to-night news that you were in pain and nigh to death, I would save you a long journey."

Sanders could not see his face, for the night was dark, and there was only a tangle of stars in the sky above to give light to the world.

"I know you to be a cunning man, Bosambo," he said quietly; "and I listen to you without doubt. Now you shall tell why this is, and after I will do that which is best."

"Lord," said Bosambo quietly, "I am your man, and by all things which men swear by I am ready to die for you, and it seems likely that I shall die one way or the other. For though I vex you, and you have cursed me many times, yet I desire that I and all my house should die before you suffered pain."

"That I believe," said Sanders shortly.

"Therefore, lord, trust me without the *palaver*."

"That I will do also," said Sanders.

At five o'clock in the morning—as we count time—Bosambo went swiftly to the forest, taking with him a long-handled native spade. He reeled a little in his walk; the farther he got the more unsteady became his gait.

There was a clearing less than a mile along the forest path, a notable rendezvous for lovers in the soft hours of the evening, and by night the feeding place of devils.

To this spot Bosambo made his way; for this was the place where the Silent Ones awaited report. He came staggering into the clearing, his spade on his shoulder, and five men watching him from the shadows knew that he was drunk.

He came to a halt by the tree of the Weaver Birds, and sat down heavily. From the fold of his cloak he produced a bottle, and this he raised to his lips.

"Bosambo," said Tambeli, coming noiselessly before him, "this is a good sight, for something tells me that you have done what should be done."

"He was my father," whined Bosambo, "and of my blood; he was a great lord, and now that he is dead the white people will come with the guns and say '*Ha-ha-ha!*' and eat me up."

He rolled his drooping head in misery.

"None shall know," soothed Tambeli the strong one, "for here are we all, the five silent men of the good order, and no man knows but us—we say nothing." He paused, and then added carefully: "So long as you do that which we bid, and send us tributes of women and corn."

Bosambo heard this programme for his enslavement without visible sign of distress.

"Why have you brought the spade?" asked Tambeli suddenly; "you do not bury Sandi here?"

"Who knows?" said the listless Bosambo.

He took the bottle from his pocket. It was a small square bottle, in which liquor, such as gin, illicitly and secretly trafficked, comes to the backlands.

"This I will take," said Tambeli. He reached out his hand and wrenched the bottle from the reluctant grasp of the other. "Men who drink spirits talk boastfully, and you shall not talk, Bosambo, till there are many rivers between me and Sandi's soldiers."

He took the little wooden stopper from the neck.

"Also," he said, "it is a long time since *ginni* came to me."

He waved his hand to his four shadowy companions.

"These are my brethren," he said, "and yours; therefore, in the way of the white people of the coast, let us drink for happiness."

He lifted the bottle and drank, then handed it to the man nearest him. One by one they took long draughts, then the bottle came to Bosambo.

"Tell me, did Sandi die in pain?" asked Tambeli.

"He died peacefully," said Bosambo.

Tambeli nodded.

"That is the proper way," he said, "for if he died with a great shouting there would come soldiers. Now none can say but that he died of the sickness *Mongo*, (literally the True Sickness, *i.e.*, any sickness which ends life.) There is no medicine like this, being prepared by a celebrated witchdoctor."

Bosambo said nothing for a while; then he spoke.

"Who is there to betray me?" he asked; "for if it comes to the ears of the High Lords at the Coast that I slew Sandi—"

"Have no fear," said Tambeli, with a little cough, "for there are none but these"—he waved his hand unsteadily—"and—they—speak—never." Indeed he spoke the truth, for the men were lying comfortably as though composing themselves for sleep.

"Up—up!" muttered Tambeli.

He went to kick the nearest sleeper, but his legs gave way, and he fell on his knees.

Bosambo watched him, deeply interested.

"Dog!"

Tambeli half turned his body toward the Chief of the Ochori, and spat out the word. He gathered all the great strength that was within him and leapt to his feet, launching himself straight at the other's throat.

But Bosambo was prepared.

His left hand shot out, caught Tambeli's shoulder, and half twisted him till he fell.

The man tried to rise, went down again, and soon he, too, fell asleep, uneasily at first, then calmly like a man tired.

Bosambo sat patiently.

After a decent interval, he looked round for the spade he had brought.

"Tambeli," he said as he went about his business—a hard business, for the digging of a grave big enough for five men needs much muscular strength—"you were foolish, or you would know that no man of my faith slays his friend and patron. And no man of very high temperament sits in the shadow of death. Oh, Silent Ones, you are very silent now!"

He covered up his work and wiped his steaming forehead, standing irresolutely by the grave. Then he scratched his chin thoughtfully. He had an uneasy recollection of a mission-school a thousand miles away and of sad-eyed fathers who had taught him certain rituals.

He dropped the spade and knelt awkwardly.

"Blessed Marki and Luko and Johann," he prayed, closing his eyes conventionally, "I have slain five men by poison, though they themselves took it without my invitation. Therefore they are dead, which is a good thing for us all. Amen."

CHAPTER 6

The Village of Irons

Sanders was used to the child-like buttering of his people, and accepted their praise without conviction. It was part of the game. He expected to be termed "Protector of Persecuted People," "Lord of Wisdom," and the like, and would have been suspicious if these terms were omitted, because that was all part of the game, and meant no more than the prefix "dear" in the epistles of the civilised.

Just so long as flattery and sycophancy ran along conventional lines, just so long as politeness followed a normal course, Sanders was satisfied; if compliment fell short or slopped over, all his intellectual bristles stood on end, and he looked around with narrowed eyes and a growl in his throat for the danger which lay somewhere to hand.

He was overlord of a million black people, subdivided by language, dialect, prejudice, custom, jealousy, and temperament into twenty-three distinct nations. The Bangeli, who lived close to the headquarters and were a selfish, bastard people, made up by accidental unions between Krooman, Congolaise, Angola folk, and Coast peoples, he did not heed, for they were civilised up to a point, and were wise in the way of white men. Also they were fearful of punishment, and just as the fear of the Lord is the beginning of wisdom, so is the fear of the Law the beginning of civilisation.

But beyond this people lay the fighting tribes, untouched by the trader, only slightly affected by the missionary. Warlike, unreasoning children, with a passion for litigation and a keen sense of justice. And it was Sanders' business and his pleasure to know these as they were—to study them as you study your own children, perhaps more carefully, for you take your children and their peculiarities for granted—and to adjust his attitude as he adjusted theirs, which rearrangement was usually made once in every twenty-four hours.

Sanders differed from ready-made Empire-builders in this respect, that, whilst his pompous superiors treated native people as an aggregate problem, Sanders dealt with them as individuals.

A certain Excellency once addressed him through a secretary's secretary, asking him to explain the prevalence of crime among the people of the Lesser Isisi, and Sanders answered naively (as it seemed to the superior folk of His Excellency's entourage) that the increase in crime was due to the dreams of a certain man named M'dali.

Sanders did not believe in clairvoyance, and when an agent brought him news that M'dali of Tembolini, in the Isisi country, had dreamt a dream in which he saw the river rising so that it flooded the middle island, which lay immediately opposite the village, he paid no heed.

Because he knew that the rains had been very heavy and that all the lesser rivers were swollen, and would in course of time swell the big river, and because the village of Tembolini stood so far above the level of the river that there was no danger to the people.

When a week later he learnt that all that M'dali dreamt had come to pass, he was neither impressed nor greatly interested. He thought M'dali was a shrewd guesser, and let it go at that.

When later he was told that on such and such a night M'dali had dreamt that E'timgolo, his second wife, would die—as she did—Sanders was mildly puzzled till he remembered that he had seen the woman the last time he was in the village, and that then she was in an advanced state of sleeping sickness. He gathered that M'dali had sufficient data at hand to justify his imagining.

News of other dreams came down the river—some first hand, and these were fairly commonplace; some, more wonderful, from mouth to mouth—and these were obviously exaggerated.

Sanders was a busy man about this time, and had neither leisure nor inclination to bother himself about such matters.

But one morning at break of day a canoe came swiftly, bearing Ahmed, chief of Sanders' secret spies.

"Lord," he said, presenting himself at Sanders' bedside and squatting on the floor, "there is a dreamer in the Isisi country."

"So I have heard," said Sanders in Arabic, and wearily. "I, too, am a dreamer, and I should have dreamt for another hour if you had not disturbed me."

"God knows I would not destroy your gracious sleep," said Ahmed. "And I pray God every morning and every night that you may slumber kindly; but this M'dali sells his dreams, and has a great following.

230

For he says to such an one, 'You shall give me a bag of salt or I will dream that you will die,' and, being afraid, the people pamper him in his desires."

"I see," said Sanders thoughtfully.

He dismissed his spy and rose.

In a little while he sent for his sergeant of police.

"Go you with three men, Abiboo," he said, "to the village of Tembolini, by the crocodile creek, and bring me M'dali, a dreamer of dreams."

"On my head and by my life," said Abiboo, and departed joyfully in a canoe.

He was ten days absent, and came back empty-handed.

"For the people threatened to kill me," he said, "M'dali having dreamt a dream that I was coming, and saying that if I took him every man of the village would be stricken blind. And, lord! knowing your disposition I did not desire a killing *palaver*, so came back without him, though, as you know, I am fearless of death."

"You did that which was right," said Sanders.

In an hour his steamboat was ready and had cast off, her sharp bows cleaving the black waters of the river, her little stern revolving rapidly.

In two days and a night the *Zaire* reached the village, and was met in mid-stream by the chief, one Kambori, an intelligent man.

"Lord," he said. "I tell you that if you take the dreamer the people will rise—not only the people of my village, but of the country round about—for he is regarded by all as a very holy man."

"I'll 'holy man' him," said Sanders in English, and continued his way to shore.

He entered the village with two Houssas at his elbow, and walked straight to the hut where M'dali sat in state.

Now M'dali had been a very ordinary man as Sanders knew him in the days before he began to dream.

He had been a spearer of fish, no more and no less well-to-do than hundreds of others.

Now he sat upon the carved stool that Lalinobi of Kusau had presented to him for dreaming that his wife would bear a male child, and he wore about his shoulders a robe of monkeys' tail which Tonda, chief of the Lulangu River, had presented when M'dali dreamt that he would outlive his brother.

He had various other gifts displayed—the carved stick in his hand, the string of iron beads about his neck, the worked copper bracelets about his arm, the little French mirror within reach, all testified mutely to the excellence of his clairvoyance.

He did not rise as Sanders came up.

Five hundred pairs of eyes were watching the Commissioner; all the countryside had assembled, for M'dali had dreamt of the Commissioner's coming.

"Hi, white man!" said M'dali loudly, "have you come for my dreams?"

Then he stood up quickly.

Twice Sanders landed at him with his pliant cane, and each blow got home.

Sanders heard the rustle of spears behind him, and turned—a heavy black automatic pistol in his hand.

"I had a dream," snarled Sanders, his pistol covering the nearest group. "I dreamt that a man raised his spear to me and died. And after he died his soul lived in a place filled with fishes, and every morning the fishes fed little by little upon it, and every night the soul grew again."

They dropped their spears. With their knuckles to their teeth—a sure sign of perturbation—they regarded him with horror and consternation.

"I dreamt," said Sanders, "that M'dali came with me to the Village of Irons, and when he left, all his property and all the rich presents of the foolish were divided amongst the people of this village."

There was a little murmur of approval, but some there were who regarded him sullenly, and Sanders judged these to be the country folk.

He turned to M'dali, a dazed man rubbing the growing weals on his shoulder with a shaking hand.

"*Ih*, dreamer!" said Sanders softly, "speak now, and tell these people how, when you leave them, all things shall be well."

The man hesitated, raised his sulky eyes to the level of the Commissioner's, and read the cold message they carried.

"People," he said shakily, "it is as our lord says."

"So you dreamt," suggested Sanders.

"So I dreamt," said M'dali, and there was a big sigh of relief.

"Take him to the boat," said Sanders. He spoke in Arabic to Abiboo. "Let none speak with him on your life."

He followed the Houssas with their crestfallen prisoner, and losing no time, cast off.

This ended the episode of the dreamer—for a while.

But though M'dali worked in the Village of Irons for the good of the Empire, his work went on, for he had been a busy man. There were unaccountable deaths. Men and women lay down in health and woke only to die. And none thought it remarkable or made report, for M'dali had dreamt thus, and thus it happened.

Yet rumour has feet to carry and mouth to tell; and in course of time Sanders went up country with a hastily-summoned doctor from headquarters, and there were people who were sorry to see him.

Men who had lost inconvenient wives, others who had buried rich relations, wives who found freedom by the fulfilment of M'dali—his dreams—sat down and waited for Sanders, gnawing their knuckles.

Sanders administered justice without any other evidence than his doctor could secure in unsavoury places; but it was effective, and M'dali, a chopper of wood in the Village of Irons, saw many familiar faces.

The Village of Irons stands on a tongue of land which thrusts the Isisi River to the left and the Bokaru River to the right. It is the cleanest village in Sanders' land, save only headquarters; but nobody appreciated its cleanliness except Sanders.

Here the streams run so swiftly that even strong swimmers dare not face them. At the base of the triangle a broad canal had been cut for five or six hundred yards connecting the two rivers, so that the little tongue of land was less a peninsula than an island, and a difficult island to leave—since a barbed-wire fence had been erected on both sides of the canal. Moreover, this canal was the abiding-place of three croco-diles—thoughtfully placed there by Mr. Commissioner Sanders—and their egress at either end of the canal was barred by stout stakes.

The village itself was divided into three parts, one for men, one for women, and a third—and this overlooking the only landing-place—for half a company of Houssas.

Though it was called the Village of Irons, none but shameless or hardened men wore the shackles of bondage, and life ran smoothly in this grim little village, save and except that the men were on one side of a tall wire and the women on the other. M'dali arrived, and was given a number and a blanket. He was also told off to a hut with six other prisoners.

"I am M'dali of Isisi," he said, "and Sanders has sent me here be-cause I dreamt."

"That is strange," said the headman of the hut, "for he sent me here because I beat one of his spies—I and my brother—till he died."

"I came here," said another man, "because I was a chief and made war—behold I am Tembeli of the Lesser Isisi."

One by one they introduced themselves and retailed him their discreditable exploits with simple pride.

"I am a dreamer of dreams," said M'dali in explanation. "When I dream a thing it happens, for I am gifted by devils and see strange things in my sleep."

"I see," said Tembeli wisely. "You are mad."

It is not difficult to explain how it came about that M'dali secured a hold upon the credulity and faith of his new companions.

There is a story that he predicted the death by drowning of one of the guards. Certainly such a fatality occurred. Every new prisoner from Tombolini was a fresh witness to his powers.

And in his most fluent manner M'dali dreamt for them. And this is one great dream he had:

It was that Sandi came to inspect the Village of Irons, and that when he reached a certain hut six men fell upon him and one cut his throat, and all the soldiers ran away terrified, and the prisoners released themselves, and there was no more bother.

He dreamt this three nights in succession.

When he retailed his first dream, Tembeli, to whom he related it, said thoughtfully:

"That is a good thought, yet we are without any weapon, so it cannot come true."

"In my dream tonight it will be revealed," said M'dali.

And on the next morning he told them how he had seen in his vision a Congo man among the prisoners, and how this Congo man carried a little razor stuck in his hair.

And, truth to tell, there was such a Congo man who carried such a razor.

"Who struck the blow?" asked Tembeli. "That is a matter which requires great revelation."

Accordingly M'dali dreamt again, and discovered that the man who killed Sanders was Korforo, a half-witted prisoner from Akasava.

All things were now ready for the supreme moment. There was a certain missionary lady, a Miss Ruth Glandynne, who had come to the Great River to work for humanity.

There were reasons why Sanders should not be on excellent terms with her, not the least of these being his ever-present fear for her safety, and the knowledge that she did not know as much about native people as she thought she knew—which was the gravest risk.

One day he received a letter from her asking permission to visit the Village of Irons.

Sanders groaned.

He was not proud of the village—it advertised the lawlessness of a section of his people, and he was absurdly sensitive on this point. Moreover, he was, as he knew, a gauche showman.

With some ill-grace, he replied that he would be ready to show her the village at any time that was convenient, except—here followed a maddening list of forbidden dates.

In the compilation of this list Sanders showed more than usual guile. He racked his brain for exceptions. On such a date she could not visit the village because of "quarterly inspection," on another because of "medical inspection"; yet another forbidden day was the "inspection of equipment."

With great ingenuity he concocted thirty-five periods in the year, varying from one to seven days, when the convict establishment was not visible; and he hoped most earnestly that she would be sufficiently annoyed to give up the visit altogether.

To his despair, she replied immediately, choosing a day that was sandwiched between a spurious "appeal day" and a "mending week"— both of which occasions were the products of Sanders' fertile imagination.

She came downstream in her canoe, paddled by twenty men, and Sanders met her half-way and transferred her to his steamer.

Sanders in dazzling white, but a little stiff and very formal.

"If you don't mind my saying so," he said, "I'd much rather you hadn't attempted this little jaunt."

"It is hardly a jaunt, Mr. Sanders," she replied coldly. "I have a duty to these people—you admit that they are seldom seen by missionaries—and I should feel that I had tailed in that duty if I did not take the opportunity which you so kindly offer me" (Sanders swore to himself at her brazen effrontery) "of visiting them."

From under the shade of his big helmet Sanders glanced at her. .

"I shouldn't like you to go through life under the impression that I wanted you to come," he said bluntly—and Ruth Glandynne's nose rose ever so slightly, for if she was a missionary she was also a woman.

They reached the Village of Irons at eight o'clock one blazing morning.

"Now what the devil does this mean?" said Sanders. For there were only two Houssas on the beach—one of them on sentry duty and the other his relief.

"Lord!" said this man when Sanders stepped ashore. "The men of the company have journeyed downstream to a Place of Palms."

"By whose orders?" asked Sanders.

"It was revealed them, lord," said the man, "they being of the Sufi sect, that the blessed son of the Prophet would appear to them in this place and show them many miracles."

A light dawned on the Commissioner, and he half smiled, though in his heart he raged.

"It seems that M'dali the Dreamer still dreams," he said. "There will be some whipping here tomorrow."

His first impulse was to send the girl straight back; he had no fear that the temporary withdrawal of the guard would lead to any serious consequence—that thought never for one moment entered his head—but he was a cautious man, and his instinct was against taking risk of any kind.

He was half-way back to the boat when he decided that, as the girl was here and had, moreover, come a long way, he had better get the thing over.

"You had best confine yourself to the women's quarters," he said. "I will send Abiboo with you—for myself, I have a little *palaver* with one M'dali."

He unlocked the steel gate that led to the women's compound, and stood watching the slim white figure of the girl as she moved up the tiny street—the straight, broad-shouldered Houssa at her elbow.

Then he crossed the lane which separated the men from the women, opened the gate, and entered, double-locking it behind him.

None came to speak to him, which was strange. Usually they clamoured to him for a hearing, good-naturedly calling him by his familiar name—which in English is "The-Little-Butcher-Bird-Who-Flies-by-Night."

Now they sat before their huts, chins on knees, watching him silently, fearfully.

"I don't like this," said Sanders.

He slipped his hand carelessly in his pocket and pushed down the safety catch of his Browning.

His second finger searched carefully for the butt of the pistol to feel if the magazine was pushed home.

He stood on a bare patch of well-swept roadway, and had an unin-

236

terrupted view of the street.

One quick glance he gave to the right. He could see Ruth talking to some native women—a group of three who squatted at her feet.

Behind her, clear of the group, was Abiboo, his Winchester carbine—a gift of Sanders—in the crook of his arm.

As the Commissioner looked he saw the Houssa furtively bring the lever back.

"Abiboo is loading," said something in Sanders' brain.

His eyes came back to the men's village. There was no move. The convicts sat before their huts, silent and expectant. A thrill of apprehension ran through his frame. He glanced again at Abiboo. He had unostentatiously withdrawn still further from the women and now he was holding the rifle with both hands—the right gripping the butt, the left supporting the barrel.

Then he turned his head slightly and nodded, and Sanders knew the signal was for him.

Sanders turned swiftly. Whatever danger there was lay in the women's village. He walked quickly back the way he came. Four men who had sat quietly rose and came out to meet him, showing no sign of haste.

"Lord, we have a petition," began one.

"Go back to your hut, Tembeli!" said Sanders steadily. "I will come again for your petition."

"*Crack!*"

Abiboo was firing into a hut, and the girl was flying along the street towards the gate.

All this Sanders saw as he turned his head, and then the four men were upon him.

A great hand covered his face, a cruel thumb fumbled for his eye. Tembeli went down shot through the heart, and Sanders tore himself free. He raced for the gate, taking out the key as he went.

He turned and shot at two of his pursuers, but they had no heart for the fight.

His steady hand unlocked the gate and closed it behind him. He saw Abiboo on the ground in the midst of a swaying tangle of men. The girl had disappeared. Then he saw her struggling with two of the women, and the half-witted Koforo slashing at her over the shoulders.

He reached the women as one grasped the girl by her hair and pulled back her head.

Koforo saw him coming, and dropped his hand.

"*Ho*, father!" he said, in his foolish, jocose way. "I am to kill you because you are a devil!"

The women shrank back, and Sanders caught the fainting girl by the waist and swung her out of reach.

Koforo came at him mouthing and grimacing, the little spade-shaped razor in his hand.

Sanders shot definitely because he had only five more cartridges, then he turned his attention to Abiboo.

He was lying on the ground insensible; his assailants had fled, for the sentry and his relief were firing through the wire-netting—and your trained Houssa is a tolerably good shot.

Together they bore the girl to the boat, and Abiboo was revived, stitched, and bandaged.

At four in the afternoon the crestfallen guard returned, and Sanders made an inspection of both camps.

"Lord," said one who had been but a passive conspirator, "it was the plan to take you in the women's quarters. Therefore certain men concealed themselves in the huts, thinking your lordship would not carry your little gun amongst women. All this was dreamt by M'dali, who has escaped."

"No man escapes from the Village of Irons," said Sanders. "Which way did M'dali go?"

The man pointed to the wire fence by the little canal.

Sanders made his way to the fence and looked down into the weed-grown stream.

"I saw him climb the first fence," said his informant; "but the second I did not see him climb."

The Commissioner stooped, and, picking up a handful of grass, threw it at a green log that lay on the water.

The log opened a baleful eye and growled hatefully, for he had fed well, and resented the interruption to his slumbers.

CHAPTER 7

The Thinker and the Gum-Tree

There are three things which are beyond philosophy and logic.

Three things which turn mild men to rage and to the performance of heroic deeds. The one is love, the other is religion, and the third is land.

There was a man of the Isisi people who was a great thinker. He thought about things which were beyond thought, such as the stars and the storms and time, which began and ended nowhere.

Often he would go to the edge of the river and, sitting with his chin on his knees, ponder on great matters for days at a time. The people of the village—it was Akalavi by the creek—thought, not un-naturally, that he was mad, for this young man kept himself aloof from the joyous incidents of life, finding no pleasure in the society of maidens, absenting himself from the dances and the feasts that make up the brighter side of life on the river.

K'maka—such was this man's name—was the son of Yoko, the son of N'Kema, whose father was a fierce fighter in the days of the Great King. And on the dam side he went back to Pikisamoko, who was also a strong and bloody man, so that there was no hint of softness in his pedigree. "Therefore," said Yoko, his father, "he must be mad, and if the matter can be arranged without Sandi knowing, we will put out his eyes and take him a long way into the forest. There he will quickly die from hunger or wild beasts."

And all the relations who were bidden to the family *palaver* agreed, because a mad son is an abomination. He wanders about the village, and in his wanderings or in the course of his antics, he breaks things and does damage for which the family is legally responsible. They talked this matter over for the greater part of the night and came to no decision. The *palaver* was resumed the next day, and the elder of

239

the family, a very old and a very wise chief from another village, gave his decision. "If he is mad," he said, "by all laws and customs he should be destroyed. Now I am a very clever man, as you all know, for I have lived for more years than any of you can remember. Let me, therefore, test K'maka, lest he be not mad at all, but only silly, as young men are when they come to the marrying age."

So they summoned K'maka to the council, and those who went in search of him found him lying on a soft bank in the forest. He was lying face downwards, his head in his hands, watching a flower.

"K'maka," said the man who sought him out, "what do you do?"

"I am learning," said K'maka simply; "for this weed teaches me many things that I did not know before."

The other looked down and laughed.

"It is a weed," he said, "bearing no fruit, so therefore it is nothing."

"It is alive," said K'maka, not removing his eyes from the thing of delicate petals; "and I think it is greater than I because it is obedient to the law."

"You are evidently mad," said his cousin, with an air of finality; "this is very certain."

He led him back to the family conference.

"I found him," he said importantly, "looking at weeds and saying that they were greater than he."

The family looked darkly upon K'maka and the old chief opened the attack.

"K'maka, it is said that you are mad; therefore, I, being the head of the family, have called the blood together that we may see whether the charge is true. Men say you have strange thoughts—such as the stars being land afar."

"That is true, my father," said the other.

"They also say that you think the sun is shining at night."

"That also I think," said K'maka; "meaning that it shines somewhere. For it is not wise to believe that the river is greater than the sun."

"I perceive that you are indeed mad," said the old man calmly; "for in what way do the sun and the river meet?"

"Lord," said the young man earnestly, "behold the river runs whether it is day or night, whether you walk or sleep, whether you see it or whether it is unseen. Yet the foolish think that if they do not see a thing, then that thing does not exist. And is the river greater than the

240

sun? For if the river runs by night, being part of the Great Way, shall the sun, which is so much mightier and so much more needful to the lands, cease to shine?"

The old chief shook his head.

"None but a man who is very mad would say such a thing as this," he said; "for does not the sun become the moon by night, save on the night when it sleeps? And if men sleep and goats sleep, and even women sleep, shall not the sun sleep, creeping into a hole in the ground, as I myself have seen it?"

They dismissed K'maka then and there. It seemed useless to talk further.

He slept in a hut by himself. He was late in returning to his home that night, for he had been watching bats in the forest; but when he did he found six cousins waiting. They seized him; he offered no resistance.

They bound him hand and foot to a long pole and laid him in the bottom of a canoe. Then his six cousins got in with him and paddled swiftly downstream. They were making for the Forest of Devils, which is by the Silent River—a backwater into which only crocodiles go to lay their eggs, for there are sandy shoals which are proper for the purpose.

At dawn they stopped, and, lighting a fire, cooked their meal. They gave their prisoner some fish and *manioc*.

"There is a hungry time waiting you, brother," said one of the cousins; "for we go to make an end of you, you being mad."

"Not so mad am I," said K'maka calmly, "but that I cannot see your madness."

The cousin made no retort, knowing that of all forms of lunacy that which recognised madness in others was the most hopeless.

The sun was well up when the canoe continued its journey, K'maka lying in the bottom intensely interested in the frantic plight of two ants who had explored the canoe in a spirit of adventure.

Suddenly the paddles ceased.

Steaming up stream, her little hull dazzling white from a new coat of paint, her red and white deck awning plainly to be seen, came the *Zaire*, and the tiny blue ensign of Mr. Commissioner Sanders was hanging lazily from the one stub of a mast that the vessel boasted.

"Let us paddle nearer the shore," said the chief of the cousins, "for this is Sandi; and if he sees what we carry he will be unkind."

They moved warily to give the little steamer a wide berth.

But Sanders of the River, leaning pensively over the rail of the forebridge, his big helmet tilted back to keep the sun from his neck, had seen them. Also, he had detected concern in the sudden cessation of paddling, alarm in the energy with which it was resumed, and guilt confessed in the new course.

His fingers beckoned the steersman, and the helm went over to port. The *Zaire* swung across to intercept the canoe.

"This man," said the exasperated chief cousin, "has eyes like the *okapi*, which sees its enemies through trees."

He stopped paddling and awaited the *palaver*.

"What is this, Sambili?" asked Sanders, as the steamer came up and a boat hook captured the tiny craft.

Sanders leant over the side rail and addressed the cousin by name.

"Lord," said Sambili, "I will not lie to you; this man is my cousin, and is mad; therefore we take him to a witchdoctor who is famous in such matters."

Sanders nodded, and flecked the white ash of his cheroot into the water.

"I know the river better than any man, yet I do not know of such a doctor," he said. "Also I have heard that many mad people have been taken to the Forest of Devils and have met a doctor whom they have not seen. And his name is *Ewa*, which means Death."

Two of his Houssas hauled the trussed man aboard.

"Release him," said Sanders.

"Lord," said the cousin, in agitation, "he is very mad and very fierce."

"I also am fierce," said Sanders; "and men say that I am mad, yet I am not bound to a pole."

Released from his bondage, K'maka stood up shakily, rubbing his numbed limbs.

"They tell me you are mad, K'maka," said Sanders.

K'maka smiled, which was a bad sign, for native men, far gone in sleeping sickness and touching the verge of madness, often smile in this way. Sanders watched him curiously.

"Master," said K'maka, "these cousins of mine think I am mad because I think."

"What manner of things do you think, K'maka?" asked Sanders gently.

The other hesitated. "Lord, I fear to say, lest you, too, should believe in my madness."

"Speak," said Sanders, "and have no fear; for I am as your father and your king, being placed here to rule you by a man who is very high in the council of kings."

K'maka drew a long breath.

"I think of life," he said, "and of the stars; of why men do certain acts. I think of rivers. Lord," he asked, "why does a stone thrown into still water make little ripples in true circles widening, widening until the waves reach beyond sight?"

Sanders looked at him narrowly. He had heard of this thinker.

"Go on," he said.

"Lord, this also I think," Said K'maka, encouraged, "that I am nothing, that all is nothing"—he waved his hand to the white hot world—"that you, our lord, are nothing."

"This is a shameful thing to say," said the chief cousin, shocked, "and proves beyond doubt that he is mad."

"Why am I nothing, K'maka?" asked Sanders quietly.

"Lord," said the man gravely, "that-which-is-not-always is nothing."

"Hear him!" appealed Sambili in despair. "Hear this madman. Oh *ko ko!* Now, K'maka, you have shown your madness to our lord beyond doubt."

He waited for Sanders to summon the Man of Irons to shackle K'maka to the deck. Instead, Sanders was leaning against the rail, his head sunk in thought.

"K'maka," he said at last, "it appears to me that you are a strange man; yet you are not mad, but wiser than any black man I have seen. Now you are so wise that if I leave you with your brethren they will surely kill you, for stupid men hate the learned, and it seems to me that you have too much learning."

He gave orders that K'maka should be housed with the crew.

As for the cousins, he turned them into their canoe.

"Go in peace," he said, "for you have rid yourself of your 'madman' and have saved yourself a hanging—I will have no putting out of eyes in this land."

Sanders had no man handy to whom he might speak of the thinker, for his two subordinates were down with fever and on leave at the coast. He was inclined towards experiments. Bosambo of Monrovia had been an experiment, and a most successful one. Just now Bosambo was being a nuisance, as witness this journey which Sanders was making.

Contiguous to the land of the Ochori was a narrow strip of territory, which acted as a tiny buffer state between the Ochori and the Isisi. It occupied a peculiar position, inasmuch as though completely unimportant, it was desired by both the Ochori and the Isisi, and had at various times been absorbed by both, only to be ruthlessly restored to its neutrality by the iron hand of Sanders. There was no reason in the world why both nations should not have free access and passage through the Lombobo—as it was called—and a wise chief would have so ordered things that whilst Ochori man and Isisi moved in and through it, neither nation should claim the right to lordship.

This chief Sanders had been long in finding. He had appointed many. Kombanava the N'Gombi, who sold his kingship to the Isisi for a thousand rods and twenty bags of salt; Olambo of Akasava, who had hardly been installed before he bartered away his rights to Bosambo of the Ochori; M'nabo, the coast man; Tibini, the Lesser Isisi man; a whole string of little chiefs of Lombobo had come and gone.

Sanders thought of these, sitting under the awning of the bridge, as the *Zaire* drove through the black-yellows waters of the Big River.

He was very patient, and his was the patience of years. He was not discouraged, though the bitterness of a recent failure still rankled. For he had placed one Sakadamo in the seat of chieftainship, and he had known Sakadamo for years.

Yet once Sanders was out of sight, the mild Sakadamo, stiff with pride, had gathered his fighting men, and had led them with fine impartiality against Ochori and Isisi, and in the end had sold the country to both.

For which offence Sakadamo was at the moment working out a sentence of two years' labour in the Village of Irons, and Lombobo was chiefless.

Sanders smoked two cigars over the matter, then he sent for K'maka the Thinker.

They brought him, a tall young man, inclined to thinness. Sanders took him in from the broad crown of his woolly head to the big feet which ended his thin legs. He had knobby knees, and the skin cloak which partially covered him revealed the same tendency to thinness.

Sanders put his age at nineteen, which was probably an accurate estimate.

"K'maka," he said, after his survey, "such a man as you it is not usual to meet, nor have I met your like. Now I know you to be a man above ambition, above hates, and understanding large matters of life."

"Lord, I am one who thinks, and I myself do not know whether my thoughts be mad thoughts or whether they are high above the common thoughts of men."

"Take to yourself the pleasure of knowing that you are not mad," said Sanders drily. "Surely I believe this, and to give you a sign of my faith I am for making you chief of Lombobo, standing in my place, giving and taking justice, and laying over the fiery spirit of your people the waters of your wisdom."

"Lord, I will do as you wish," said K'maka.

And so it came about that at a great *palaver* at which the headmen and lesser directors of the people were assembled, Sanders made the Thinker paramount chief and lord of the Lombobo tribe, hanging about his neck the steel chain and medal of his rank and office. To a separate *palaver* Bosambo and the Ring of the Isisi were summoned, and plain words were spoken.

After the Isisi had departed Sanders took the young chief a journey to the very edge of his new domain, and with them went Bosambo.

In a clearing on the very border, and by the side of the path which connected the two little countries, grew a great gum-tree, and here the party halted.

"Bosambo and K'maka," said Sanders, "this tree shall mark which is Ochori and which is Lombobo. For all that is on one side belongs to one and all that is on the other belongs to the other."

They looked at the tree, the two chiefs; they regarded it long and attentively.

"Lord," said Bosambo at length, "your meaning is clear, yet in whose country does this tree stand?"

It was a question worthy of Bosambo.

"That half which faces the Ochori is in the Ochori country; that half which faces Lombobo is in the Lombobo country," said Sanders.

One last warning he gave to K'maka.

"To Ochori and to Isisi," he said, "you will give communion and freedom of trade; you shall hinder none, nor help any at the expense of the other. You shall be wise and large."

"Lord, I will do this," said K'maka, nodding his head, "for the things that grow and perish are nothing and only the spirits of men endure."

With which wise saying in his ears Sanders took his departure, happy in the belief that Providence had sent him at last the solution of the buffer state problem.

It is placed on record that K'maka began his rule with wisdom.

The Lombobo people, used by now to strange chiefs, did their best to help him to destruction. They brought forward litigation for his judgment—litigation which would have taxed the sagacity of a Supreme Court or the Judicial Committee of the Privy Council. As for instance:

"If a man buys a wife, paying for her with two bags of salt, and she be a vixen, and, moreover, undesirable from many points of view, how shall he recover the price he paid for her when the salt has been capsized out of his own canoe, rowed by two of his own paddlers and two of his father-in-law's paddlers?" Also:

"A man has borrowed a neighbour's spear to go hunting, and has invariably paid for the loan by a proportion of the kill. One day he went hunting with a defective spear, and became lamed by a leopard. Can he claim compensation because the spear was a bad one if the lender can prove that its defective condition is due to the carelessness of a mutual cousin?"

These were two of the problems they propounded, sitting in a solemn circle at *palaver*, and the Thinker judged at length. He was four days delivering his judgment in the first case. His people sat spellbound, hypnotised by words. They did not understand his philosophy; they could not follow his reasoning; they were altogether fogged as to whether he decided upon the one side or the other; and at the end, when he raised his two hands according to custom and said, "The *palaver* is finished," they went away pleasantly confounded.

"We have a chief," said the headman of the fishing village by the river, "who is wiser than all other men; so wise that we cannot understand him."

K'maka busied himself with mundane affairs. He even took a girl of the Isisi to wife. Also he allowed free passage to Isisi and Ochori alike. Both nations sent him presents, which he accepted. On the third day of his chieftainship his headman had come to tell him that the Ochori were fishing in Lombobo waters, and that the Isisi were hunting in the Lombobo forests.

"Let this be," said M'maka, "for the forests and the rivers are for all, and there are no boundaries to necessity. For this is not my land nor my river; nor is it yours; being rather for all men, who find therein certain requirements."

This was as Sanders required, and when the news came to the Commissioner, as it did, he was pleased.

Then an evil gossip brought to K'maka stories of his girl-wife, who was attractive.

"I am no man to set a fence about desire," said K'maka; "nor shall man or woman in this, my land, be enslaved by custom."

Two months passed smoothly. K'maka grew in influence daily, his crowning achievement being a judgment which took nine days to deliver.

Then a headman came with a plaint against the Ochori.

"Lord, they cut wood in the Lombobo country and carry it to their city," he said.

"The wood is free to all," said K'maka.

He sat on the little carved stool in the centre of the half-moon of huts which constituted his administrative headquarters.

"Yet," he went on, "since this is my land and the people my people, and since I have been set to guard them, it is a shameful thing that robbers should spoil this land."

A fortnight after this a party of Ochori hunters came into the Lombobo country hot on the trail of an elephant. K'maka sent a regiment to seize them and impound the elephant.

"For this I say," said he to his captives, "and my words are of such wisdom that even Sandi bows before them: That which is on one side of a certain tree on the Ochori side is mine and what is on the other side is your master's."

"Lord," said the chief huntsman, "it was a *palaver* that there should be free hunting in your land."

"And free fishing," said K'maka with savage sarcasm, "and free wood-cutting by Death! And that thief, your master, would spoil my beautiful land, sucking it I dry, and make mock of me—a chief of a thousand spears! Go back to Bosambo and summon him to meet me by the gum-tree on the road."

The empty-handed huntsmen returned home to meet with the wrath of their lord.

Bosambo swore in Karo, in Arabic, in Bomongo, in Swahili, and in English, calling K'maka a "dam black nigger," and casting reflections upon his parentage. At an appointed time the two chiefs met, K'maka being late in arriving.

"Lord Bosambo," said he, speaking from a place which was on the Lombobo side of the gum-tree, "I have shame in my heart that I did not come at the hour. But I have a wife who had a lover, putting shame on me, and this day I killed her and him according to the law."

"These things happen," said Bosambo. "Now have I come to you,

K'maka the Thinker, because of certain strange occurrences which have come to my ears. It is said that you have forbidden the Ochori to hunt or chop wood in your territory."

"That is true," said K'maka, "for the land this side of the gum-tree is mine, and I am chief of the country as far as your eye sees."

"The land is for all," said Bosambo with some unction.

"The world is for all," corrected the Thinker; "yet rabbits do not nest in trees or eagles burrow in the earth. Each kind lives in the place appointed, and it is appointed the Ochori should live on the one side and the Lombobo on the other."

Bosambo was aroused.

"It seems that you are an avaricious dog," he said, "and if I chop wood to the edge of my country, behold I begin!"

He called for an axe, and they brought him one thin of blade and very sharp.

He struck twice at the tree.

"Bosambo," said K'maka, quivering with rage, "what do you do?"

"Dispenser of Justice," mocked Bosambo, "former of fat words, talking fish and breeder of wisdom as a dirty hut breds vermin, I go to cut my tree."

"It is my tree!" roared K'maka and reached behind him for a throwing spear.

"One half is yours," said Bosambo, chopping steadily, yet with an eye to danger, "and behold! I cut down that half which is mine. And if by your wisdom you keep your half standing, then you are a prince amongst thinkers."

He continued cutting whilst K'maka watched, boiling with rage.

"If you continue in your evil practice," he said, "what shall prevent the tree falling."

"Nothing," said Bosambo significantly, "for the nights of wind are coming, and the wind blows towards the Ochori—and behold! when the tree falls it shall belong to me!"

K'maka drew back his hand swiftly and threw his spear.

★★★★★★

"They are in that clump of bush," said Sanders. His face was reeking wet, and there was a thin trickle of blood on his face.

"I'll put a couple of shells into 'em," said the Houssa captain. "These Lombobo people fight fairly well."

Sanders said nothing. He bared his white teeth in a smile, but he was not really amused.

"Ahmet," said the Houssa captain, kneeling on the deck and keeping his field glasses fixed on the little patch of wood that hid the enemy, "as you love the faith and hate all Kaffirs, do not drop your shell short again, or I will beat you on the feet."

"Lord, the light is bad," said the gunner. He brought the muzzle of the gun a little higher and fired.

This time the shell fell true. Over the trees a white ball of smoke came into existence, and they heard the "*krock*" of its shell as it burst.

The Houssa captain rose and walked to where Sanders stood.

"Exactly what is all the bother about?" he asked.

Sanders said nothing for a while.

"Bosambo had something to do with it," he said, "yet the rascal was only acting according to his rights. K'maka is raising Cain. He has fought the Isisi and raided their territory; he has pushed back the Ochori to the edge of their city—they had to fight like the devil to save it. K'maka has proclaimed himself king of the Ochori, the Isisi, and the Lombobo, and has sent to the Akasava and the N'Gombi to bring him presents and do homage."

His voice choked; then the humour of it appealed to him, and he laughed.

He went ashore with the Houssas, and led the section which stormed the last stockade. Revolver in hand, he raced across the little clearing, the Houssas, with fixed bayonets, flanking him.

K'maka, surrounded by the remnant of his captains, made a fierce resistance, but it was futile.

Suddenly his men flung down their spears and bolted.

"Take that man!"

A group of Houssas flung themselves upon the struggling philosopher and bore him down.

They brought him, bleeding but defiant, before Sanders, and for the space of two minutes they looked at one another.

"K'maka," said Sanders at length, "you have done a terrible thing, for you have brought war to this land by your arrogance and pride."

"White man," said K'maka haughtily, "I am a king and the master of these countries—I do not speak with servants—therefore, little man, bring me before your king that we may speak, equal to equal."

Sanders said nothing, then:

"Catch him!" he said quickly.

For K'maka went suddenly limp, his knees gave way and he slid down to the earth.

He was wounded to death, as Sanders saw when he examined him.

They carried the man to the shade of a tree, and Sanders sat by him.

The man looked up at the Commissioner.

"Lord," he said faintly, "I think I go beyond your punishment."

"That is true, K'maka," said Sanders softly, "and I could have wished you had gone before you brought all this sorrow to the Lombobo people."

K'maka shook his head.

"This is the way," he said drowsily, "for the living things prey upon the living things, birds upon insects, leopards upon birds, men upon leopards, and, since there is nought greater than man, then man preys upon himself. This is ordained—"

They gave him water and he opened his eyes again.

"Lord," he said, and now he spoke with difficulty, "I have discovered in my thinking the greatest truth in the world."

A strange light came into his eyes; they danced eagerly with the greatness of his discovery.

"All your wise men do not know this," he whispered; "death is——"

Sanders waited, but K'maka the Thinker carried his secret with him to the land of sleep.

CHAPTER 8

Nine Terrible Men

There were nine terrible men in the Forest of O'tomb', so native report had it.

Nine terrible men who lived on an island set in a swamp. And the swamp was hard to come by, being in the midst of a vast forest. Only a monkey or a leopard could find a way to the inhabitants of this island—they themselves being privy to the secret ways.

No man of the Isisi, of the N'Gombi, of the Akasava, or of the river tribes, attempted to track down the nine, for, as it was generally known, most powerful *ju-jus* guarded all paths that led to the secret place.

Nine outlawed men, with murder and worse upon their souls, they came together. God knows how, and preyed upon their world.

They raided with impunity, being impartial as to whether Isisi or N'Gombi paid toll.

By night they would steal forth in single file, silent as death, no twig cracking in their path, no word spoken. As relentless as the soldier ant in his march of destruction, they made their way without hindrance to the village they had chosen for the scene of their operations, took what they wanted and returned.

Sometimes they wanted food, sometimes spears—for these lords of the woods were superior to craftsmanship—sometimes a woman or two went and never came back.

Such lawless communities were not uncommon. Occasionally very ordinary circumstances put an end to them; some there were that flourished, like the People-Who-Were-Not-All-Alike.

The Nine Terrible Men of the O'tomb' existed because nothing short of an army corps could have surrounded them, and because, as Sanders thought, they were not a permanent body, but dispersed at times to their several homes.

Sanders once sent two companies of Houssas to dislodge the nine, but they did nothing, for the simple reason that never once did they get within shooting distance. Then Sanders came himself, and caught little else than a vicious attack of malarial fever.

He sent messages to all the chiefs of the people within a radius of a hundred miles to kill at sight any of the nine, offering certain rewards. After three palpably inoffensive men of the Ochori tribe had been killed, and the reward duly claimed, Sanders countermanded the order.

For two years the nine ravaged at will, then a man of the Isisi, one Fembeni, found grace.

Fembeni became a Christian, though there is no harm in that. This is not satire, but a statement with a reservation. There are certain native men who embrace the faith and lose quality thereby, but Fembeni was a Christian and a better man—except—

Here is another reservation.

Up at Mosunkusu a certain Ruth Glandynne laboured for the cause, she, as I have previously described, being a medical missionary, and pretty to boot.

White folk would call her pretty because she had regular features, a faultless complexion, and a tall, well-modelled figure.

Black folk thought she was plain, because her lips were not as they should be by convention; nor was she developed according to their standards.

Also, from N'Gombi point of view, her fair, long hair was ridiculous, and her features "like a bird."

Mr. Commissioner Sanders thought she was very pretty indeed—when he allowed himself to think about her.

He did not think about her more often than he could help, for two reasons—the only one that is any business of yours and mine being that she was an enormous responsibility. He had little patches of white hair on either side of his temple—when he allowed his hair to grow long enough for these to become visible—which he called grimly his "missionary hairs." The safety of the solitary stations set in the wilds was a source of great worry.

You must understand that missionaries are very good people. Those ignoramuses who sneer at them place themselves in the same absurd position as those who sneer at Nelson or speak slightingly of other heroes.

Missionaries take terrible risks—they cut themselves adrift from the material life which is worth the living; they endure hardships incomprehensible to the uninitiated; they suffer from tempestuous illnesses which find them hale and hearty in the morning and leave their feeble bodies at the edge of death at sunset.

"And all this they do," said Bosambo of Monrovia, philosophically and thoughtfully, "because of certain mysteries which happened when the world was young and a famous Man called Hesu. (The Third Person of the Trinity is so called in some dialects.) Now I think that is the greatest mystery of all."]

Sanders appreciated the disinterestedness of the work, was immensely impressed by the courage of the people who came to labour in the unhealthy field, but all the time he fretfully wished they wouldn't.

His feelings were those of a professional lion-tamer who sees a light-hearted amateur stepping into the cage of the most savage of his beasts; they were feelings of the skilled matador who watches the novice's awkward handling of an Andalusian bull—a troubled matador with a purple cloak held ready and one neatly-shod foot on the barrier, ready to spring into the ring at the *novello's* need.

The "missionary patches" grew larger and whiter in the first few months of Ruth Glandynne's presence at Musunkusu, for this village was too near to the wild N'Gombi, too near the erratic Isisi, for Sanders' liking.

Sanders might easily have made a mistake in his anxiety. He might have sent messengers to the two peoples, or gone in person—threatening them with death and worse than death if they harmed the girl.

But that would have aroused a sense of importance in their childlike bosoms, and when the time came, as it assuredly would come, when their stomachs were angry against him, some chief would say:

"Behold, here is a woman who is the core of Sandi's eye. If we do her harm we shall be revenged on Sandi."

And, since children do not know any other tomorrow than the tomorrow of good promise, it would have gone badly with the lady missionary.

Instead, Sanders laid upon Bosambo, chief of the Ochori, charge of this woman, and Bosambo he trusted in all big things, though in the matter of goods movable and goods convertible he had so such confidence.

When Fembeni of the Isisi was converted from paganism to Christianity, Sanders was fussing about the little creeks which abound on the big river, looking for a man named Oko, who after a long and mysterious absence had returned to his village, killed his wife, and fled to the bush.

The particular bush happened to be in the neighbourhood of the mission station, otherwise Sanders might have been content to allow his policemen to carry out the good work, but no sooner did news come that Oko had broken for that section of the N'Gombi country which impinges on Musunkusu, than Sanders went flying up river in his steamer because something told him he had identified one of the nine men.

Wrote Sergt. Ahmed, the Houssa, who prided himself on his English, to his wife at headquarters:

> At daylight, when search for murderer was officially resumed, came our Lord Sundah very actively angry. By orders I took left bank of Kulula River with three men, being ordered to shoot aforesaid Oko if resistance offered. Abiboo (sergeant) took right or other bank, and our lord searched bush. Truly Oko must be a very important man that Sundah comes officially searching for same, saying bitter reproach words to his humble servants.

Ahmed's picture of his chief's agitation may be a little exaggerated, but I do not doubt that there was a substratum of fact therein.

On the second day of the hunt, Sanders' steamer was tied up at the mission station, and he found himself walking in the cool of the evening with Ruth Glandynne. So he learnt about Fembeni, the Isisi man who had found the light and was hot and eager for salvation.

"H'm!" said Sanders, displaying no great enthusiasm.

But she was too elated over her first convert to notice the lack of warmth in his tone.

"It is just splendid," she said, her grey eyes alight and her pretty face kindling with the thought, "especially when you remember, Mr. Sanders, that I have only an imperfect knowledge of the language."

"Are you sure," asked the incredulous Sanders, "that Fembeni understands what it is all about?"

"Oh, yes!" She smiled at the Commissioner's simplicity. "Why, he met me half-way, as it were; he came out to meet the truth; he—"

"Fembeni?" said Sanders thoughtfully. "I think I know the man; if I remember him aright he is not the sort of person who would get religion if he did not see a strong business end to it."

She frowned a little. Her eyebrows made a level line over resentful eyes.

"I think that is unworthy of you," she said coldly.

He looked at her, the knuckle of his front finger at his lips.

She was very pretty, he thought, or else he had been so long removed from the society of white women that she seemed beautiful only because she stood before a background of brutal ugliness.

Slim, straight, grave-eyed, complexion faultless, though tanned by the African sun, features regular and delicate, hair (a quantity) russet-brown.

Sanders shook his head.

"I wish to heaven you weren't monkeying about in this infernal country," he said.

"That is beside the question," she replied with a little smile. "We are talking of Fembeni, and I think you are being rather horrid."

They reached the big square hut that Sanders had built for her, and climbed the wooden steps that led to the *stoep*.

Sanders made no reply, but when she had disappeared into the interior of the hut to make him some tea, he beckoned to Abiboo, who had followed him at a respectful distance.

"Go you," he said, "and bring me Fembeni of the Isisi."

He was stirring his tea whilst the girl was giving him a rosy account of her work, when Fembeni came, a tall man of middle age, wearing the trousers and waistcoat which were the outward and visible signs of his inward and spiritual grace.

"Come near, Fembeni," said Sanders gently.

The man walked with confidence up the steps of the *Stoep*, and without invitation drew a chair towards him and seated himself.

Sanders said nothing. He looked at the man for a very long time, then:

"Who asked you to sit in my presence?" he said softly.

"Lord," said Fembeni pompously, "since I have found the blessed truth——"

Something in Sanders' eyes caused him to rise hurriedly.

"You may sit—on the ground," said Sanders quietly, "after the manner of your people, and I will sit on this chair after the manner of mine. For behold, Fembeni, even the blessed truth shall not make black white or white black; nor shall it make you equal with Sandi, who is your master."

"Lord, that is so," said the sullen Fembeni, "yet we are all equal in the eyes of the great One."

255

"Then there are a million people in the Isisi, in the N'Gombi, the Akasava, and the Ochori, who are your equals," said Sanders, "and it is no shame for you to do as they do."

Which was unanswerable, according to Fembeni's sense of logic.

The girl had listened to the talk between her novitiate and the commissioner with rising wrath, for she had not Sanders' knowledge of native people.

"I think that is rather small of you, Mr. Sanders," she said hotly. "It is a much more important matter that a heathen should be brought to the truth than that your dignity should be preserved."

Sanders frowned horribly—he had no society manners and was not used to disputation.

"I do not agree with you, Miss Glandynne," he said a little gruffly, "for, whilst the Isisi cannot see the ecstatic condition of his soul which leads him to be disrespectful to me, they can and do see the gross materialism of his sotting body."

A thought struck him and he turned to the man. That thought made all the difference between life and death to Fembeni.

"Fembeni," he said, relapsing into the language of the Isisi, "you are a rich man by all accounts."

"Lord, it is so."

"And wives—how many have you?"

"Four, lord."

Sanders nodded and turned to the girl.

"He has four wives," he said.

"Well?"

There was a hint of defiance in the questioning "Well?"

"He has four wives," repeated Sanders. "What is your view on this matter?"

"He shall marry one in the Christian style," she said, flushing. "Oh, you know, Mr. Sanders, it is impossible for a man to be a Christian and have more wives than one!"

Sanders turned to the man again.

"In this matter of wives, Fembeni," he said gently; "how shall you deal with the women of your house?"

Fembeni wriggled his bare shoulders uncomfortably.

"Lord, I shall put them all away, save one," he said sulkily, "for that is the blessed way."

"H'm!" said Sanders for the second time that morning.

He was silent for a long time, then:

"It is rather a problem," he said.

"It presents no difficulty to my mind," said the girl stiffly.

She was growing very angry, though Sanders did not realise the fact, being unused to the ways of white women.

"I think it is rather horrid of you, Mr. Sanders, to discourage this man, to put obstacles in his faith——"

"I put no obstacle," interrupted the Commissioner. He was short of speech, being rather so intent upon his subject that he took no account of the fine feelings of a zealous lady missionary. "But I cannot allow this to happen in my district; this man has four wives, each of them has borne him children. What justice or what Christianity is there in turning loose three women who have served this man?"

Here was a problem for the girl, and in her desperation she used an argument which was unanswerable.

"The law allows this," she said. "These things happen all over the world where missionary work is in progress. Perhaps I could bring the women to understand; perhaps I could explain——"

"You couldn't explain the babies out of existence," said Sanders brutally.

That ended the discussion, for with a look of scorn and disgust she passed into the hut, leaving Sanders a prey to some emotion.

He turned a cold eye to the offending Fembeni.

"It seems," he said, "that a man by becoming a Christian has less mouths to fill. Now I must investigate this matter."

Fembeni regarded him apprehensively, for if a woman is questioned, who knows what she will say? And it was fairly unimportant to the man if he had one wife or forty.

There was no possibility of searching any farther that night for the erring Oko, and Sanders was rowed across the river in his canoe to interview the wives of the new convert.

He found one woman who viewed the coming change with considerable philosophy, and three who were very shrill and very voluble.

"Lord," said one of these three in that insolent tone which only native women assume, "this white witch has taken our man——"

"I do not hear well," said Sanders quickly, "yet I thought I heard a word I do not like."

He whiffled a pliant stick till it hummed a tune.

"Lord," said the woman, dropping her voice and speaking more mildly, "this God-lady has taken our man."

"God-ladies do not take men," said Sanders; "rather they influence

257

their spirits that they may be better men."

"Fembeni will be no better and no worse," said the woman bitterly, "for he goes to the forest by night; often he has risen from my side, and when he has gone, behold the Nine Terrible Men have come from nearby and taken that which they wanted."

She stopped abruptly. There was horror in the eyes which met the Commissioner's; in her anger she had said too much.

"That is foolish talk," said Sanders easily.

He knew there would be no more information here and he played to quieten her fears.

He strolled through the village, talked awhile with the headman, and returned to his canoe.

Once on the *Zaire* he summoned Abiboo.

"Take three men and bring Fembeni to me," he said, "and be very ready to shoot him, for I have heard certain things."

He waited for ten minutes, then Abiboo returned—alone.

"Fembeni has gone into the forest," he said; "also the God-lady."

Sanders looked at him.

"How?"

"Lord, this Fembeni is a Christian, and desired to speak with the God-woman of the new magic. So they walked together, the God-woman reading from a book. Also he had a gift for her, which he bought from a Frenchi trader."

"I see," said Sanders.

He poured himself out a stiff glass of whiskey, and his hand shook a little.

Then he lifted down a sporting rifle that hung on the wall of his cabin, broke open two packets of cartridges, and dropped them into his coat pocket.

"Let the men come on quickly," he said, "you commanding."

"Lord, there are other Sergeants," said Abiboo. "I will go with you, for I am at your right hand, though death waits me."

"As you will," said Sanders roughly.

He went through the missionary compound, stopping only that a boy should point out the direction the two had taken, then he moved swiftly towards the forest, Abiboo at his heels.

He followed the beaten track for a hundred yards. Then he stopped and sniffed like a dog.

He went on a little farther and came back on his tracks.

He stooped and picked up some pieces of broken glass and turned aside from the path, following his nose.

★★★★★★

Ruth Glandynne had supreme faith in the power of the Word which makes martyrs.

"You must have no doubt, Fembeni," she said in her halting Isisi, "for with Light, such things as the Word brings, all things will be made plain to: you."

They were beyond the confines of the little mission station, walking slowly towards the forest.

She read little extracts from the book she carried, and so full of her subject was she that she did not observe that they had passed the straggling trees, the outposts of the big forest.

When she did notice this she turned.

"More I will tell you, Fembeni," she said.

"Lady, tell me now," he begged, "for Sandi has made me doubt."

She frowned. What mischief can a materialist work! She had liked Sanders. Now for one resentful moment she almost hated him.

"There are white men who doubt," she said, "and who place pitfalls in the way—"

"Also this have I bought for you," said Fembeni, "paying one bag of salt."

From the leather pouch at his side he produced a long flat flask.

She smiled as she recognised the floral label of the abominable scent beloved of the natives.

"This I bought for you, teacher," he said, and removed the stopper so that the unoffending evening reeked of a sudden with the odour of musk, "that you might protect me against Sandi, who is no God-man but a devil."

She took the bottle and hastily replaced the stopper.

"Sandi is no devil," she said gently, "and will do you no harm."

"He has crossed the river," said Fembeni sulkily, and there was a curious glitter in his eyes, "and he will speak with my wives, and they will tell him evil things of me."

She looked at him gravely.

"What evil things can they say?" she asked.

"They can lie," he said shortly, "and Sandi will bring his rope and I shall die."

She smiled. "I do not think you need fear," she said, and began to walk back; but he stood in front of her, and at that instant she realised

259

her danger, and the colour faded from her face.

"If Sandi comes after me to kill me," he said slowly, "I shall say to him: 'Behold, I have a woman of your kind, and if you do not pardon me you will be sorry.'"

She thought quickly, then of a sudden leapt past him and fled in the direction of the station.

He was after her in a flash. She heard the fast patter of his feet, and suddenly felt his arm about her waist.

She screamed, but there was none to hear her, and his big hand covered her mouth.

He shook her violently.

"You live or you die," he said; "but if you cry out I will beat you till you die."

He half carried, half dragged her in the direction of the forest.

She was nearly dead with fear; she was dimly conscious of the fact that he did not take the beaten path, that he turned at right angles and moved unerringly through the wood, following a path of his own knowing.

As he turned she made another attempt to secure her liberty. She still held the scent flask in her hand, and struck at him with all her might. He caught her arm and nearly broke it.

The stopper fell out and her dress was drenched with the vile perfume.

He wrenched the flask from her hand and threw it

Grasping her by the arm he led her on. She was nearly exhausted when he stopped, and she sank an inert heap to the ground.

She dare not faint, though she was on the verge of such a break-down. How long they had been travelling she had no idea. The sun was setting; this she guessed rather than knew, for no sunlight penetrated the aisles.

Fembeni watched her; he sat with his back to a tree and regarded her thoughtfully.

After a while he rose.

"Come," he said.

They moved on in silence. She made no appeal to him. She knew now the futility of speech. Her mind was still bewildered. "Why, why, why?" it asked incoherently.

Why had this man professed Christianity?

"Fembeni," she faltered, "I have been kind to you."

"Woman," he said grimly, "you may be kinder." She said no more.

The horror of the thing began to take shape. She half stopped, and he grasped her arm roughly.

"By my head you shall live," he said, "if Sandi gives his word that none of us shall hang—for we are the Terrible Men, and Sandi has smelt me out."

There was a gleam of hope in this speech. If it was only as a hostage that they held her——

Night had fallen when they came to water,

Here Fembeni halted. He searched about an undergrowth and dragged to view a section of hollow tree-trunk.

Inside were two sticks of iron wood, and squatting down before the *lokali* he rattled a metallic tattoo.

For ten minutes he played his tuneless rhythm. When he stopped there came a faint reply from somewhere across the lake.

They waited, the girl and her captor, for nearly half an hour. She strained her ears for the sound of oars, not knowing that the water did not extend for more than a hundred yards, and that beyond and around lay the great swamp wherein stood the island headquarters of the Nine.

The first intimation of the presence of others was a stealthy rustle, then through the gloom she saw the men coming toward her.

Fembeni grasped her arm and led her forward. He exchanged a few words with the new-comers in a dialect she could not understand. There was a brief exchange of questions, and then the party moved on.

The ground beneath her feet grew soft and sodden. Sometimes the water was up to her ankles. The leader of the men picked his way unerringly, now following a semi-circular route, now turning off at right angles, now winding in and out, till she lost all sense of direction.

Her legs were like lead, her head was swimming and she felt she was on the point of collapse when suddenly the party reached dry land.

A few minutes later they reached the tumbledown village which the outlaws had built themselves.

A fire was burning, screened from view by the arrangement of the huts which had been built in a crescent.

The girl was shown a hut and thrust inside.

Soon afterwards a woman brought her a bowl of boiled fish and a gourd of water.

In her broken Isisi she begged the woman to stay with her, but she was evidently of the N'Gombi people and did not understand.

A few minutes later she was alone.

Outside the hut about the fire sat eight of the Nine Terrible Men. One of these was Oko of the Isisi, a man of some power.

"This woman I do not like," he said, "and by my way of thinking Fembeni is a fool and a son of a tool to bring her unless she comes as other women have come—to serve us."

"Lord Oko," said Fembeni, "I am more skilled in the ways of white folk than you, and I tell you that if we keep this woman here it shall be well with us. For if Sandi shall catch you or me, or any of us, we shall say to him: 'There is a woman with us whom you greatly prize, and if you hang me, behold you kill her also.'"

Still Oko was not satisfied.

"I also know white people and their ways," he said. "Sandi would have left us, now he will not rest till we are scattered and dead, for Sandi has a memory like the river, which never ceases to flow."

A man of the Akasava suggested an evil thing.

"That we shall consider," said Oko.

He had already decided. He had none of the subtlety of mind which distinguished Fembeni. He saw an end, and was for crowding in the space of life left to him as much of life as his hand could grasp.

They sat in *palaver* till early in the morning, the firelight reflected on the polished skin of their bodies.

Then Oko left the circle and crept to the girl's hut. They saw him stoop and enter, and heard a little scream.

"Oko has killed her," said Fembeni.

"It is best," said the other men.

Fembeni rose and went to the hut.

"Oko," he called softly, then stooped and went in.

Facing him was a ragged square of dim light, where a great hole had been cut in the farther side of the hut.

"Oko," he called sharply, then two hands of steel caught him by the throat and two others pulled his legs from under him.

He went to the ground, too terrified to resist.

"Fembeni," said a soft voice in his ear, "I have been waiting for you."

He was rolled on to his face and he made no resistance. His hands were pulled behind, and he felt the cold steel bands encircle his wrist and heard a "snick" as they fastened.

He was as expeditiously gagged.

"As for Oko," said Sanders' voice, "he is dead, and if you had heard

262

him cry you also would have been dead."

That ended the one-sided conversation, Sanders and his sergeant sitting patiently in their little lair waiting for the rest of the men to come.

With the morning arrived a detachment of Houssas under Sergeant Ahmed, following the trail Sanders had followed. There were four dead men to be buried—including him who had stood on guard at the edge of the swamp.

There was a white-faced girl to be guarded back across the swamp to the seclusion of the forest, and with her went the women of the outlaws' village.

Fembeni and his four companions stood up for judgment.

"One only thing I would ask you, Fembeni," said Sanders, "and that is this: you are by some account a Christian. Do you practise this magic, or are you for the *ju-jus* and gods of your fathers?"

"Lord," said Fembeni eagerly, "I am a Christian in all ways. Remember this, master, I am of your faith."

Sanders, with his lips parted, and his eyes narrowed, looked at the man.

"Then it is proper that I should give you time to say your prayers," he said. "Abiboo, we hang this man last."

"I see that you are a devil," said Fembeni, "otherwise you would not follow us in the night with none to show you the way. Now I tell you, Sandi, that I am no Christian, for all God-folk are foolish save you, and I know that you are no God-man. Therefore, if I am to, hang, let me hang with the rest."

Sanders nodded.

CHAPTER 9

The Queen of the N'gombi

There are certain native traits, certain inherent characteristics, which it is inexpedient to describe in print.

The N'Gombi people had a weakness for forbidden fruit; they raided and burnt and pillaged, but in the main the treasure which they carried away with them took the shape of eligible women.

Sanders was at some pains to teach them that this was one of the forms of hunting which his soul loathed. He pointed his lesson with whippings, banishments, and once, after a particularly unpleasant episode, by a hanging from a gallows which he caused to be erected in the N'Gombi city of Shusha.

Here, before the duly impressed people, in the presence of a *puisne* judge brought especially from the coast—there had been a little trouble over a summary execution—and in a space kept clear by a half-battalion of Houssas (imported for the occasion), Lombasi, a king of the N'Gombi, died the death amidst the plaudits of his fickle subjects. And this happened in the sight of every chief, every headman, and the new king of the N'Gombi.

Yet three weeks later the offence for which the king suffered was repeated by his successor.

"Make your own arrangements," telegraphed the Administration when a despairing Sanders had reported the fresh crime. "Hang Bogali at your discretion; if necessary, burn crops and village."

Sanders did neither. He deposed the king as he had deposed half a dozen other kings, thrashed him publicly, distributed his property, and appointed—whom should be appoint?

He had half a mind to send for Bosambo of the neighbouring Ochori, but that would be a dangerous experiment.

The deposed Bogali had two sons and a daughter. One of the sons was far gone in sleeping sickness, and the other was a fairly easy-going, foolish youth, who would be in the hands of his councillors.

"It shall be the woman," decided Sanders; and so, against all precedent, he set up E'logina as Queen of the N'Gombi.

A tall, resolute girl of sixteen, she was at that time with a husband of no great character and several lovers, it there was any truth in popular rumour.

With fitting solemnity Sanders placed her in the chair of state, and she was very grave and very stately—accepting her new position as by right.

"E'logina," said Sanders, "you shall rule this country, and there shall be no women *palavers*. And I am behind you to enforce your order. If any man say to you: 'I will not obey you because you are a woman,' behold! he shall obey because I am a man; and whosoever sets your authority at defiance shall suffer very painfully."

"Lord!" said the girl, "I will rule wisely."

"As for your lovers," said Sanders, "of whom I have heard, you shall give them no preference over other councillors, or they will lead you to destruction."

"Master!" said the girl, "it is said in the N'Gombi country, 'A lover has strong arms, but no brains.'"

"That is true in other countries," said Sanders.

There were no more women *palavers* in the N'Gombi from that day. A minor chief who raided an outlying village and carried away girls was summoned to her presence, and certain things happened to him which changed his habits of life, for this lady of the N'Gombi was elementary but effective.

Sanders heard of the happening, and wisely pretended ignorance. The art of government lies in knowing nothing at the proper moment.

She ruled as she had promised—with wisdom. There came the inevitable moment when her chief lover sought to influence affairs of state.

She sent him a long green leaf, which meant that she was in mourning for him. He accepted this as an augury of what might happen and left the city with commendable expedition.

The chiefs and kings of other countries paid her visits of ceremony, bringing her rich presents. Not least of these was Bosambo of the Ochori.

His state rivalled in magnificence a combination of the sunset and the morning star, but the girl on her dais was not noticeably affected.

"Lady Queen," said Bosambo, "I have come a long journey because I have heard of your greatness and your beauty, and, behold, you are wonderful to see, and your wisdom blinds me like the sun on still water."

"I have heard of you," said E'logina. "You are a little chief of a little people."

"The moon is little also, when seen from a muck-heap," said Bosambo calmly. "I return to my moon."

He was ruffled, though he did not betray the fact.

"To-morrow," he said, as he prepared to depart, "I send word to Sandi, who, as all the world knows, is my nephew—being the son of my sister's husband's brother, and therefore of my blood—and I will say to him that here in the N'Gombi is a queen who puts shame upon our house."

"Lord Bosambo," said the girl hurriedly, "we know that you are nearly related to Sandi, and it would be wrong if my foolish tongue made you ashamed."

"We are proud men, Sandi and I," said Bosambo, "and he will be very terrible in his anger when he knows in what way you have spoken."

The girl rose and came toward him.

"Lord Bosambo," she said, "if you leave me now it will be dark and there will be no sun. For often I have spoken of you till my councillors weary of your name and deeds. Therefore, stay with me a little that I may drink of your understanding."

But Bosambo was dignified and obdurate.

"Also, Lord Bosambo," she said, "there are many presents which my people are gathering for you, for it would be shameful if I sent you back to your great nation empty-handed."

"I will stay," said Bosambo, "though presents I do not value—save meal and a little water—and my hut is filled with presents from Sandi." He observed the look of relief on the girl's face, and added without a tremor, "So that I have room only for precious gifts as your ladyship will give me."

He stayed that day, and the queen found him agreeable; he stayed the next day, and the queen was fascinated by his talk. On the third day he was indispensable.

Then came Bosambo's culminating effort.

He had a passion for discussing his kinship with Sanders, and she was an attentive listener. Also she had that day given him many tusks of ivory to carry with him to his home.

"My brother Sandi," said Bosambo, "will be pleased already; he loves you and has spoken to me about you. Now I will not doubt that his love will be greater than it is for me—for you are a woman, and Sandi has sighed many days for you."

She listened with a kindling eye. A new and splendid thought came into her head. Bosambo departed that evening, having compressed more mischief into three days than the average native man crowds into a lifetime.

It was six months before the result of Bosambo's extravagance was seen. Sanders came north on a tour of inspection, and in due course he arrived at Shusha.

All things were in order on the river, and he was satisfied. His experiment had worked better than he had dared to hope.

"Queen," he said, as he sat with her in the thatched *palaver*-house, "you have done well."

She smiled nervously.

"Lord, it is for love of you that I did this," she said; and Sanders, hardened to flattery, accepted the warmth of her pronouncement without blushing.

"For I have put away my lovers," she went on, "and my husband, who is a fool, I have banished to another village; and, my lord, I am your slave."

She slipped from the seat which was by her side, and knelt before him in the face of the city and before all the people.

She grasped his foot with her strong young hands and placed it on her head.

"Phew!" said Sanders, breaking into a sweat—for by all custom this was not an act of fealty, but the very act of marriage.

"Stand up, queen!" said the Commissioner when he had got his breath, "lest your people think foolish thoughts."

"Lord," she murmured, "I love you! and Bosambo, your nephew, looks favourably upon our marriage."

Sanders said nothing. He reached down, and catching her by the arm, drew her to her feet.

"Oh, people!" he said loudly to the amazed throng at the foot of the little hill on which the *palaver* house stood, "your queen is, by her act, wedded to my government, and has sworn to serve me in all matters of queenship—be faithful as she is. The *palaver* is finished."

It was an ingenious escape—though the girl's eyes narrowed as she faced him, and her bare bosom rose and fell in her anger.

"Lord," she breathed, "this was not as I meant."

"It is as I mean," said Sanders gently.

She faced him for a moment; then, turning swiftly, walked to her hut, and Sanders saw her no more that day.

"We stay till tomorrow," said Sanders to his sergeant as he went on board the *Zaire* that evening. "Afterwards we go to Ochori—I will have a *palaver* with Bosambo."

"Master," said Abiboo, "Bosambo will be pleased."

"I doubt it," said Sanders.

He went to bed that night to sleep the sleep of one who had earned the daily two pounds with which a grateful government rewarded him.

He was dead tired, but not too tired to slip the fine-meshed wire fly-door into its place, or to examine the windows to see if they were properly screened.

This must be done in the dark, because, if by chance a window or a door is open when a light appears, certain it is that the cabin will be filled with tiny little brothers of the forest, a hundred varieties of flies, winged beetles, and most assuredly *musca*—which, in everyday language, is the fever-carrying mosquito. With the habit formed of long practice, Sanders' hand touched the three windows, found the screens in their place and latched.

Then he switched on the electric light—a luxurious innovation which had come to him with the refitment of the *Zaire*. Leading from his cabin was a tiny bathroom. He pulled his pyjamas from under his pillow and disappeared into the cupboard—it was nothing more—to reappear at the end of five minutes arrayed in his grey sleeping kit.

He turned on a light over his pillow, switched out the other, and pulled back the clothes.

He did not immediately jump into bed, because, carefully arranged at regular intervals in the centre of the bed, were three round thorns.

Sanders turned on the other light, opened his desk, and found a pair of tweezers. With these he removed the uncomfortable burrs, placing them under a glass on his table.

After this he made a very thorough search of the room—especially of the floor. But whosoever had placed the thorns had evidently forgotten the possibilities of a man walking bare-footed—nor was there any sign of the unknown's thoughtful attention in the bathroom.

He pulled the bed to pieces, shaking every article carefully; then he remade his couch, turned out the lights, climbed into bed, and went to sleep.

Two hours before dawn he woke. This was the time he intended waking. He sat up in bed and groaned—deliberately and inartistically. He groaned at intervals for five minutes, then he was quiet.

He listened and thought he heard a slight movement on the bank to which the *Zaire* was moored.

He bent his head and waited. Yes, a twig snapped.

Sanders was out of the door in a second; he flew across the gangway which connected the steamer with the bank, and plunged into the forest path that led to the village of E'tomolini. Ahead of him he heard a patter of bare feet.

"Stop! O walker of the night," called Sanders in the Bomongo dialect, "or you die!"

The figure ahead halted and Sanders came up with it.

"Walk back the way you came," he said, and followed the shadowy form to the boat.

Sanders observed that the night-wanderer was a little taller than a boy, and had a method of walking which was not inconsistent with the theory that it was a girl.

"Go straight to my cabin," said the Commissioner, "if you know it."

"Lord, I know it," quavered the other, and Sanders learnt that it was indeed a girl.

A girl of fifteen, he judged, as she stood in the glare of the electric light—shapely of build, not bad-looking, and very frightened.

"I am plagued by women," said Sanders wrathfully. "You shall tell me how it comes about that you spy upon me in the night, also how you come to be abroad so early."

The girl hesitated, casting a bewildered glance round the cabin.

"Lord," she said, "I did that which seemed best."

"Who sent you here?"

Again she hesitated.

"I came for no reason, lord, but that I wish to see the strange devil-light."

This was a reasonable excuse, for the new electric installation had proved irresistibly fascinating to the raw folk of the upper river.

Sanders uncovered the three thorn burrs, and she looked at them curiously.

"What do they call you?" asked Sanders.

"Medini, the woman with nine lovers," she said simply.

"Well, Medini," said Sanders with a grim little smile, "you shall pick up those thorns and hold them in your hand—they will wound you a little because they are very sharp."

The girl smiled.

"A little thorn does not hurt," she quoted, and stretched out her hand fearlessly.

Before she could touch the thorns Sanders' hand shot out and caught her wrist.

The girl was puzzled and for a moment a look of apprehension filled her eyes and she shrank back, dragging her wrist from the Commissioner's hand.

"Sit down," said Sanders. "You shall tell me before you go who sent you to the bank to watch my boat."

"None, lord," she faltered.

Sanders shook his head.

"I have a *ju-ju*," he said slowly, "and this *ju-ju* has told me that somebody said, 'Go you, Medini, to the bank near where Sandi lies and listen. And when you hear him groan aloud like a man in great pain, you shall come and tell me.'"

Consternation and horror were on the girl's face.

"Lord," she gasped, "that is true—yet if I speak I die!"

"Also, if you do not speak, I shall take you away from here to a place far from your own people," said Sanders.

The girl's eyes dropped.

"I came to see the devil-lights," she said sullenly.

Sanders nodded.

He went out from the cabin and called up the guard—an alert guard which had watched a flying Commissioner in pyjamas cross the plank gangway and reappear with a prisoner.

"Keep this woman under your eyes," he said. "Let none speak with her."

When daylight came he removed a spike from the thorn and placed it under his microscope. What he saw interested him, and again he had recourse to the microscope—scraping another spike and placing the shavings between two slides.

Native people have a keen sense of humour, but that humour does not take the form of practical joking.

Moreover, he had detected blood on the spike, and an organism which old blood generates.

Thus the bushmen poison their arrows by leaving them in the bodies of their dead enemies.

He sent a guard for the queen and brought her on board.

"I shall take you away," he said, "because you have tried to kill me by placing poisoned thorns in my bed."

"Medini, my woman, did this, because she loved me," said the queen, "and if she says I told her to do the thing she lies."

"You have said enough," said Sanders. "Abiboo, let there be steam quickly, for I carry the queen with me to the Ochori country."

Bosambo was not prepared for the Commissioner's arrival. He was a man singularly free from illusions, and when they brought him word that Sanders was accompanied by the Queen of the N'Gombi he had no doubt in his mind that the times ahead were troublesome.

So they proved.

Sanders cut short the flower of his welcome. He nipped it as the frost nips young buds, and as coldly.

"You have put foolish ideas into this woman's head," he said, "and I have brought her here that you might do that which is honourable."

"Lord, I am your man," said Bosambo, with proper humility.

"And my uncle also," said Sanders, "if all that you said to her was true."

The girl stood by listening.

"Now you have told her that she should marry into my house," said Sanders, "and, being a woman, her mind is set upon this matter."

Bosambo saw what was coming, and hastened to avert the evil.

"Lord," he said, in his agitation dropping into the English he had spoken on the coast, "she be number one women; dem wife she not be fit for nudder woman."

"I do not speak that monkey talk," said Sanders calmly. "You marry this woman today and she goes back to rule the N'Gombi—tonight."

"Lord," pleaded Bosambo, "I am of the Faith—the one Prophet of the one God."

"But not the one wife, I think," said Sanders. "You marry her or I whip you."

"Lord, I will be whipped," said Bosambo promptly.

"Also, I will place another chief over the Ochori."

"That is too great a shame," said Bosambo aghast. "For as you know, lord, my father and his father were chiefs of this tribe, and I have the blood of kings in my veins."

"You have the blood of Monravian thieves, and your fathers you never knew," said Sanders patiently. "You marry today!"

"It is as you will, oh, my uncle!" said Bosambo.

Sanders said nothing, though his hands clutched his stick the tighter.

After all, he had brought that insult upon himself.

CHAPTER 10

The Man on the Spot

Once upon a time a man went up to the Calali River to buy rubber from the natives. He had a permit signed by the new Administrator and a licence to trade, and he had come into Sanders' territory by a back way and did not trouble to have this permit visaed.

Now the permit bore the signature of His Excellency the Administrator, him and none other, and the name of His Excellency "goes," and people have been known to bow their heads most respectfully at the mention of his name.

Sanders did not respect him, but called him "your Excellency," because it was lawful.

Anyway, this trader to whom I have referred went up the Calali River and bought rubber. He bought it and sometimes paid for it. He did not give its exact value, and after three weeks of bartering his business came to an end, because native folk would not bring any further rubber to his big canoe. Whereupon Tinkerton—such was his name—had recourse to other methods. He sat down in a likely village and instructed the headman to produce for him so many kilos of rubber in so many days, promising remuneration which by every standard was absurd. The head-man refused, whereupon Tinkerton tied him up to a tree and whipped him with a *chicotte*.

"Now you'll change your point of view," said Tinkerton, "and fetch me rubber—quick!"

The chief sent twenty young men into the forest to find rubber, and four men who were his best paddlers to find Mr. Commissioner Sanders, collecting hut tax with some labour in the Akasava country.

Rubber and Sanders arrived at the Calali River at the same time.

Tinkerton explained his position and the chief exhibited his back.

"My permit is quite in order, I think," said Tinkerton.

273

"Up to a point," admitted Sanders carefully, "it is. But, as you know, a licence to trade becomes invalid when the holder is convicted of any breach of the common law."

Tinkerton smiled uneasily.

"That doesn't affect me, I think," he said.

He always added "I think" to everything he said, lest the hearer should labour under the impression that he spoke without thinking.

"It affects you considerably," said Sanders; "for I am sentencing you to six months' hard labour for your assault on this native, and I am sending you to the coast to serve that sentence."

Tinkerton went crimson with rage.

"Do you know what I think of you?" he asked loudly.

"No," said Sanders, "but I can guess it, and if you open your mouth uncivilly I shall take you by the scruff of the neck and kick you into the river."

Tinkerton went down to the coast under escort, and he never forgave the Commissioner.

The major portion of his sentence was remitted by the Administrator, because it happened that the Administrator was a sort of cousin to Tinkerton's father.

So that to the patent fury of Tinkerton was added the coldly polite disapproval of an Administrator who is remembered best on the coast by his mistakes.

Now, although it is amusing to recall the blunders of a high official after his departure, it is not so entertaining to furnish material for subsequent anecdote, and one must be possessed of a peculiarly poignant sense of humour to thoroughly appreciate the travail in which these jests were born.

The Administrator may or may not have deliberately set himself the task of annoying Sanders.

From a strictly service aspect, a service which has for its ideal the perfection of British administration, to the exclusion of all personal ambition, the idea is preposterous. From the standpoint of one who has some knowledge of human nature, it seems very likely that there was something in the suggestion that His Excellency had his administrative knife in the executive ribs of Mr. Commissioner Sanders.

One spring morning Sanders received a big blue letter. It came in his mail bag with other communications but bore, in addition to the notification that it was "*On His Majesty's Service*," the legend "*Department of His Excellency the Administrator*," and was moreover subscribed

"Strictly confidential."

Now, when a high official of state writes in strictest confidence to his subordinate, he is not telling him his troubles or confessing his guilt, or even trying to borrow money.

He is, as a rule, delivering a kick with all the force of his strong right leg.

Sanders looked at the letter, picked it up gingerly, held it up to the light, and weighed it in his hand. It was heavy. The bulk of it was eloquent of reproof, because administrators do not expend overmuch energy in praising the works of their underlings.

Sir Harry Coleby, K.C.M.G., had a reputation which he had acquired in Bermuda, Jamaica, and the Straits Settlements. It was not a reputation for loving kindness exactly. His nickname—he came by this when he was a secretary of Legation at Madrid—was *"Calliente,"* which he pronounced "Cally-enty," and means "hot." And hot he was of head and temper, and the men who worked for him and with him lived in a mild perspiration.

He was extravagant of speech and quick of temper, and he wrote letters which were vitriolic without being offensive within the meaning of the act.

Sanders opened the blue envelope reluctantly and smoothed out the typewritten sheets and read:

"Sir,—I have the honour to inform you that His Excellency the Administrator has received your half-yearly report on the conditions of the tribes and peoples under your honour's administration.

"His Excellency regrets that the reports you send concerning the spread of sleeping sickness in the Calali district are not as satisfactory as His Majesty's Government could wish. The measure framed for the restriction of this disease does not seem to have been effectively applied, and he requests that a further report on this matter should be furnished at the end of the present quarter."

Sanders read so far without being seriously troubled. The Administration was covering itself against any kicks which might come from Downing Street, and by Sanders' code was justified.

He read on:

"The state of lawlessness which prevails in the Akasava and Ochori countries is, in His Excellency's opinion, a matter for regret, and he expects your honour to take immediate steps to deal drastically with this condition of affairs. A suggestion which His Excellency makes is that the chief Bosambo should be deposed, and that the Akasava and

Ochori should be combined under one chief."

Sanders, who knew the Ochori and Akasava for hereditary enemies, mopped his forehead with a gaudy bandana handkerchief and swore softly.

"His Excellency desires me to state that considering the natural resources of the lands under your honour's dominion, the amount of taxes collected would appear to be inadequate and he sends you herewith a revised scale of taxation which shall come into operation as from July 1st of the current year."

That was all.

The reference to the Akasava and Ochori crime left him unmoved. The crime was of no great importance, and was, in point of fact, less serious than in previous years. He could afford to ignore the suggestion concerning Bosambo, though he knew it was made to annoy Bosambo's patron. But the taxation was another matter—a very serious matter indeed, and he sat down to write on the subject. He pointed out the consequences of increasing the demand upon uncivilised people. He reported means by which an increased revenue might be secured without adding to the burden of the individual, and he ended his letter by expressing his absolute disagreement with the Administration.

"Whilst noting your Excellency's instructions," he said, "I decline to accept any responsibility whatsoever for the effect the new imposition may produce."

In reply, he received a most unpleasant letter which told him, in the stilted and official language of special correspondence, to do as he was bid.

"You will make whatsoever arrangements you deem necessary, without any further reference to His Excellency, to deal with the disorder which in your view will arise as a result of the new taxation. I am to say that in His Excellency's opinion no such danger is to be apprehended."

Now Sanders' position was a difficult one. He was bound hand and foot by service regulations. He knew that the new Administrator was acting off his own bat, and that were the Home Government aware of the innovation of the new taxes, it would make short work of them.

But Sanders could not communicate with Downing Street direct. It would be an unpardonable thing to go behind his superior. In another land where white men were, a newspaper correspondent might reveal the trouble brewing without Sanders being in any way responsible; such things are done—as I know. But the only white men in Sanders' territory were three missionaries, separated from him by hundreds of miles, a captain of Houssas and himself.

Sanders thought the matter over day and night for a week. Once he almost decided to break through all rules, notify the Government, and resign. He was in the act of penning the cablegram when an inspiration came to him.

"You will make whatsoever arrangements . . ."

The concluding paragraph of the Administrator's letter occurred to him.

Very slowly and thoughtfully he tore up the draft of his cable into little pieces and called his orderly, who was half-asleep on the verandah outside.

"Tell Yoka," he said, "that I will have fire in the *Zaire* by sunset—take food on board for three weeks. I go to make *palaver* with the God-men."

When the sun was throwing mile-long shadows upon the beach, he began his cruise.

His first call necessitated a twenty-mile march through the Isisi country to a place called Konshinda.

Here was the mission station of the Jesuits, and he found Father Wells, a tall, spare man in white, superintending the erection of a new hut.

He was a middle-aged man, grey-haired and cleanshaven, and he greeted Sanders with a smile. Together they went to the mission-house with its big cool *stoep*.

"Sit down, Commissioner," said the missionary. He took off his white *topee* and produced a well-burnt pipe, and Sanders, declining the jar of tobacco the other pushed toward him, lit a cheroot.

"Well," said the first, "what is the trouble? Have some of my converts been raiding or is this a visit of ceremony? If it is, I am sorry Father Vettechi is not here—he's rather keen on ceremonies."

He laughed with the happy boyish laugh of one who has no cares.

"I'm going to turn you out of the country," said Sanders calmly.

The other looked up quickly, with a smile which was half quizzical and half earnest.

"What is this?" he asked, "a new Expulsion of the Jesuits?"

"Something like that," said Sanders, "it is a long time since I persecuted anybody."

"But seriously——"

Sanders told the story of the new taxation. He was immensely serious, painting the consequence of the new tariff with vividness of detail.

"I am inclined to agree with you," said the Jesuit; "but I shall have to protest against being sent down, even though I know that you are acting in my best interest."

"Protest away," said Sanders cheerfully.

Father Wells was troubled.

"But I shall have to wire my protest to England," he said.

"I will give you every facility," said Sanders.

He left, carrying with him the Jesuit's cablegram, and when he reached the river sent a special courier to headquarters with orders to dispatch it.

A day later, he entered the narrow river which leads to the Modern Baptist Mission Station.

Along this stream for forty miles Sanders proceeded with caution. It was not easy to navigate. Beneath the smiling surface of smooth waters lay the gentle, sloping crests of sandbanks. These in themselves were fairly innocuous. But the Tembolini River flowed in its earlier stages through miles of primeval forest, and trees would sometimes float down to be caught and embedded in the sand, a blunt branch peeping from its sandy covering. Woe betide the steamer that struck these "snags"; for a mahogany brand backed and supported by a buried tree offered more resistance than anything smaller than an Atlantic steamer could resist, and striking at full speed, the bottom would be ripped from the best of steamers.

Tiny fishing villages were met at rare intervals, for this is part of the Isisi, isolated from the main country for many reasons, not the least of which was *M'shimba-M'shamba*, the green devil who walks by night and is very terrible to the dwellers of cities.

Sanders, who never wasted a journey if he could help it, stopped at each village for an hour, adjusted such differences as needed his help (there was a very bad murder *palaver* at one to which he had to return later) and on the morning of the second day he arrived at the Baptist Mission.

He had different material to deal with here. A little man, immensely important as little men sometimes are, slightly aggressive in the name of the Lord and "not quite."

You meet people who are "not quite" in all branches of life, but curiously enough they are to be met with most frequently in a certain type of foreign mission. God forbid that I should speak disparagingly of the devoted men and women who sacrifice health and life in the execution of their duty and in the fulfilment of their faith.

Mr. Haggins, of the Modern Baptist Mission, was "not quite," however.

He had been a London street preacher, hot for glory, and a radical constitutionally opposed to government, whatsoever and whichever party was for the moment in power. Sanders represented government, was popularly supposed to be antagonistic to the Word and its carriers. He whipped people, hanged a few with scanty trial, and had been accused by Mr. Haggins' predecessor of having committed atrocities. It cost the proprietors of the Modern Baptist Mission, which printed the wild and whirling accusation, exactly a thousand pounds, and if Mr. Haggins ever wrote tremendous things about Sanders you may be sure that the editor of the magazine never published them.

"I am glad to see you, Mr. Sanders," said the missionary with ominous politeness, as Sanders stepped ashore; "there are one or two matters on which I wished to see you. Particularly in regard to your atrocious treatment of one of my native evangelists, Balibi—"

"He can keep," said Sanders shortly; "your evangelist amused himself in his spare time with certain women of the Akasava——"

"That's not true," said Mr. Haggins rudely.

Sanders looked at him queerly.

"If you call me a liar," he said, "I shall—"

He checked himself.

"It isn't true," said Mr. Haggins with vehemence. "I believe in our brother—"

"That is neither here nor there!" interrupted Sanders. "What I have come to tell you is that you are to close up your station and bring all your belongings to headquarters."

Mr. Haggins was dumbfounded.

"Close—my—station?" he repeated.

"That is it," said Sanders blandly; "I expect trouble with my people over the new taxation."

"But I will not go," said Mr. Haggins, very wrathful and suspecting the worst; "it is an outrage; it is an attempt to ruin my station—I shall make representations to England, Mr. Sanders—we are not without friends in Parliament—"

He said much more in the same strain, speaking with great heat.

"If you like to send a telegram," said Sanders, calling into play all his patience, "I shall be most happy to send it."

Sanders made other calls, including one upon that medical missionary lady, Miss Glandynne, and at each station he met with an unpleasant reception.

Sir Harry Coleby, K.C.M.G., occupied a magnificent white palace at a coast town, with the name of which you are tolerably sure to be familiar. It was set on the side of a great mountain and looked down upon a town of broad streets, in the main populated and inhabited by coal-black negroes who spoke English and affixed "Mr." to their name.

Sir Harry was stout, white of hair, bristling of moustache, and pink of face. He referred to himself as the "man on the spot"; this was an idiosyncrasy of his.

He worked as a motor engine worked, by a series of explosions. He exploded at his overworked secretary, he exploded at his officers; he exploded at anything and anybody that thwarted or annoyed him.

He damned people's eyes with a persistency and a fury which suggested that he had a near and dear relative in the optical line of business, and was trying to do him a turn.

I add the indisputable fact that though he had only been six months on the coast he was cordially hated.

Mr. Commissioner Sanders of the Isisi, Mr. Commissioner *de la* Court of the Kroo River, numerous deputy commissioners, inspectors and officers of state, living meanly along a hot slip of coast, daily thought of him and cherished next to their hearts the news—it was cut from an impudent Lagos journal—that His Excellency found the climate very trying.

Sir Harry came into his office one day—it was the morning after the official dinner at Government House and he was lively—to find Sanders' final letter on the subject of taxation.

"By God, if I have any more of that fellow's insolence I will pack him off to England!" he roared, and proceeded to invoke Divine interference with Sanders' eyesight.

"Tell him—" he shouted, banging his desk with his clenched knuckles.

"I'm sorry to interrupt your Excellency," said the secretary, "but ought we not to notify the Colonial Office about this change—"

He was a permanent official who had spent his life on the coast, and he knew more about West Central Africa than most secretaries.

"Notify nothing," snapped his chief, "I administrate here, I am the man on the spot; I am going to increase revenue, sir."

"There will be trouble, your Excellency," said the secretary quietly.

Sir Harry drew a long breath, and in one long and comprehensive sentence consigned the secretary, Sanders, and the native peoples of his kingdom to the devil.

A negro clerk brought in a cablegram and handed it to the Administrator.

"Here's a 'confidential,' Browne," he snarled; "decode the damn thing and don't bother about matters which do not concern you."

The secretary took the four closely written forms.

It began:

"Airlight, Transport, Divine, Sunlight, Meridan."

"Airlight" meant "confidential"; "transport" meant "act at once"; this he knew, and settled down to decode the wire.

The further he got, consulting the two books with the double code, the higher rose the spirits of His Excellency's secretary. When he had finished he laid the decoded message before his chief, and Sir Harry read:

Very urgent. Act at once. Representation made by missionary societies that their stations being closed in Isisi, Akasava, Ochori, N'Gombi countries by order Sanders. Understand he fears disturbances as a result of new taxation. Before enforcing new taxation communicate particulars to Colonial Office.

It is said that Sir Harry Coleby went stark, staring mad when this communication was read. He was not used to being dictated to from Downing Street. He was of a regime which held the Colonial Office in good-natured contempt. Whether he went mad or whether this is an exaggerated description of the secretary, I do not know. Certainly he sent a wire to His Majesty's Secretary of State for Colonial Affairs which reminded that gentleman of communications which came to him in the stormy days of the first Home Rule Bill. It was not a mad wire, or a bad wire, it was penned in Sir Harry's best style, and it hinted to the Colonial Office in London that Sir Harry was the man on the spot and would use his own discretion, and he would not submit to outside interference, and that if anybody interfered with him—my word!

Sir Harry had once sent such a wire before and the Colonial Secretary of the day had surrendered. Unhappily for the Administrator, there was a man at the Colonial Office.

At ten o'clock that night a cable was received by His Excellency. It was in plain English and the Administrator read it and sat looking at it for quite a long time before he understood it. It ran:

> Your successor sails on ninth. Hand over your work to your attorney-general and return by first available steamer.

It was signed "Chamberlain."

CHAPTER 11

The Rising of the Akasava

A native alone may plumb the depths of the native mind with any accuracy. Sanders was remarkable because he was possessed of a peculiar quality—the quality of comprehension.

He made few mistakes because he applied no rules. He knew, for instance, that native memory is short, yet he was prepared to hear a greybeard of forty contest his finding in some particular suit with a precedent created twenty years before and entirely obliterated from Sanders' memory.

A scientific expedition once again went through the Ochori country—and I think it had to do with astronomical observation—and in the language of Kipling:

What they thought they might require, They went an' took.

Bosambo, the chief, complained, for he knew the value of money to such an extent that he never accepted a Spanish *douro* without biting it, or confused a mark with a shilling.

Sanders was secretly annoyed with the behaviour of the expedition, but felt it necessary to keep up the end of his fellow-countrymen.

"They were of the Government," he said at the time; "and, moreover, white men. And it is the white man's way."

Bosambo said nothing, but remembered.

Years later something happened in the Akasava, and by a distressing string of circumstances Sanders found himself confronted with a two-million-pound war, the undoing of all his work, and a most ignominious death.

This happened in the autumn of the year. At the time of harvest the lands under Mr. Commissioner Sanders were quiet and peaceable. The crop had been a good one, the fish plentiful in the river, serious sickness of no account.

"And no crime," said Sanders to himself, and pulled a little face. "I would welcome a little earthquake just now."

The European reader might stand aghast at this callousness, but Sanders knew.

The reports that came downriver were satisfactory—if one gained satisfaction from the recital of virtuous behaviour. Isisi, N'Gombi, Akasava, Bolegi, Bomongo—all these peoples were tranquil and prosperous.

The only adverse report was from the Ochori. There a mysterious fire had destroyed one-half of the crops—a fire that had appeared simultaneously in twenty gardens. Also it was reported that Bosambo, the chief, was treating his people with unusual severity.

Sanders grew very thoughtful when this news came, for Bosambo was a wise and cunning man, who knew native folk as well as Sanders himself. Sanders drew his own conclusions, and made preparations for a long cruise.

He stepped on board his little stern-wheeler at dawn one day.

For days previous men had been piling wood on the lower deck till the *Zaire* looked for all the world like a timber ship. On the steel deck below, in double banks, in the well before the tiny bridge deck, in the space at the stem which is usually occupied by drowsy Houssas, wood was piled to the height of a man's head.

In addition there were many stacks of a bright, black stone, which Yoka, the engineer, regarded with unusual pride; as well he might, for coal is not a customary sight on the big river.

The *Zaire* had recently come newly furnished from the slips. White workmen, brought at great expense from Lagos or Sierra Leone, or one of those far-distant and marvellous cities, had replaced certain portions of the machinery and had introduced higher power, and, most wonderful of all, a new engine which worked from the main boiler and which by magic turned a strange, clumsy wheel at an incredible speed. From this coiled two fat ropes of wire, covered so that no wire could be seen.

They disappeared through a hole in the deck and came to light again in the bridge, being attached to a big lamp working on a swivel.

Nor was this the only innovation. The two Maxims which had stood on either corner of the bridge deck had been moved to amidships, and in their places were long steel-barrelled Hotchkiss guns with rubber-covered shoulder pieces. Beneath, by the bulwarks, were polished wooden chests, where fat brass cartridges lay stored like wine in bins.

Sanders went aboard with a picked crew and half a company of Houssa rifles, and set forth with little idea as to where his journey would end.

He had not left headquarters far behind when the steersman who stood by his side uttered an exclamation, and Sanders looked up.

Overhead in the blue, two birds were wheeling and circling frantically.

The smaller bird darted this way and that.

Sanders sprang into his cabin and snatched up a shot-gun.

The bigger bird was a hawk, going about his proper business; but his quarry, as the Commissioner recognised at a glance, was a faithful servant of the Government—a carrier-pigeon.

The birds had closed in one furious bunch of whirling feathers and talons when Sanders raised his gun and fired. The first barrel missed, but the second brought them down to the water.

A dozen men sprang overboard and swam to the spot where the birds struggled convulsively in their death-grip.

One of the men reached them, deftly wrung the neck of the hawk, and came back to the boat.

The pigeon was dead—had probably died before the shots hit him. Round one red leg was a rubber band and a torn piece of paper.

Sanders smoothed it out and read. It was in Arabic, and all that was left consisted of three words:

. . . Akasava . . . war . . . King.

"H'm!" said Sanders.

He had a man watching the Akasava, a reliable spy whose judgment was beyond doubt. There was urgency in the fact that the message had been sent by carrier-pigeon, and Sanders put the nose of his steamer to the north and prepared for the worst.

At two o'clock in the afternoon, two days' steaming from headquarters, he came to the junction of three rivers where, according to all plans, his spy should have waited him with further intelligence.

But there was no sign of the man, and, though the steamer cruised about, crossing from one bank to the other, the spy did not put in an appearance. Sanders had no other course than to continue his voyage. He arrived at the Akasava city at midnight, picking his way through the shoals and sand-banks without difficulty, thanks to his new search-light.

He "tied up" to one of the many middle islands in the centre of the river and waited for light. At dawn the *Zaire* came sidling to the Akasava bank, her soldiers sitting on the iron lower deck, their legs dangling over the side, their loaded rifles at their knees.

Yet there was no sign of perturbation amongst the people. They flocked down to the beach to watch the steamer come to her moorings, and in half an hour Toloni, the King, came in state with his drummers, his spearmen and his councillors—to pay their respects.

Sanders went ashore with an orderly, walked through the city's street by the King's side, and listened to such news as he had to tell him.

Sanders made no inquiry as to his spy, because that would be futile, but he kept a sharp lookout.

The scene was a peaceful one. The women ground corn before their huts, naked babies strutted daringly in the streets, their shrill laughter rising as hut called to hut, and, best of all, the men were in good humour.

"Lord," said the King as Sanders took his departure, "all things are well, as you see, and my people are full of food and lazy. There is no sickness, and no man injures another."

"Thus it is," said Sanders, who never failed to take advantage of any opportunity for drawing a moral, "because my lord the king has given you his protection so that every man may live fearless of his enemies."

"That is so," said the other humbly. "We are dogs before your presence, and blinded by the bright face of the Great King our master."

Sanders took a short cut to the *Zaire*.

There was a little path which led through the tall, rank, elephant grass.

"Lord," said Toloni, hesitating at the entrance of the path, "this is not a proper way for your greatness, for there is water in the path, and many snakes who live in the marsh."

"This is the way," said Sanders briefly.

The Akasava monarch hesitated, then led the way.

It was, as he had said, an unpleasant road, for the rains had been very heavy and in places the path was ankle-deep in ooze.

Sanders was regretting his obstinacy when, halfway to the beach, he came upon a place where the earth had been recently dug, and there was a raised mound.

"What man is buried here?" asked the Commissioner.

The King looked at him steadfastly.

"One Karama," he said.

"This is not the place of burying," said Sanders; "for if my memory serves me your dead people sleep in one of the middle islands."

"That is so, lord," replied the chief, "yet this man was dead a long time, and only his bones were left. And because my people feared his spirit they buried him where he was found."

The explanation was satisfactory and Sanders passed on, though the grave was the grave of Ali Hazrah, a reliable spy of his, who had been caught by the King's men and speared to death whilst the pigeon he had just released was still circling above in the blue sky.

"My lord goes far?" asked the King as he stood by the gangway of the ship.

"I go north," said Sanders. "Why do you ask?"

"There have been heavy rains," said the King, "and many rivers are swollen. And in such times strangers from the Frenchi and Portagasi lands come into these territories; also, I have heard of an Arabi who is buying people, ten days' journey from here, on the Calali River."

Was this the message Ali had sent? The possibility struck Sanders as being a reasonable one.

The man might have heard something of the sort, sent his message, and gone north in search of further news.

Sanders cast off, and, leaving the Isisi River on his right, took the Calali—a little-known stream.

Toloni, the King, might be sending him on a fool's errand, but he had to take that chance. As it happened, the Akasava overlord had spoken the truth for a certain purpose.

El Mahmud, a notorious trader, found his way into Sanders' territory one spring-time when the rivers were flooded and when certain streams were navigable which had never before known canoe, much less El Mahmud's gay *felucca*.

He brought with him rich bales of merchandise, secret bottles of gin, tobacco, hemp, and his own elegant person.

He was a sallow-faced man who sat under an awning on a silken cushion and smoked, and he was possessed of an insatiable curiosity.

He had large ideas, and was a man of many schemes.

He was engaged in arming a Calali village with rifles which had rendered good service to France in '75, when Sanders came suddenly upon him.

El Mahmud was warned, and put his craft, with all sails set, in the direction of safety, which was represented by a creek four miles up-river, into which no steamer of the *Zaire* size could penetrate.

His little plan, admirable in intention, was somewhat upset by the disconcerting fact that the *Zaire* had recently been re-equipped. The first shot from Sanders' new Hotchkiss gun smashed the side of the *felucca* as a rifle bullet would smash a match-box. The second carried away the roof of El Mahmud's private cabin.

The *Zaire* swung up to the sinking *felucca*, and a rope being passed she was towed to shallow water.

Taking all things into consideration. El Mahmud, who knew something of the English-speaking people and their peculiar ways, would much rather have seen his boat sunk.

"*Sheik*," said his headman as the *Zaire* took the boat in tow, "there is time to get rid of much that will do us harm when the Englishman inspects this boat."

El Mahmud was silent, and his headman drew a long knife from his belt and tested its edge.

He looked inquiringly at his master, but El Mahmud shook his head.

"You are a fool! This *Americano* will hang you like a pig if he smells a spot of blood. Let us wait—what is written must be."

He had not long to wait. As soon as the *Joy of Night*—such was the felicitous name of the craft—was beached, he was escorted before Sanders.

"How came you here?" demanded the Commissioner, and El Mahmud explained calmly and logically that owing to the heavy rains he had adventured along a new river which had never before existed, and thus had come to the Isisi. That was a good excuse, as Mahmud knew. It was more difficult to explain the selling of rifles, for it is a practice which all civilised nations very properly hold as unpardonable. Much more difficult was it to account for twenty-one slaves discovered in the bottom of the *felucca*. Yet the man had a permit to "recruit labour," signed by one Dom Reynaldo de Costa y Ferdinez, Portuguese governor of a coast colony.

Sanders had a horror of "complications," especially with Portuguese authorities, for complications meant long, long letters, reports, minutes, memoranda, and eventually blue books. This meant years of correspondence, official investigations, and a kick at the end, whether he was right or wrong.

"By all laws. El Mahmud," he said, "you have forfeited your life, yet I accept part of your story, though, God knows, I believe you lie! My steamer shall take you to a place which is twenty miles from the Portuguese, and there you shall be set free with food and arms."

"What of my ship and cargo?" asked El Mahmud.

"I shall burn the one and confiscate the other," said Sanders.

El Mahmud shrugged his shoulders.

"All things are ordained," he said.

Sanders took him on board and steamed to a place indicated by the trader—it was nearer his camp—and released him with rifles and ammunition for his followers and ten days' supply of food.

"Go with God," said Sanders in the vernacular.

El Mahmud stood on the bank and watched the steamer sweeping out to midstream.

He waited till its nose was turned down-stream and Sanders was plainly to be seen on the bridge, then sat down carefully, raised his rifle, taking deliberate aim, and fired.

Sanders was giving instructions to Abiboo concerning the repacking of Hotchkiss cartridges which had been laid on the deck in preparation for eventualities.

"These—" he said, then stumbled forward.

Abiboo caught him in his arms, and lowered him to the deck.

"The man—do not let him escape," said Sanders faintly.

Abiboo picked up a cartridge, opened the breech of the long-barrelled Hotchkiss, and slipped it in.

El Mahmud was running swiftly toward the cover of the forest. He had two hundred yards of bare ground to cover, and Abiboo was firing a gun which was as accurately sighted as a rifle. Moreover, he had plenty of time, and was not flurried.

The terrified followers of El Mahmud, returning that night to search for their master, were constantly finding him.

The moon came up over the forest and fretted the river with silver, and Toloni, King of the Akasava, watched from the shore for the omen which Tilagi, the witchdoctor, had promised.

He had long to wait before he saw the ripple which a swimming crocodile makes, but when it came into view, crossing the river in a straight line from shore to shore, he had no eyes for aught else.

Straight as an arrow it sped, undeviating by a single curve from the true line.

"That is a good omen," said Toloni, and rose from the shadow of the bush which hid him from view.

He waited a little while, then struck noiselessly into the forest, swinging his spears.

He came upon his six councillors sitting patiently by the side of the forest path.

"All is as should be," he said. "Tilagi has spoken the truth, for the crocodile crossed from bank to bank, and the day of the Akasava has come."

He led the way back to the sleeping city and gained his big hut. It was empty, by his orders. A fire smouldered in the centre of the hut, and his bed of skins was ready for him on the raised frame bedstead.

He went out again into the open.

"Send Tilagi to me," he said to the waiting headman.

When the old man came—a skinny old man, walking laboriously by the aid of a stick, Toloni called him into the hut.

"Father," he said, "at the full of the moon, as the tide was high, I saw the black crocodile leave his pool on the Isisi bank, and he swam from shore to shore even as you said."

The old man said nothing, nodding his head.

"All this is favourable to my plans," said the King, "and it shall fall out as you say."

"You are a great king," croaked the old man. "There never was in this land so great a king, for you have the mind of a white man, and are greater than Sandi. Other kings and chiefs of the Akasava were fools, and died like fools on a certain high tree, Sandi putting a rope about their necks; but they had black men's brains."

The King walked up and down the length of his hut. He was a tall man, splendidly built, and he carried his head high.

"All men are with me," he said. "Isisi, N'Gombi, Bomongo——"

He paused.

"And the Ochori, lord king," said the witchdoctor. "Yes, they are with you, though the foreigner who rules them is one with Sandi."

"That is a matter which needs settlement," said the King; "yet we must move quickly, for Sandi will soon be back. It is now three days since he left, and the boat-with-the-wheel travels swiftly."

Messengers came and went all that day. Five times was the King aroused from his slumbers to receive messages and to answer questions. The Isisi people were nervous; they feared Sandi.

Would the King swear by death that if the plan did not prosper he would tell Sandi that he forced the Isisi to act by threats and cruelties? The N'Gombi had a queen of Sandi's house; should they slay her?

She had a lover who would kill her very quickly, having access to her hut.

"Do not kill her," was the message Toloni sent, "for I know she is very beautiful. She shall have a hut in the shadow of my great house."

The Lesser Isisi people were impatient. There were two mission stations in their country; should they stay and burn?

"These are small matters," said Toloni the King. "First we must take Sanders, and him we will sacrifice according to ancient practice. Then all other matters will be simple and easy."

That night when darkness came and his unconscious people gossiped about the fires—none were in the secret of the coming great events save Toloni's councillors and certain headmen of other tribes—a *lokali* rattled musically on the outskirts of the town.

The King, in his hut, heard the signal-drum, and knew from its note that it answered some far-off fellow.

Very faintly the distant drum was sounding news from village to village, every roll, every *staccato* tap, every *crescendo* having its special meaning.

Before his hut, with both hands to his ears, the King listened.

Three rolls, rising and falling, a slow rattle, a roll, a tattoo, another roll.

That stood for Sandi—Sandi the swift, Sandi the sharp in anger, Sandi the alarmer, Sandi the giver of justice.

All these qualities and characteristics were expressed by the distant drummer.

Twice the far-away *lokali* spoke Sandi's name, then a long roll, a short roll, and silence.

Again—a long roll, a short roll—silence.

"Sandi dies!"

Toloni's voice was harsh and exultant.

"Listen!" he whispered.

A metallic tattoo, punctuated by an irregular procession of low, deep notes—that stood for the Arabi.

"*Tap—tap—tap—tap.*"

There had been more shooting.

Then Sanders' name occurred again—the long roll, the short roll, and silence.

It was clear to those who could read the message—the message that ten miles away had been received by the *lokali* man and hammered forth from his hollow tree trunk to yet another village.

Even now Toloni's signaller was sending the message on. All night long, through the length and breadth of the land, the message would be repeated till it came to the edges of wild lands, where Sandi was unknown and the message itself incomprehensible.

"All gods and devils are with me," said the King of the Akasava. "Now is the time."

Stretched on his bunk, Sanders, with the aid of Abiboo and a small hand-mirror, located his injury.

He had suffered the slightest of wounds—the bullet had struck a steel chain purse he carried in his pocket and had deflected and taken a piece of flesh out of his left forearm, and had fetched up in the roof of the cabin before which he had been standing.

Beyond a pained bruised side and the wound in his arm, he had suffered no hurt. Abiboo dressed both places from the medicine chest, and there the matter should have ended, for Sanders was a healthy man.

But the next morning found him in a highly feverish condition. The arm had swollen to twice its normal dimensions, and was terribly painful. Sanders suspected a poisoned bullet, and was probably justified. He did not consider the matter very fully, for he was too busily engaged in an impossible argument with the Administration to give much heed to such trivialities. It was a tedious argument about a tall hat. Should Sanders wear a tall hat for the Coronation Naval Review, or should he not? The Administration was firm, but Sanders was equally determined.

"I've a shocking headache, and you ask me to wear a tall hat, your Excellency," he said in anger, and burst into tears.

It was so unlike Sanders, and he knew it was so unlike him, that by a tremendous effort of will, he came back to actualities.

He was lying in his cabin. His head and his arm ached diabolically. His face was wet with perspiration and his tongue was like a strip of leather.

Abiboo, squatting by the side of the bed, rose as Sanders opened his eyes.

"Where do you go?" asked Sanders.

"To the God-woman who gives medicine," said. Abiboo, without any display of emotion. "For I fear that you will die, and I wish for a book that I did everything properly."

"Cautious devil," muttered Sanders, and relapsed again into unconsciousness.

When he awoke again he did not hear the beat of the steamer's paddles. It was to a surprising calm and ease he awoke. He was lying in a big room in a small bed, and the sheets were of the finest linen—which on the steamer they had not been. 'There was a big bowl of blue flowers on a table near the bed, and a strange fragrance.

It cannot be said that he recognised the place, because he had never before seen the interior of Miss Glandynne's bedroom; but he had a dim recollection that somebody had said he was to be taken to her. His first conscious emotion was one of extreme annoyance that he had been a nuisance to somebody, his second was one of doubt as to his own condition.

He turned his head slowly to view the erring arm. He would not have been surprised if he had found it missing. It was here safe enough, and he sighed his relief. Also it was near enough to normal size to be comforting.

He ventured to move the hand of the injured limb, and to his great pleasure found no difficulty to and experienced no pain.

Then Ruth Glandynne came in—-a beautiful vision in that dark land.

She smiled, lifted a warning finger, shifted his pillow a little, and sat down by his side.

"What is wrong with the Akasava?" he asked suddenly. It was apropos of nothing; he had not even been thinking of the Akasava, but something impelled the question.

He saw her face go suddenly grave.

"I—I think you had better not bother about the Akasava," she faltered. "You must keep very quiet."

"I must know!" he said.

His voice was cracked and weak, but she knew that, whatever might be the result, she must tell him.

He lay quietly with closed eyes while she spoke, and when she had finished he lay silent—so silent that she thought he had relapsed into unconsciousness.

Then he opened his eyes.

"Send a messenger to the Ochori," he said, "and bid Bosambo the chief come to me."

Bosambo was immensely unpopular amongst all other chiefs and peoples.

Bosambo was an alien—being a Krooman who had fled from Liberia owing to the persecutions of the government of that model

293

republic. If you should ask how it came about that the majestic machinery of state came to be put into motion against so insignificant a man as Bosambo—a common man, if you might judge him by his place in the state—I enlighten you by offering the explanation that Bosambo had killed a warder at the convict settlement whither he had been sent for theft. The adventurer wandered across Africa till he came to the milk-hearted Ochori, in which he became paramount chief of the tribe on the sudden and inexplicable death of its rightful chief.

It is sufficient to say that this ex-convict made men of a timid people, giving them pride and a sort of spurious courage which was made up as to three-parts of fear—for Bosambo had pliant whips of rhinoceros hide, and was very quick to take offence.

One morning, in the spring of the year, Bosambo came out of his hut to find the world exquisitely beautiful—being covered with the freshest green of growing things, the sky flecked with white clouds, and a gentle breeze wrinkling the surface of the big river.

The city of the Ochori was built on the slope of a hill, and you looked across the N'Gombi Forest to the faint blur of the mountain of trees, which is in the Akasava territory.

Bosambo, who was no poet and admired only those beauties of nature which were edible, glanced disconsolately along the broad street of his city, where women were preparing the morning meals, and where the smoke of a score of little fires drifted lazily. Bosambo's three common wives were engaged before the next hut in a similar operation; his chief wife was not visible, being of the faith which requires that woman shall have no existence save to her lord.

He turned his face to the western end of the city and walked slowly.

Bosambo was no fool. He had lived amongst civilised people, he spoke English, he was a thief who had made his living in a nation of thieves.

He was aware of the happenings in the Akasava. There had been a rising—a section of the people which had declared against rebellion and had been wiped from the face of the earth. Also the Isisi had joined in the general movement, had destroyed the timid of their number, and forced the folk of the Bolenzi to servitude.

Bosambo had received an invitation to do homage to Toloni, the King, and had sent back a message which was at once comprehensive and coarse. He was safe from reprisals for a week or so. Between him and the Akasava lay the mission station where Sandi was—dying, by all accounts, but certainly there. And tied up to the mission bank was the *Zaire* and half a company of Houssas, to say nothing of two immense guns.

But if Bosambo was contemptuous of the self-appointed King of the World—as Toloni called himself—there were men of the Ochori who, remembering Bosambo's pliant whip, and his readiness to exercise it, corresponded with Toloni, and Bosambo knew that half the Ochori people were far gone in sedition.

Yet he was not over-distressed—that worried him less than another matter.

"Light of my life and joy of my soul," he said to the woman who shared the gaudy magnificence of his thatched *harem*. "If Sandi dies there is no virtue in religion, for I have prayed to all gods, to the Prophets, and to the lords Marki, Luko, and Johanni—also to the Virgin of whom the Marist Brothers told me; and I have prayed to crosses and to *ju-jus*, and have sacrificed a goat and a chicken before the Ochori fetish."

"Mahomet," she said reprovingly, "all this is evil, for there is but one God."

"He will praise my diligence in seeking Him," said Bosambo philosophically. "Yet, if Sandi recover, I will thank all gods lest I miss the Him who benefited my master."

His position was a delicate one, as he knew. Only the previous night he had caught a secret messenger from Toloni, who came to call upon the Ochori to attack Sandi's men from the north, driving them towards the waiting legions of the rebel king. Bosambo extracted the full message from the courier before he disposed of him.

Two more days of anxious waiting followed. A headman of the Ochori, who had been promised the chiefship of the tribe, decided to rush matters, and crept into Bosambo's hut one evening to create the necessary vacancy.

Bosambo, who was waiting for him, clubbed him into insensibility with promptitude and dispatch, dragged him in the darkness of the night to the river bank, and slid him into the water with a rope about his neck and a stone attached to the rope.

It brought matters to a head in one sense, for, missing their leader, his faction called upon Bosambo and demanded that the missing man be handed over to them. Their chief's reply was an emphatic one. The spokesman carried the marks of Bosambo's eloquence to the grave. How matters might have developed it is difficult to guess, but Sandi's summons came to Bosambo, and he called his people together.

"I go to Sandi," he told them, "Sandi who is my master and yours, in addition to being my relative, as you know. And behold I leave behind me a people who are ungrateful and vicious. Now I say to you that in my absence you shall go about your work and do nothing evil—that you shall neither attend to the council of fools nor follow your own wicked fancies—for when I return I shall be swift to punish; and if any man disobey me, I will put out his eyes and leave him in the forest for the beasts to hunt. I will do this by *Ewa*, who is death."

After which Bosambo departed for the mission station, taking with him his favourite wife and fifty fighting men.

He came to Sandi's within forty-eight hours of the Commissioner's summons, and squatted by his master's bedside.

"Bosambo," said Sandi, "I have been very ill, and I am still too weak to stand. And whilst I am lying here, Toloni, King of the Akasava, has risen, and with him the countryside."

"Lord, it is as you say," said Bosambo.

"In time there will come many white men," said Sandi, "and they will eat up this foolish king; but in the meantime there will be much suffering, and many innocent people will be slain. I have sent for you because I trust you."

"Lord," said Bosambo, "I am a thief and a low man, and my heart is full of pride that you should stoop toward me."

Sandi detected the tremor in Bosambo's voice, and he knew he was sincere.

"Therefore, O chief, I have placed you in my place, for you are skilled in war. And I give over to you the command of my ship and of my fighting men, and you shall do that which is best."

Bosambo sprang noiselessly to his feet, and stood tense and erect by the bedside. There was a strange light in his eyes.

"Lord Sandi," he said in a low voice, "do you speak true—that I"—he struck his broad chest with both his clenched fists—"I stand in your place?"

"That is so," said Sandi.

Bosambo was silent for a minute, then he opened his mouth to speak, checked himself, and, turning without a word, left the room.

Which was unlike Bosambo.

They were prepared for his coming. Abiboo stood at the end of the gangway and raised his hand in salute.

"I am your man, chief," he said.

"Abiboo," he said, "I do not lie when I say that I am of your faith; and by Allah and his Prophet I am for doing that which is best for Sandi, our master."

"So we both desire," said Abiboo.

Bosambo's preparations were quietly made.

He sent half of his fighting men to the mission house to guard Sandi, and with them twenty Houssas under a sergeant.

"Now we will call upon Toloni the king," he said.

The King of the Akasava sat in *palaver*. His force was camped on the edge of the N'Gombi country, and a smoking village spoke of resistance offered and overcome—for the N'Gombi had at last declined to join the coalition, and the lover, who had undertaken to persuade the queen, and, failing persuasion, to take more effective action, had failed.

The queen notified his failure by sending his head to Toloni.

Not even the news that Sandi was sick to death served to shake them in their opposition. It may have been that the vital young queen cherished ambitions of her own.

The king's *palaver* was a serious one.

"It seems that the N'Gombi people must be eaten up village by village," he said, "for all this country is with me save them only. As to this queen, she shall be sorry."

He was within striking distance of the N'Gombi queen. His legions were closing steadily in upon the doomed city. By nightfall he was within reach, and at dawn the following morning Toloni carried the city by assault and it was a beastly business.

They carried the queen back to the king's headquarters, and there was a great dance.

By the light of a dozen fires the king sat in judgment.

The girl—she was little more—stood up before him, stripped of her robes, and met the king's eyes without fear.

"Woman," he said, "this night you die!"

She made no answer.

"By fire and by torment I will kill you," said Toloni, and told her the means of her death.

He sat on his carved stool of state beneath a tree. He was naked, save for the leopard robe that covered one shoulder, and his cruel eyes glittered in anticipation of the spectacle she would afford.

She spoke calmly enough.

"If I die tonight and you die tomorrow, O king, what is a day? For

Sandi will come with his soldiers."

"Sandi is dead," said the king thickly. He had drunk heavily of the maize beer that natives prepare. "And if he lived—"

There came to his hearing a faint wail that grew in shrillness until it became a shriek. Shrieking it passed over his head and died away.

He struggled to his feet unsteadily.

"It was a spirit," he muttered, then—

The wailing sound came again—a shriek this time of men. Something struck the tree, splintering the bark.

The faint and ghastly light of dawn was in the sky; in a second the world went pearl-grey and, plain to be seen, hugging the shore on the opposite bank, was the *Zaire*.

As the king looked he saw a pencil of fire leap from the little ship, heard the whine of the coming shell, and realised the danger.

He gave a hurried order, and a regiment ran to the river-bank where the canoes were beached. They were not there. The guards left to watch them lay stretched like men asleep on the beach, but the canoes were in mid-stream five miles away, carried down by the river.

In the night Bosambo's men had crossed the river.

The story of the fall of Toloni is a brief one. Trapped on the middle island, at the mercy of the long-range guns of the *Zaire*, Toloni surrendered.

He was conducted to the *Zaire*.

Bosambo met him on the bridge.

"Ho, Bosambo!" said Toloni, "I have come to see Sandi."

"You see me who am as our lord," said Bosambo.

Toloni spat on the deck.

"When a slave sits in the king's place only slaves obey him," he quoted a river saying.

"Kings have only one head, and the slave's blood is also red," said Bosambo readily. "And it seems to me, Toloni, that you are too full of life for our lord's happiness. But first you shall tell me what has come to the Queen of the N'Gombi."

"She died," said Toloni carelessly; "very quickly she died."

Bosambo peered at him. It was a trick of Sandi's this peering, and the Chief of the Ochori was nothing if not imitative.

"You shall tell me how she died," said Bosambo.

The king's face twitched.

"I took her by the throat," he said sullenly.

"Thus?" said Bosambo, and his big hand closed on the king's strong neck.

"Thus!" gasped the king, "and I struck her with my knife—ah!"

"Thus?" said Bosambo.

Twice his long, broad-bladed knife rose and fell, and the king went quivering to the deck.

★★★★★★

Sandi was strong enough to walk to the beach to meet the *Zaire* on its return—strong enough, though somewhat dazzled by his splendour, to greet Bosambo, wearing a sky-blue robe laced with tinsel, and a tall and napless hat.

Bosambo came mincing down the gangway plank swinging a brass-headed stick and singing a low song such as Kroomen sing on the coast when they receive their pay and are dismissed their ships.

He was beautiful to behold—feathers were in his hair, rope after rope of gay beads about his neck.

"I have slain Toloni," he said, "even as your lord would have done—he turned his face from me and said, 'It is honourable to die at your hands, Bosambo,' and he made little moaning noises thus—"

And Bosambo, with his heart in the task, made an admirable effort of mimicry.

"Go on," said Sandi hastily.

"Also I have sent the Isisi and the Akasava to their homes to await your honour's judgment, even as you would have done, master."

Sandi nodded.

"And these?" he asked, indicating the chief's finery.

"These I stole from the camp of Toloni," said Bosambo. "These and other things, for I was working for government and lord," he said with becoming simplicity. "It is according to the white man's custom, as your lordship knows."

CHAPTER 12

The Missionary

This is a moral story. You may go to the black countries for your morals and take from cannibal peoples a most reliable code of ethics. For cannibal folk are fastidious to a degree, eminently modest—though a photograph of the average Bogra native would leave you in some doubt—clean of speech and thought and habit. If they chop men it is because they like food of that particular type. They are no better and no worse than vegetarians, who are also faddy in the matter of foodstuffs.

Native peoples have a code of their own, and take some account of family obligations.

There were two brothers who lived in the Isisi country in a small village, and when their father died they set forth to seek their fortune. The name of the one was M'Kamdina, and of the other M'Kairi. M'Kamdina being the more adventurous, crossed the border of the lawful land into the territory of the Great King, and there he sold himself into captivity.

In those days the Great King was very great and very ancient; so great that no British Administrator did more than reprove him mildly for his wanton cruelty.

This M'Kamdina was a clever youth, very cunning in council, very patient of abuse. He had all the qualities that go to the making of a courtier. It is not surprising, therefore, that he gained a place in the King's household, sat at his right hand at meat, and married such of the King's light fancies as His Majesty was pleased to discard.

He grew wealthy and powerful; was the King's Prime Minister, with power of life and death in his master's absence. He went afield for his lord's dancing girls and, having nice taste in such matters, was considerably rewarded.

So he lived, happy and prosperous and content.

The other brother, M'Kairi, had no such enterprise. He settled in a small village near the Pool of Spirits, and with great labour, being a poor man and only affording one wife, he cleared a garden. Here he sowed industriously, and reaped with a full measure of success, selling his stock at a profit.

News came to him of his brother's prosperity, and once, in contempt of all Sanders' orders, the painted canoe of the Great King's Premier came flashing down the river bearing gifts to the poor brother.

Sanders heard of this when he was on a tour of inspection and went out to see M'Kairi.

"Lord, it was so," said the man sadly. "These rich gifts come from my brother, who is a slave. Salt and corn and cloth and spearheads he sent me."

Sanders looked round at the poor field the man worked.

"And yet, M'Kairi," he said, "this is not the garden of a rich man, nor do I see your fine cloth nor the wives that salt would bring you."

"Lord," said the man, "I sent them back, for my heart is very sore that my brother should be a slave and I a free man, toiling in the fields, but free; and I would give my life if I could pay the price of him."

He told Sanders he had sent a message asking what that price was, and it happened that Sanders was close at hand when the Great King, for his own amusement, sent back word saying that the price of M'Kamdina was ten thousand *matakos*—a *matako* being a brass rod.

Now it is a fact that for seven years—long, patient, suffering, lean years—M'Kairi laboured in his garden, and sold and bought and reared and bargained until he had acquired ten thousand *matakos*. These he put into his canoe and paddled to the edge of the land where the Great King ruled, and so came to the presence of his brother and the master of his brother.

The Great King was amused; M'Kamdina was not so amused, being wrathful at his brother's simplicity.

"Go back with your rods," he said. He sat in his grand hut, and his smiling wives and his slaves sat about him. "Take your rods, M'Kairi my brother, and know that it is better to be a slave in the house of a king than a free man toiling in the fields."

And M'Kairi went back to his tiny plantation sick at heart.

Three weeks later the Great King died. That is the station where the moral of this little story steps off. For according to custom, when the Great King lay stretched upon his bier, they took the principal slave of the great one—and that slave was M'Kamdina—and they cut off his head that his body might be buried with his master to serve his soul's need in another land.

And the son of the Great King reigned in his stead, and in course of time died violently.

"There's the basis of a good Sunday school yarn in that story," said the Houssa captain.

"H'm!" growled Sanders, who was innocent of any desire to furnish material for tracts.

"Rum beggar, that old king!" said the Houssa thoughtfully, "and the new fellow was a rummer. You hanged him or something, didn't you?"

"I forget," said Sanders shortly. "If your infernal troops were worth their salt there would be no hangings. What is it?"

His orderly was standing in the doorway of the Houssa skipper's hut.

"Lord, there is a book," said the man.

Sanders took the soiled envelope from the man's hand. It was addressed in flowing Arabic:

"The Lord Commissioner, Who is at the town where the river is broadest near the sea. Two flagstaffs standing up and many soldiers will be seen. Go swiftly, and may God be with you."

It was an address and an instruction.

"Who brought this?"

"An Arabi," said the man, "such as trade in the high land."

Sanders tore open the letter. He sought first the signature at the top of the letter and found it to be that of Ahmed, a reliable chief of his secret service.

Sanders read the letter, skipping the flowery introduction wherein Ahmed asked Providence and its authorised agents to bring happiness to the house of the Commissioner.

"It is well that I should tell you this, though I hide my face when I speak of a woman of your house."

(Sanders accepted the innuendo which coupled the name of an innocent missionary lady with himself.)

"Of this God-woman, who is at present on the river, many stories come, some being that she cries at night because no men of the Akasava take God-magic.

"And I have heard from an Isisi woman who is her servant that this God-woman would go back to her own land, only she is ashamed because so few have learnt the new God. Also, she has fever. I send this by an Arabi, my friend Ahmed, who is my messenger, being five days in search of an Akasava man who has stolen goats."

Sanders laughed helplessly. "That girl will be the death of me," he said. He left for the mission station that very hour.

The girl was well enough, but very white and tired; she was obviously glad to see Sanders.

"It was so good of you to come," she said. "I was getting a little dispirited; I had half made up my mind to go back to England."

"I wish I hadn't come if that's the case," said Sanders bluntly.

The girl smiled.

"That isn't very nice of you, Mr. Sanders," she said.

"Nice! Look here."

He took off his helmet and pointed to his closely cropped head.

"Do you see those?" he asked.

She looked curiously.

She saw nothing except a face burnt brick-red by the sun, two steady grey eyes in such odd contrasts to the tan that they seemed the lightest blue.

She saw the lean face, the straight thin nose, the firm jaw and the almost hairless head.

"What am I looking for?" she asked.

"Grey hairs," said Sanders grimly.

She frowned in pretty perplexity.

"It is difficult to see any hair at all," she confessed. "But will you turn your head a little? Yes, I see something which might be grey."

"They're grey enough," said Sanders with a little smile. He was more at home with her than he had ever been with a white woman.

"And exactly what do they signify?" she asked.

"Worry—about you," said Sanders. "Good Lord! Haven't you had enough of these infernal people? I seem to spend half my life running up and down this river keeping people in order who are anxious to chop you. You cannot build on sand, and you are trying to lay a foundation on water."

"You mean religious teaching must have a basis of civilisation?" she asked quietly.

"Something like that. Look here, Miss Glandynne; that man who is working in your garden, he's one of your converts, isn't he?"

She nodded.

"He is the most helpful man I have; he goes into the outlying villages and holds services."

"What is his name?"

"Kombolo," she said.

Sanders called the man to him. He was a stout, good-humoured native, the "outward and visible sign of whose inward and spiritual grace" was a pair of trousers and a waistcoat.

"Kombolo," said Sanders in the Isisi dialect, "they tell me you are a fine God-man."

"Lord, that is so," said the man, beaming, "for I have the blessed Spirit in me which makes me talk wonderfully."

"And you go to many villages?"

"Preaching the Word, master," said the man, nodding.

"And do you go ever to the people of the Forest-of Happy-Thought?" asked Sanders quietly.

The man shuddered.

"Lord, I do not go there," he said.

"Why?"

Kombolo shuffled his bare feet and stood on one leg in his embarrassment.

"Lord, there are devils and ghosts in the wood, as you know," he said.

"Do you ever go to the people of the N'Gombi Forest?" asked Sanders innocently.

Again the man shivered.

"Never do I go there, Sandi," he said, "because, as your lordship knows, *M'shimba-M'shamba* walks therein."

The girl was following the conversation with knitted brows.

"Who is *M'shimba-M'shamba?*" she asked.

"He is the green devil who walks by night," said Sanders blandly, "and he is very terrible."

Kombolo nodded his head vigorously.

"That is true, mamma," he said earnestly. "I myself have seen him."

The girl's face wore a look of shocked surprise.

"But, Kombolo," she said in distress, "you know there are no such things as devils."

Kombolo was frankly puzzled.

"Lady," he said slowly, "it is certain that there are devils, for do we not read of him—the Devil, the old One—who fills us with bad thoughts?"

"But that is different," she began helplessly.

"A devil is a devil," said Kombolo philosophically, "and, though there be only one devil in your land, there are many here; for, lady, here, as you have told me, there are many flies and many beasts such as you do not see in your own country. So also there must be devils, though perhaps not so mighty as the lord Devil of the white people."

Sanders dismissed him with a nod, and sat whistling cheerfully to himself whilst the girl laid reason under tribute to fact.

"Well?" he said at last.

"You don't make things easy," she said, and Sanders, to his horror, discovered that she was on the verge of tears. "I think it was unkind of you to sow doubt in Kombolo's mind. It is hard enough to fight against their superstition—"

"But—" protested the agitated Commissioner.

"—without having to combat superstition and ignorance fortified by authority."

She checked a sob.

"But, Miss Glandynne—"

"I know what you are going to say—you want me to go home. I'm too much bother to you. I give you grey hairs and take up all your time. But I'm going to stay."

She rose and stamped her foot vehemently.

"Don't get angry—"

"I'm not angry—"

"Don't be annoyed—"

"I'm not annoyed. I know I'm unfitted for the work; I never intended doing evangelical work. I came out for the medical side, and if I'd known I had to work alone I shouldn't have come at all."

"Then go back," said Sanders eagerly; "go back to the life you ought to be living. I'll get Father Wells to come up and take over your station."

"A Catholic!" she said scornfully.

"Is he?" asked Sanders, who never worried about creeds. "Anyway—"

"And besides," she said, and her voice shook, "I've nothing to hand over. I've been here nearly a year, and my only convert is a man who believes in green devils. Oh, Mr. Sanders!"

She broke down and tugged furiously for a handkerchief in her belt.

"Oh, Lord!" said Sanders, and beat a hasty retreat.

He saw her again in the evening. She was calmer and inclined to listen to reason.

"Give the station another three months," he said. "The country has been a bit upset since you've been here. I can understand you not wishing to admit your failure."

She caught her breath ominously.

"Not that you've been a failure," Sanders went on with frantic haste; "far from it. But it would be different, wouldn't it, if you could point to some work——"

"Of course it would," she said shortly; then, realising that she was being a little ungracious, she smiled through the gathering tears. "I'm afraid I'm too worldly for this work. I'm not satisfied with the knowledge that I am doing my best. I want to see results."

Sanders, in his intense astonishment, patted her hand. More to his astonishment, he told her the story of the two brothers, and she was greatly impressed.

"That is the best missionary moral I have ever heard," she said.

"I am leaving tomorrow," he said, after he had stopped to curse himself under his breath. "I go to Lukalela for a wife-beating *palaver*, and afterwards to the black country."

He did not mention the fact that he was going to the Ochori—for reasons of his own. Yet it was to the Ochori country that he headed. It was peculiar to his office that no man knew to whither the Commissioner was bound. He stood by the steersman, and by a wave of his hand, this way or that, set the steamer's course.

If he so willed, the *Zaire* would deviate to the left or right bank—if he wished the steamer kept a straight course till night fell, when the nearest wooding was his apparent objective.

Before night came, late in the afternoon, he fetched up at a wooding where a year before he had felled ten trees, leaving them to season and to dry. For two hours the men of the *Zaire* sawed and chopped at the fallen trunks, stacking the wood on the well-deck below.

At night the *Zaire* resumed her journey. The big lamp on the right of the steersman hissed and spluttered as Sanders switched on the current, and a white fan of light shot ahead of the ship.

It searched the water carefully—a great unwinking eye which looked closely for shoal and sandbank.

At midnight Sanders tied up to give himself a little rest.

He reached the Ochori city in the afternoon, and his interview with Bosambo was a brief one.

By evening he was gone, the steamer sweeping back to Lukalela.

Bosambo held a court every morning of his life, save on those mornings when work and pleasure were forbidden by the Koran, which he imperfectly knew, but which he obeyed at second hand—his wife was of the faith, and had made an obedient, if a careless, convert in her husband.

In the time of the Ramadhan, Bosambo did no work, but fasted in the privacy of the forest—whither on the previous day he had removed a store of food and water sufficient to last him over a very trying twenty-four hours. For, though it was his pleasure to humour his wife, it was not his wish to humour her to his own discomfort.

On the morning after Sanders' visit, Bosambo sat upon a wooden chair—a gift of Sanders—painted alternately red, green, and yellow—the paint also being a gift of Sanders, though he was unaware of the fact—and dealt with the minor offences and the little difficulties of his people.

"Lord Bosambo," said a thin young man from an outlying village, "I bring salt to your justice, (a river saying, meaning: "I am so certain of the meal, I have brought the flavouring.")"

"Speak, my brother," said Bosambo; "you shall have your meal."

"I have two wives, lord; one I bought from her father for three skins, and one came to me after the great (Akasava) war. Now the woman I bought has put shame upon me, for she has a lover. In the days before you came, lord, it would be proper to put her to death; but now she and other women laugh at our beatings, and continue in sin."

"Bring the woman," said Bosambo.

The young man dragged her forward, a comely girl of sixteen, with defiant laughter in her eyes, and she was unabashed.

"Woman," said Bosambo severely, "though no death awaits you by Sandi's orders, and my pleasure, yet there are ways, such as you know, of teaching you wisdom. I have built a prison in the Forest of Dreams, where devils come nightly, and it seems a proper place for you."

"Lord," she gasped, "I am afraid."

"Yet I will not send you there, for I love my people," said Bosambo. "Now you shall go to the God-woman who dwells by Kosumkusu, and you shall do as she tells you. And you shall say that you have come to learn of the new God-magic, and you shall do all the strange things she desires, such as shutting your eyes at proper moments and saying 'Ah-min.'"

"Lord, I will do this," said the girl.

"It will be well for you if you do," said Bosambo.

The next case was that of a man who claimed goats from his neighbour in lieu of other benefits promised.

"For he said, speaking with an evil and a lying tongue, 'If you help me with my fishing for a year I will give you the first young of my goat after the rains,'" said the man.

The dispute centred in the words "after the rains," for it would appear that the goats were born before the rains came.

"This is a difficult *palaver*," said Bosambo, "and I need time to take the counsel of Sandi. You, Kalo, shall go to the God-woman by Kosumkusu; and you too," he said, addressing the other party to the dispute, "and there you shall learn the God-magic and do all the things she desires, telling her that you come to learn of her wisdom, and in course of time it shall be revealed to me who is right and who is wrong."

And for every man and woman who came before him he had one solution, one alternative to punishment—a visit to the God-woman and the cultivation of a spirit of humility. Some there were who demurred.

"Lord, I will not go," said a man violently, "for this God-woman speaks slightingly of my god and my *ju-ju*, and I do not want to know the new God-magic."

"Tie him to a tree," said Bosambo calmly, "and whip him till he says '*Ah-min*.'"

Willing hands bound the unfortunate to a tree, and a rhinoceros whip whistled in the air and fell once, twice, thrice—

"*Ah-min!*" yelled the malcontent, and was released to make his pilgrimage to Kosumkusu.

At the close of the *palaver*, Bosambo, with his chief councillor, Olomo, a wise old man, walked through the street of the city together.

"Lord," said Olomo, shaking his head, "I do not like this new way of government, for it is not proper that the young people of the Ochori should—"

Bosambo stopped and looked at him thoughtfully.

"You are right, Olomo," he said softly; "it is not wise that only the young people should go. Now I think it would please me if you went with them that they might feel no shame."

"Lord, I do not desire," said the alarmed old man.

"For I should like you to bring me news of my people," Bosambo went on, "and you could teach them, being so full of wisdom, how to shut their eyes and say 'Ah-min' when certain words are spoken; also, you could prevent them running away."

"By *Ewa*, I will not go!" said the old man, trembling with passion.

"By *Ewa*, you will go," said Bosambo, "or I will take you by the beard, old he-goat, and pull you through the village."

"I am your slave," muttered Olomo, and tottered off to make preparations for the journey.

Sanders made a longer stay in Kukalala than he had expected. And there had been an outbreak of *beriberi* in an interior village which made his presence necessary.

He came to the mission station, wondering, hoping, and a little fearful.

He went ashore and walked up the little path and through the garden she had made for herself; the girl came to meet him half-way.

A radiant, happy girl, showing no sign of her illness. Sanders' heart smote him.

"Oh, Mr. Sanders," she said, stretching out both hands in welcome, "I cannot tell you how glad I am to see you! I have wonderful news!"

Sanders blushed guiltily, and felt monstrously uncomfortable.

"Indeed!" was all he could say.

And then she told him the splendid happening. How her little flock had grown with a rapidity which was little short of marvellous; how the news had gone out, and pilgrims had arrived—not singly, but in fours and fives—for days on end—men and women, old and young.

"Extraordinary!" said Sanders. "Now I suppose you will not object to handing over the station to Father———"

"Hand it over!" she exclaimed in amazement. "Leave all those poor people! Abandon them! Of course, I shall do nothing so criminal."

Sanders did not swoon.

"But—but," he said, "do they want to stay?"

"They did not at first, but after I had told them your story they understood something of their position."

"Oh!" said Sanders. He gathered himself together and walked back to the boat.

Bosambo paddled downstream to meet the Commissioner and lay his troubles before him. "Lord," he said ruefully, "I did not know that this new *palaver* would be pleasing to my people. I have sent the flower of my nation to the God-woman, and they will not come back."

"It is written," said Sanders.

They had met in the middle of the river. Just as the *Zaire* was turning Bosambo had come alongside, and now they stood on the deck together, silent in the consciousness of their mutual failure.

From the shore came a sound of singing. It was the evening hymn of the new converts.

The music came to an end, there was a pause, and then a sharp roll of melody.

"*Ah-min!*" echoed Bosambo bitterly. "And, lord, I taught them that word."

CHAPTER 13

A Maker of Spears

North of the Akasava country and on the left bank of the Isisi is a veritable forest of elephant grass. Here in the cool of the evening, and later, the hippo come to wallow and for social intercourse. Here, too, buck and the small but terrible buffalo come to bathe and drink.

For ten miles without a break the jungle runs and there is no tree or hill behind the green curtain to reveal what manner of country lies beyond.

It is a marsh for fifty miles and in the centre is an island unapproachable save by secret ways such as a few Akasava men know and jealously preserve.

No corporation working under a charter or great seal of state is so close, so exclusive as is that of "The Keepers of the Water Path."

The secret is kept in one family and is known only to the male members. There is a story that a woman once discovered the mystery of the open water—for open water there is in the maze of grass—and that she unwittingly betrayed her knowledge. They took her, so the story runs, her own brothers and blood kindred, and they drowned her in the water. This must have been *cala cala*—long ago—before keen-eyed and swift-handed justice made its appearance in the shape of Mr. Commissioner Sanders.

To the uninitiated it might seem that the secret way was not of any great importance. True, the best fish came into the creek and the family had that advantage.

But as Sanders discovered, the marsh land was of some strategical importance, for it effectively separated the Akasava from the Isisi. It made sudden raidings such as are common between tribes with contiguous frontiers impossible, also it offered no hiding place to malefactors, and for this reason alone it was wiser to preserve the Keepers of the Marsh in their mystery.

Sanders was in the Akasava territory, in the village nearest the marsh, when an unfortunate thing occurred.

There was a woman of the frontier who had been married to an old chief whose name was Likilivi. He was chief not only of the village, but of the family which kept the marsh, and he was an important man—but old.

Now all men know that the makers of spears, and of iron work generally, are the N'Gombi people.

They are born craftsmen, skilful and very cunning. Also, in parenthesis, they are great thieves and once stole a little anvil from the *Zaire*, which was converted into spear heads and steel cups before the anvil was missed.

Yet Likilivi, a man of the Akasava, was the most famous worker of spears on the river. So famous that hunters and warriors came from all parts to buy his weapons. His father before him, and his father, had also made spears, but none equal in keenness or in temper to those which Likilivi made in his big work hut. And he made them with extraordinary rapidity, he and the two sons of his house, so that he grew rich and powerful.

He was old, too old for the girl his wife, who hated him from the first, hated him fiercely till her young heart nearly burst with the fury of her emotions.

She ran from him, was brought back and beaten. She sat down to brood and find a way out, whilst from the adjoining hut came the "*tink—tink—tink*" of hammered steel, as Likilivi and his grown sons pounded spear heads into shape.

If you take a piece of glass no bigger than the top of your thumb, place it in a mortar and industriously pound and grind at it, you will, in course of time, produce a fine white powder smooth to the touch and, though insoluble, yet easily administered to man.

You must be patient, and have plenty of time to make your powder "fit," as they say on the coast, but M'ciba (this was the girl's name) had all the time there was to prepare her release.

Old Likilivi came from his workshop one afternoon; he was a little soured because some innocent villager with a taste for crude arithmetic had asked him how it came about that so few men made so many spears.

He was at best an old and sour man, he was no more amiable because of this embarrassing question.

"The sun has come to me," his wife should have said politely, as he came to the hut where she sat crushing corn. (The white powder and the mortar and iron-wood pestle were discreetly hidden.)

She said nothing.

"If you do not speak to me," said the old man sourly, "I will break your head."

The girl did not speak. She went about her work, which was the preparation of his food. She made him a mess of *manioc*, and fish, and she added a judicious quantity of fine white powder.

The old chief ate his meal, muttering to himself and casting evil eyes at her.

When he had finished he beat her for no particular reason save that he felt like beating her, then he went to bed.

He woke up in the night. She was not lying at his side as was her duty. By the dull red light of the fire he saw her sitting with her back against the hut wall, her hands clasping her knees, watching him with grave eyes.

"M'ciba," he gasped, and the sweat was standing on his forehead, "I have the sickness–*mongo*."

She said nothing and he did not speak again.

An hour later she covered her body with dust and sitting down before the hut wailed her grief, and the awakened village hurried forth to find Likilivi near to death, with his face twisted painfully.

By the aid of an extraordinary constitution and the employment of a drastic but effective native remedy the chief did not die. M'ciba had wailed too soon.

It was many weeks before Likilivi recovered. He suspected nothing. As soon as he was well he took the pliant half of his hunting spear and thrashed her.

"For you are a fool," he said, "or you would have called for help sooner, and I should have recovered more quickly."

She took her beating meekly, knowing that she deserved more, but her hatred grew.

Her treatment by her husband was scandal in the village, for native folk are kind, and it is not customary or good form to beat one's womenkind.

Then M'ciba committed her crowning indiscretion.

Likilivi, his cousin and his sons, prepared to make one of their periodical visits to the marsh—a matter of some importance and considerable secrecy. There was to be a great netting of fish, and other high mysteries were to be enacted—foolish mysteries, you might think them, such as the sacrificing of chicken and the like, but which were very real and important to Likilivi and his kin. Also there were other matters to be seen to.

By some means M'ciba came to know of the intended visit, and spoke to a woman about the event. It was unforgivable. It was against all tradition. Likilivi, for the honour of his house, ordered a public whipping.

And at sunset one evening, before the assembled visitors, with the chief sitting on his stool, M'ciba was led forth, and whilst his sons held her the chief took the hide.

"Woman," he said, "I do this that all the world may know you as shameless and a destroyer of honour—behold..."

So far he got, when the crowd opened to allow of the passage of a dapper man in white, a broad and spotless helmet on his head, an ebony stick in his hand.

Likilivi was staggered.

"Lord Sandi," he said in confusion, "this woman is my wife, and I go to whip her because of certain abominations." Sanders eyed him unpleasantly.

"Release this woman," he said, and the two sons obeyed instanter.

"It seems," he said to the embarrassed chief, "that you are old and evil. And when I place a man above others to be chief of those people, I desire that he shall so live that all common people shall say 'Lo! as our lord lives, so shall we.' And if he is evil, then all the village is evil. You are certainly no chief for me."

"Lord," said the old man tremulously, "if you take from me my chieftainship I shall die of shame."

"That I shall certainly do," said Sanders, "and whip you also if you injure this woman, your wife." And Sanders meant it, for he respected only the law which has neither age nor sex.

He took the girl apart.

"As to you, M'ciba," he said, "be pleasant to this man who is your husband, for he is old and will soon die."

"Lord, I pray for his death," she said passionately.

Sanders looked at her from under his brows.

"Pray," he said drily, "yet give him no glass in his food, or I shall come quickly, and then you will be sorry."

She shivered and a look of terror came into her eyes.

"You know all things, master," she gasped.

Sanders did not attempt to disabuse her mind. The faith in his omnipotence was a healthy possession.

"You shall be beaten no more," he said, for she was in a state—being prepared for a further whipping—that revealed something of her husband's previous ferocity.

Sanders dismissed the people to their homes—some had departed quickly on his appearance, and he had a few words with Likilivi.

"O chief," he said softly, "I have a mind to take my stick to you."

"I am an old man," quavered the other.

"The greater evil," said Sanders, "that you should beat this child."

"Lord, she spoke with women of our Marsh Mystery," said the chief.

"More of this mystery," warned Sanders, "and I will bring my soldiers and we will clear the grass till your infernal mystery is a mystery no longer."

In all his long life Likilivi had never heard so terrible a threat, for the mystery of the Marsh was the most sacred of his possessions.

Sanders was smiling to himself as the *Zaire* went speeding down the river. These childish mysteries amused him. They were part of the life of his people.

Admitting the fact that the Marsh was an impenetrable buffer state between Isisi and Akasava, it was less a factor in the preservation of peace than it had been in the bad years of long ago.

Sanders' trip was in a sense a cruise of leisure. He was on his way to the N'Gombi to make an inquiry and to point a lesson.

N'Gombi signifies forest. When Stanley first penetrated the interior of the great land, he was constantly hearing of a N'Gombi city of fabulous wealth. Not until he had made several ineffective expeditions did he discover the true significance of the name.

Though of the forest, there are N'Gombi folk who live on the great river, and curiously enough whilst they preserve the characteristic which distinguishes them from the riverain people in that they cannot swim, are yet tolerable fishermen.

Sanders was bound for the one N'Gombi town which stands on the river, and his *palaver* would be, as he knew, an unsatisfactory one.

He saw the smoke of the N'Gombi fires—they are great iron workers hereabouts—long before he came in sight of the place.

As he turned to give directions to the steersman, Abiboo, who stood on the further side of the helmsman, said something in Bomongo, and the man at the wheel laughed.

"What was that?" asked Sanders.

"Lord, it was a jest," said Abiboo; "I spoke of the N'Gombi people, for there is a saying on the river that N'Gombi crocodiles are fat."

The subtlety of the jest may be lost to the reader, but to Sanders it was plain enough.

The town is called Oulu, but the natives have christened it by a six-syllable word which means "The Town of the Sinkers."

Sanders nodded. An extraordinary fatality pursued this place. In the last four or five years there had been over twenty drowning accidents.

Men had gone out in the evening to fish. In the morning their waterlogged canoes had been found, but the men had disappeared, their bodies being either carried away by the swift stream, or, as popular legend had it, going to some secret larder of the crocodile in the river bed.

It was on account of the latest disaster, which had involved the death of three men, that Sanders paid his visit.

He swung the *Zaire* to shallow water and reached the N'Gombi foreshore.

The headman who met him was grimed with smoke and very hot. He carried the flat hammer of his craft in his hand, and was full of grievances. And the least of these was the death of three good workmen by drowning.

"Men who go on the water are fools," he said, "for it is not natural that any should go there but fish and the dogs of Akasava."

"That is not good *palaver*," said Sanders sharply. "Dogs are dogs and men are men; therefore, my man, speak gently in my presence of other tribes or you will be sorry."

"Lord Sandi," said the man bitterly, "these Akasava would starve us and especially Likilivi the chief."

It was an old grievance between the two villages, the N'Gombi holding themselves as being chartered by Providence to supply all that was crafty and cunning in iron work.

"For as you know, master," the man went on, "iron is hard to come by in these parts."

Sanders remembered a certain anvil stolen at this very village, and nodded.

"Also it is many years before young men learn the magic which makes iron bend. How it must be heated so, cooled so, tapped and fashioned and hammered."

"This I know," said Sanders.

"And if we do not receive so much salt and so many rods for each spear head," the headman continued, "we starve, because . . ."

It was the old story, as old as the world, the story of fair return for labour. The N'Gombi sold their spears at the finest margin of profit.

"Once we grew fat with wealth," said the headman, "because for every handful of salt we ate, when we worked two handfuls came for the spears we made. Now, lord, few spears go out from the N'Gombi and many from Likilivi, because he sells cheaper."

Sanders sighed wearily.

"Such things happen in other lands," he said, "and folks make *palaver*—just as you, M'Kema. Yet I know of no way out."

He inspected the town, received two oral petitions, one for the restoration to liberty of a man who had stolen government property (to wit the aforesaid anvil) and one for a dissolution of marriage, which he granted. He stayed at the town, holding a *palaver* in the cool of the evening, in the course of which he addressed the people on the necessity for learning to swim.

"Twenty men have been drowned," he said, "and yet none learn the lesson. I say that you either do not go upon the water at all, or else learn to walk-in-water as the Isisi and the Ochori and the Akasava walk."

After dinner, that night, being in a frame of mind agreeable to the subject, he sent again for the headman.

"O chief," he said, looking up from the book he was reading, "I have been thinking about this matter of spears. For it seems to me that Likilivi, for all his skill, cannot make so many spears that you are inconvenienced."

"Master, I speak the truth," said the man emphatically.

"Yet the people hereabout are hunters," said Sanders, puzzled.

"Lord," said the headman with considerable emphasis, "if all the world wanted spears Likilivi would supply them."

That was an exaggeration, but Sanders passed it over. He dismissed the man and sat down in solitude to reason the matter out.

Likilivi was an old man, and if he were of our faith we should say that he would be well employed if he were engaging himself in the preparation for another and a better world. Certainly he should not be considering means of reprisal against his young wife. She had put him to shame before his people. She had called down upon him a public reproof from Sandi, moreover, had caused Sandi to threaten an end to the Marsh Mystery and that was the worst offence of all.

Likilivi calmly considered in what way be might bring about her death without Sandi knowing by whose instrumentality she perished. There were many ways suggested to his mind. He could easily bring about her disappearance ... there would be no inquiries, but the matter might be readily explained.

He came back from his workplace and found her in the hut he had set aside for her, for she was no longer a Wife of the House—degradation for most women, but happiness for little M'ciba. She looked up apprehensively as he stooped to enter the hut.

"M'ciba, my wife," he said with a twisted smile; "you sit here all day as I know, and I fear that you will have the sickness mongo, for it is not good for the young that they should shun the sunlight and the air."

She did not speak but looked at him, waiting.

"It will be good," he said, "if you go abroad, for though my heart is sore within me because of your ingratitude, yet I wish you well. You shall take my little canoe and find fish for me."

"If I find no fish you will beat me," she said, having no illusions as to his generosity.

"By my heart and my life," he swore, "I will do none of these things; for I desire only your health, knowing that if you die of sickness Sandi will think evil things of me."

Thus it came about that M'ciba became a fisher girl. From her babyhood she had been accustomed to the river and its crafts. She made good catches and pleased her husband.

"You shall find me a great fish," he said to her one evening; "such as few fisherfolk find—that which is called Baba, the father of fish."

"Master and husband," said M'ciba sulkily, "I do not know where such fish are found."

He licked his thin lips and stroked his little grizzled beard.

"I, Likilivi, know," he said slowly. "These fish come in the dark of the night to the edge of the Mystery. And when the moon is newly risen you shall take your canoe to the place of elephant grass which hides my marsh and catch such a fish. And if you do not catch it, M'ciba, I shall not beat you, for such fish are very cunning."

When night came she took food and drink and placed it in the tiny canoe, Likilivi helping her.

"Tell none that you go to find the fish," he said, "lest the people of the village discover where the fish feeds and trap it for themselves."

It was then moonlight when she pushed off from the shore. She paddled close to the shore, keeping to the slack water until she was out

318

of sight of the village, then brought her canoe out into the river as it sweeps around the little headland which marks the beginning of the Mystery Marsh.

Again she sought for slack water and having found it paddled leisurely to the place which her husband had indicated.

She saw a hippo standing belly high in mud; once she crossed the path of a cow hippo swimming to shore with a little calf on its back.

She steadied the canoe and waited for it to pass, for a cow hippo with young is easily annoyed.

At last she found the spot. The water was calm and almost currentless and she threw over her lines and sat down to wait.

Such drift of the water as there was set toward the shore, very slowly, imperceptibly. Hereabouts there was no sign of solid earth. The green reeds grew thickly from the water. Once the canoe drifted till its blunt bow went rustling amongst the grass and she was forced to take her paddle and stroke away for a few yards.

Once she thought she heard a sound in the bushes, but there was a gentle night wind and she paid no heed to the noise.

She pulled in her lines, baited them again with the little silver fish such as is used for the purpose and threw them out again.

This made a little noise and drowned the click of a tiny steel grapnel thrown by somebody hiding in the grass.

She felt the boat drifting in again and paddled. But there were two strong arms pulling the canoe. Before she realised her danger, the boat was pulled into the rushes, a hand at her throat strangled her screams.

"Woman, if you make a noise I will kill you!" said a voice in her ear, and she recognised the elder son of her husband.

He stepped from the darkness into the canoe ahead of her—he must have abandoned his own—and with strong strokes sent the boat into the darkness of the marsh. She could not see water. The jungle surrounded them. Putting out her hand she could touch the rank grass on either side.

This way and that the canoe went deeper and deeper into the marsh, and as he paddled her stepson sketched with frankness the life which was ahead of her.

Strapped to her thigh, hidden by the dyed grass waist skirt, was a thin knife. She had kept it there for reasons of her own. She slipped it out of its case of snake skin, leant forward and with the other hand felt his bare back.

"Do not touch me, woman!" he snarled over his shoulder.

"I am afraid," she said, and kept her hand where it was, a finger on each rib.

Between her fingers she pushed the thin knife home.

Without a word he slid over the side of the canoe, and she threw her weight on the other gunwale to prevent it filling.

His body fell into the water with a loud "plop" and she waited for him to come up again. He gave no sign, though she peered into the water, the knife in her hand. Then she paddled back the way she came, driving the canoe stern first.

There was little mystery about the waterway save the mystery of the spot where creek and river met, and she had little difficulty in reaching open water. She had nearly come to safety when a sound reached her and she stopped paddling. Behind her she could hear the beat of another canoe, the very swishing of the grass as it forced its passage.

With quick silent strokes she sent her tiny craft the remainder of the journey, and came into the river just as the moon was sinking behind the N'Gombi Forest. Keeping to the shadow of the jungle she passed swiftly along to the north. They could not see her, whoever the mysterious "they" were, and had she reasoned clearly she was safe enough. But she could not reason clearly at the best of times, being but an Isisi girl whose mental equipment found no other stimulus than the thought of lovers and their possibilities. Her breath came quickly in little sobs as she plied her paddles. She skirted the grass until she reached the second headland—the horn of the bay in which the marsh stands.

Clear of this she paddled boldly into midstream. Looking behind her she saw nothing, yet there were vague, indefinite shadows which might have been anything.

Her nerve had gone; she was on the point of collapse, when suddenly ahead of her she saw something and dropped her paddles.

A steamer was coming toward her, its funnel belching sparks, and ahead, as though to feel its way through the darkness, a broad beam of light, a dazzling whiteness.

She sat spellbound, breathing quickly, until the current carried her into the range of the searchlight.

She heard the voice of Sanders in the black darkness behind the light, and the tinkle of the engine telegraph as he put the *Zaire* astern.

★★★★★★

Likilivi believed in the impenetrability of the Marsh as whole-heartedly as he believed in *M'shimba-M'shamba* and other strange gods.

"The woman is dead," he said to his son, "and your brother Okora also, for M'ciba was a wicked woman and very strong."

He did not doubt that somewhere in the depths of the lagoon the two lay locked in the grip of death.

The villagers accepted the drowning of M'dba philosophically and made no inquiries.

"I will report this matter to Sandi," said Likilivi.

"Father," said his son, "Sandi passed on the night of the killing, which was six nights ago, for men who were fishing saw his devil light."

"So much the better," said Likilivi.

There had been other deaths in the Marsh, for sickness readily attacks slaves who are chained by the leg and beaten, and who moreover do their work by night, lest the smoke of their fires invites suspicion.

Likilivi, his two remaining sons and two cousins, set themselves to recruit new labour.

Three nights they waited on the edge of the Marsh, and on the fourth they were rewarded, for two men came paddling carelessly with trailing fish lines.

They sang together a N'Gombi song about a hunter who had trusted an Akasava spear and had died from over-confidence.

Listening in the darkness Likilivi cursed them silently.

The canoe was close in shore when the elder of the chief's sons threw the grapnel, and the canoe was drawn into the rushes.

Two canoes closed in upon it.

"You come with us or you die," said Likilivi.

"Lord, we go with you," said the N'Gombi promptly.

They were transferred to the chief's canoe carrying their blankets, and their boat was taken by the other canoe, turned bottom upwards, and allowed to drift.

The chief waited until the canoe returned, then the two boats made for the heart of the Marsh.

For an hour they twisted and turned along the meandering fairway until at length the nose of the foremost canoe grounded gently on a sandy beach.

They were on the island. The pungent smell of smoke was in the air—Likilivi had wood to spare—and to the ears of the captives came a monotonous "*clank, clank, clank*," of steel against steel.

Likilivi hurried them along a narrow path which ended abruptly in a clearing.

By the light of many fires the prisoners saw. There were two big huts—long and low roofed. They were solidly built on stout, heavy stakes, and to each stake a man was fastened. A long chain clamped about his legs gave him liberty to sleep on the inside of the hut and work at the fire outside.

There they sat, twelve men without hope, hammering spear heads for Likilivi, and each man was a skilled N'Gombi workman, artistically "drowned" for Likilivi's profit.

"Here shall you sit," said Likilivi to the two silent watchers, "and if you work you shall be fed, and if you do not work you shall be beaten."

"I see," said one of the captured.

There was something strange in his tone, something dry and menacing, and Likilivi stepped back showing his teeth like an angry dog.

"Put the chain upon them," he commanded, but his relatives did not move, for the prisoner had dropped his blanket from his arm, and his revolver was plain to be seen.

Likilivi saw it too and made a recovery. .

"You are one of Sandi's spies," he said thickly. "Now I swear to you that if you say nothing of this I will make you rich with ivory and many precious things."

"That I cannot do," said the man, and Likilivi, peering at the brown face closely, saw that this N'Gombi man had grey eyes, and that he was smiling unpleasantly, just as Sanders smiled before he sent men to the Village of Irons to work in bondage for their crimes.

Chapter 14

The Praying Moor

Abiboo told Sanders that an Arabi had come to see him, and Arabs are rare on the coast, though certain dark men of Semitic origin have that honorary title.

Sanders came out to his *stoep* expecting to find a Kano, and was surprised to see, squatting by the edge of the raised verandah, a man of true Moorish type. He sat with his hands about his knees wrapped in a spotless white *djellab*.

"You are from Morocco," said Sanders in Arabic, "or from Dacca?" The man nodded.

"The people of Dacca are dogs," he said, in the singsong voice of a professional storyteller. "One man, who is a cousin of my mother's, stole twenty *douros* from my house and went back to Dacca by a coast boat before I could catch him and beat him. I hope he is killed and all his family also. Bismallah. God is good!"

Sanders listened, for he knew the Tangier people for great talkers.

The man went on. "Whether a man be of the Ali or Sufi sect, I do not care. There are thieves of both kinds."

"Why do you come here?" asked Sanders.

"Once I knew a man who sat in the great *sok*." (Sanders let him tell his story in his own way.) "And all the country people who brought vegetables and charcoal to the market would kiss the edge of his *djellab* and give him a penny.

"He was an old man with a long white beard, and he sat with his beads in his lap reciting the *Suras* of the *Koran*.

"There was not a man in Tangier who had not kissed the edge of his *djellab*, and given him five *centimes* except me."

"When the people from far-away villages came, I used to go to a place near the door of his little white house and watch the money

323

coming to him.

"One day when the sun was very hot, and I had lingered long after the last visitor had gone, the *Haj* beckoned me and I went nearer to him and sat on the ground before him.

"He looked at me, saying no word, only stroking his long white beard slowly. For a long time he sat like this, his eyes searching my soul.

"'My son,' he said at last, 'how are you called?'

"'Abdul az Izrael,' I replied.

"'Abdul,' he said, 'many come to me bringing me presents, yet you never come.'

"'Before God and His prophet,' I swore, 'I am a poor man who often starves; I have no friends.'

"'All that you tell me are lies,' said the holy man, then he was silent again. By and by he spoke. "'Do you say your prayers, Abdul?' he asked." 'Four times every day,' I replied. "'You shall say your prayers four times a day, but each day you shall say your prayers in a new place,' and he waved his hand thus."

Abdul Azrael waved his hand slowly before his eyes. Sanders was interested. He knew the Moors for born story-tellers, and was interested. "Well?" he said.

The man paused impressively. "Well, favoured and noble master," he said, "from that day I have wandered through the world, praying in new places, for I am cursed by the holy man because I lied to him, and there is that within me which impels me. And, lord, I have wandered from Damaraland to Mogador, and from Mogador to Egypt, and from Egypt to Zanzibar."

"Very pretty," said Sanders. "You have a tongue like honey and a voice like silk, and it is written in the *Sura* of the *Djinn*, '*Truth is rough and a lie comes smoothly. Let him pass whose speech is pleasing.*'"

Sanders was not above taking liberties with the Koran, as this quotation testifies.

"Give him food," said Sanders to his orderly, "later I will send him on his way."

A little later, the Commissioner crossed over to the police lines, and interrupted the Houssa Captain at his studies—Captain Hamilton had a copy of *Squire's Companion to the British Pharmacopaeia* open before him, and he was reading up arsenic (1) as a cure for intermittent fever; (2) as an easy method of discharging himself from the monotony of a coast existence.

Sanders, who had extraordinary eyesight, comprehended the study at a glance and grinned.

"If you do not happen to be committing suicide for an hour or so," he said, "I should like to introduce you to the original Wandering Jew from Tangier."

The Houssa closed his book with a bang, lit a cigarette and carefully extinguished the match.

"This," he said, addressing the canvas ceiling of his hut, "is either the result of overwork, or the effect of fishing in the sun without proper head protection."

Sanders threw himself into a long seated chair and felt for his cheroots.

Then, ignoring the Houssa's insult, he told the story of Abdul Azrael, the Moor.

"He's a picturesque mendicant," he said, "and has expressed his intention of climbing the river and crossing Africa to Uganda."

"Let him climb," said the Houssa; "from what I know of your people he will teach them nothing in the art of lying. He may, however, give them style, and they stand badly in need of that."

Abdul Azrael accordingly left headquarters by the store canoe which carried government truck to the Isisi villages.

There was a period of calm on the river. Sanders found life running very smoothly. There were returns to prepare (these his soul loathed), reports from distant corners of his little empire to revise; acts of punishments administered by his chiefs to confirm—and fishing.

Once he ran up the river to settle a bigger *palaver* than the new king of the Akasava could decide upon, but that was the only break in the monotony. There was a new Administrator, a man who knew his job, and knew, too, the most important job of all was to leave his subordinates to work out their own salvation.

Sanders finished his *palaver* with the Akasava, gave judgment, which was satisfactory to all parties, and was returning to the enjoyment of that contentment which comes to a man who has no arrears of work or disease of conscience.

He left the Akasava city at sunset, travelling through the night for his own convenience. The river hereabout is a real river, there being neither sand-bank nor shoal to embarrass the steersman. At five o'clock he passed Chumbiri.

He had no reason to believe that all was not well at Chumbiri, or cause to give it anything but a passing glance. He came downstream in the grey of dawn and passed the little village without suspicion. He saw, from the bridge of the *Zaire*, the dull glow of a fire on the distant foreshore—he was in midstream, and here the river runs two miles wide from bank to bank. Day came with a rush. It was little better than twilight when he left the village to starboard, and long before he came to the sharp bend which would hide Chumbiri from view, the world was flooded with strong white light.

One acquires the habit of looking all ways in wild Africa. It was, for example, a matter of habit that he cast one swift glance backward to the village, before he signalled to the helmsman with a slight bend of his head, to bring the helm hard-a-port. One swift glance he threw and frowned. The tiny town was clearly to be seen. Three straight rows of huts, on a sloping bank, with Isisi palms running the length of each street.

"Turn about," he said, and the steersman spun the wheel.

The little steamer listed over as the full power of the swift current caught her amidships, then she slowly righted and the waters piled themselves up at her bows as she breasted the current again.

"Abiboo," said Sanders to his sergeant, "I see no people in the streets of this village, neither do I see the smoke of fires."

"Lord, they may go hunting," said Abiboo wisely.

"Fishermen do not hunt," said Sanders, "nor do women and old people."

Abiboo did not advance the preposterous suggestion that they might sleep, for if the men were sluggards they would not be sufficiently lost to shame to allow their womenfolk to escape their duties.

Sanders brought the steamer into slack water near the beach and none came to meet him.

There was no dog or goat within sight—only the remains of a big fire still smouldering upon the beach.

His men waded ashore with their hawsers and secured the steamer, and Sanders followed.

He walked through the main street and there was no sign of life. He called sharply—there was no response. Every hut was empty; the cooking pots, the beds, every article of necessity was in its place. The rough mills for the grinding of corn stood before the huts, the match-ets and crude N'Gombi axes for the cutting of timber, the N'Gombi spades, all these things were in evidence, but of the people, young or old, man or woman or child, well or sick, there was no trace. The only living being he saw was Abdul Azrael. He came upon that pious man on a sheltered beach near the village; his praying carpet was spread and he faced toward Mecca in rapt contemplation.

Sanders waited for the prayers to finish and questioned him.

"Lord, I have seen nothing," he said, "but I will tell you a story. Once—"

"I want no stories," snapped Sanders.

He put the nose of the steamer across the river. Exactly opposite was Fezembini, a larger town, and since constant communication was maintained between the two places, some explanation of the people's absence might be secured.

Fezembini was alive and bustling, and all that could walk came down to the beach to say "O ai!" to the Commissioner, but Mondomi, the chief, had no solution.

He was a tall, thin man, with a thin curl of beard on his chin.

"Lord, they were there last night," he said, "for I heard their drums beating and I saw their fires; also I heard laughter and the rattle of the dancers' little cages." (A sort of wicker-work dumb-bell, containing stones—not unlike a double-headed baby's rattle.)

"H'm!" said Sanders.

He pursued his inquiries at the neighbouring villages, but was no nearer a satisfactory explanation of the vanishing of three hundred people at the end of his investigation.

He sat down in the cool and quiet of his cabin to reason the matter out. The Chumbiri folk were as law-abiding as Akasava people can be; they had paid their taxes; there was no charge against any of them, yet of a sudden they had left their homes and gone into the forest. That they had not made for the river was evident from the discovery of their canoes, carefully docked in a convenient creek.

"I give it up," said Sanders. He had to be at headquarters for a day or two. When he had finished his work there he returned to Chumbiri and its problem.

The people had not returned, nor had any of his spies news of them.

He sent Abiboo into the forest to find their trail, and the Houssa sergeant had no difficulty, for two miles into the forest he found an old man who had died by the way, and a little further he found an old woman, also dead.

Sanders went out to see the bodies. There was no sign of wound or injury. They had obviously died from fatigue.

"When daylight comes we will follow," said Sanders, "I will take ten men, and you will choose swift walkers."

He snatched a few hours' sleep, and before dawn Abiboo brought him the cup of tea without which Sanders never began a day.

Sanders, who had not an ounce of superfluous flesh, was an indefatigable walker, and the party covered twelve miles before noon—no easy task, for the forest path was little more than a grass track. The party rested through the three hot hours of the day, and resumed its journey at three o'clock.

They came upon a camping place with the ashes of the fires hardly cold and two newly-made graves to testify to the fate of age and infirmity suddenly called upon for effort.

At nine o'clock that night, just when Sanders was considering the advisability of camping, he saw the light of fires ahead and pushed on.

There were many young trees which hid the view of the camp, and the party had to take a circuitous route to reach the clearing where the people were.

It was an extraordinary view which met the eyes of our dumbfounded Commissioner.

Line upon line of kneeling forms were revealed by the light of the fire. They faced in one direction, and as they swayed backwards and forward, one knelt in advance, whom Sanders had no difficulty in recognising as the chief headman.

"Lala is a great one," he sang.

"*O Gala!*" droned his people.

"Lala is high!"

"*O Gala!*" they repeated and bowed their heads.

The chief did not see Sanders, because Sanders came up behind him. He knew that Sanders was there, because Sanders kicked him very hard. "Get up, O foolish man!" said Sanders. He did not use those exact words, because he was very annoyed, but whatever he said had the desired effect.

"Now you shall tell me," said Sanders, "why you are so much bigger a fool than I ever thought you were."

"Lord," said the chief humbly, "we go to seek new lands, for an Arabi taught us that we should pray in a certain way, and that if we prayed in a different place every night, great blessings would come to us—"

A light dawned on Sanders.

"We will go back tomorrow," he said, after swallowing something in his throat, "and I will take my steamer and search for this Arabi."

Two days brought him to the village. He left the judgment of the chief to another day and hurried aboard.

As the *Zaire* was casting off that woebegone individual came running to the beach.

"Master," he gasped, "we ask for justice!"

"You shall have it," said Sanders grimly.

"Lord, all our homes are stolen, nothing is left." Sanders swore at him fluently, in a language which allows considerable opportunities for such exercise. "Speak quickly, father of monkeys."

"Lord, they are gone," said the agitated headman, "all our good pots and our mills, our spears, our hatchets and our fishing lines."

"Why did you leave them, O father of tom-cats?" said Sanders in exasperation.

"The Arabi told us," said the headman, "and we did that which we thought was best."

Sanders leant on the rail and spoke to the man. They were not words of kindness and cheer, nor words of hope or comfort. Sanders drew upon forest and river for his illustrations. He told the headman all about his life and sketched his existence after death. He referred to his habits, his morals and his relations. He spoke feelingly of his head, his feet and his bodily infirmities, and the interested Houssas on the *Zaire* drew closer lest one word should escape them.

"And now," said Sanders in conclusion, "I call all men to witness that you and your people are bush-men."

"*O Ko!*" said the horrified villagers who had come to the beach at the heels of their headman, for "bush-man" is the very summit of insults.

"Bushmen!" repeated Sanders bitterly as the boat drifted from the shore; "root-eaters, who talk with monkeys in their own language. . ."

He left the people of the village considerably depressed.

First he crossed the river to Fezembini. Yes, the chief had seen the Arabi, had indeed hired him two large canoes and six paddlers to each.

"He said he was of the Government, lord, on secret service," said the chief, "and desired to collect the things which the people of Chumbiri had left behind them."

These canoes had gone up river and they had some six days' start of the Commissioner. Sanders lost no time. From a coop which was erected aft he took two pigeons. One had a red and the other had a tiny blue band about its leg. He wrote identical messages on sheets as thin in texture as a cigarette paper, bound them to the legs of the birds and released them. One pigeon he released, and that went north. He waited till it was out of sight, then he let the other go. That went north also, but a point or two west to its fellow.

Sanders sent the *Zaire* in the same general direction. Later in the afternoon he reached the Akasava city.

"What strangers have been here?" he asked the hastily-summoned chief.

"Master, no stranger," said the chief, "save only the new Arabi, whom your lordship has sent to sell us pots and knives."

Sanders gripped the rail of the boat, not trusting himself to speak.

"He sold you pots?" he asked chokingly.

"And spears," said the chief, "and many desirable things, and they were very cheap and all the people praised you, master, that you had done this kindness. For thus said the Arabi: 'Our lord Sandi desires that you should pay only a little for these precious articles—he himself has paid me that I should benefit you.'"

"Anything else?"

The chief hesitated.

"Lord, he told us a story about a certain evil devil who tormented the ungrateful, and my people were frightened lest they did not accept the benefits your lordship offered and—"

"Cast off!" roared Sanders.

Naked men jumped into the shallow water and waded ashore to where the wire hawsers were fastened.

"As for you," said Sanders to the chief, "go tell your master the king that he has set up a child as chief of this city. For when was I so mad that I gave gifts to lazy people? Have I sickness that I should pay a thieving Arabi money to benefit evil and foolish men?"

"Lord," said the chief simply, "knowing that you were a mean and cruel man we felt great joy, thinking that the gods had touched your hard heart."

Sanders looked round for something to throw at him, for time was precious.

He found only valuable things and allowed the matter to drop.

At a village ten miles away he found further evidence of the Moor's perfidy. Here the praying pilgrim had rested for a night and had borrowed three bags of salt, some dried fish and a store of *manioc*. He had done this in the name of the Government.

"And gave me," said the wizened headman, "a book with devil

marks."

He handed a paper to Sanders. It was in Arabic, and the Commissioner read it with some emotion.

"From Abdul Azrael, the servant of God, the one, true, beneficent and merciful.

"To the *giaour* Sanders whom may God preserve and lead to the true faith.

"Peace be on your house. This is written on the fourth day of the third week following Ramazin.

"I go to my brethren who live beyond the Cataracts of the Great River. I pray for you, therefore pay these people for all that I have taken."

Sanders read it again.

If Abdul took the river which passes Ochori and turned sharply to the right into the creek of Bamboo he would come in time to the Arab settlements which were beyond the Commissioner's jurisdiction. Moreover, he would be beyond his reach, for the *Zaire* drew a fathom and a half of water and the creek of Bamboo averaged half a fathom.

"Did this Arabi say which way he would go?" asked Sanders.

The old man nodded.

"By the Ochori country, lord," he said, and Sanders groaned. "And he asked what manner of people the Ochori were."

"And what said you?" asked Sanders, interested.

"I said they were fools," said the headman, "and very fearful."

"And how long have you sat in this village?" asked Sanders.

"Lord, I was born here and here I have lived."

There was a twinkle in the eyes of Mr. Commissioner Sanders. This old man had never heard of Bosambo the chief. Suppose Abdul yielded to temptation and arrested his flight at the city of that great man?

Abdul Azrael came to the Ochori village singing a song. He was cheerful because a few miles up the river was a crocodile creek, broad enough and deep enough for a fast canoe, but having neither depth nor the width for a steamer such as the *Zaire*.

He had intended going straight to his hiding-place, but judged very shrewdly that so far he had a day the better of the chase.

It would have been wiser of him to continue his journey, but this he did not know. He was in high spirits, for a few hours before he had sold one of the canoes he had borrowed to a N'Gombi chief, who had, moreover, paid him in *Frankies*. (The *franc* was the only coinage known in Sanders' territory, and on the Upper River. It came from the adjoining French territories.)

In various portions of his attire Abdul Azrael secreted the result of many pilgrimages. He had dirty Turkish notes, golden coins of Tunis, English sovereigns, *marks*, twenty-*peseta* pieces, heavy golden eagles from a land he had never seen, not a few black and chocolate hundred-*franc* notes of the Bank *Nationale de Belgique* (these he had come by on the Congo), to say nothing of the silver coinage of dubious quality which the Shereefian Government issue at odd moments.

He strutted through the main street of the Ochori city and came before Bosambo. "Peace be upon your house," he said, and Bosambo, who had a working knowledge of Arabic, bade him welcome.

"I have come from Sandi, our lord," said Abdul gravely; "he has sent me with these words, 'Give unto Abdul Azrael the best of your hospitality and regard him as me.'"

"I am Sandi's dog," said Bosambo, "though he is, as you know, my half-brother of another mother."

"This he has often told me," said Abdul.

They exchanged compliments for twenty minutes, at the end of which time the Moor excused himself.

"For I must say my prayers," he said.

"I will also say my prayers," said Bosambo promptly, "according to my custom, and I thank *Allah* that you are here that I may pray in peace."

Abdul had been on the point of telling his story of the Holy Man of Tangier, but stopped.

"That is strange talk," he said, "for there is one custom as there is one God. And all men pray in peace."

Bosambo shook his head sadly.

"I live amongst thieves," he said, "and I am a rich man. It is the custom in this part of the country to remove all clothes, placing them before the door of the dwelling, then to enter the hut and pray."

"That is a good custom," said Abdul eagerly. "It is one I have often practised."

"Yet," Bosambo went on, "how may a believer go about his proper business? For if I leave my clothes, with all my precious jewels concealed, my people will rob me."

"*Bismallah!*" cried the pious Moor, "this is a happy day, for we will pray together, you and I. And whilst I am at prayers you shall guard my robes, and whilst you are at your prayers, behold, I will be Azrael, the

Angel of the Sword, and none shall touch your jewels by my life."

It is said that they embraced. Abdul in the excess of his emotion running his deft fingers lightly over the other's waist, noting certain bulky protuberances which were unknown to nature.

"I will pray first," said Abdul, "and I will pray for a long time."

"I also will take a long time," said the simple Bosambo.

Abdul stripped to his under robe, collected his *djellab* and his long gabardine into a convenient bundle and placed them on the ground before the hut and entered.

Sanders arrived six hours later and Bosambo awaited him.

"Lord," said the chief, "the Arabi I have arrested as your lordship directed, for your pigeon was a cunning one and came swiftly though there are many hawks."

"Where is he?" asked Sanders.

"He is in my hut," said Bosambo, "and, master, deal gently with him, because he is of my faith; also he is a little mad."

"Mad?"

Bosambo nodded his close-cropped head. "Mad, master," he said sadly, "for he says I have robbed him, taken from him such as gold and book money—a large fortune."

Sanders eyed him keenly.

"Did you?" he asked.

"Lord," said Bosambo with simple dignity, "he was my guest and of my faith, how could I rob him?"

Sanders' interview with the wrathful Moor was not a protracted one.

"I send you to labour in the Village of Irons for a year," he said, "for you are a liar, a thief, and a maker of mischief."

"I will go to your prison, lord," said Abdul; "but tell this black man to restore the money he has stolen from me; lord, it was hidden in my clothes, and by a trick—"

"That is not my *palaver*," said Sanders shortly. The Houssas were marching the Moor away when he turned to Bosambo.

"After I come back from the Village of Irons," he said, "I will come to you, Bosambo, thou infidel, and eater of pig. And—"

Bosambo waved his hand with an airy gesture. "You will never come from the Village of Irons," he said, "for Sandi, who is my cousin, has told me secretly that you will be poisoned. As to the money, I think you are an evil liar."

"Six hundred Spanish dollars!" hissed Abdul.

"Four hundred and half a hundred," corrected Bosambo blandly, "and much of the silver breaks when you bite it. Go in peace, O my angel!"

CHAPTER 15

The Sickness Mongo

Sanders taught his people by example, by word of mouth, and by such punishment as occasion required. Of all methods, punishment was the least productive of result, for memory lasts only so long as pain, and men who had watched with quaking hearts a strapped body as it swayed from a tree branch, straightway forgot the crime for which the criminal died just as soon as the malefactor was decently interred.

Sanders taught the men of the *Zaire* to stack wood. He showed them that if it was stacked in the bow, the vessel would sink forward, or if it was stacked all on one side, the vessel would list. He stood over them, day after day, directing and encouraging them, and the same men were invariably his pupils because Sanders did not like new faces.

He was going up river in some haste when he tied to a wooding to replenish his stock.

At the end of six years' tuition he left them to pile wood whilst he slept, and they did all the things which they should not have done.

This he discovered when he returned to the boat.

"Master," said the headman of the wooders, and he spoke with justifiable pride, "we have cut and stored the wood for the *puc-a-puc* in one morning, whereas other and slower folk would have worked till sundown, but because we love your lordship we have worked till the sweat fell from our bodies."

Sanders looked at the wood piled all wrong, and looked at the headman.

"It is not wise," he said, "to store the wood in the bow, for thus the ship will sink, as I have often told you."

"Lord, we did it because it was easiest," said the man simply.

"That I can well believe," said Sanders, and ordered the restacking, without temper.

You must remember that he was in a desperate hurry: that every hour counted. He had been steaming all night—a dangerous business, for the river was low and there were new sandbanks which did not appear on his home-made chart. Men fret their hearts out, dealing with such little problems as ill-stacked wood, but Sanders neither fretted nor worried. If he had, he would have died, for things like this were part of his working day. Yet the headman's remissness worried him a little, for he knew the man was no fool.

In an hour the wood was more evenly distributed and Sanders rang the engines ahead. He put the nose of the boat to the centre of the stream and held on his course till at sunset he came to a place where the river widened abruptly, and where little islands were each a great green tangle of vegetation.

Here he slowed the steamer, carefully circumnavigating each island, till darkness fell, then he picked a cautious way to shore, through much shoal water. The *Zaire* bumped and shivered as she struck or grazed the hidden sandbanks.

Once she stopped dead, and her crew of forty slipped over the side of the boat, and wading, breast high, pushed her along with a deep-chested song.

At last he came to a shelving beach, and here, fastened by her steel hawsers to two trees, the boat waited for dawn.

Sanders had a bath, dressed, and came into his little deck-house to find his dinner waiting.

He ate the tiny chicken, took a stiff peg of whiskey, and lit his cigar. Then he sent for Abiboo.

"Abiboo," he said, "once you were a man in these parts."

"Lord, it is so," said Abiboo. "I was a spy here for six months."

"What do you know of these islands?"

"Lord, I only know that in one of them the Isisi bury their dead, and of another it is said that magic herbs grow; also that witchdoctors come thither to practise certain rites."

Sanders nodded.

"Tomorrow we seek for the Island of Herbs," he said, "for I have information that evil things will be done at the full of the moon."

"I am your man," said Abiboo.

It happened two nights following this that a chief of the N'Gombi, a simple old man who had elementary ideas about justice and a considerable faith in devils, stole down the river with twelve men and with labour they fastened two pieces of wood shaped like a St. Andrew's Cross between two trees.

They bent a young sapling, trimming the branches from the top, till it reached the head of the cross, and this they made fast with a fishing line. Whatever other preparations they may have contemplated making were indefinitely postponed because Sanders, who had been watching them from behind a convenient copal-tree, stepped from his place of concealment, and the further proceedings failed to yield any satisfaction to the chief.

He eyed Sanders with a mild reproach.

"Lord, we set a trap for a leopard," he explained, "who is very terrible."

"In other days," mused Sanders aloud, "a man seeing this cross would think of torture, O chief—and, moreover, leopards do not come to the middle island—tell me the truth."

"Master," said the old chief in agitation, "this leopard swims, therefore he fills our hearts with fear."

Sanders sighed wearily.

"Now you will tell me the truth, or I shall be more than any leopard."

The chief folded his arms so that the flat of his hands touched his back, he being a lean man, and his hands fidgeted nervously.

"I cannot tell you a lie," he said, "because you are as a very bat, seeing into dark places readily and moving at night. Also you are like a sudden storm that comes up from trees without warning, and you are most terrible in your anger."

"Get along," said Sanders, passively irritable.

"Now this is the truth," said the chief huskily.

"There is a man who comes to my village at sunset, and he is an evil one, for he has the protection of the Christ-man and yet he does abominable things—so we are for chopping him."

Sanders peered at the chief keenly.

"If you chop him, chief, you will surely die," he said softly, "even if he be as evil as the devil—whichever type of devil you mostly fear. This is evidently a bad *palaver* indeed, and I will sit down with you for some days."

He carried the chief and his party back to the village and held a *palaver*.

Now Sanders of the River in moments such as these was a man of inexhaustible patience; and of that patience he had considerable need when two hours after his arrival there came stalking grandly into the

337

village a man whose name was Ofalikari, a man of the N'Gombi by a Congolaise father.

His other name was Joseph, and he was an evangelist.

This much Sanders discovered quickly enough.

"Fetch this man to me," he said to Sergeant Abiboo, for the preacher made his *palaver* at the other end of the village.

Soon Abiboo returned.

"Master," he said, "this man will not come, being only agreeable to the demands of certain gods with which your honour is acquainted."

Sanders showed his teeth.

"Go to him," he said softly, "and bring him; if he will come for no other cause, hit him with the flat of your bayonet."

Abiboo saluted stiffly—after the style of native noncommissioned officers—and departed, to return with Ofalikari, whom he drew with him somewhat unceremoniously by the ear.

"Now," said Sanders to the man, "we will have a little talk, you and I."

The sun went down, the moon came up, flooding the black river with mellow light, but still the talk went on—for this was a very serious *palaver* indeed.

A big fire was built in the very middle of the village street and here all the people gathered, whilst Sanders and the man sat face to face.

Occasionally a man or a woman would be sent for from the throng; once Sanders dispatched a messenger to a village five miles away to bring evidence. They came and went, those who testified against Ofalikari.

"Lord, one night we gathered by his command and he sacrificed a white goat," said one witness.

"We swore by the dried heart of a white goat that we would do certain abominable things," said another.

"By his order we danced a death dance at one end of the village, and the maidens danced the wedding dance at the other, then a certain slave was killed by him, and . . ."

Sanders nodded gravely.

"And he said that the sons of the White Goat should not die," said another. .

In the end Sanders rose and stretched himself.

"I have heard enough," he said, and nodded to the sergeant of Houssas, who came forward with a pair of bright steel handcuffs.

One of these he snapped on the man's wrist, the other he held and led him to the boat.

The *Zaire* swung out to midstream, making a difficult way through the night to the mission station.

Ill news travels faster than an eight-knot steamboat can move up stream.

Sanders found the missionary waiting for him at daybreak on the strip of white beach, and the missionary, whose name was Haggin, was in one of those cold passions that saintly men permit themselves, for righteousness' sake.

"All England shall ring with this outrage," he said, and his voice trembled. "Woe the day when a British official joins the hosts of Satan."

He said many other disagreeable things.

"Forget it," said Sanders tersely; "this man of yours has been playing the fool."

And in his brief way he described the folly.

"It's a lie!" said the missionary. He was tall and thin, yellow with fever, and his hands shook as he threw them out protestingly. "He has made converts for the faith, he has striven for souls ... "

"Now listen to me," said Sanders and he wagged a solemn forefinger at the other. "I know this country. I know these people—you don't. I take your man to headquarters, not because he preaches the gospel, but because he holds meetings by night and practises strange rites which are not the rites of any known Church. Because he is a son of the White Goat, and I will have no secret societies in my land."

If the truth be told, Sanders was in no frame of mind to consider the feelings of missionaries.

There was unrest in his territories—unrest of an elusive kind. There had been a man murdered on the Little River and none knew whose hand it was that struck him down.

His body, curiously carved, came floating down stream one sunny morning, and agents brought the news to Sanders. Then another had been killed and another. A life more or less is nothing in a land where people die by whole villages, but these men with their fantastic slashings worried Sanders terribly.

He had sent for his chief spies.

"Go north to the territory of the killing, which is on the edge of the N'Gombi country and bring me news," he said.

One such had sent him a tale of a killing *palaver*—he had rushed north to find by the veriest accident that the threatened life was that of a man he desired most of all to place behind bars.

He carried his prisoner to headquarters. He was anxious to put an end to the growth of a movement which might well get beyond control, for secret societies spread like fire.

At noon he reached a wooding and tied up.

He summoned his headman.

"Lobolo," he said, "you shall stack the wood whilst I sleep, remembering all the wise counsel I gave you."

"Lord, I am wise in your wisdom," said the headman, and Abiboo having strung a hammock between two trees, Sanders tumbled in and fell asleep instantly.

Whilst he slept, one of the wooders detached himself from the working party, and came stealthily towards him.

Sanders' sleeping place was removed some distance from the shore, that the noise of chopping and sawing and the rattle of heavy billets on the steel deck should not disturb him.

Noiselessly the man moved until he came to within striking distance of the unconscious Commissioner.

He took a firmer grip of the keen steel machette he carried and stepped forward.

Then a long sinewy hand caught him by the throat and pulled him down. He twisted his head and met the passionless gaze of Abiboo.

"We will go from here," whispered the Houssa, "lest our talk awake my lord."

He wrenched the machette from the other's hand and followed him into the woods.

"You came to kill Sandi," said Abiboo.

"That is true," said the man, "for I have a secret *ju-ju* which told me to do this, Sandi having offended. And if you harm me, the White Goat shall surely slay you, brown man."

"I have eaten Sandi's salt," said Abiboo, "and whether I live or die is ordained. As for you, your fate is about your neck . . ."

Sanders woke from his sleep to find Abiboo squatting on the ground by the side of the hammock.

"What is it?" he asked.

"Nothing, lord," said the man. "I watched your sleep, for it is written, 'He is a good servant who sees when his master's eyes are shut.'"

Sanders heard the serious undertone to the proverb; was on the point of asking a question, then wisely checked himself.

He walked to the shore. The men had finished their work, and the wood was piled in one big, irregular heap in the well of the fore deck. It was piled so that it was impossible

(1) for the steersman on the bridge above to see the river;

(2) for the stoker to get anywhere near his furnace;

(3) for the *Zaire* to float in anything less than three fathoms of water.

Already the little ship was down by the head, and the floats of her stem wheel merely skimming the surface of the river.

Sanders stood on the bank with folded arms looking at the work of the headman's hands. Then his eyes wandered along the length of the vessel. Amidships was a solid iron cage, protected from the heat of the sun by a double roof and broad canvas eaves. His eyes rested here for a long time, for the cage was empty and the emissary of the White Goat gone.

Sanders stood for a few moments in contemplation; then he stepped slowly down the bank and crossed the gangway.

"Be ears and eyes to me, Abiboo," he said in Arabic, "find what has become of Ofalikari, also the men who guarded him. Place these under arrest and bring them before me."

He walked to his cabin, his head sunk in thought. This was serious, though he reserved his judgment till Abiboo returned with his prisoners.

They arrived under escort, a little alarmed, a little indignant.

"Lord, these men have reason," said Abiboo.

"Why did you allow the prisoner to go?" asked Sanders.

"Thus it was, master," said the senior of the two; "whilst you slept the God-man came—him we saw at daybreak this morning. And he told us to let the prisoner come with him, and because he was a white man we obeyed him."

"Only white men who are of the Government may give such orders," said Sanders; "therefore I adjudge you guilty of folly, and I hold you for trial."

There was nothing to be gained by lecturing them. He sent for his headman.

"Lobolo," he said, "ten years you have been my headman, and I have been kind to you."

"Lord, you have been as a father," said the old man, and his hand was shaking.

"Yonder," said Sanders, pointing with his finger, "lies your land and

341

the village you came from is near enough. Let the storeman pay you your wages and never see me again."

"Lord," stammered the headman, "if the stacking of wood was a fault——"

"Well, you know it is a fault," said Sanders; "you have eaten my bread and now you have sold me to the White Goats."

The old man fell sobbing at his feet.

"Lord master," he moaned, "I did this because I was afraid, for a certain man told me that if I did not delay your lordship I should die, and, lord, death is very terrible to the old, because they live with it in their hearts."

"Which man was this?" asked Sanders.

"One called Kema, lord."

Sanders turned to his orderly.

"Find me Kema," he said, and Abiboo shifted his feet.

"Lord, he has died the death," he said simply, "for whilst you slept he came to slay you. And I had some *palaver* with him."

"And?"

"Lord, I saw him for an evil man and I smote his head from his body with a machette."

Sanders was silent. He stood looking at the deck, then he turned to his cabin.

"Master," said the waiting headman, "what of me?"

The Commissioner stretched his finger towards the shore, and with bowed shoulders Lobolo left the ship that had been his home for many years.

It took the greater part of an hour to trim the vessel.

"We will make for the mission station," said Sanders, though he had no doubt in his mind as to what he would find. ...

The mission house was still burning when the *Zaire* rounded the river's head.

He found the missionary's charred body among the smouldering wreckage.

Of Ofalikari he found no trace.

There had been a secret society suppressed in Niger-land, and it had been broken by three regiments of native infantry, a battery of mountain guns and some loss of life. The "British victory" and the "splendid success of our arms" had given the people of the islands a great deal of satisfaction, but the Commissioner who let the matter get to the stage of war was a ruined man, for governments do not like spending the millions they have put aside for the creation of a national pension scheme which will bring them votes and kudos at the next election, on dirty little wars which bring nothing but vacancies in the junior ranks of the native army.

Sanders had a pigeon post from headquarters containing a straight-away telegram from the Administrator.

"Your message received and forwarded. Ministers wire settle your *palaver* by any means. For God's sake keep clear necessity employing army. Sending you one battalion Houssas and field gun. Do the best you can."

There was not much margin for wastage. The whole country was now rotten with rebellion. It had all happened in the twinkling of an eye. From being law-abiding and inoffensive, every village had become of a sudden the headquarters of the White Goats. Terrible rites were being performed on the Isisi; the N'Gombi had danced by whole communities the dance of the Goat; the Akasava killed two of Sanders' spies and had sent their heads to Sanders as proof of their "earnest spirits"—to quote the message literally.

There was a missionary lady at Kosumkusu. Sanders' first thought was for her. He steamed direct from the smouldering ruins of Haggin's hut to find her.

She was amused at the growth of the secret societies, and thought it all very interesting.

Sanders did not tell her the aspect of the situation which was not amusing.

"Really, Mr. Sanders," she smiled, "I'm quite safe here—this is the second time in three months you have tried to bring me into your fold."

"This time you are coming," said Sanders quietly. "Abiboo has turned my cabin into a most luxurious *boudoir*."

But she fenced with him to the limits of his patience.

"But what of Mr. Haggin and Father Wells?" she asked. "You aren't bothering about them."

"I'm not bothering about Haggin," said Sanders, "because he's dead—I've just come from burying him."

"Dead!"

"Murdered," said Sanders briefly, "and his mission burnt. I've sent an escort for the Jesuits. They may or they may not get down. We pick them up tomorrow, with luck."

The girl's face had gone white.

343

"I'll come," she said, "I'm not afraid—yes, I am. And I'm giving you a lot of worry—forgive me."

Sanders said something more or less incoherent, for he was not used to penitent womankind.

He took her straight away, and the *Zaire* was hardly out of sight before her chief convert set fire to the mission buildings.

Sanders picked up the Jesuits. His rescue party had arrived just in time. He landed his guests at headquarters and went back to the Upper River to await developments.

The *Zaire* had a complement of fifty men. They were technically deck hands and their duty lay in collecting wood, in taking aboard and discharging such stores as he brought with him and in assisting in the navigation of the boat.

He went to a wooding on the Calali River to replenish his stock of fuel and very wisely he "wooded" by daylight.

The same night the whole of his men deserted, and he was left with twenty Houssas, Yoka, the engineer, and a Congo boy, who acted as his cook.

This was his position when he dropped down stream to an Isisi river where he hoped news would await him.

For all the volcano which trembled beneath his feet, he gave no outward sign of perturbation. The movement could be checked, might indeed be destroyed, if Ofalikari were laid by the heels, but the "missioner" had vanished and there was no reliable word as to his whereabouts.

Somewhere in the country he directed the operations of the society.

There was a lull; a sudden interval of inactivity That was bad, as bad as it could be.

Sanders reviewed the position and saw no good in it; he remembered the Commissioner who brought war to the Niger and shivered, for he loved the country and he loved his work.

There were two days of heavy rains, and these were followed by two days of sweltering heat—and then Bosambo, a native chief, with all a native's malignity and indifference to suffering grafted to knowledge of white men, sent a message to Sanders.

Two fast paddlers brought the messenger, and he stood up in his canoe to deliver his word.

"Thus said our lord Bosambo," he shouted, keeping a respectful distance from the little boat. "'Go you to Sandi, but go not on board his ship on your life. Say to Sandi:The White Goat dies, and the people of these lands come back to wisdom before the moon is full.'"

"Come to the ship and tell me more," called Sanders. The man shook his head.

"Lord, it is forbidden," he said, "for our lord was very sure on that matter; and there is nothing to tell you, for we are ignorant men, only Bosambo being wiser than all men save your lordship."

Sanders was puzzled. He knew the chief well enough to believe that he did not prophesy lightly, and yet—

"Go back to your chief," he said, "tell him that I have faith in him."

Then he sat down at the junction of the Isisi and Calali Rivers for Bosambo to work miracles.

Bosambo, chief of the Ochori, had had in his time many gods. Some of these he retained for emergencies or because their possession added to his prestige. He neither loved nor feared them. Bosambo loved or feared no man, save Sanders.

The White Goats might have the chief of the Ochori in a cleft stick; they might seduce from their allegiance half and more than half of his people, as they had done, but Bosambo, who knew that weak men who acquire strength of a sudden, invariably signalise their independence by acquiring new masters, accepted the little troubles which accompany the chieftainship of such a tribe as his with pleasing philosophy.

It was a trying time for him, and it was a period not without some excitement for those who tried him.

A dish of fish came to him from his chief cook one morning. Bosambo ate a little, and sent for the same cook, who was one of his titular wives.

"Woman," said Bosambo, "if you try to poison me, I will burn you alive, by *Ewa!*"

She was speechless with terror and fell on her knees before him.

"As matters are," said Bosambo, "I shall not speak of your sin to Sandi, who is my sister's own child by a white father, for if Sandi knew of this, he would place you in boiling water till your eyes bulged like a fish. Go now, woman, and cook me clean food."

Other attempts were made on his life. Once a spear whizzed past his head as he walked alone in the forest. Bosambo uttered a shriek and fell to the ground and the thrower, somewhat incautiously, came to see what mischief he had wrought, and if need be to finish the good work. . . . Bosambo returned from his walk alone. He stopped by the river to wash his hands and scour his spears with wet sand, and that was the end of the adventure so far as his assailant was concerned.

But the power of the society was growing. His chief councillor was slain at meat, another was drowned, and his people began to display a marked insolence.

The air became electric. The Akasava had thrown off all disguise, the influence of the White Goat predominated. Chiefs and headmen obeyed the least of their hunters, or themselves joined in the lewd ritual celebrated nightly in the forest. The chief who had brought about the arrest of Ofalikari was pulled down and murdered in the open street by the very men who had lodged complaints, and the first to strike was his own son.

All these things were happening whilst Sanders waited at the junction of the Isisi and Calali Rivers, his Houssas sleeping by the guns.

Bosambo saw the end clearly. He had no illusions as to his ultimate fate. "Tomorrow, light of my eyes," he said to his first wife, "I send you in a canoe to find Sandi, for men of the White Goat come openly— one man from every tribe, calling upon me to dance and make sacrifice."

His wife was a Kano woman; tall and straight and comely. "Lord," she said simply, "at the end you will take your spear and kill me, for here I sit till the end. When you die, life is death to me."

Bosambo put his strong arm about her and patted her head.

The following day he sat at *palaver*, but few were the applicants for justice. There was a stronger force abroad in the land; a higher dispenser of favour.

At the moment he had raised his hand to signify the *palaver* was finished a man came running from the forest. He ran unsteadily, like one who was drunken, throwing out his arms before him as though he was feeling his way.

He gained the village street, and came stumbling along, his sobbing breath being audible above the hum of the Ochoris' wondering talk.

Then suddenly a shrill voice cried a word in fear, and the people went bolting to their huts—and there was excuse, for this wanderer with the glazed eyes was sick to death, and his disease was that dreaded bush plague which decimates territories. It is an epidemic disease which makes its appearance once in twenty years; it has no known origin and no remedy.

Other diseases: sleeping sickness, *beriberi*, malaria, are called by courtesy the sickness *mongo*—"The Sickness Itself"—but this mysterious malady alone is entitled to the description.

The man fell flat on the ground at the foot of the little hill where Bosambo sat in solitude—his head-men and councillors fleeing in panic at the sick man's approach.

Bosambo looked at him thoughtfully.

"What may I do for you, my brother?" he asked.

"Save me," moaned the man.

Bosambo was silent. He was a native, and a native mind is difficult to follow. I cannot explain its psychology. The coils were tightening on him, death faced him as assuredly as it stared hollow-eyed on the Thing that writhed at his feet.

"I can cure you," he said softly, "by certain magic. Go you to the far end of the village, there you will find four new huts and in each hut three beds. Now you shall lie down on each bed and after you shall go into the forest as fast as you can walk and wait for my magic to work."

Thus spake Bosambo, and the man at his feet, with death's hand already upon his shoulder, listened eagerly.

"Lord, is there any other thing I must do?" he asked in the thin whistling tone which is characteristic of the disease.

"This you must also do," said Bosambo, "you must go to these huts secretly so that none see you; and on each bed you shall lie so long as it will take a fish to die."

Watched from a hundred doorways, the sick man made his way back to the forest; and the men of the village spat on the ground as he passed.

Bosambo sent his messengers to Sanders then and there, and patiently awaited the coming of the emissaries of the Goat.

At ten o'clock that night, before the moon was up, they arrived dramatically. Simultaneously twelve lights appeared, at twelve points about the village, then each light advanced at slow pace and revealed a man bearing a torch.

They advanced at solemn pace until they arrived together at a meeting place, and that place the open roadway before Bosambo's hut. In a blazing semicircle they stood before the chief—and the chief was not impressed.

For these delegates were a curious mixture. They included a petty chief of the Ochori—Bosambo marked him down for an ignominious end—a fisherman of the Isisi, a witch doctor of the N'Gombi, a hunter of the Calali, and, chiefest of all, a tall, broad-shouldered negro in the garb of white men.

This was Ofalikari, sometime preacher of the Word, and supreme head of the terrible order which was devastating the territories.

As they stood the voice of a man broke the silence with a song. He led it in a nasal *falsetto*, and the others acted as chorus.

"The White Goat is very strong and his horns are of gold."

"*Oai!*" chorused the others.

"His blood is red and he teaches mysteries."

"*Oai!*"

"When his life goes out his spirit becomes a god."

"*Oai!*"

"Woe to those who stand between the White Goat and his freedom."

"*Oai!*"

"For his sharp feet will cut them to the bone and his horns will bleed them."

"*Oai!*"

They sang, one drum tapping rhythmically, the bangled feet of the chorus jingling as they pranced with deliberation at each "*O ai!*"

When they had finished, Ofalikari spoke.

"Bosambo, we know you to be a wise man, and acquainted with white people and their gods, even as I am, for I was a teacher of the blessed Word. Now the White Goat loves you, Bosambo, and will do you no injury. Therefore have we come to summon you to a big *palaver* tomorrow, and to that *palaver* we will summon Sandi to answer for his wickedness. Him we will burn slowly, for he is an evil man."

"Lord Goat," said Bosambo, "this is a big matter, and I will ask you to stay with me this night, that I may be guided and strengthened by your lordships' wisdom. I have built you four new huts," he went on, "knowing that your honours were coming; here you shall be lodged, and by my heart and my life no living man shall injure you."

"No dead man can, Bosambo," said Otalikari, and there was a rocking shout of laughter. Bosambo laughed too; he laughed louder and longer than all the rest, he laughed so that Ofalikari was pleased with him.

"Go in peace," said Bosambo, and the delegates went to their huts.

In the early hours of the morning Bosambo sent for Tomba, an enemy and a secret agent of the society.

"Go to the great lords," he said, "tell them I come to them to-night by the place where the Isisi River and the big river meet. And say to them that they must go quickly, for I do not wish to see them again, lest our adventure does not carry well, and Sandi punish me."

At daybreak with his cloak of monkey tails about him—for the dawn was chilly—he watched the delegation leave the village and each go its separate way.

He noted that Tomba accompanied them out of sight. He wasted half an hour, then went to his hut and emerged naked save for his loin cloth, his great shield on his left arm, and in the hand behind the shield a bundle of throwing spears.

To him moved fifty fighting men, the trusted and the faithful, and each carried his wicker war shield obliquely before him.

And the Ochori people, coward at heart, watched the little company in awe. They stood waiting, these fierce, silent warriors, till at a word they marched till they came to the four huts where Bosambo's guests had lain. Here they waited again. Tomba came in time and stared uneasily at the armed rank.

"Tomba," said Bosambo gently, "did you say farewell to the Goat lords?"

"This I did, chief," said Tomba.

"Embracing them as is the Goat custom?" asked Bosambo more softly still.

"Lord, I did this."

Bosambo nodded.

"Go to that hut, O Tomba, great Goat and embracer of Goats."

Tomba hesitated, then walked slowly to the nearest hut. He reached the door, and half turned.

"Slay!" whispered Bosambo, and threw the first spear.

With a yell of terror the man turned to flee, but four spears struck him within a space of which the palm of a hand might cover and he rolled into the hut, dead.

Bosambo selected another spear, one peculiarly prepared, for beneath the spear head a great wad of dried grass had been bound and this had been soaked in copal gum.

A man brought him fire in a little iron cup and he set it to the spear, and with a jerk of his palm sent the blazing javelin to the hut's thatched roof.

In an instant it burst into flame—in ten minutes the four new houses were burning fiercely.

And on the flaming fire, the villagers, summoned to service, added fresh fuel and more and more, till the sweat rolled down their unprotected bodies. In the afternoon Bosambo allowed the fire to die down. He sent two armed men to each of the four roads that led into the village, and his orders were explicit.

"You shall kill any man or woman who leaves this place," he said; "also you shall kill any man or woman who, coming in, will not turn aside. And if you do not kill them, I myself will kill you. For I will not have the sickness *mongo* in my city, lest our lord Sandi is angry."

Sanders, waiting far he knew not what, heard the news, and went steaming to headquarters, sending pigeons in front asking for doctors. A week later he came back with sufficient medical stores to put the decks of the *Zaire* awash, but he came too late. The bush plague had run its course. It had swept through cities and lands and villages like a tempest, and strange it was that those cities which sent delegates to Bosambo suffered most, and in the N'Gombi city to which Ofalikari stumbled to die, one eighth of the population were wiped out.

"And how has it fared with you, Bosambo?" asked Sanders when the medical expedition came to Ochori.

"Lord," said Bosambo, "it has passed me by."

There was a doctor in the party of an inquiring mind. "Ask him how he accounts for his immunity," he said to Sanders, for he had no knowledge of the vernacular, and Sanders repeated the question.

"Lord," said Bosambo with simple earnestness, "I prayed very earnestly, being, as your lordship knows, a *bueno Catolico*."

And the doctor, who was also a "good Catholic," was so pleased that he gave Bosambo a sovereign and a little writing pad—at least he did not give Bosambo the latter, but it is an indisputable fact that it was in the chief's hut when the party had gone.

CHAPTER 16

The Crime of Sanders

It is a fine thing to be confidential clerk to a millionaire, to have placed to your credit every month of your life the sum of forty-one pounds thirteen shillings and fourpence.

This was the experience of a man named Jordon, a young man of considerable character, as you shall learn. He had a pretty wife and a beautiful baby, and they were a contented and happy little family.

Unfortunately the millionaire died, and though he left "£100 to my secretary, Derik Arthur Jordon," the sum inadequately compensated young Jordon for the forty-one pounds thirteen shillings and fourpence which came to his banker with monotonous regularity every month.

A millionaire's confidential clerk is a drug on the market which knows few millionaires, and those admirably suited in the matter of secretaries. The young man spent six months and most of his money before he came to understand that his opportunities were limited.

Had he been just an ordinary clerk, with the requisite knowledge of shorthand and typewriting, he would have found no difficulty in securing employment. Had he had an acquaintance with a thousand and one businesses he might have been "placed," but he had specialised in millionaires—an erratic millionaire whose memory and purse and Times he was—and the world of business had no opening for his undisputed qualities. He had exactly £150 left of his savings and his legacy, when the fact was brought home to him.

Then it happened, that returning to his suburban home one evening, he met a man who had just met another man, who on a capital of a few pounds had amassed a fortune by trading on the West Coast of Africa.

Jordon sought an introduction to the friend and they met in the splendour of a West End hotel, where the trader drank whiskey and talked of his "little place at Minehead."

"It's dead easy," he said, "especially if you get into a country which isn't overrun by traders, like Sanders' territory. But of course that's impossible. Sanders is a swine to traders—won't have them in his territory. He's a sort of little god. . . ."

He drew a picture of the wonderful possibilities of such a field, and the young man went home full of the prospect.

He and his pretty wife sat up till the early hours of the morning discussing the plan. They got a map of Africa showing the territory over which Mr. Commissioner Sanders had dominion. It seemed absurdly small, but it was a little map.

"I wonder what he is like?" asked the girl thoughtfully. She concealed her own agony of mind at the prospect of parting with him, because she was a woman, and women are very extraordinary in their unselfishness.

"Perhaps he would let you go in," she said wistfully. "I am sure he would if he knew what it meant to us."

Jordon shook his head a little ruefully.

"I don't suppose that our position will have much influence with him. Ammett says that he's a very strict man and unpleasant to deal with."

They went into the cost of the expedition. By selling up the furniture and moving into lodgings it could be done. He could leave her fifty or sixty pounds, sufficient to last her with economy for a year. The rest he would sink into goods—a list of which the successful trader had given him.

Some weeks later Jordon took the great step. He sailed from Liverpool with a stock of *gew-gaws* and cloth, and, as the tiny figure of his weeping girl-wife grew more and more indistinct on the quay, he realised, as all men realise sooner or later, that death is not the most painful of humanity's trials.

He changed his ship at Grand Bassam for the accommodation of a small steamer.

He did not confide his plans to the men he met on board—harddrinking men in white duck—but what he learnt of Sanders made his heart sink.

Sanders went down to the beach to meet the steamer, which usually brought the mails.

A tall young man in white sprang from the boat and a portmanteau followed. Sanders looked at the newcomer with suspicion. He did not love strangers—his regulation in this respect was known from Dacca to Mossamades and the phrase "Sanders' Welcome" had become idiomatic.

"Good morning," said Jordon, with his heart quaking.

"Good morning," said Sanders; "do you want to see me? I am afraid you will not have much time, the boat does not stay very long."

The newcomer bit his lip.

"I am not going on yet," he said, "I—I want to stay here."

"Oh!" said Sanders, without enthusiasm.

In the cool of the verandah over an iced drink the young man spoke without reserve.

"I've come out here to make a fortune, or at any rate a living," he said, and the thought of her he had left in her tiny lodging gave him courage.

"You've come to a very unlucky place," said Sanders, smiling in spite of his resentment at this intrusion on his privacy.

"That is why I came," said the other with surprising boldness; "all the likely places are used up, and I have got to justify my existence somehow." And without attempting to hide his own poverty or his inexperience, he told his story.

The Commissioner was interested. This side of life, as the young man recited it, was new to him; it was a life which he himself did not know or understand, this struggle for existence in a great uncaring city.

"You seem to have had the average kind of bad luck," he said simply. "I can't advise you to go back because you have burned your boats, and in the second place because I am pretty sure that you would not go. Let me think."

He frowned at the police huts shimmering in the morning heat: he sought inspiration in the glimpse of yellow sands and thundering seas which was obtainable from whence he sat.

"I could find work for you," he said, "if you spoke any of the languages, which of course you do not, or if—" He was silent.

"I am supposed to have an assistant," he said at last, "I could appoint you—"

The young man shook his head.

"That's good of you, sir," he said, "but I'd be no use to you. Give me a trader's licence. I believe you've got authority to do so, in fact nobody else seems to have that authority."

Sanders grinned. There was a licence once issued by the Administrator's secretary to an Eurasian trader—but that story will keep.

"I'll give you the licence," he said after a pause, and the young man's heart leapt; "it will cost you a guinea to start with, all the money you've got eventually, and in course of time you will probably add to the bill of costs your health and your life."

He issued the licence that day.

For a couple of weeks the young man remained his guest whilst his stores came on from Sierra Leone.

Sanders found an interpreter and headman for him, and the young man started off in his new canoe to wrestle with fortune, after a letter to his wife in which he described Sanders as something between a Peabody and an angel.

Before he went Sanders gave him a few words of advice.

"I do not like traders," he said, "and I never issue a licence unless I can help it: do not upset my people, do not make any kind of trouble. Avoid the N'Gombi, who are thieves and the bush people, who are chronically homicidal. The Isisi will buy salt with rubber—there is plenty of rubber in the back country. The Ochori will buy cloth with gum—by the way, Bosambo, the chief, speaks English and will try to swindle you. Good-bye and good luck."

He watched the canoe till it disappeared round the bluff, and went back to his hut to record the departure in his diary.

After which he sat himself down to decipher a long despatch in Arabic from one of his intelligence men—a despatch which dealt minutely with three other strangers who had come to his land, and arriving mysteriously, had as mysteriously disappeared.

These were three men who dwelt by the River, being of no village, and of no denned race, for they were settled on the border-line between Akasava, Isisi, and Ochori, and though one had the lateral face-marks of a Bogindi man, yet there was little doubt that he was not of that people.

They lived in three huts set side by side and they fished and hunted. A strange fact was that none of these men had wives.

For some reason which the psychologist will understand, the circumstances isolated the three from their kind. Women avoided them, and when they came to the adjacent village to sell or to buy, the girls and the young matrons went into their huts and peered at them fearfully.

The chief of the three was named M'K-aroka—or so it sounded—

and he was a broad, tall man, of surly countenance, sparing of speech, and unpleasant in dispute. He accounted himself outside of all the village laws, though he broke none, and as he acted and thought so did his fellows.

Their lives if strange were inoffensive, they did not steal nor abuse the privileges which were theirs. They were honest in their dealings and cleanly.

Sanders, who had made inquiries through channels which were familiar enough to those who understand the means by which a savage country is governed, received no ill-report, and left the three to their own devices. They fished, hunted, grew a little maize in a garden they won from the forest, sought for and prepared manioc for consumption, and behaved as honest husbandmen should do.

One day they disappeared. They vanished as though the earth had opened and swallowed them up. None saw their going. Their huts were left untouched and unspoiled, their growing crops stood in the gardens they had cultivated, the dying fish hung on lines between poles just as they had placed them, and the solitary canoe they shared was left beached.

But the three had gone. The forest, impenetrable, unknown, had swallowed them, and no more was heard of them.

Sanders, who was never surprised and took it for granted that the most mysterious of happenings had a natural explanation, did no more than send word to the forest villages asking for news of the three men. This was not forthcoming, and the matter ended so far as the Commissioner was concerned.

He heard of Jordon throughout the year. Letters addressed to his wife came to headquarters, and were forwarded. His progress from village to village was duly charted by Sanders' agents. Such accounts as reached Sanders were to the effect that the young man was finding it difficult to make both ends meet. The rubber that arrived at irregular intervals for shipment was not of the best quality, and one load of gum was lost in the river by the overturning of a canoe. Sanders, knowing the young man's story, was worried, and caused word to go up river that patronage of the trader would be pleasing to the Commissioner.

Then one day, a year after he had set forth, he unexpectedly turned up at headquarters, thinner, burnt black by the Sun, and the possessor of a straggling beard.

He came in an old canoe with four paddlers, and he brought nothing with him save his rifle, his cooking pots and bedding.

His clothes were patched and soiled, he wore clumsy moccasins of skins, and a helmet which was no longer white and was considerably battered.

He had learnt something and greeted Sanders fluently in the Bomongo dialect.

"*Chasi o!*" he said, with a bitter little laugh, as he stepped from the canoe, and that word meant "finished" in a certain River dialect.

"As bad as that?" said Sanders.

"Pretty nearly," replied the other. "I'm no trader, Mr. Sanders, I'm a born philanthropist."

He laughed again and Sanders smiled in sympathy.

"I've seen a lot of life," he said, "but it doesn't pay dividends."

Sanders took him to the residency and found a suit that nearly fitted him.

"I'll have just one more try," Jordon went on, "then I light out for another field."

There were letters awaiting him—letters of infinite sweetness and patience. Letters filled with heroic lies—but too transparent to deceive anybody.

The young man read them and went old-looking.

There were remittances from his agent at Sierra Leone—very small indeed these were, after commission and the like had been subtracted.

Still there was enough to lay in a fresh trading stock, and three weeks later the young man again disappeared into the unknown.

His departure from headquarters coincided with the return of one of the mysterious three.

He came back alone to the place by the River. The huts had disappeared, the garden was again forest, the canoe rotted on the beach—for none had dared disturb it.

He set to work to rebuild a hut. He cleared the garden unaided, and settled down in solitude to the routine of life. He was the chief of the three men, M'Karoka, and like the two men who had disappeared, a man of splendid physique.

Sanders heard of his return and the next time he passed that way he landed.

The man was squatting before his fire, stirring the contents of a steaming pot as Sanders came into sight round the hut which had screened his landing.

He leapt to his feet nimbly, looked for a moment as though he would run away, thought better of it, and raised his hand palm outward in salute.

"*Inkoos,*" he said in a deep booming voice.

It was an unusual greeting, yet dimly familiar.

"I bring happiness," said Sanders, using a form of speech peculiar to the Ochori. "Yet since you are a stranger I would ask you what you do, and why do you dwell apart from your own people, for I am the King's eye and see for him?"

The man spoke slowly, and it was evident to Sanders that the Ochori was not his speech, for he would sometimes hesitate for a word and sometimes fill the deficiency with a word of Swaheli.

"I am from a far country, lord chief," he said, "and my two cousins. Many moons we journeyed, and we came to this place. Then for certain reasons we returned to our land. And when we did that which we had to do, we started to come back. And one named Vellim was killed by a lion and another died of sickness, and I came alone and here I sit till the appointed time."

There was a ring of truth in the man's speech.

Sanders had an instinct for such truth, and he knew that he had not lied.

"What are your people?" he asked; "for it is plain to me that your are a foreigner and like none that I know save one race, the race of the great one Ketchewayo."

"You have spoken, lord," said the man gravely; "for though I eat fish, I am of the Zulu people, and I have killed men."

Sanders eyed him in silence. It was an astounding statement the man made, that he had walked four thousand miles across desert and river and forest, through a hundred hostile nations, had returned thence four thousand miles with his companions and again covered the distance. Yet he was indisputably a Zulu—Sanders knew that much from the moment he had raised his hand in salute and greeted him as a "prince."

"Rest here," he said, "keep the law and do ill to none, and you shall be as free as any man—it is finished."

Sanders pursued a leisurely way down the river, for no pressing matter called him, either to headquarters or to any particular village.

He passed Jordon's canoe going up stream, and megaphoned a cheery greeting. The young man, though the reverse of cheerful, responded, waving his hand to the white-clad figure on the bridge of the *Zaire*.

It was with a heavy heart he went on. His stock was dwindling, and he had little to show for his labours. Not even the most tempting and the most gaudy of Manchester goods had induced the lazy Isisi to collect rubber. They offered him dried fish, tiny chickens and service for his desirable cloth and beads, but rubber or gum they were disinclined to collect.

Night was coming on when he made the hut of the solitary stranger.

He directed his paddlers to the beach and landed for the night. Whilst his four men lit a fire he went on to the hut.

M'Karoka with folded arms watched his approach. No other man on the river but would have hastened forward to pay tribute, for black is black and white is white, whether the white man be commissioner or trader.

Jordon had been long enough on the River to see in the attitude of indifference a hint of ungraciousness. Yet the man was polite.

Together they sat and haggled over the price of a piece of cloth—M'Karoka had no use for beads—and when Jordon set his little tent up on the shore, the man was helpful and seemed used to the peculiar ways of tents.

But the most extraordinary circumstance was that M'Karoka had paid for his purchase in money. He had entered his hut when the bargain had been completed and reappeared with a golden sovereign.

He paid four times the value of the cloth, because the negotiations were conducted on a gum basis.

Jordon was thinking this matter out when he retired for the night. It puzzled him, because money, as he knew, was unknown on the River.

He went to sleep to dream of a suburban home and the pale face of his pretty wife. He woke suddenly. It was still night. Outside he could hear the swish-swish of the river and the faint murmur of trees. But these had not awakened him.

There were voices outside the tent, voices that spoke in a language he could not understand.

He pulled on his mosquito boots and opened the fly of the tent.

There was a moon, and he saw M'K-aroka standing before his hut and with him was another. They were quarrelling and the fierce voice of the newcomer was raised in anger. Then of a sudden, before Jordon could reach his revolver, the stranger stepped back a pace and struck twice at M'Karoka.

Jordon saw the gleam of steel in the moonlight, stooped and found his revolver, and dashed out of the tent. M'Karoka lay upon the ground, and his assailant had dashed for the river.

He leapt into Jordon's canoe. With a stroke he severed the native rope which moored the craft to the shore, and paddled frantically to midstream.

Three times Jordon fired at him. At the third shot he slid overboard like a man suddenly tired.

"Swim out and bring the canoe," ordered Jordon and turned his attention to M'Karoka. The man was dying; it was not necessary to have an extensive knowledge of surgery to see that he was wounded beyond recovery.

Jordon attempted to plug the more terrible of the chest wounds and to arrest the bleeding. The Zulu opened his eyes.

"*Baas*," he said faintly, "what came of Vellim?" (This man's name was probably Wilhelm or William.)

"I think he is dead," said Jordon.

M'Karoka closed his eyes.

"Listen, *baas*," he said after a while, "you will tell Sandi that I lied when I said Vellim was dead, though all else was true—we each took our share of the stones—then we went back because they were no use to us in this far land—and some we changed for money—then we had to fly—and Vellim tried to kill us so that he might have all—and we beat him, taking from him his stones, and he ran into the forest—"

He paused, for he found difficulty in speaking.

When he spoke again it was in a language which Jordon could not understand—the language the men had spoken when they quarrelled. He spoke vehemently, then seemed to realise that he was not understood, for he changed his speech to the Ochori dialect.

"Under the fire in my hut," he gasped, "are many stones, master—they are for you, because you killed Vellim—"

He died soon afterwards.

In the morning Jordon cleared away the ashes of the fire, and dug through the baked earth. Two feet below the surface he came upon a parcel wrapped in innumerable coverings of native cloth. He opened it eagerly, his hands shaking. There were twenty or thirty pebbles varying in size from a marble to a pea. They were of irregular size and mouse-coloured. Jordon found his training as secretary to a South African millionaire helpful, for he knew these to be uncut diamonds.

Sanders listened to the story incoherently told.

Jordon was beside himself with joy.

"Think of it, Mr. Sanders," he said, "think of that dear little wife of mine and that dear kiddie. They're nearly starving, I know it—I can read between the lines of her letter. And at a moment when everything seems to be going wrong, this great fortune comes—"

Sanders let him rave on, not attempting to check him. The homeward-bound steamer lay in the roadstead, her launch bobbed and swayed in the swell by the beach.

"You arrived in time," said Sanders grimly; "if I were you I should forget that you ever told me anything about this affair—and I shouldn't talk about it when you get home if I were you. Goodbye."

He held out his hand and Jordon gripped.

"You've been kindness itself," he began.

"Goodbye," said the Commissioner; "you'd better run or the launch will go without you."

He did not wait to see the last of the trader, but turned abruptly and went back to the residency.

He opened his desk and took out a printed document.

To all Commissioners, Magistrates, Chiefs of Police, and
Deputy Commissioners:

Wanted on a warrant issued by the Chief Magistrate of Kimberley, Villim Dobomo, Joseph M'Karoka, Joseph Kama, Zulus, charged with illicit diamond buying, and believed to be making their way northward through Baroskeland, Angola and the Congo. Accused men disappeared from Kimberley two years ago, but have been seen recently in the neighbourhood of that town. It is now known that they have returned north.

At the foot of the communication was a written note from Sanders' chief:

Please state if anything is known of these men.

Sanders sat staring at the document for a long time. It was of course his duty to report the matter and confiscate the diamonds in the possession of Jordon.

"A young wife and a baby," said Sanders thoughtfully; "how infernally improvident these people are!"

He took up his pen and wrote:

Unknown: Sanders.

CHAPTER 17

Spring of the Year

The life of one of His Britannic Majesty's Commissioners of Native Territories is necessarily a lonely one. He is shut off from communion with those things which men hold most dear. He is bound as by a steel wall to a life which has no part and no harmony with the life to which his instincts call him, and for which his early training, no less than the hereditary forces within him, have made no preparation. He lives and thinks with black people, who are children of thought, memory and action.

They love and hate like children; they are without the finesse and subtlety which is the possession of their civilised brethren, and in their elementary passions rather retrograde toward the common animal stock from whence we have all sprung, than progress to the nicenesses of refinement.

And white men who live with them and enter into their lives whole-heartedly become one of two things, clever children or clever beasts. I make this bald statement; the reader must figure out the wherefore.

Sanders came down the river in the spring of the year, in a thoughtful mood. Under the striped awning which covered the bridge of his stern-wheeler he sat in a deep-seated lounge chair, his book on his knees, but he read little.

His eyes wandered idly over the broad, smooth surface of the big river: they followed the line of the dark N'Gombi forest to the left, and the flat rolling land of the Isisi to the right. They were attracted by the blue-grey smoke which arose from this village and that. The little fishing canoes, anchored in likely places, the raucous call of the parrots overhead, the peering faces of the little monkeys of which he caught glimpses, when the *Zaire* moved to deep water in shore, all these things interested him and held him as they had not interested him since—oh, since quite a long time ago.

As he came abreast of a village he pulled the cord which controlled the siren, and the little steamer hooted a welcome to the waving figures on the beach.

With his fly whisk in his hand, and his unread book on his knee, he gazed by turns absently and interestedly at the landscape.

Bogindi, the steersman, who stood in the shadow of the awning with his hand on the wheel, called him by name.

"Lord, there is a man in a canoe ahead who desires to speak with your lordship."

Sanders shaded his eyes. Directly in the course of the steamer a canoe lay broadside on, and standing upright was a man whose outstretched arms spoke of desire for an urgent *palaver*.

Now only matters of great moment, such as rebellion and the like, justify holding up the King's ship on the river.

Sanders leapt forward in his chair and pulled over the handle of the telegraph to "Stop," then to "Astern Easy."

He rose and took a survey of the man through his glasses.

"This is a young man, Abiboo," he said, "and I think of the Isisi people; certainly he is no chief to bid me halt."

"He may be mad, lord," said Abiboo; "in the spring of the year the Isisi do strange things, as all men know."

The *Zaire* came slowly to the canoe, and its occupant, wielding his paddles scientifically, brought his little craft alongside and stepped aboard.

"Who are you?" asked Abiboo, "and what great matter have you in hand that you stop our lord on his splendid way?"

"I am Kobolo of the Isisi, of the village of Togo-bonobo," said the young man, "and I love a chief's daughter."

"May God send you to the bottom of the waters," swore the wrathful Abiboo, "that you bring your vile body to this ship; that you disturb our lord in his high meditations. Come thou, Kaffir, and whilst you speak with Sandi, I go to find the whip he will surely order for you."

Thus Kobolo came before Sanders and Abiboo introduced him in words which were not flattering.

"This is a strange *palaver*," said Sanders not unkindly, "for it is not the practice for young men to stop the ship of the King's Commissioner because they love maidens."

The young man was tall, straight of back, and well made of shoul-

362

der, and he showed no remorse for his outrageous conduct. Rather there was an air about him of desperate earnestness.

"Lord," he said, "I love Nimimi, who is the daughter of my chief, the chief of the village of Togo-bonobo. And because she is a beautiful dancer, and men come from afar to see her, her father demands two thousand rods for her, and I am a poor man."

"'The father is always right,'" quoted Sanders, "for it is said on the River, 'A thing is worth its price and that which you give away is worth nothing.'"

"This woman loves me," said the youth, "and because of her I have saved a thousand *matakos*, which, as your lordship knows, is a great fortune."

"What can I do?" asked Sanders, with one of his rare smiles.

"Lord, you are all-powerful," said the agitated young man, "and if you say to the chief her father——"

Sanders shook his head.

"That may not be," he said.

There was something in the spring air, something responsive in his blood, that inclined him to act as he did, for after a moment's thought he turned to Abiboo.

"Take this man," he said, "and give him——"

"Lord, I have the whip ready," said Abiboo complacently. "For I knew that your lordship would be offended by this foolish one."

"Give him a thousand *matakos* from the store, that he may buy the woman of his desire."

Abiboo, a little dazed, went slowly to do his master's bidding.

"Lord," said Kobolo, and fell at the Commissioner's feet, "you are as my father and mother, and I will repay you with good words and thoughts."

"Repay me with *matakos*," said the practical Sanders. "Go, take your girl, and God help you!"

Yet he was in no cynical mood. Rather there was a gentleness, a mild stirring of emotions long repressed, a strange tenderness in heart, which harmonised with the tenderness of the young green trees, with the play of budding life about him.

He stood watching the native as he paddled to shore, singing a loud song, tuneless save for the tune of joy that ran through it. Wistfully Sanders watched. This man, little better than an animal, yet obedient to the inexorable laws which Sanders in his wisdom defied; hastening, with his brass rods, to a glorious life, to a hut and a wife, and the raising of young children to manhood. To toil and the dangers and vicissitudes of his peculiar lot; but to the fulfilment of his highest destiny.

The Commissioner stood watching him until he saw the canoe ground on the beach, and the man leap lightly ashore and make the boat fast.

Sanders shook his head and turned the handle of the telegraph to "full speed."

He made no pretence at reading; his gaze was abstracted. Presently he rose and walked into his cabin. He pulled the curtains across the door as though he desired none to witness his folly, then he took a key from his pocket and unlocked the little safe which was let into the wall over the head of his bunk, He opened a drawer and took out a fat brown book.

He laid it upon his desk and turned the leaves.

It was his bank book from the coast agent of Cox, and the balance to his credit ran into five figures, for Sanders had been a careful man all his life, and had bought land at Lagos in the days when you could secure a desirable building lot for the price of a dress suit.

He closed the book, and replacing it in the safe resumed his seat on the bridge.

In the course of the next day he arrived at headquarters.

It was late in the afternoon when the *Zaire* went slowly astern into the little dock, which Sanders with much labour had built.

It was a pretentious little dock, the pride of his days, for it had walls of concrete and a big sluice gate, and it had been erected at the time when the *Zaire* had undergone her repairs. Sanders never saw that dock without a feeling of intense gratification. It was the "child" which awaited his return; the creation of his mind which welcomed him back.

And there was a concrete footpath from the dock to the residency—this he had built. On each side Isisi palms had been planted—the work of his hands. They seemed pitiably insignificant.

He surveyed the residency without joy. It stood on a little rise; from its corrugated root to its distempered stoep, a model of neatness and order.

"God bless the place!" said Sanders irritably.

For its old charm had departed; the old pleasant home-coming had become a bleak and wearisome business. And the house was lonely and needed something. It needed a touch which he could not supply. He walked disconsolately through the rooms, lit a pipe, knocked it out again, and wandered vaguely in the direction of the Houssas lines.

Captain Hamilton, of the King's Houssas, in white shirt and riding breeches, leant over the rail of the stoep and watched him.

"Back again," he said conventionally.

"No," said Sanders disagreeably, "I'm on the top river catching flies."

Hamilton removed his pipe.

"You've been reading the American Sunday Supplements," he said calmly, "which is either a sign of mental decrepitude or the awakening of a much-needed sense of humour."

He called to his servant. "Ali," he said solemnly, "prepare the lord Sandi such a cup of tea as the *houris* of paradise will prepare for the *Khalifa* on the great day."

"What rot you talk, Hamilton!" said Sanders irritably when the man had gone. "You know well enough the *Khalifa* would drink nothing but Turkish coffee on that occasion."

"Who knows?" asked the philosophical Hamilton. "Well, and how are all your good people?"

"They're all right," said Sanders, seating himself in a big chair.

"The usual murders, witchcraft and pillage," Hamilton grinned. "Bosambo the virtuous sitting on the foreshore of the Ochori, polishing his halo and singing comic songs!"

"Bosambo—oh, he's subdued just now!" said Sanders, stirring the tea which the man had brought, "he's the best chief on this river, Hamilton," the other nodded, "if I had my way—if I were the British Government—I'd make him paramount chief of all these territories."

"You'd have a war in ten minutes," said the Houssa skipper, "but he's a good man. Depressed, was he?"

"Horribly—I've never seen him so worried, and I'm blest if I know why!"

Hamilton smiled. "Which shows that a poor devil of a soldier, who is not supposed to be au courant with the gossip of the River, may be wiser than a patent stamped-in-every-link Commissioner," he said. "Bosambo is very fond of that Kano wife of his."

"I know that, my good chap," said Sanders, "and a good wife is half the making of a man. Why, what is a man without—"

He saw the curious laughing eyes of the other watching him, and stopped, and under the tan his eyes went red.

"You're singularly enthusiastic, Sandi Labolo," he said, using the Commissioner's native name; "you're not thinking—"

"What about Bosambo's wife?" interrupted Sanders loudly.

The Houssa was eyeing him suspiciously. "Bosambo's wife," he repeated, "oh—she goes the way of womankind! Bosambo hopes and fears—after the way of men. He has no child."

"Oh!—I didn't know that, who told you?"

"My men: they are singing a little song about it—I must introduce you to the regimental poet."

There was a long silence after this, neither men talking; then Hamilton asked carelessly:

"You went to Kosumkusu of course?"

"I went—yes," Sanders seemed reluctant to proceed.

"And Miss Glandynne, that medical missionary of ours?"

"She—oh, she was cheerful."

Hamilton smiled.

"I sent her a wad of letters which came by the last mail," he said; "you probably passed the mail canoe on your way down?"

Sanders nodded and there was another pause in the conversation.

"She's rather pretty, isn't she?" asked Hamilton.

"Very," responded Sanders with unnecessary emphasis.

"A very nice girl indeed," Hamilton continued absently.

Sanders made no response for a time—then: "She is a charming lady, much too good for—"

He checked himself.

"For——?" enticed Hamilton.

"For—for that kind of life," stammered Sanders, hot all over. He rose abruptly.

"I've got some letters to write," he said and took a hurried departure. And Hamilton, watching the dapper figure stride along the path toward the residency, shook his head sorrowfully.

Sanders wrote no letters. He began many, tore them up and put the scraps in his pocket. He sat thinking till the servants came to put lights in the room. He hardly tasted his dinner, and the rest of the evening he spent on the stoep staring into the darkness, wondering, hoping, thinking. In the near-by village a wedding feast was in progress, and the mad tattoo of the drum was a fitting accompaniment to his thoughts.

Nor did the next day bring him nearer to a decision, nor the next, nor the next.

She was too good for him—he could not ask her to share his life in a country where none knew what the day would bring forth—a country filled with every known tropical disease, and populated by cannibal peoples who were never certain from day to day to retain their allegiance. It would not be fair to ask it—and yet she had said she loved the country; she was beginning to understand the people. And she could go home in the hot months—he would take his arrears of leave.

And a man ought to be married; he was getting on in years—nearly forty.

A panic seized him.

Perhaps he was too old? That was a terrible supposition. He discovered that he did not know how old he was, and spent two busy days collecting from his private documents authentic evidence. Thus three weeks passed before he wrote his final letter.

During all the period he saw little of the Houssa Captain. He thought once of telling him something of his plans, but funked it at the last.

He turned up at Hamilton's quarters one night.

"I am going up river tomorrow," he said awkwardly. "I leave as soon after the arrival of the homeward-bound mail as possible—I am expecting letters from the Administration."

Hamilton nodded.

"But why this outburst of confidence?" he asked. "You do not often favour me with your plans in advance."

"Well," began Sanders, "I think I was going to tell you something else, but I'll defer that."

He spent the rest of the evening playing picquet and made remarkable blunders.

In the morning he was up before daybreak, superintending the provisioning of the *Zaire*, and when this was completed he awaited impatiently the coming of the mail steamer. When it was only a smudge of black smoke on the horizon, he went down to the beach, though he knew, as a reasonable man, it could not arrive for at least an hour.

He was standing on the sand, his hands behind his back, fidgeting nervously, when he saw Abiboo running toward him.

"Master," said the orderly, "the God-woman is coming."

Sanders' heart gave a leap, and then he felt himself go cold.

"God-woman?" he said, "what—which God-woman?"

"Lord, she we left at the last moon at Kosumkusu."

Sanders ran back across the beach, through the Houssa barracks to the river dock. As he reached the stage he saw the girl's canoe come sweeping round the bend.

He went down to meet her and gave her his hand to assist her ashore.

She was, to Sanders' eyes, a radiant vision of loveliness. Snowy white from head to foot; a pair of grave grey eyes smiled at him from under the broad brim of her *topee*.

"I've brought you news which will please you," she said; "but tell me first, is the mail steamer gone?"

He found his tongue.

"If it had gone," he said, and his voice was a little husky, "I should not have been here."

Then his throat grew dry, for here was an opening did he but possess the courage to take it; and of courage he had none. His brain was in a whirl. He could not muster two consecutive thoughts. He said something which was conventional and fairly trite. "You will come up to breakfast," he managed to say at last, "and tell me—you said I should be pleased about some news."

She smiled at him as she had never smiled before—a mischievous, happy, human smile. Yes, that was what he saw for the first time, the human woman in her. "I'm going home," she said.

He was making his way towards the residency, and she was walking by his side. He stopped. "Going home?" he said.

"I'm going home." There was a sparkle in her eyes and a colour he had not seen before. "Aren't you glad? I've been such a nuisance to you—and I am afraid I am rather a failure as a missionary."

It did not seem to depress her unduly, for he saw she was happy.

"Going home?" he repeated stupidly.

She nodded. "I'll let you into a secret," she said, "for you have been so good a friend to me that I feel you ought to know—I'm going to be married."

"You're going to be married?" Sanders repeated.

His fingers were touching a letter he had written, and which lay in his pocket. He had intended sending it by canoe to her station and arriving himself a day later.

"You are going to be married?" he said again.

"Yes," she said, "I—I was very foolish, Mr. Sanders. I ought not to have come here—I quarrelled—you know the sort of thing that happens."

"I know," said Sanders.

She could not wait for breakfast. The mail steamer came in and sent its *pinnace* ashore. Sanders saw her baggage stored, took his mail from the second officer, then came to say good-bye to her.

"You haven't wished me—luck," she said.

At the back of her eyes was a hint of a troubled conscience, for she was a woman and she had been in his company for nearly an hour, and women learn things in an hour.

"I wish you every happiness," he said heartily and gripped her hand till she winced.

She was stepping in the boat when she turned back to him.

"I have often wondered—" she began, and hesitated.

"Yes?"

"It is an impertinence," she said hurriedly, "but I have wondered sometimes, and I wonder more now when my own happiness makes me take a greater interest—why you have never married?"

Sanders smiled, that crooked little smile of his.

"I nearly proposed once," he said. "Good-bye and good-luck!"

He left that morning for the Upper River, though the reason for his visit was gone and the ship that carried her to happiness below the western horizon.

Day by day the *Zaire* steamed northward, and there was in her commander's heart an aching emptiness, that made time and space of no account.

One day they came to a village and would have passed, but Abiboo at his side said: "Lord, this is Togobonobo, where sits the man who your lordship gave a thousand *matakos*."

Sanders showed his teeth.

"Let us see this happy man," he said in Arabic, "for the Prophet hath said, 'The joy of my friend cleanseth my heart from sorrow.'"

When the *Zaire* reached the shore, Sanders would have sent for the bridegroom, but that young man was waiting, a woe-begone figure that shuffled to the bridge with dejected mien.

"I see," said Sanders, "that the father of your woman asked more than you could pay."

"Lord, I wish that he had," said the youth, "for, lord, I am a sorrowful man."

"Hath the woman died?"

"Lord," said the young man, "if the devils had taken her I should be happy: for this woman, though only a girl, has a great will and does that which she desires, taking no heed of me. And when I speak with her she has a bitter tongue, and, lord, this morning she gave me fish which was not cooked, and called me evil names when I corrected her. Also, lord!" said the youth with a catch in his voice, "the cooking-pot she threw at me before the whole village."

"That is a bad *palaver*," said Sanders hastily; "now you must give way to her, Tobolo, for she is your wife, and I cannot stay—"

"Lord," said the young man, catching his arm, "I am your debtor, owing you a thousand *matakos*—now if your lordship in justice will divorce me I will repay you with joy."

"Go in peace," said Sanders, and when the youth showed a reluctance to leave the ship, Abiboo threw him into the water.

The incident gave Sanders food for thought—and there was another matter. Two days further up the River he came to the Ochori and found Bosambo's people in mourning. The chief waited his master's coming in the dark of his hut and Sanders went in to see him.

"Bosambo," he said, soberly, "this is bad hearing."

"Lord," moaned the chief, "I wish I were dead—dead as my first-born who lies in the hut of my wife."

He rocked to and fro in his grief, for Bosambo had the heart of a child, and in his little son, who had counted its existence by days, was centred all the ambition of his life.

"God be with you, Bosambo my brother," said Sanders gently, and laid his hand on the black man's heaving shoulder; "these things are ordained from the beginning of time."

"It is written," whispered Bosambo, between his sobs, and caught his lord's hand.

Sanders turned his steamer downriver, and that night, when he prepared for bed, the sorrow of his chief was fresh in his mind.

Before he turned in, he took a letter from his pocket, tore it deliberately into a hundred scraps and threw it from the door of the cabin into the river. Then he got into his bunk and switched out the light. He thought of the young man of the Isisi, and he thought of Bosambo.

"Thank God I'm not married," he said, and went to sleep.